BELFAST

A Novel of the Troubles

Douglas Clark

"Belfast, A Novel of the Troubles," by Douglas Clark. ISBN 1-58939-628-6 (softcover), 1-58939-629-4 (hardcover).

Library of Congress Control Number: 2004111051

Dedicated to Josie, whose support, encouragement,
and editing made *Belfast* possible.

"There can never be peace in Ireland until the foreign, oppressive British presence is removed, leaving all the Irish people as a unit to control their own affairs and determine their own destinies as a sovereign people, free in mind and body, separate and distinct physically, culturally and economically."

-Bobby Sands, 1954-1981

Chapter One

Belfast, Northern Ireland – John Malone had been sitting alone at a back table in the pub for half an hour nursing a Guinness. He would give it a little more time. Patrick Coogan was not often punctual.

"Good to see ya, John," Coogan greeted Malone as he took a seat and shook Malone's hand.

"Been keeping well, Patrick?"

"Well enough considering."

"So what's this important information that brings me out on a night like this?"

"Major piece of intelligence, John. We need you to feed certain information to the R.U.C. brass about a weapons conduit to the U.F.F. We've also identified a major weapons depot. Rather have the coppers do their job and seize it instead of us."

"Why do you need me? Why not just give them the intel yourself,"

"Ah, there's the rub. We have information that implicates certain high-ranking R.U.C. officers cooperating with the U.F.F. We'll tell you who they are so you can go over their heads. The fuckers will sweep it under the rug coming from us. Can't do that with you blokes have'n the story."

"The last information you fed me was useless. We could not confirm, therefore we didn't publish. That's the rules," Malone said. "So what do'ya give me on this that's different?"

"Knowing what sticklers you are, there's information here that you can trace that will confirm the R.U.C. officials' involvement. Should be a real story in here somewhere for you blokes, especially if the coppers raid the arms cache. Should be able to get some front- page pictures. "

Coogan handed Malone a thick envelope.

"Implicating the R.U.C. supporting the Protestant paramilitaries is the real I.R.A. interest isn't it, Patrick? "

"Of course, John — — —-"

Patrick Coogan was cut off in mid-sentence as the entire front of the pub exploded inward.

Mason Devereux sat on his apartment balcony having coffee. It was mid-morning, promising already to be a warm autumn day on the Mediterranean. The view was magnificent. He looked down from the cliffs of the old town sector of the tiny French principality. Sailing craft and yachts were in abundance. The water was a deep, rich blue. It was relatively quiet, the beaches being some distance away. In general, Monaco was quieter than the other adjoining Riviera beaches of France on its western border, or Italy to the east.

He had moved to Monaco soon after the death of his wife and joining the Reuters news agency as a correspondent. Assignments usually placed him closer to Europe anyway. He had wanted a new start far away. What better place than Monaco. The sun, the Mediterranean, the urbane elegance, and no income tax. Furthermore, he spoke French.

The apartment was in an older building, under extensive remodeling when he came across it. It had cost him an extraordinary amount of money to purchase, and even then it had been a lucky find. It had more than tripled in value in the ten years he had owned it, but there was no interest in selling. It was convenient. The building manager and his wife looked after things during his long absences, and took care of the housekeeping.

He had been home almost two months. The first draft for his latest book had been completed and sent off to his agent the previous week. Devereux was satisfied with the result. Two years in Haiti, Peru, and Mexico had produced a compelling photographic work. It was an eclectic mix of violence played against a backdrop of differing social situations and politics. His publisher was enthused with the galleys, his agent was ecstatic. Devereux was equally as pleased with the writing as he was with the photographs. None of this however dispelled a depression he was unable to shake.

On the patio table a single picture lay next to his coffee cup. It was not one of the photographs included in the book. He had taken the shot as the Mexican Army overran the guerrilla band. It was one of the last shots taken before he was captured. It showed a young Mexican army officer, probably in his mid-twenties. It was the face of the only man that Devereux had ever killed.

The book captured a sequence of horrific photographs of the executions of several Mexican Army officers by the Zapatista rebel band Devereux was with. Captured later by the Mexican Army, the remaining rebels were subjected to torture and anticipated execution. A foreign journalist could not be allowed to witness the retribution. The justification of the act did little to attenuate the continual reliving of the image of killing the man up close with a knife.

Since his business was world strife, Devereux kept up with events by receiving newspapers from New York, London, and Paris. His procedure was to scan the entire paper quickly. He knew the major areas of international conflict and had a good understanding of the background. He reviewed all the paper but tended to focus more on articles several pages inside which gave a broader perspective when followed over a period of time.

Major news events started out on the front page, but progressed deeper into the paper as the event value waned. Subsequent information had a half-life as news value, quickly becoming relegated to the inside pages. Such an article appeared on the fourth page of the London Times.

Most homicides never make a major paper, but Northern Ireland always had a newsworthy potential in London that would result in publishing accounts of almost anything violent that happened. A comparable murder in Devonshire would receive no space.

Devereux could have easily overlooked the small quarter column article. Perhaps it was the mention of a journalist's murder in the title that drew his eye. The story reported a bombing of a West Belfast pub the previous day. Several were injured, three killed. One of those killed was identified as John Malone, a journalist for a Dublin newspaper.

Devereux didn't know John Malone, but he knew his brother, Egan. Egan Malone had been a close friend during graduate school at UCLA. Malone was Irish, studying at UCLA on a fellowship. Malone had flown in from Ireland and stayed with Devereux for a couple of weeks after the death of Devereux's wife. Devereux knew this must be Egan's brother. The article indicated that John Malone worked for Egan's newspaper.

Devereux called Dublin immediately, leaving messages for Egan Malone at his office and on his answering machine at home. A few hours later, Malone returned his call.

"Mason, thanks for calling. I guess you've heard," Malone said. The hurt in his voice was apparent.

"Jesus, Egan, I'm so sorry to hear about your brother."

"Thanks, Mason. You know, he was only thirty-three. Married with two beautiful kids."

"I guess being a reporter puts you at some greater risk than other professions. But Christ, this is not like what you do, Mason. Hearing about your death would grieve me terribly, but wouldn't be a surprise. But Johnny was only a reporter. Sure the *troubles* make the North a meaner place, but it's not a war zone," Malone burst forth in a release of frustration."

"I didn't think of it as was a war zone, but I guess it is. The fucking violence has been going on for so long it may never change."

Malone was quiet for a few moments. Devereux could almost hear the tears.

"Egan, it's been years since I've seen you. I'm coming up tomorrow,"

"That's kind of you, Mason, but you really don't have to."

"Of course I don't have to, Egan. I want to. Maybe even need to. I know you've got Jenny and your kids. You're got your family to help you through this. But I remember when Angela died. You were there for me. I didn't even want you there. I wanted to crawl into a hole. But you came anyway. I've thought about that often, Egan, because I think about Angela often. I've got to come, Egan."

Tears came to Devereux's eyes. He hadn't talked with Malone for almost two years. Had not seen him for almost ten years. Had never met his family. He felt guilty as hell. They had been very close friends for several years. Devereux made few close relationships, but Malone was important in his life. Malone had been his only other real friend, other than Angela. The fact that they had fallen out of touch did nothing to change that.

Devereux arrived in Dublin in the early afternoon the next day. Malone had insisted he stay at his home. Devereux had insisted that he would make his own way from the airport. Malone lived in the seaside village of Malahide, to the north of Dublin, and only about ten kilometers from the airport.

The taxi driver extolled the virtues of this delightful village. Everything here was history. In particular, Devereux would certainly enjoy the local attraction, Malahide Castle. The place that was Malone's own house was a grand structure, built one hundred-fifty years ago Devereux learned later.

Malone's wife Jenny greeted him at the door with a hug and kiss on the cheek. She was somewhat embarrassed at her own display of affection. She had never met Devereux.

"My Lord, it seems like I know you, but I've never met you Mr. Devereux. No, I shall call you Mason. I do know you well enough to call you Mason," Jenny Malone said. "Do come in. Egan's in Belfast, but he'll be back this evening."

Devereux liked her instantly. His old friend had been as lucky as he had been. Jenny Malone made coffee and took the opportunity to get to know this Mason Devereux she had heard so much about for so long. Devereux thoroughly enjoyed their conversation, almost forgetting the reason for his visit.

"Thank you for coming, Mason. I know this will help Egan. We both hurt deeply. Johnny was like one of my own brothers."

Jenny Malone started to cry softly. Devereux held her hand.

Malone's two teenage daughters returned from school in the afternoon. They had heard their father speak about Mason Devereux. At first shy, the girls quickly warmed to him and asked him all sorts of questions. He was rescued by Egan Malone's return around six o'clock.

"Mason," Malone said, embracing Devereux. Tears streamed down both their cheeks with no self-consciousness.

Devereux and Malone talked for two hours, catching up on news of each other, graduating soon from coffee to whiskey. Jenny Malone and her daughters retreated to the background, eventually leaving to the kitchen to prepare a late dinner.

The next day they spent a few hours at Malone's office in Dublin. Late in the afternoon, Malone took him to his favorite pub.

"Egan, we heard about your brother. Can't tell you how sorry we are," the barkeeper said, extending his hand to Malone.

"Thanks, Pat, I appreciate that. I'd like you to meet an old friend of mind from my college days, Mason Devereux," Malone said.

The barkeeper extended his hand to Devereux. "Pleased to have you in my establishment, Sir. Any friend of Egan Malone is always welcome here, Sir. Devereux? Don't sound Irish. Perhaps French?"

"The name is French, and I speak French, but I'm from the U.S.," Devereux answered, extending his hand.

"Well French or American, it's alright by me. Just so as you're not British, or a Protestant from the North," the barkeeper said, firmly shaking Devereux's hand.

At Malone's request, Pat pulled two pints of Guinness. The proper drawing of Guinness was a slow process taking several minutes. After the ritual, Malone and Devereux took their drinks to a table in the corner of the pub.

"The story in the London Times indicated that a Protestant paramilitary group was suspected. Was your brother working on a story?" Devereux asked.

"I don't know. I talked with Kevin Flanagan, a friend of Johnny's, and also a reporter for the paper. If he was, Kevin didn't know about it. Hard to say. Could be he was just in the wrong place at the wrong time. It was a Catholic bar, in a Catholic working class neighborhood. But it wasn't near where he lived. Kevin didn't know the place as somewhere Johnny went to. Who knows. Could have been following a lead. Could have been just fishing around," Malone said.

"You know what Belfast is like," Malone blurted out, looking intently at Devereux. "It's like air travel. The statistics say it's safe. But when something happens, it occurs at random, and you're usually dead."

Devereux didn't quite see the analogy, but didn't comment.

"It's not a crime ridden place. There's far less of a drug problem than here in Dublin. Yet when you're there you can feel the tension. Like something could happen at any moment. I imagine it's something like those drive-by shootings that happen in Los Angeles. The randomness, the unexpectedness."

"Johnny used to talk about what it was like. Said it was a pleasant place, a vibrant place. Friendly people. Economically in better shape than here in the Republic," Malone said, motioning to the barkeeper for two more.

"Then how do you account for the continuing violence. Christ, we've been hearing about I.R.A. terrorism for years," Devereux said.

"It wasn't the I.R.A. who killed Johnny, Mason. Don't get me wrong. I've never approved of the I.R.A.'s methods. I think they're terrorists. But it's not just the I.R.A. There's the other side that does much the same. The police suspect a faction of the U.F.F. They're outlawed too. I.R.A. are Catholic, the U.F.F. Protestant. Except religion has nothing to do with it."

"I've often wondered why the world press doesn't give them the same attention to their acts of violence. I.R.A. violence gets at least three times the copy space as the comparable attack by one of these Protestant paramilitary groups."

"And you're right, it has been going on forever. Everybody says over twenty-five years. But it's been much longer. The I.R.A. goes way back. The modern *troubles* seem to use the 1969 riots in Derry, as the demarcation point."

Malone continued. "You know, all the world thinks this is only about some rebellion to join the North to the Republic. Make Ireland whole so to speak. To the average Catholic in Northern Ireland, it's often much more basic and personal. The

I.R.A. gets much of its continuing support because of simple discrimination if not outright persecution."

"The average working class Catholic, and that's essentially all there are, experiences virtually the same discrimination as did blacks in America during the fifties and sixties. It's as blatant as apartheid in South Africa. Catholics are a minority in the North and they have all the problems minorities have everywhere."

"With the disbanding of the old parliament in 1972 there has been some progress. Direct rule from London has been better than the Protestant dominated Northern Ireland Parliament."

Devereux asked a few questions, letting Malone go on. It was cathartic. Along with his monologue, Malone ordered several whiskeys with Guinness chasers.

"Are you going to Belfast with us for the funeral, Mason?" Malone asked.

"Of course, Egan."

"God, I'm glad to see you, Mason," Malone gripped Devereux's shoulder.

The next day, the Malones, their two daughters, and Devereux drove the two hours to Belfast. Jenny Malone was glad for the diversion that Devereux brought.

With copies of Devereux's books in the house, the Malone girls knew of his exploits into war zones. The entire ride was filled with a constant barrage of questions from the teenagers, taking up where they had left off the day before. By the time they arrived, both were madly in love with this handsome, romantic friend of their father's.

Devereux's first glimpse of Belfast was a revealing shock. He understood the security checkpoint at the border of the Republic of Ireland with Northern Ireland, which was part of the United Kingdom. However, an army checkpoint as they entered Belfast was unexpected.

"Thought things had eased here, Egan," Devereux said as they came to a stop in a queue at a security checkpoint.

"Not entirely, Mason. Note that these are British army personnel. That's at the crux of the turmoil. Not that long ago, the British army patrolled the streets of Belfast in full combat dress and armored personnel carriers. That's eased, but not the British presence."

"The British sure as hell don't see this as a pleasant place with friendly people, Egan," Devereux commented.

Devereux spent an uncomfortable first two days in Belfast. As much as everyone welcomed him, including Johnny Malone's widow, he still felt like an outsider. He reminded himself that he was here for Egan's sake, the same as Egan had done for him. He could feel that his being here had helped. Jenny Malone had touched his shoulder, and smiled into his eyes at a poignant moment, acknowledging her thanks simply by her expression.

The funeral turned out to be a much larger affair than planned, even though John Malone's widow had declined the suggestion to have a joint funeral with the others killed in the bombing. Hundreds turned out. Obviously, most could not have known John Malone. Egan speculated to Devereux that I.R.A. sympathizers undoubtedly organized the turnout. Catholic deaths were an important I.R.A. propaganda instrument.

The day after the funeral, Egan invited Devereux to a wake for his brother. A number of his friends had arranged the traditional celebration at Johnny Malone's favorite pub.

The concept of a wake was to celebrate the life of the deceased and how that life touched others. It was not devoted to grieving over the loss.

Malone and Devereux entered the pub late in the afternoon. They were greeted first by Kevin Flanagan, John Malone's friend from the paper. Flanagan made the introductions round the pub. Pints and whiskeys were in full flow. After a time, Devereux, Malone, and Flanagan found a table.

Flanagan was in his late twenties. Slender, even gaunt, with unfashionably longish hair, leather jacket and jeans. John Malone had been his boss, mentor, and friend.

"Well, Mason, what do you think of us Irish?" Flanagan said, raising his beer and downing the remaining half glass.

"Probably thinks we're stereotypical drunkards," Egan Malone quipped. "Seems I've had him drinking ever since he arrived in Ireland."

"I'm meanin' about the *troubles*, Egan" Flanagan said.

"It's a curiosity, Kevin," Devereux said. "Most people think the I.R.A. is some old-time terrorist group that continues to do some violence. But to be honest, Kevin, Northern Ireland is lost in a long list of troubled spots in the world. Many parts of the world are suffering horrific slaughter and brutality of thousands of people. "

"Egan says the fundamental issue is discrimination against Catholics in Northern Ireland. That being so, it's hardly unique in the world today. Real bad shit is genocide. Discrimination isn't in the same league, Kevin."

Flanagan was already well into his fourth pint and at least two whiskeys. "So what you're saying is, unless there's a lot of violence with hundreds dying, the rest of the world will pay little attention."

"The rest of the world doesn't even care about those hundreds that are dying. It's just news. The people just don't have any connection. They're not touched by it."

"Shit. This is a wake for my brother. Let's forget the goddamn politics, Kevin" Egan Malone said.

"Ah Jesus, Egan, I'm sorry. It's the liquor talking. I don't mean to go on. It's just that—well, I report on what's going on, but it's bloody hard to stand apart from it," Flanagan said.

"I'm sorry, Mason. I didn't mean to attack you. I'm just so fucking mad. Johnny Malone was the best. He was a great newspaperman. He was a Catholic, but he reported things the way they were, whether it was pro-republican or pro-unionist."

"He taught me a lot. Taught me about reporting. Taught me about objectivity. Taught me about the craft. Most of all, he taught me how to think. Then some asshole fanatic, probably too stupid to have ever read a newspaper, kills him. Kills him with a fucking bomb. Doesn't even give a shit who he kills as long as they're Catholics."

Flanagan cried. It was not embarrassing. His were not the only tears shed for Johnny Malone that evening.

After a few moments, Kevin Flanagan regained his composure. "You know, this here's the third wake I've been to for someone I've known killed by the Prods or Brits. This isn't how most of the world lives, at least not in Europe or the United States. It's not Africa or the Balkans."

Flanagan took a long swig of another whiskey, "You know what it's like here in the six counties, it's like the civil rights struggle with your blacks in the U.S. Read a book by a black man, James Baldwin. What he describes from decades ago is what goes on in Northern Ireland in the nineties of today. You've got internment, which is imprisonment without trial. Or you have simple murder. Contrary to world opinion about the I.R.A., more Catholics die than anyone else."

"Listen, Mason. I'm a newspaperman. I know what's going on in the world, all the bad shit, all the wars, all the genocide," Flanagan was showing the effects of his liquor intake. "But look at this. What country in the West, what industrialized country, has such a war going on? Unrelenting violence for decades? No country does. That's the answer. What has gone on here for years is unique," Flanagan continued passionately.

"Goddamn it, Egan will attest that I don't agree with the I.R.A.'s methods, but the Prods' killers, the British backed killers, are as much a part of the problem. They make this a war."

"You know why the I.R.A. gets all the negative press?" It's their acronym. It's as simple as that. The fucking I.R.A. should give the enemy an acronym, and make it easy on the press," Flanagan said.

By now Kevin Flanagan was getting drunk. He excused himself to go to the lavatory.

"There's no getting away from politics here, Mason. Everybody has a position. You can't just take what happens here as a natural course of events. There's always the politics. There's always the history," Egan Malone said.

"How do you feel, Egan? Do you hate the group responsible for John's death? Or do you just hate the circumstances?" Devereux asked Malone.

"Both, goddamn it! I'd like to see the bastards that killed Johnny hung. People of good cause don't set bombs in public places," Egan too was feeling the drink. His anger was surfacing.

"I'll tell you my feelings, Mason. I think England is an occupying power in the North. So do most Irish. I would like to see them gone. They've a terrible history here in Ireland."

"I don't think the majority of the Protestants want to discriminate against the Catholic's. Like everywhere in the world, it's some faction that's the cause of the violence and the misery. Fucking fanatics have always shaped history. Most people just want to survive."

Malone continued. "God, I'm sick, Mason. Johnny's dead. Killed by some thugs. An I.R.A. bombing could have just as easily killed Johnny. He could have been doing a story in a Protestant pub. So who do I blame?"

"There's nothing I could say to ease your pain, Egan. You blame the environment here that causes violence. It's exactly that kind of thinking that separates you from those that need to lay blame on some group they've been taught to hate," Devereux said.

"The masses, huh? You make me out to be what the communists would call a bourgeoisie. An elitist I guess," Malone remarked. "I hate all the murdering bastards here."

"Bullshit, Egan. You share the same opinion I do that the majority of people anywhere just follow some sort of lead. Most often based on some prejudice."

"You're a thinking person. Are you an elitist because of that? Maybe, but what thinking person would follow the kinds of nonsense we see in the world today? The fanatics can only move the stupid, the blind, or the willing. Don't chastise yourself because you're not one of the sheep," Devereux said.

Kevin Flanagan navigated back to the table with some difficulty. He downed the remainder of his whiskey. "God, I loved Johnny. He was my best friend."

With that, both Flanagan and Malone held each other and cried softly. Devereux went to the bar and ordered another round, leaving them alone for a few minutes.

Upon his return, Flanagan said, "Mason, I've seen your books. You follow the violence in the world. You've got the eye. The photos make me angry. Not at you, but at what is going on.

Some make me want to cry. That's why they're good. What about doing a book about Northern Ireland?"

Devereux was slightly surprised by the suggestion. As a journalist, as a photographer, he knew the potential of Northern Ireland, but the thought had never entered his mind.

"Come on, Kevin, a book is a major project. There's arrangements, advances to be negotiated, not to mention devoting months of your life. Big step. Big decision. Besides, I just completed a book. I'm not sure I'm ready to jump off to start a new one," Devereux said.

"What's the last book about, Mason?" Flanagan asked. Malone too was curious.

"It's about rebellion, oppression, violence in the Americas. Specifically, the book uses Peru, Haiti, and Mexico as subjects," Devereux answered.

"And the book I recall seeing was about Africa? Flanagan said. "And you've published others?"

"One other. My first. It was about El Salvador," Devereux said.

"You like the warm climates. Do you live where it's warm, like in Florida?" Flanagan joked.

Devereux laughed, "The Mediterranean, Kevin. And yes, I like it warm. I'll tell you, the Emerald Isle's climate sucks. I've only been here a few days, and only once it didn't rain. I haven't seen the sun at all. It's no wonder the Irish drink," Devereux said good-naturedly.

"Kevin makes an interesting point about a book, Mason," Malone said. "Consider the uniqueness of such violent, unrelenting civil strife, in a so-called western democracy. The historical perspectives may share common elements with Eastern Europe, but Ireland is part of the West. The violence is more like from Central American. But this is an industrialized nation, even though a very poor one. Ireland, both Irelands, are so-called Western democracies. It's also the only Western country where terrorism is practiced on a continuing basis. And it goes on for decades."

Malone continued, "There are the classic socio-political issues. Geopolitical boundaries created contrary to the ethnic composition of the people. The Catholic population in the North historically and culturally identifies with those of the Republic. You've got repressive government, bigotry, institutionalized discrimination. You've got civil rights abuses every bit as blatant as those of the old South Africa. You've got the last remnant of colonialism with occupying military troops. The equivalent of marshal law, the suspension of civil rights, imprisonment without trial. And, you have the inherent interest of a huge expatriate Irish population living outside of Ireland."

"Jesus Christ, Egan, give you a little whiskey and you do get on your soapbox," Devereux said. There were interesting elements, but it wasn't something he had done before. Past work was in virtual war zones. Great visual stuff. Northern Ireland, even with the *troubles*, would be far subtler.

"Seriously, Mason, this could be a major opportunity," Malone said, having convinced himself with his own arguments. "Spend a couple days up here. I'm sure Kevin would show you around."

"Egan's right, Mason. Like I said, you've got the eye. You could do a hell of book here. Show the fucking world what goes on here. Show them why my friend Johnny Malone died."

Flanagan was getting drunker. Tears rolled down his cheeks.

Devereux was in better shape than either Malone or Flanagan. He helped both of them up. They shook hands with everyone and left the bar. Devereux hailed a taxi. They dropped Kevin off at his flat. It was midnight when they got back to the Europa Hotel on Great Victoria Street in the center of the city. It was the centerpiece hotel in Belfast. Extensive remodeling had followed a recent I.R.A. bombing.

The next morning, Devereux had a slight headache from the previous night's drinking, but he was ravenously hungry. It was another gray day with a light drizzle. He slipped on the same sweater he had worn for the last two days. It was the only one he had brought. He grabbed his brown leather jacket, and made a mental note to consider purchasing more warm clothes. It was early October so it would only be getting colder.

Egan, Jenny, and the girls were already in the dining room when Devereux came down. The Malone girls beamed. He ordered a traditional Irish breakfast of sausages, bacon, and eggs, with generous portions of soda bread. Bad for the cholesterol, but it suited Devereux's appetite just fine. He preferred red meat anyway, and loved bread. The coffee was excellent.

"How are you doing this morning, Egan?" Devereux asked.

"Drinking tea instead of coffee. Dry toasted bread. I feel like hell. Can't drink whiskey like that anymore," Malone answered. His looks reflected how he was feeling. Jenny shook her head, but smiled. As for Devereux, the hearty meal made him feel much better.

"You're going back home today?" Devereux asked.

"Yeah. Nothing more we can really do for Sarah and the kids. We'll have them down probably in a couple of weeks. Right now, she'll have to come to terms with Johnny's death. Better for the kids to get back into school to give them a diversion away from the grief. There're plenty of friends to make sure she's getting along,"

"I thought about what you and Kevin suggested last night. You remember?"

"Of course I remember. I wasn't that drunk," Malone protested. "About doing a book on the *troubles*? So what are you going to do?"

"Get in touch with Kevin. Have him show me around if he can spare the time. Thought I'd spend a couple of days, see if it feels right for a project. See if I want to spend a lot of time in this god-awful climate."

Good-byes said, the Malones left the hotel mid-morning. Devereux found himself alone. Before contacting Kevin Flanagan, Devereux decided to do a bit of research on Ireland. The concierge suggested the Linenhall Library, a few blocks walk from the hotel on the northwest corner of Donegal Square. It was a nasty day, with a freezing rain out of a miserable gray sky. The kind of day that left no doubt for the cause of the Irish tendency to strong drink, and sad poetry.

The Linenhall Library faced the City Hall, at the center of Donegal Square. City Hall represented the physical center of Belfast. The quadrangular building was typical of the Victorian British style. At the main entrance, stands a statue of Queen Victoria herself.

Entering the library, Devereux stopped at the information desk to inquire if there was someone who could make recommendations on books of Irish history. The young woman smiled broadly at Devereux. Somewhat flustered, she went to a small middle-aged man seated at a desk. After introductions, the small bespectacled man took him in charge, delighted to have the opportunity to exercise his expertise. He asked all sorts of questions, praising Devereux for his wisdom and character to become familiar with the history of his country.

He seated Devereux at a table then made off mumbling to himself, running through a mental list of potential titles. Within ten minutes, the man had scurried about the shelves, returning with four books.

"These should be a good group from which you might start, Sir. There are of course many others. If you have any questions, please don't hesitate to ask," The librarian said, leaving Devereux to his research.

Devereux started by locating a chronology of Irish historical events in R. F. Foster's, *Modern Ireland*. An interesting fact leapt out, no doubt intended by the author. The population of Ireland was over eight million in 1841. By the turn of the century, it had dropped to four and a half million. It continued to decline through the first half of the century, and in 1970 was still no greater than in 1900, considering both the Republic and Northern Ireland.

Devereux of course knew about the great potato famine of the last century, and the large immigrations of Irish, particularly to the United States. But this statistic was staggering. And in a predominately Catholic country, with the attendant high birth rate due to the Vatican's prohibitions against artificial contraception. What would make such vast numbers of people emigrate? What was wrong with this Ireland that held such fervent ethnic pride but drove its children away?

Perhaps this fact alone, piqued Devereux's interest. He was a rapid reader, and waded through most of two books. Getting hungry, he asked his librarian friend to hold the books for his return. Inquiring as to a recommended place for a late lunch, the librarian suggested several within the immediate area. Devereux opted for the library's own tearoom. The tea was excellent, and the scones were just enough to stave off hunger until dinner. Much more conducive to his reading than a pint or two of beer and typically heavy Irish fare.

It was Thursday, the day the library stayed open until 8:30pm. Devereux was the last to leave. He thanked the librarian, and promised to return.

Acting on the librarian's recommendation, Devereux stopped at the Crown Liquor Saloon for a whiskey. It was actually a national trust property, but still open for drinking. The Crown was certainly something to experience. Only its golden scrolled ceiling, ornate appointments, and stained glass surpass an incongruous glittering tiled exterior. The decor was more befitting a church, or maybe an old-fashioned whorehouse. It too had recovered from an I.R.A. bombing. Devereux concluded his evening with dinner at a cozy restaurant, the waitress being particularly attentive since Devereux was dining alone.

Devereux reflected on his day's research. No question about it, he was intrigued. He knew himself. Something would spark his interest, then he would get inside it, absorb it, feel the essence of what was happening. The French Foreign Legion had been the first. Many wars and much experience later, Devereux knew what interested him and knew what sold.

Northern Ireland, the *troubles* did have those elements. Malone had been right. The social strife, the unrelenting sectarian violence, played against a backdrop of a western industrialized nation, did invite the potential of a dramatic photographic project. Could he show that in his photographs? Could he capture compelling photographs? More importantly, did he want to stay here and do this work?

On the plus side for doing the project was the continuing violence, inherently of interest to the world. Devereux himself was intrigued by the violence practiced by pro-unionist, Protestant paramilitary groups against I.R.A., republicans, and Catholics in general. While practicing essentially the same violence, these people were able to avoid the international notoriety the I.R.A. had acquired.

On the other hand, it would be harder to capture the violence than in places actually engulfed in open warfare. The background to the violence would be a challenge to illustrate in photographs. For all the publicity Belfast had received, it was not a dangerous city. It was statistically much safer than most American major cities.

It would be a dramatically different environment than those war zones that had been his past venues. Conditions would be much more comfortable than locations of his previous work. Decent food and drink, a shower, a toilet, and a clean bed. On the down side, it was cold, damp, and overcast.

What probably persuaded him to take the project further was the Irish character, or at least those here in Belfast. There was a charm and genuine warmth. People went out of their way to assist the outsider. These were good people with a terrible affliction.

Chapter Two

Devereux spent the next two days at the library. He arranged to meet Kevin Flanagan for lunch on Sunday. Flanagan would pick him up at the hotel at noon, suggesting they get out of the downtown area and see another face of Belfast.

"So what have you been up to since the funeral, Mason? Seeing Belfast?" Flanagan asked, after greeting Devereux in the lobby of the Europa. They walked to Flanagan's Volkswagen.

"Not at all. In fact I haven't left downtown for the last few days. Been doing research at the library."

"Research? Thinking seriously about doing a book?"

"Maybe. I'll admit that you and Egan have got me interested, but I need to work the idea further. That's why I wanted to have lunch with you. I'd need your help. After all, it was originally your suggestion."

Flanagan left the parking lot turning left onto Grosvenor Road and headed west.

"My suggestion? Lord, you can't hold a man accountable for everything he says when he's into his whiskey, especially at a wake. Lots of puffed up talk at a wake," Flanagan said affably. More seriously he asked, "What kind of help could I be?"

"Two things. The first is what we're doing today — showing me around. The second is tougher. I'll need to talk to people. I'll need introductions."

"No problem, Mason. I'll be glad to show you around. I've got time, and no commitments right now other than my job.

Broke up with my girlfriend a couple of months ago. Getting drunk too much anyway. Might as well have company."

"Where're we going?"

"Andersonstown, the heart of the Falls area. Working class Catholic section of Belfast. There's a pub there that serves an excellent lunch. The bartender is a real character. Good local color. It'll give you a flavor for the tough side of life in Belfast."

"Over there's the Royal," Flanagan said as they drove west along Grosvenor Road, pointing to a group of red brick buildings. "Officially the Royal Victoria Hospital, but everyone calls it the Royal."

"They do a hell of a job fixing up victims of the *troubles*. If you're Catholic and you've been shot, bombed, or beaten, they'll most likely bring you to the Royal. Good people there. They're not political. Treat Catholic and Protestant alike. Many a time I've been there after some incident, getting information on the victims from the hospital staff."

They turned left onto the Falls Road, traveling southwest. A short distance later a prominent mural appeared on the left. Mason had Flanagan stop the car in order to photograph the mural. It said, 'I have always believed we had a legitimate right to take up arms and defend our country and ourselves against the British occupation. Mairead Farrell.'

"Who was Mairead Farrell?" Devereux asked.

"A prominent member of the I.R.A. Killed by a British S.A.S. hit team in Gibraltar along with two others in nineteen eighty-eight. Big stink at the time. Some called it murder. Anyway, it gives you a sense of the feeling here. This is the heart of republicanism in Belfast."

About a mile further on, Flanagan pointed out the Milltown Cemetery. Across the road was a British army encampment.

"This is the main burial ground for republicans. Even had a firefight here once. Violence broke out at the funeral of one of those I.R.A. lads killed in Gibraltar. Some loyalist assholes started shooting and throwing grenades."

Less than a mile further on, they were in the Andersonstown area. Flanagan made a couple of turns. They passed a British army patrol in a jeep. "There's the pub," Flanagan indicated by pointing.

"Where?" There were no signs.

"Behind the sand bags and chicken wire."

"Christ, that's where we're having lunch? Really knocked yourself out, Kevin. Guess the owner expects trouble?"

"Just precautions. Place has been bombed by Protestants twice. The owner's not being paranoid. That's how I came to know him. Covered the story after the last attack. The chicken wire protects against thrown bombs or grenades. The sand bags would absorb a good measure of the force of a car bomb. And for that eventuality, the area in front of the pub effectively prohibits any parking. Tough to get close with a car bomb."

Flanagan found a place to park further down the block. They walked to the rear of the pub, passing through a fence of barbed wire closing off the alleyway. They entered the pub through a heavy metal door. Heads turned abruptly, but relaxed quickly when it was obvious to the patrons that Devereux and Flanagan were not bent on killing everyone.

The barkeep came out from the backroom and noticed Flanagan sitting down.

"Kevin Flanagan, me lad, good to see you. Been keeping well?" The barkeep asked, coming from around the bar to shake hands with Flanagan. The man was short and stocky, with a protruding belly. Over his left eye, he wore a black patch. Below the eye was a nasty patchwork of scars.

"It could be worse, Tim. See you've still got the place walled up like a fortress. Any more trouble since the last time?" Flanagan asked.

"No. Things have been quiet."

"Tim, I'd like you to meet my friend here, Mason Devereux. Mason, this is Tim Whitely."

"Pleased to meet you, Mr. Devereux."

Whitely shook Devereux's hand.

"You in the newspaper business, too, Mr. Devereux?"

"Not really. I know Kevin here through a mutual friend down in Dublin. We met, unfortunately at a funeral of a mutual friend."

"Sad thing, Tim. My mate at the paper, Johnny Malone, got killed in that bombing a week ago."

Whitely made the sign of the cross. "My condolences, Kevin, and to you, too, Mr. Devereux. Bombs are for cowards. Don't care which side you're on. That's how I lost my eye here, back in eighty-three. Bomb killed two people over there to the right of what used to be the front door. Car bomb. Injured most everyone in here. Hit me again in ninety-one, grenade this time, through the window. That's when I changed the outside to make it tougher on the bastards. They'll have to come in the back now, and look us in the face if they want to be killing us. And we ain't exactly defenseless. Bastards come in here looking for trouble, we'll send them back north of the Falls Road in a box."

"Tough on business, I'd imagine," Devereux commented.

"Not really. I've been here a long time. My customers' been here a long time. The bastards are not scaring any of us away. But enough of this talk of violence. It's a pleasant Sunday afternoon. You lads here for drinking, or eating? Best place for both." Whitely said.

"Exactly what I told Mason here. How about a couple of Guinness. Food's always tops here, Mason, but what do you recommend today, Tim?"

"Stew's particularly good today, if I do say so myself. Fresh bread. The lamb chops look good too, perhaps with some potato cakes," Whitely suggested.

Both Devereux and Flanagan ordered the Irish stew and bread. There was no such thing as a light lunch in Ireland. Typical fare was most often meat oriented. The food was served with generous portions. In spite of a plain and even tacky decor, not to mention the fortress-like exterior, the food was particularly delicious. After another round of Guinness and refusing the apple pie desert, they got down to discussing possible plans.

"Tell me Kevin, what are your views, your politics? Once I start, if I start this project, I could step on toes."

"What you mean is Catholic toes, republicans, maybe even the I.R.A.?" Flanagan asked.

"Maybe."

"I'm a newspaper man, Mason. I step on toes all the time. I have strong feelings about the history of Ireland and strong feelings about the problems here in the North. But I do my job by reporting what I see, not what I feel."

Flanagan continued, "I'm from Belfast. I'm Catholic. I was lucky enough to go to university, Queen's, here in Belfast. My father owns a moderately successful food distribution company. Most of my classmates were Protestant. It was hard. I had my share of fights."

"I think Catholics are discriminated against in jobs, housing, certainly in lending. I think the six counties are the first and last British colony. We call them the Protestants, but it's not a religious thing. It's a convenient way of labeling unionists. Most Protestants are poor, just like most Catholics. Just trying to get along. Most don't give a shit about politics."

"I hate the violence. I hate how it effects everyone's life here. I hate how it makes us out to be something like a third world country. The Republic advertises the charm of the Emerald Isle. Northern Ireland is known only for its violence, a place where people are routinely in danger of being killed by a bomb. Christ, I saw the news footage of the 1992 Los Angeles riots. It's never been that bad here. Even the beginning of the *troubles*, up in Derry, 'Bloody Sunday in 1972, only thirteen people were killed. Nothing like what goes on in other places."

"I'll tell you, Mason. I don't hate the I.R.A. itself. At the heart of it, most I.R.A. are patriots. I know that sounds naive, but their cause is as right as any in history. The injustices are a damn sight greater than those that caused the American colonies to rebel."

"Come on, Kevin. The I.R.A. are a bunch of thugs and zealots. One and the same to the victims."

"I understand that must be the prevailing view. Some of these fanatical bastards have no remorse when they're in the dock. Necessary casualties, and all that. But that's not the typical I.R.A. soldier, but that's what makes the headlines.

What really is unfair is the way the world ignores what the Protestant paramiltaries do. Christ Almighty, they kill as many as the I.R.A."

Flanagan paused to drain his glass, then motioned to Whitely to pull two more.

Devereux said, "Look, Kevin, all I'm saying is that I'm not going to set out to build a case favoring any perspective, anymore than you would in reporting a story. I don't live here. I don't have any preconceived bias. Like most of the outside world, I would envision Northern Ireland to be a fortress, with heavily armed patrols and people avoiding the streets. Clearly, that conception is not the way things are. But it is also clear that there is a terrible undercurrent of fear and sectarian hatred that dominates life here."

"If you help me, Kevin, I don't want any misunderstandings as to my motives. Like you, I'm really just a journalist. In fact, I'm just a picture taker. I try to show things that reveal as much as possible about the event. Most causes are flawed and eventually become corrupted. What I have seen, what I have photographed, is the people at the bottom suffering and dying for someone else's cause. If there is a universal truth, it is that."

"If you're going to help me, Kevin, you need to understand that I am apolitical. I see most organizations professing high purpose but acting with a self-serving reality. Most governments don't even espouse high purpose. To put it bluntly, I don't care who my work irritates or even who it hurts."

"I understand, Mason, and I have no problem with that. If it's pictures you want, everything here can't help but to tell what life is like for the Catholic poor."

"Probably. But I won't be doing a commentary on the social deprivations in Northern Ireland, Kevin. It's the unrelenting violence that's the story. To the extent I can illustrate the backdrop, I will. But it is the uniqueness, the things you yourself have pointed out, that make the story. It's not statistics of how many are killed, Kevin. It's the mystique of this unrelenting violence."

"You make it sound like nothing more than fucking business," Flanagan said sarcastically.

"Get off it, Kevin. It is business. It's my business. No different than your business as a journalist. Don't expect a champion or a crusade. This is a story, nothing more."

Flanagan sighed. "I know, Mason. We're both professionals. But if you live with this, if it's part of your life, you can't separate your feelings. Being a journalist doesn't separate you from thinking and feeling. You can't feel the same things I do."

"So? Do I have to feel those emotions? Remember, Kevin, the rest of the world can't either. If I do a book, a photographic essay, then it's going to say many things. Like a painting, I hope it evokes feeling and thought. But it won't evoke what someone living inside the experience feels. And it sure as hell won't be biased to a preconceived perspective."

"Jesus Christ, Mason, you want my help or not?"

"Depends, Kevin. I want no misunderstandings where the project might lead. I don't want to deceive a friend, Kevin," He was sincere about referring to Flanagan as a friend.

Flanagan softened. "Those are kind words, Mason. I consider you a friend too, even not knowing you very long. I know what you're saying and I'm willing to help you. I've seen your work. Whatever you do, it's honest. I'm OK with the world seeing the *troubles* through your lens."

"Thanks, Kevin. So what's next?"

"First, I think you might want to get familiar with Belfast, maybe some other places like Derry, too. I'll also work on trying to set up some interviews for you."

"Interviews?"

"Sure. Various people to give you some ideas. Maybe even some Protestant loyalists for journalistic balance," Flanagan remarked jokingly.

"What about contacting someone in the I.R.A.?" Devereux asked.

"Possibly. I'll see what I can do."

They left the pub several whiskeys, later. Flanagan arranged to pick Devereux up on Tuesday, and do a proper tour of Belfast as he put it. Devereux spent Monday riding buses all over Belfast on his own, following a map and notes from his research. The solitary time allowed him to develop a feeling for the place.

Flanagan picked him up early in the morning on Tuesday. "Thought we'd start by journeying up to Derry first. Show you where the *troubles* started. Actually, they started hundreds of years ago, but this is where the last twenty-five years of violence got their beginning. It's about two hours. We'll get some breakfast along the way."

Around noon they arrived in Derry, or officially, Londonderry. In the distance could be seen the rise of the city's two hillsides and the spread of the River Foyle emptying into Lough Foyle. Flanagan took the Craigavon Bridge east across the river to the famous Derry City walls, the marvelously intact seventeenth century defensive fortifications. Evidence of more modern dangers was suggested by strategically located iron sheeting, and rolled barbed wire laid down by the British and Northern Ireland security forces.

"Built in the early sixteen hundreds with financing from London guilds. Last construction of a walled city in Europe, if my memory serves me," Flanagan said. "Walls are twenty feet thick. Big-assed cannon controlled the river. Protected London's mercantile interests here in the north."

"You're a walking history book, Kevin," Devereux joked.

"All right, but you've got to have some background. At any rate, I won't bore you with the area inside, unless you're interested. Museums, cathedral, shops, but there is a R.U.C. barracks."

"Maybe later."

"Well it may have happened a long while ago, but I'll tell you my friend, the Protestants still talk of history here like it was just yesterday."

"What do you mean?"

"The Battle of the Boyne. They talk like it happened in their own lifetime. It was before 1700. Actually the fighting began here in Derry. Protestants, loyal to William of Orange, held out against forces of the Catholic King James. Soon after, James was defeated at the battle of the Boyne, cementing Protestant domination of the northern Ireland counties."

"And that's the origin of orange being the color of the Protestants. I've been reading up on the history, Kevin," Devereux teased good-naturedly.

"Very well, we'll be getting along to the so-called Bogside area. In modern times, the current violence that now plagues us began there in the late sixties."

The Bogside area was to the northwest of the ancient walls. The area dropped off into a valley from the promontory of the walled city. Flanagan pointed out the signal mast with cameras atop the west wall, which had been taken over by the British army. They soon came upon an isolated wall with the slogan "YOU ARE NOW ENTERING FREE DERRY."

Flanagan parked the car nearby. He suggested they walk the area. Devereux slung his camera supplies bag over his shoulder, and draped two cameras around his neck.

"Back in the early days of the *troubles*, it was a warning to the police and security forces to keep out on fear of being fired on. They would have, too. The I.R.A. owned things in there, still does in a less overt show. Police have decided not to provoke the issue by removing the sign."

"Was that when 'Bloody Sunday' happened?" Devereux asked.

"Yeah, in seventy-two. But before that there were other events that really started things. The first event was a civil rights march in sixty-eight that probably started it all."

"You see, Derry is somewhat unique in Northern Ireland. While collectively the six counties are something like sixty percent Protestant, Derry is two-thirds Catholic. Yet here the Protestants control the government and economy of the city by defining the voting districts."

"So what brought things to a head that day?"

"I don't know exactly. But about two thousand marchers took to the streets that day. They demanded equality in employment and housing. The Royal Ulster Constabulary and B-Specials met them. The police busted a lot of heads that day with riot batons. They also showed the Catholics whose side they were on. After that, the R.U.C. was the enemy to the Catholics."

"A year or so later, the I.R.A. was reborn with the so-called Provincial wing breaking away from the older, less military oriented, Official Irish Republican Army," Flanagan said.

"The B-Specials? Seems I read about them, but refresh me," Devereux said.

"Yeah, well the B-Specials got their name from a Lord Brookeborough back in the twenties, during the war for independence. To be honest, I can't recall their history, but they were the first of the Protestant and Unionist paramiltaries. Government sponsored to boot. The British semi-official militia. They were still around until the nineties. Provided the British with extra resources, and a convenient way to disavow excesses."

Some portions of the area had undergone attempts at redevelopment. But still in evidence, were the turn-of-the-century blocks of two-story brick tenements, stained with decades of industrial soot. The dull, sunless sky cast even more gloom over this depressed area.

Flanagan continued his narrative, "Then about a year later, in 1969, there was another incident. 'Battle of the Bogside' they called it. Hell of a thing it was to hear from those that were there. Did a story once about it. Interviewed some people who were there at the time."

"There was this Protestant march that provoked the Catholics. The Catholics started throwing stones, then all manner of forces, the R.U.C., B-Specials, and mobs of Protestants attempted to enter the Bogside. It was like a siege from the middle ages. Know what one old timer told me it reminded him of? The Warsaw ghetto during the war, especially the news footage of the Nazis trying to root out the resistance.

The Catholics erected barricades. They kept the security forces at bay for several days, but at a cost. There were some killed. Hundreds more were injured. Eventually caused London to commit more British troops. Britain again appeared to enforce Protestant sympathies. Things got so bad that the Irish prime minister sent Irish soldiers to the border in a threat to prevent genocide of Catholics here in the North."

Flanagan continued, "Then in 1972 you had 'Bloody Sunday.' British paratroopers fired on an unarmed civil rights procession. Thirteen people were killed. The soldiers claimed they were fired on first. An official inquiry exonerated them. But it forever changed how Catholics thought of the British army."

"Other places have had the same kind of background as Ireland. The hatreds never die, but they have not perpetuated a continued armed struggle. Why have the Irish waged such an unrelenting violent struggle against the British for so long, Kevin?"

"Don't know, Mason. That's the grand question. Wives and mothers have asked that throughout Irish history as they grieved at the loss of their men. Irishmen are either too dumb or too brave to shy away from the fight."

"What do you feel, Kevin?"

Flanagan stopped walking and faced Devereux. "In my heart I hate the British and those that control things here in the north. It's not always rational, but it's too much a part of our history. The British have always shit on us Irish. They subjugated us by ruling the land through local landowners loyal to the Crown. Ireland became a land of tenant farmers. When that didn't work, they simply killed us," Flanagan said with passion. "I grew up hearin' my own Pa tell about how he was treated by his Protestant foreman. He was a machinist. A proud man. I remember crying with hate and shame overhearing him tell my Ma about what went on at the factory."

"How do the British figure into that?"

"Because the Protestants are the ancestors of the English and Scotch colonists of the past. They think of themselves as British. They fear the Catholic minority here in Northern Ireland. They fear being absorbed into the predominately Catholic south. Why? Because of religious differences? Shit no. Most don't go to church any more than most Catholics go to mass. It's as simple as not wanting to lose power. And by now, it's evolved into a conditioned prejudice on both sides. I can feel it in myself. Many times it's stronger than any logic."

They had walked the Bogside area slums for close to two hours. Devereux shot up several rolls of film. He thought about the photographs he had taken so far. Nothing of real value. Dirt, poverty, slum dwellings, some barbed wire, some barricades, but certainly nothing 'book-worthy.' His publisher wouldn't do a pictorial book on Northern Ireland social commentary. It was the violence that set Northern Ireland apart. It was the violence he must capture.

They arrived back at the car. As they drove off, Devereux asked, "What's next on the agenda, Kevin?"

"Back to Belfast, a drink or two, then you can treat me to dinner."

"I think there is a book here, Kevin, but it's going to be tough. I'm not sure the sectarian violence in Northern Ireland has the power of a predominately photographic work. The story has to have a visual impact. Obviously it's not like an overt war zone. All the pictures I've seen in the library are from the street violence mostly during the seventies. So the question is, how can I get shots that are telling of what goes on here today?"

Flanagan headed the car east back toward Belfast.

After a few moments, Flanagan asked, "What kind of material would you want, Mason?"

Devereux considered his response. Flanagan's tone had changed slightly. "If I could get some candid material, illegal activities, things beyond news photo shots, something with some meat in it. Don't imagine your friends in the I.R.A. would like photographs of bomb-making, or training exercises, though."

"You think I have friends in the I.R.A.?"

"I don't know, Kevin, but you're a newspaper man. You're obviously pro-Catholic, so I'm sure you have your contacts. I suspect you know somebody that knows somebody, that sort of thing."

Flanagan was quiet for several minutes, then said, "What about activities of the Protestant paramilitaries? Would that be as good as shots of the I.R.A.?"

"Perhaps. What are you suggesting?"

"Nothing specific, but like you said, maybe I know somebody who knows somebody."

Chapter Three

It was a beautiful morning. Sun poured through the thin curtains, announcing what was to be a spectacular spring day. To Garrett O'Donovan, slightly hung over, it was a harsh call back to work and reality.

Beside him, covered to her neck with the bedding, was the source of an exquisite night of love making. Passive now, she was breathing with a total depth of sated relaxation. He climbed out of bed to look out the window onto the early morning activity in the street. The woman rolled over, partially awake.

"What are you doing, Luv? Come back to bed," she said groggily. She had turned and sat upright, the sheets falling down, revealing her ample breasts.

O'Donovan felt himself growing hard.

He climbed back onto the bed and grabbed her breasts. She in turn stroked his erect member. O'Donovan soon pushed her back down on the bed. She responded by guiding him into her with her hand.

"Like that, Luv?" the woman whispered in a throaty rasp. "Deeper."

O'Donovan responded by holding her legs out at arms length.

"Oh, that's it!" she said loudly.

Having spent himself, he rolled off of her.

"You do like to fuck don't you?" O'Donovan said. The woman was an insatiable lover. As much as he liked sex, he thought it fortunate that he saw her only about once a month. She could suck a man dry.

"With you I do, Luv."

"No one else?"

"Come on now, Luv, a girl's got to live. It's weeks sometimes between your visits. But you're special. I look oh so forward to your visits," she said as she rose from the bed and gave O'Donovan a long look at her body before pulling on a robe.

She made him breakfast before he returned to Belfast. This had been their routine for almost a year.

"So why can't you stay longer, Luv? A girl needs more than just the occasional sweet time in bed. Wish your business here in Armagh was more regular."

"Told you how it is. Wife and all. Business to run. Not complaining are you?" There was a slight edge to his voice.

O'Donovan intrigued her. Tall, strong, handsome, and mysterious. In Northern Ireland, mysterious might translate as involvement somehow with the I.R.A. She could fancy that. Shacking up with a real Provo man had a ring of adventure.

Then again, he might be into drugs or some such thing.

"No. Just would like to see more of you."

It was an hour drive back to the pub in Belfast. O'Donovan arrived during the lunch hour trade. He kissed the portly matron behind the bar, "Hi, Mum," then made the rounds to greet the working class patrons. Most were regulars.

His mother shook her head. His absences were nothing new, but a continuing concern.

O'Donovan rejoined his mother back behind the bar.

"Mary Catherine and I expected you back yesterday." Her tone was mildly accusatory.

"Business, Mum. You know how it is."

By 'business,' he knew his mother understood what he meant. His mother assumed his absences were associated with the I.R.A. She knew he was active in some way. The details she did not want to know.

O'Donovan's wife appeared from the kitchen. She acknowledged his presence coldly by simply saying "Garrett," then going about her duties.

O'Donovan took lunch with a couple of the pub's regulars. After doing his social duties with the noontime patrons, he went upstairs to the living quarters over the pub. With a meeting of the 'unit' that night, he needed a nap. There had been little opportunity for that the previous night.

Mary Catherine entered the bedroom as he was undressing. "You know, Garrett, your mother and I can't run this business without help. There's all manner of things that haven't been done. There's the cooling unit to the cold storage that needs fixing. There's the light fixture in the corner. There's the —"

"All right, enough, woman. I'll get to it when I can. There's other things that are more important. But you wouldn't be understandin' that would you?"

He looked at her. Mary Catherine perhaps could have been attractive. But O'Donovan found her unexciting. She took no pains in her looks. No makeup. Matronly dresses. She was lousy in bed. Mostly he resented her. O'Donovan stood naked in front of her. She slightly averted her gaze away from him.

"I'm going to take a nap for a while. I'll be busy tonight."

"Useless bitch," he thought as she left. Couldn't remember when they last had sex. Didn't matter anyway since she made it seem like a favor. Not like it was in the beginning. She had not been experienced, but she fucked enthusiastically and as often as he liked. Then she got herself pregnant. That was the first time he hit her. Stupid bitch should have known better.

He thought back on that early time not so long ago before things turned sour.

Mary Catherine Mullins had been working at the pub for two months. His father had hired her to replace some fat girl that had somehow found a husband. Mary Catherine was not married. She had apparently been taking care of her father and brothers until the old man died. O'Donovan paid her little mind since he was rarely around the pub except to sleep.

When his father suddenly died of a heart attack, Garrett O'Donovan's life abruptly changed. There was no choice but to quit his job. It was a choice job, with one of the few successful Catholic owned firms in Belfast. O'Donovan had been to a trade school, receiving a certification as an electrician.

O'Donovan's pub was in the west of Belfast. The surrounding neighborhoods were Catholic, with strong republican sympathies. Both the R.U.C. and the British army moved with considerable caution on these streets. It was the poor of Belfast, Catholics who lived here. Unemployment was high, the likelihood of improved prospects low.

His father took great pride in the fact that he was a businessman. As a tavern keeper, he was at the center of social and political life, one in the same in Catholic Belfast. To the young O'Donovan, life did not seem much different from his mates at school, most of which had blue-collar fathers, many were unemployed, all were poor. He too was poor, his father's pub bringing in profits no better than an average laborer's wages. From as far back as he could remember, he worked in the pub, picking up tables, washing dishes, mopping, cleaning the lavatories.

His father had loved the business. It was also a forum for him to hold forth to a receptive audience. Any prestige of being a businessman was short-lived for Garrett O'Donovan. He acutely felt the loss of freedom that his factory job had afforded. It allowed for various affairs and one night stands with willing women. With running your own business came twelve and fourteen hour days and doing labor he thought he had left behind.

He had not paid Mary Catherine much notice previously. Fairly good body, if perhaps a little on the skinny side. Somewhat plain.

Being around her each day, he looked at her differently. Availability was the primary factor even if she did not seem a hot number. He also discovered he liked talking to her.

"Your Da was a grand man. He had a melodious voice," Mary Catherine said to O'Donovan during a break in work one day soon after his father's death.

"Melodious? Now there's a grand word."

"I read a lot. You pick up lots of words that way," she said a little self-consciously. "But that's how I remember his voice. He could talk for hours, all the while pulling pints and pouring whiskies. It was like entertainment for the customers."

"Was he with the I.R.A., Garrett?"

"That's a bold question, girl."

"Well there was no secret about how he felt about the Brits and Prods. Praised the I.R.A. openly. Walking history book he was too."

"You could say my Da was I.R.A. Most everybody knew that. My brother was I.R.A. too."

"Your brother?"

"Yeah. Name was Joseph, just like my Da he was. Died some years ago. Killed he was by the British. Da hated them enough before, but after that it was worse."

"What happened?"

"Joe was part of an I.R.A. Active Service Unit. That's the boys that do all those things you read about. He was part of a team of four who tried to blow up an R.U.C. barracks with a car bomb. British soldiers gunned them down at a roadblock. Killed my brother and another guy. Shot Joe in the face. Casket had to be closed. My mother couldn't even look at her dead son."

"How old were you when this happened?"

"Fifteen. I remember when we heard. It was Father Maloney that brought the news around one winter afternoon. It was cold and raining. The day was made for melancholy. I was cleaning tables. He came around the bar then gently grabbed my father by the arm and whispered something. My mother was there too. Then all three went into the back room. Next thing I hear is my mother wailing. Knew then it was bad. Knew it was about Joseph."

He did not tell Mary Catherine how his father then came over to tell him. How his knuckles were white from gripping the broom fearing the worse. How tears flowed down his cheeks uncontrollably as his father hugged him and sobbed as well. How the pub was absolutely silent. How his father turned to his patrons, his friends and said, "They've killed my boy. The bloody bastards have killed my boy."

The funeral was a major event. All such funerals of I.R.A. men killed in action were. The I.R.A. saw to it. Funerals were the most visible evidence of the *war*. What else could strike such a responsive cord in those Irish who held republican sentiments than a funeral? Never mind that the dead person may have been committing an act that you could not conscionably condone. The hard fact remained, the enemy had claimed another victim.

The I.R.A. turned out people in the thousands for such events. After every such a funeral, requests for enlistments poured in at elevated rates. Martyrs were essential to sustaining the Irish Republican Army.

Such press also made the international news. The Northern Ireland situation had to compete for world attention. Millions of people of Irish descent lived outside the Republic of Ireland, or Northern Ireland. No other ethnic group had quite the expatriate population in the same proportions as the Irish. Major funding and arms smuggling to the I.R.A. came from support from the United States. Funerals of dead heroes were their poster children. The funeral of Joseph O'Donovan and his colleague drew several thousand marchers to the place of internment. It was the I.R.A.'s form of public relations.

O'Donovan had become momentarily lost in the memory.

"I'm sorry. I can tell it still hurts," Mary Catherine said.

O'Donovan certainly did not want her to feel sympathy toward him.

"Sure, I loved my brother, but that was a long time ago. Joe was a soldier. He died a soldier's death for the Cause and there's good in that."

"Is it your cause too?"

"If you mean do I hate the Protestants and the British, I do."

"Are you I.R.A. too, Garrett?"

"Jesus, woman! You can't be asking questions like that!"

That conversation had taken place only a week after his father's funeral and a conversation with Padraig McCullough.

His father's wake had naturally been held at the pub. It was there that Padraig McCullough, commander of a Belfast I.R.A. unit, recruited the now twenty-four year old Garrett O'Donovan into the I.R.A. McCullough had been close to O'Donovan's father for years. Garrett O'Donovan knew him only as a close friend of his father's and somehow connected to the I.R.A. After several whiskies, and knowing the young O'Donovan's sympathies, McCullough, told him of his father's and brother's roles in the continuing war.

"You know about the things your brother was into. Things that were in the papers when he was killed. Most of it was true. A real hero. Your father's heart was torn out when he died, but he couldn't have been prouder," McCullough said. "But did you ever know what your father did for the Cause himself?"

"Not really. He never talked about anything specific. I remember him being arrested a couple of times. Said it was because of his sympathies and because of my brother. I remember my mother being scared."

"Joseph O'Donovan senior was more than a sympathizer. He was full-blooded I.R.A. Joe was a valuable logistical conduit for money, weapons, and intelligence. Your father was always the man to be trusted, always the one to be relied on," McCullough said.

McCullough lowered his voice and made sure no one was in earshot, then continued.

"I shouldn't tell you this, but a son should know what his father was. Your father channeled money coming from America to the Army Council. Lots of money, and weapons too. He was brilliant and never got caught."

"I remember people at the back tables talking in low voices. Me Da always spent a lot time with you particularly, Paddy. Yeah, I wondered what he was part of."

"Told me he would never allow you to join," McCullough said. "Said he couldn't take it if anything were to happen to his only son. But I also know it was a promise he made to your mother. Told me she had laid down the law telling him that his family could survive if he was sent off to prison since they had the pub, but they couldn't survive another dead son."

"Choice is for you to make now. We need good men like you, Garrett. Like your father, you're more than just a tavern keeper. There's a history of fighting for Ireland in your family. Your father told me once that your great-grandfather had also been killed in the civil war in twenty-one."

O'Donovan told McCullough he would think on it. But there was really little to consider. He was eager for a change in a life that was already becoming suffocating. McCullough was right, he was more than a tavern keeper.

The I.R.A. was part of his family. He probably would have become involved sooner had his brother not been killed, and his father not blocked any such thoughts. His hatred for the British and the Protestants was well ingrained.

It was a week later that he had his first real conversation with Mary Catherine. They were closing the pub as usual, his mother having retired earlier as was her habit. It was after two o'clock in the morning on a Friday night. O'Donovan had good-naturedly kicked out the last of the diehards.

"So you liking it here, Mary Catherine?"

She looked up from washing the last of the glasses. "Very much. Your Mum's a real dear."

"And me?" O'Donovan asked with a broad smile as he sat himself on a stool directly across the bar from Mary Catherine.

She blushed and smiled back averting his gaze saying, "I like you too, Garrett."

When she did look at him, her eyes did not conceal much. He knew when a woman was ready.

He came around the bar next to her. Still with her hands in the soapy water, he gently put his hands on her shoulders and turned her toward him. She could not resist his kiss as he embraced her.

"I'm getting you all wet," Mary Catherine said as she eventually pulled back having put her wet hands on his shirt.

"That you are, lass, but not in the way you mean."

O'Donovan pulled her against him again. He could sense she had turned the corner, that decision to drop all inhibition as she returned his kiss greedily. He knew she could feel his erection against her and cemented the seduction by rubbing her breasts.

"Upstairs," was all he said. Mary Catherine complied without comment.

She was a virgin that first night, but aggressive. It got better over time. She really seemed to like sex. Naive and inexperienced, she was willing to be taught what he liked her to do. She was his only bed partner for the next several months.

Much had happen during those months. Only three weeks after the funeral of his father, Garrett O'Donovan was formerly accepted into the Provincial Irish Republican Army. The ceremony was held in the back room of the pub. Attending were many of the patrons, some of which Garrett had always suspected were I.R.A. members.

McCullough administered the oath. O'Donovan was given a typed card from which to read the official oath.

"I, Garrett Michael O'Donovan, declare that to the best of my knowledge and ability I will support and defend the Irish Republic against all enemies, foreign and domestic, that I will bear true faith and allegiance to the same. I do further declare that I do not and shall not yield a voluntary support to any pretended Government, Authority, or Power within Ireland hostile or inimical to that Republic."

"I take this obligation freely without any mental reservation or purpose of evasion - so help me God."

Beyond the official oath of allegiance, McCullough added his own more immediate, more direct declaration of purpose.

"Before you is the shamrock, symbol of our believed Eire. Also before you is the gun, symbol of our resolve to wrest our freedom from an oppressive authority."

On a table before O'Donovan was a four leafed shamrock encased in a Lucite cube, next to it, an old thirty-eight caliber revolver laid out on a square of green velvet. O'Donovan was instructed to grasp both objects.

"This weapon is particularly sacred to our Cause. It was the personal sidearm of Patrick Pearse, Commander-in-Chief of the Army of the Irish Republic who led the Easter uprising of 1916. He died for Ireland at the hands of a British firing squad. It symbolizes our war that goes back over three hundred years before even that time, and shall continue until there is a united Ireland."

McCullough intoned, "The inductee, will repeat after me. I, Garrett Michael O'Donovan, do swear to follow all lawful orders issued by the Provincial Irish Republican Army command, to deny the enemy access to any information injurious to its cause or its members, and to be prepared to sacrifice my life in the struggle for freedom."

O'Donovan repeated the oath, then replaced both objects on the table. O'Donovan was not one normally moved by religious or patriotic ceremony. This was something else however. He could feel a shuddering sensation on taking the oath. For the first time in his life he experienced a true sense of belonging, of identifying with a group.

Holding Pearse's revolver had a more pronounced effect. He could not take his eyes off it. His hand noticeably shook. It was as if the Cause took on a physical presence in the form of some sort of energy.

O'Donovan had not only joined the Provincial Irish Republican Army, but also what was referred to as an Active Service Unit. While total I.R.A. membership was in the hundreds, only a comparatively small number were associated with Active Service Units. These were the people that committed the bombings and assassinations.

After the ceremony, there followed much backslapping and whisky drinking. Excluded from the ceremony, O'Donovan's mother brought in pints of Guinness. Looking at these men, she knew what this was about. She knew her son was now part of an inevitable cycle.

McCullough put his arm around Mrs. O'Donovan.

"He's a fine lad, your Garrett is. You should be very proud."

Her eyes were glassy.

"Mind you, Paddy McCullough, I know what you are about. Both my beloved Josephs gave their lives to the Cause. Now you say I should be proud. Proud that my only son will now go in harms way. To what fate? A British bullet? One from the U.F.F, or U.V.F., or whatever the letters are? Or maybe prison until he is an old man with no more life? I don't know anymore. Nothing has ever changed during my life, except maybe it's worse now."

"It's in God's hands now. You men will drink your whiskey, tell your stories, play your game of heroes, and many will go to their graves too soon. Then it'll be the women who'll be burying more of you and your enemies."

"They're enemies of all Irish Catholics, Mrs. O'Donovan," McCullough said.

"Aye, so you people say. Once I thought so too, but now I don't know. Just don't you be comin'' around with any sorrowful news about my Garrett, Paddy McCullough."

Two weeks after his induction into the I.R.A., Paddy McCullough asked him to meet him at a certain pub. McCullough brought another young man along to the meeting. O'Donovan had never met him before. McCullough introduced him as Seamus Devlin.

"Both of you are new to the unit. It's quite possible that you will be involved on a mission, soon. So you need to know some things, lads. After an attack, there's always hell to pay. The R.U.C. starts pulling in large numbers of suspected I.R.A. You must assume that they know you are a member. In all likelihood, they do."

Both O'Donovan and Devlin were surprised by that acknowledgment.

"You've got to prepare yourself for what happens when you're picked up. If you understand what they are trying to do, you can defeat them, and save yourself a lot of grief to boot. They're very good at this sort of thing, not as rough as in the old days, but tough just the same."

"What are you worried about, Paddy? I wouldn't tell them a thing. Spit in their eye, I would. The bloody fuckers," Devlin responded.

"And you, Garrett? You feel the same?" McCullough asked.

"Sure, that's right. Killed my brother, didn't they. Think I would give them shit? What are they going to do? Work me over a bit? Don't worry about none of that," O'Donovan answered.

"Listen, I know you're both brave lads, devoted to the Cause and all, but that won't be enough. You think they'll just bash you about some, keep questioning you for hours. Aye, that they will. But that's not the half of it." McCullough was not getting through to them.

"There is one central thing to remember if you are picked up by the police. Unless they are formally charging you, they want to get a confession out of you. I know you're thinking that they couldn't possibly get me to confess. Believe me, men better than you have broken under interrogation."

Both O'Donovan and Devlin shook their heads almost imperceptibly in protest.

McCullough banged his fist on the table, "Listen to me, and don't give me no schoolboy bullshit. First of all, they'll probably come for you in the wee hours of the morning. Catches one at the most vulnerable time. Disorientation and all that."

"Next, you'll maybe spend several days without any contact, without any questioning. That's to soften you up. Don't know what's coming. Mind plays all sorts of ugly scenarios. They may taunt you in the cell. Threats of physical torture to come. Remember, current laws allow them to detain you for up to seven days."

"Next, the first of the interrogations. They'll keep asking questions repeatedly. Different interrogators will trade off. Some may even say they are trying to help you. Do what they can to keep the others off your back. If you do not cooperate they may raise the game to physical abuse. In the old days, they really kicked the shit out of prisoners. Some even died. Today, they're more careful. Could be some kicking and punching, more likely shoving you about, between each of them, slamming you to the wall, that sort of thing. Really is more psychological than physical. When they really get mean, they use cigarettes on your body. If accused of torture, they claim the prisoner self inflicted the wounds."

"Somewhere in the interrogation cycle, they will make you strip. This is another tactic learned from history. A naked prisoner is more vulnerable, feels less personal esteem. The interrogators make remarks about the size of your cock, about your manhood, about your wife or girlfriend."

"Throughout the ordeal, and make no mistake, lads, it is an ordeal, the fuckers will make all sorts of threats against your family and friends. Lastly, they claim that one of your mates has confessed, has implicated you so as to get a lighter sentence. The offer is for you to also get a reduced sentence, provided you sign a confession."

"Don't underestimate the police interrogators. They are experts. They'll use every means at their disposal, to get only one thing: a confession. Without that, there is nothing, otherwise you would have been charged earlier on. Remember that. They're tryin' to make you hang yourself."

"So how do you survive? Did you read the copy of the *Green Book* yet?"

Both O'Donovan and Devlin nodded that they had.

The *Green Book* dealt with not only the political and historical foundation of the Irish Republican Army, but also served the more practical aspects as a military manual, dealing with training, organization, discipline, and security. Particular emphasis was placed on giving the recruit a firm psychological basis to counter police methods, including various forms of torture. In fact, the book was prepared in the wake of repeated successes by the R.U.C. and British security personnel in breaking volunteers in the late seventies.

"Well what did you think?" McCullough asked.

O'Donovan looked at Devlin, then answered, "I know the history. I know why we fight the Brits and Prods. My family has fought and died for the Cause for generations. It didn't tell me anything I didn't already know."

"I'm not talking about politics, O'Donovan. I'm talking about what you do if you're picked up. Then what you do when they start beating on you and fucking with your head.?"

McCullough continued, frustrated with his new recruits. "You've got to understand. After any attack, the security forces pick up and detain any number of people. Have no illusions, lads. Like I said, they may even already know of your membership. At the least, they certainly have your names in their files because of your family histories. It's the same with most of us."

McCullough had given this same lecture before. All new recruits felt the same. Full of anger. Full of confidence. Full of piss and vinegar. Underestimating the enemy. Thinking of the enemy as some cartoon caricature, responding only with blind, brutish force.

"What they want is information, a confession of some kind if possible. They're not even particular about the confession being real. They're only looking to put you away, and to put your mates away. If they can't do that, they'll try to muck you up so that you are no use to the Army anymore. Unreliable, can't be trusted, that sort of thing."

"Don't indulge in any conversation with them. Nothing. Not casual, not political. Nothing. Don't let them bait you. Don't debate politics with them. Keep your mouth shut. Take whatever shit they dish out. Remember, if you say anything, you hurt the Cause, and you shame yourself," McCullough continued.

"You talk like you expect us to get arrested, Paddy," O'Donovan said.

"Listen, God damn it. There's always a good chance you could be detained. Detained, not arrested. This is not bloody fucking England. You have no rights here. You're a Catholic — a piece of shit. They don't need to go through all the tidy legal formalities like you see on the telly. That's England, America, maybe even the Republic, but not here in the North. They'll pick you up, kick you in the balls, spit on you, and fuck you over any way they can. But if you keep your mouth shut, they'll eventually let you go. Remember, if they don't charge you right off, they've got no evidence. They'll eventually have to let you go."

"If you're picked up, say nothing, sign nothing, and read the goddamn book!" McCullough ordered, raising his voice to a harsh rasp.

O'Donovan did read the *Green Book*, this time with more critical consideration. It was to serve him in good stead.

Chapter Four

A few months after this conversation with McCullough, O'Donovan was ordered to drive to a farm in County Armagh, an hour drive over country roads southwest of Belfast. He was to go alone. He would receive further orders there. The instructions lead him down a narrow, unpaved lane.

There was another auto and a delivery van parked close to the old farmhouse. Before he could knock, the door opened, and a ancient wizened man with shaking, gnarled hands, bent with a cane, admitted him to the house.

"They're in the kitchen," was all he said to O'Donovan, leaving him to go off to some recess in the dimly lit house.

In the kitchen, seated around a table were three men, none of which were known to O'Donovan. The older one, probably in his mid-thirties, greeted him.

"My name is Daniel, this is John, and this is Eamonn. Of course those are not our real names. Therefore, I don't want to know yours. Adds a layer of security I'm sure you can appreciate. What will it be that we call you, then?" Daniel said, obviously the person in charge.

O'Donovan replied that they could call him, Joe.

"Good to have you with us, Joe. By the way, the old man who owns this farm is a loyal comrade, an old soldier. Fought in the civil war in the early twenties. I trust him completely," Daniel said.

"I understand that you are an electrician, Joe?"

"That's right," O'Donovan answered.

"Good. That's why we need you for this mission. I'm told you're a good lad."

Daniel continued. "Our mission is to carry out an execution sentence on a Brian Webster of the Ulster Volunteer Force. You may be aware of his name. Webster commands a group we know to be responsible for the deaths of at least three Irish Republican Army volunteers, and at least four other civilians. The Supreme military command convened a court marshal, which resulted in a verdict of guilty. Webster was sentenced to death."

"Holy Jesus," one man uttered softly. The others stared at Daniel intently, but said nothing.

"Don't you be worrying about this Webster. I know of him. If anyone deserves to die it's this sonofabitch. Like the court marshal said, he's killed our people. He's a military target. It's our mission to carry out that execution, lads," Daniel continued.

"Joe, you're here because of your background as an electrician. Here, this is a schematic. Can you understand it?" Daniel asked, unfolding the drawing.

O'Donovan took a few minutes to look at the schematic.

"Pretty simple. Not difficult to understand. You don't really need an electrician. Probably anyone could wire this," O'Donovan said.

"Right enough, Joe, but you were selected for other reasons as well. And if it's just the same to you, I'll feel better knowing an expert is dealing with the explosives," Daniel replied.

Jesus, O'Donovan thought. He wasn't an expert at explosives. Where in the hell had they got that idea. He knew almost nothing about it, but didn't say anything. O'Donovan hoped that the others had some sort of experience with whatever they were going to do. McCullough must have recommended him. Paddy was a smart old timer, so there must be a reason for him being selected.

"Right, lads, let's get to it," Daniel said.

O'Donovan felt the adrenaline surge through him. This was it. Not just talk anymore. They were going on a mission. This is what he had joined the I.R.A. for.

They shared a bottle of Bushmills as details of a previously drafted plan were hammered out over the next three hours. The plan was bold, yet simple and essentially sound. O'Donovan was assigned the key role. The attack was scheduled to take place in five days. For O'Donovan, there was a mixture of pride and apprehension. He slept little during the next few days.

It was a Friday, mid-afternoon on a chilly winter day. The four men assembled at a service garage operated by the I.R.A. O'Donovan had meticulously assembled the explosive device there the previous day using rather poor instructions. It was clear to him that there had been a mistake in his selection for his role. Whoever was running this operation had the impression that O'Donovan knew explosives. The electrical circuit and triggering method were fairly simple. It was the explosive charge about which he was totally ignorant. He was drenched in perspiration by the end of the process.

In a back storage room, the man in charge calling himself Daniel reviewed the plan for a final time. Handguns were distributed. O'Donovan was given a nine-millimeter automatic. Holding the weapon caused a sensation to run through him. He was ready. This was what he was meant to do. He did not think about how ineffectual the weapon would be in a real firefight. But it gave credibility to his identity and stature.

Apparently Webster always took a few pints in the late afternoon every Friday at a particular public house in the Ballymacarrett district on Belfast's east side. These were Protestant neighborhoods. The two volunteers calling themselves John and Eamon were to confirm Webster's presence by driving by and identifying his auto, which should be, parked somewhere close by. They were to then phone the garage.

It was five P.M. when the call was received. O'Donovan and Daniel left immediately in a service lorry from the garage. The name on the door panel had been changed by using an adhesive sign.

Later, O'Donovan would think back about that short trip across Belfast. Time seemed expanded. The colors, the sounds, even the smells were never so vivid. There was no fear, but there was an intensity like none he had ever experienced. Even sex could not duplicate this rush.

Twenty minutes later they passed the pub, identifying Webster's auto. Daniel drove around the block coming around again to the street in front of the pub. He pulled the lorry up alongside an auto parked two vehicles behind Webster's. The man called Eamonn appeared from an adjacent shop. Daniel and Eamonn pretended to converse as they opened the bonnet of someone's vehicle. If the owner were to appear within the next few minutes, the plan would be aborted.

O'Donovan, slipped beneath the vehicle. Dragging a satchel with the explosive device, he crawled underneath the vehicle, then the one directly behind Webster's, and finally under Webster's. There was one of Webster's U.V.F. people outside the pub keeping a watch. He saw the service lorry, but paid little attention after Eamonn opened the bonnet of the auto. Staying warm with a flask, and taking a smoke was occupying more of his interest. From his vantage point he could not see O'Donovan crawling beneath the vehicles.

Although it seemed many times longer, O'Donovan was under the vehicles for less than two minutes. He had practiced the maneuver in the garage repeatedly. He affixed the explosive device directly under the driver's seat. From under the car, he could see the legs of Webster's lookout man. His heart raced. Once completed, he crawled more quickly back up the line of cars. O'Donovan rose up on the side away from the lookout and got into the lorry. Daniel and Eamonn closed the bonnet of the auto. Daniel drove the lorry away. Eamon waved and walked back toward the shop until out of sight of the sentry. John picked him up and left the scene as instructed.

Daniel drove the lorry to a position at the end of the block, and parked.

It was after eight o'clock when Webster finally left the pub. Two other men accompanied him. The men talked for several minutes before all three got into the auto. O'Donovan and Daniel assumed it was Webster, but it was impossible to tell at this distance in the dark.

"Can you see them," Daniel asked excitedly as three men emerged from the pub and went to Webster's vehicle.

"Think so. Looks like they're talking - smoking now," O'Donovan said. He held a remote radio-transmitting device. He toggled the activating switch that enabled the triggering signal.

Sweat ran down his temples. "Get in the fucking car, damn you," he willed.

"They're in the car —- do it now," Daniel said softly.

"Aye," was all O'Donovan responded. He waited several seconds. This was a moment to change his entire life. He depressed the triggering button. The delayed response, probably only less than two seconds, caused a momentary concern. It was simply the sequence of the signal activating the electrical circuit, which in turn initiated a chemical reaction resulting in a large release of energy in a confined space in a compressed span of time.

The effects of the explosion were underestimated by the assailants. The sound was deafening. The force of the blast rocked the lorry even though they were over two hundred meters away. There was no fire, only smoke and the sound of debris falling to the ground from the destroyed automobile. The final, lone sound was the bonnet hitting the pavement followed by silence. A couple of dogs started barking.

Daniel hurried to pull the lorry onto the street. O'Donovan placed his hand on the steering wheel. "Steady, Daniel. Go slowly. Don't want to attract attention," O'Donovan said. His adrenaline was pumping, but he felt totally in command of what was going on.

Daniel eased the lorry onto the street in a "U" turn, leaving the area. Proceeding back east into Belfast, they passed screaming sirens of fire and police vehicles.

O'Donovan and the man called Daniel returned the lorry to the garage. Two men removed the bogus, temporary business name decals from the door panels. O'Donovan and Daniel were driven away immediately in separate vehicles.

O'Donovan was deposited back at the pub before ten o'clock that night. He helped out in the pub, being visible until closing time. Containing the excitement until closing time took an act of will. Idle barroom banter seemed so trivial, irrelevant to the extreme events earlier.

There was only fitful sleep that night. He was still high from what he had done. He also remembered what Paddy had told him about the security forces making arrests after an attack. He fully expected the dreaded knock on the door that night. Maybe even the door being broken down.

He awoke slightly disoriented at sunrise. Lingering into his consciousness was a dream of the police breaking in to arrest him. Mary Catherine lay on her side, sound asleep, breathing heavily. The rising of her breasts through the sheets aroused him.

He pulled back the sheet and blanket. The sight of his wife's form aroused him further. He never felt more alive. Running his hand under her nightgown, he clutched her mound.

Mary Catherine stirred, "No. Not now, Garrett," she said groggily.

"Come on woman, I'm hard as rock. I need to be inside you."

Without waiting for a response he rolled on top of her. Roughly he rubbed his erect penis against her vulva.

"No, Garrett —- please."

O'Donovan forced himself into her. She let out a slight sound. It hurt. She was not lubricated. It was not the first time. Mercifully, it was over in a few minutes. She was only an instrument. Little better than his hand. He probably didn't even know or care if she was actually awake.

O'Donovan rolled over and slept soundly for several more hours, no longer troubled by dreams of the security forces.

O'Donovan read every word of the newspaper stories about the bombing the next morning. What he felt was not easily described. A mixture of power, pride, accomplishment, of having found your calling, of being someone. The feeling was compelling and consuming. Never once did fear intrude. Christ he felt good.

This was what he was born to. Running a pub was work for old men or women. The work average people do. He wasn't average. He could do this—and do it well. Cool under fire. Not afraid. Back in school he was like that, too. Never shied from a fight. Always came out on top. Could take blows and keep giving them back.

He knew his father and probably his mother too liked his older brother more than him. Joe was always the darling. Joe was always there to help. Hard worker. Committed to the Cause. Praised by their parish priest. Altar boy. While he, Garrett, was frequently in trouble over something, usually fighting or taunting British troops. Girl trouble too. But he was never jealous. He just felt differently about things and he also loved his brother.

His father and brother were political. Garrett hated the Brits, hated the Protestants, and hated the discrimination like they did. He could feel that hatred just as much as they could. But he wanted things for himself, not just for the good of the Cause.

Nothing happened for the next several nights. A confidence set in even though he knew they might come for him at any time. They did, four nights later.

It was 3 A.M., just like Paddy said. Loud knocking on the door. No time to respond. The R.U.C. broke down the door. He was out of bed as they came up the stairs. Mary Catherine bolted upright in their bed. The bedroom door burst open. Two R.U.C. officers in bulletproof vests pushed through with automatic weapons.

Mary Catherine screamed.

"Fuck you!" O'Donovan yelled.

One of the two officers swung the butt of his weapon across O'Donovan's face. The blow knocked O'Donovan to the floor.

Mary Catherine shouted at the police to stop.

"Shut up, bitch," one yelled.

O'Donovan took a kick to the abdomen as he attempted to get up.

One officer held his weapon against Mary Catherine's head, pinning her to the bed. His companion held his weapon against O'Donovan's neck.

As usual, O'Donovan slept in the nude. The police refused his request to dress. He was hustled into the police van with only a blanket from the bed wrapped around him.

Wedged between two R.U.C. officers in the rear seat of the police vehicle, O'Donovan demanded to know what he was being arrested for. The best he could get in reply was, "You haven't been arrested you stupid bastard, not yet anyway. We're going to question you about what you been up to. And you'll tell us. You'll tell us every fucking thing we want to know. Now shut the fuck up."

O'Donovan was deposited into an interrogation room. There was a table and a couple of hard wooden chairs. It was four hours before he saw anyone. The blanket had been taken away when he had entered the small room. He was totally naked. The room was uncomfortably cool.

Two men entered. One sat down, the other put one foot on a chair. Both smoked cigarettes.

"I'm Detective Sergeant Greer, this is Detective Linsay. We're here to find out what part you had in that car bombing murder the other day. We know you're involved, so let's not have any stupid shit. Things will be a lot easier that way."

"Now, where were you Friday last in the evening?" The one called Linsay asked.

"I want some clothes. It's cold in here. It's my right," O'Donovan said.

"Your right? You stupid bastard. The Crown determines your rights. Not a goddamn thing in the penal code about a prisoner having the right to clothes. Guess they just didn't foresee the circumstance," Linsay replied.

"Now, where were you on Friday night?"

"At my pub. Ask any of my regulars."

"Oh, we will lad, but I suspect all we'll get is a bunch of fucking lies, from a bunch of fucking I.R.A. sympathizers. Because that's what your clientele is. Christ, your old man was up to his arse in helping the I.R.A. And your brother — well, he was one we took care of didn't we?"

O'Donovan came out of his chair. He was over six feet and well muscled, but apparently no match for a balding, fortyish Lindsay who pinned one arm, and clamped an inordinately strong hand around O'Donovan's throat, smashing him up against the wall. Greer immobilized O'Donovan's other arm and drove a fist into his midsection. O'Donovan crumpled to the floor, the wind knocked out of him.

After several minutes, he hauled himself off the floor, back into the chair.

"Don't try that again, O'Donovan. Next time we'll kick the shit out of you. And you won't be walking out of here," Greer said.

He was questioned for the next two hours.

O'Donovan tried to think of all that Paddy had told him about interrogation, and the *Green Book*. Say nothing. Do not engage in any conversation. You're a prisoner of war. Give the enemy nothing they can use.

He was tired, hungry, disoriented. He had been given only water. No food, no tea, no cigarettes. He was also still naked. He had been alone for an hour now, Greer and Lindsay having left. He wondered if he was being observed. No obvious two-way mirror. No evidence of a camera lens. In fact, he was being taped on video film from a small camera located several inches inside a ventilating grill.

He also had to relieve himself, but he wasn't going to ask permission. That was basic. Never ask for anything. Being granted even the most trivial request implied some reciprocation. He'd piss on their floor first.

O'Donovan had just dosed off with his head on the table when two new police officers entered the room. Their entrance was timed accordingly. Both officers said nothing for several minutes. One looked through pages in a folder. Paddy had been right about humiliation. Leaving him naked diminished his stature, made him feel vulnerable in a way never experienced before.

"O'Donovan, we know you're I.R.A. You were either involved in the bombing last Friday, or you know someone that was," one of the detectives said loudly. Neither of them identified themselves by name.

Just like Paddy said. They had nothing. Didn't even accuse him of being directly involved. The rest was just torment he had to endure. The questions went on for hours. The interrogators starting to look as physically bad as O'Donovan. Tempers were wearing thin. Both detectives were horse from screaming.

"Let me tell you how it is, O'Donovan. We know you're involved, or you know who is. Same thing either way to us. So we're going to get to whatever you know. We'll keep hurting you until you tell us what we want to know. It's as simple as that. Forget all this bloody shit they taught you about resisting interrogation," one of the detectives said. He was well built, with a look that suggested he may like to inflict pain.

"Fuck you, you British-loving, cock sucking whore," O'Donovan screamed, his nerves rubbed raw by stress and exhaustion.

The same detective, kicked the chair legs out from under O'Donovan. His head cracked sharply against the wall. Both detectives hoisted him up by the arms and drove their fists into his abdomen.

The beating lasted several minutes. They were experts. Nothing but body blows. No blood. No broken ribs. Just bad pain. He vomited till nothing was left to come up. Sometime during the beating he relieved himself involuntarily.

O'Donovan was hauled back onto a chair. The detectives composed themselves, recovering their breath. The younger of the two referred to the folder again.

"Says here that you like the ladies. That right O'Donovan? Women like you? Why's that? Your looks maybe? Maybe you're a good lover, eh? Your cock doesn't look all that impressive right now."

"Think about all those women you've fucked, O'Donovan. Think about what it would be like if you couldn't do that anymore," the detective said, his face close to O'Donovan's. O'Donovan turned his head slowly to meet the detective's eyes. The detective saw only a blank response in O'Donovan's eyes. Inside, the thought turned O'Donovan cold with fear at what the detective was implying might be done to him. Only exhaustion masked any emotion.

"We could have just as easily have worked over your balls instead of your gut. I've seen men go through that. Two things always happen. Number one, they always talk. Number two, they're never the same again, if you get my meaning."

The first day ended. It was dark. He caught a glimpse of a window on his way to a cell.

He was awakened at daybreak the next morning. During the night there was every attempt to prevent any prisoner from getting any real rest. Doors banged. Men shouted orders. The prisoner always wondered when he would be roused for another bout of questioning.

It was an effort to rise from the hard prison bed, the pain in his lower abdomen making it even difficult to breathe. He was given his first food since being picked up. Shoved through a slot in the door, it consisted of a cereal gruel, bread, and tepid tea with sugar.

Interrogation started again in the mid-morning. It was Greer and Lindsay, the original two detectives this time. The questioning focused around his alibi of being at the pub that night. They wanted names of the patrons that night. O'Donovan knew better. He answered nothing all day.

They showed him photographs of the dead men. Endless numbers of photographs, of the car, the bodies in the car from every angle, and close-up shots on the autopsy tables in the morgue. They were nothing like the newspaper photos. Two of the corpses had no faces left. Arms and legs were missing. Abdomens torn open. Organs spilled out. O'Donovan was only slightly effected by the horrific details, but through no sense of any guilt.

On the second morning he was roused before daybreak, before any breakfast. Disorientation tactic again. This time, it was the second team of detectives, the ones that had worked him over. After a several hour session of various forms of mild physical abuse, the detectives took another tact.

"We told you we intend to get information, O'Donovan. We don't care how we get it either. You fucking I.R.A. scum call this a war. This isn't a war. You're nothing but a bunch of terrorists. Common criminals. You're vermin to be exterminated. How it's done doesn't matter. That's why the security forces here in Northern Ireland have been given special powers," the younger of the two detectives said.

"This your wife?" he asked, passing a picture to O'Donovan. It was Mary Catherine leaving the pub.

O'Donovan did not respond. That was the training. Give them nothing. He had made a few mistakes, paid for some, but on the whole had given them nothing and he had stood up well.

"Not a bad body by the looks of it. She a good fuck, O'Donovan? You like fucking her? Want to get her pregnant and bring another little fuckin' I.R.A. terrorist into the world?"

O'Donovan made no reply.

"Dresses like an old maid though. That why you look elsewhere, O'Donovan, or isn't she a good screw?" the detective continued, looking for some response out of O'Donovan.

"What if we brought her in. She's part of your alibi isn't she? She was at the pub all that afternoon and evening wasn't she?" the detective said. They assumed this to be the case although O'Donovan had said nothing.

"Maybe we could have her strip searched. Think she'd like me checking her out?."

"Maybe we'll tell her about all your other girlfriends. We'll give her names, places, perhaps even photographs. What about that, O'Donovan?"

O'Donovan said nothing.

The second day's interrogation ended uneventfully.

By the third day, O'Donovan knew he had won. It was Greer and Lindsay again. Their questions never suggested that they actually connected him with the bombing. All this talk about an alibi was simply a reason to detain others, intimidate them, and either get information, or discredit him. Thanks to Paddy McCullough, he was mentally prepared for this ordeal. They kept him the full seven days allowed, but there were no further interrogation sessions after the third day.

There was the inevitable tearful reunion with his mother. Mary Catherine was relieved but angry.

"I can't believe you'd do something so stupid," Mary Catherine said. "What happens to us if you go off to prison?"

"Mind your tongue, if you know what's good for you," O'Donovan snapped back threateningly.

They were in the pub just prior to opening before the lunch crowd. O'Donovan's mother was behind the bar but said nothing.

"It's been a week with no word from you. Your mother and I've been worried sick. Hasn't the I.R.A. hurt your poor mother enough?"

O'Donovan slapped her sharply across the face with the back of his hand. She retreated crying.

"Garrett O'Donovan, they'll be none of that here," O'Donovan's mother yelled at him. She put her arm around Mary Catherine and patted her shoulder.

"Fat lot she cares about me. Been fucked over by the police for days and all she does is bitch."

"You'll be watching your mouth too, Garrett O'Donovan. You know I don't like that kind of language," his mother said.

"I'm sorry, Mum, but you don't know how it was there. Took a frightful lot of beating I did"

His mother started crying again, this time from despair rather than relief.

After his release O'Donovan learned that he was one of many that were picked up as a result of the Webster bombing. Seamus Devlin was also picked up, as were a dozen others. All had been comparatively new I.R.A. recruits, suggesting that the police had no leads or suspects and were looking to coerce information from those less able to counter police interrogation. Several in fact, did not fair well, breaking down and giving up information to the police unrelated to the Webster murder. But O'Donovan was the only one detained for any length of time who had any knowledge of the Webster murder. No one was ever charged.

For security, O'Donovan and McCullough were the only ones within their unit who knew of his involvement in the bombing, although several of the older veterans suspected. It was difficult for O'Donovan to be unable to talk about the event and take the accolades from his companions, especially the seasoned veterans. Privately McCullough praised him.

"Why'd you send me on that assignment, Paddy? I didn't know shit about explosives," O'Donovan asked.

"Didn't have to did ya? Figured you knew enough about electrical circuits not to blow yourself up. Main reason was to use somebody unknown. Job fell to me. Thought you might have the balls for it. Apparently I was right," McCullough said.

O'Donovan immersed himself in I.R.A. operations over the next couple of years. It made the drudgery of the pub bearable, and gave an excuse for absences, not always for I.R.A. business. He became accomplished in the secretive methods and operational details of the brigade. Paddy McCullough was a good teacher. O'Donovan was a natural.

To his surprise, O'Donovan discovered in himself an aptitude for organization and planning. Within four years he was promoted to the sensitive position of intelligence officer after the death of his predecessor in an auto crash.

The assignment to deliver the bomb under Webster's car had been followed with other bombing assignments for O'Donovan.

The I.R.A. had provided training. O'Donovan proved quite adept. He conducted many bombings of police and military barracks and restaurants in Northern Ireland.

O'Donovan found bombs an unsatisfying method of warfare. You never could be sure of effects. Many times they killed no one. Sometimes you killed the wrong people. It was impersonal. You didn't need much courage, only know-how. Nothing had equaled the rush of the Webster killing.

Unknown to him, O'Donovan was to test for a new plateau within the I.R.A. The unit had been given an assignment. It was to be another assassination. This time it would not be a bomb.

"All right, lads, here it is. Command has given us an assignment," McCullough said. Four other men including O'Donovan were in the back room of O'Donovan's pub.

"We're to kill an R.U.C. copper - a Detective Sergeant Matthew Heddly. Any of you ever heard of him?" McCullough asked. All shook their heads, no. "We're to do it within ten days, too."

"I've not heard of him either, but that's the orders. Intelligence says that he's responsible for the torture of I.R.A. prisoners, and the death of two, but they didn't give specifics. At any rate, orders are orders. I've picked you men for the job. Anyone here can't do this?" he asked. No one answered. "Good. Then lets see how we can go about this."

Over the next several days, the target was observed with the group alternating surveillance. As an R.U.C. officer constantly confronting the I.R.A., Heddly took more than cursory precautions. He varied his routines, even left for work at different times, traveling different routes. Another R.U.C. officer frequently accompanied him to and from police headquarters. Like Webster, he also lived on the east side of Belfast, in a strictly Protestant neighborhood. His flat was well back from the street, difficult to approach without being seen.

"Seems this copper is pretty careful," McCullough said to the assembled group. "Doesn't seem to be any particularly obvious place for an ambush."

McCullough had planned and participated on missions before. Killing security personnel did not bother his sensibilities in the least. His men had confidence in his abilities.

"Here's what I suggest. What we do know is he goes to work every day usually within a window of one hour, but he takes different routes. Sometimes he's picked up by another copper waiting in front of his flat. This happened on only two days. Both times the other one was there five or ten minutes early reading the paper while he waited. When he drives himself, he fetches his car from across the way here in this lot," McCullough said, indicating the location on a diagram.

"That's where we'll hit him, in the lot, before he gets into his car, day after tomorrow. If that should be a day he gets picked up by his partner, then we'll do it the next day, or the next after that until he is alone."

McCullough spent the next hour going over details.

"Now to assignments. Seamus will be in the van a few blocks away at the market. John, you'll drive the service lorry. Garrett will make the hit. Brian, you'll back him up."

Both O'Donovan and Brian Thompson were surprised at O'Donovan being selected to do the shooting.

"Paddy, no offense here against O'Donovan, but don't you think John or I should do the shooting? We've been in shit like this before. O'Donovan's been a damn fine intelligence officer these past couple of years, but he's had more experience with bombs than with attacks with guns." Thompson said.

"Paddy, you're asking him to shoot a man right up close," Thompson continued.

"Garrett will do fine," McCullough said. "I have my reasons. That's the way it'll be."

Brian Thompson was not convinced, but perhaps somewhat relieved. He didn't relish the idea of putting bullets into someone as he looked them in the eyes.

McCullough suspected O'Donovan wouldn't be so squeamish. Besides that, he didn't have the luxury of taking a conservative approach. He knew the leadership was embarked on an accelerated program of high profile attacks. He simply needed to expand experience within his unit. No telling what would happen with the inevitable detentions and arrests that would follow. O'Donovan was the best man he had. He was born to the trade. He was an excellent intelligence officer. He was skilled at constructing bombs. And he was showing an exceptional aptitude at operations planning. It was time he expanded his scope of experience.

It was close to seven o'clock in the morning, two days later. O'Donovan and Thompson had driven a stolen Renault to the parking lot across the street from the building where Heddly lived, arriving before daybreak. They confirmed Heddly's car was in the lot then parked fifty feet away. Thompson laid down on the seat of the Renault so as not to be seen. O'Donovan slipped under a parked car, two down from Heddly's. McCullough parked the getaway car well up the street. He, like Thompson, was dressed in a suit. Just businessmen starting their day.

At seven o'clock, a service lorry driven by John Dixon, and also stolen, pulled next to the Renault. Brian Thompson got out of the vehicle, and along with John Dixon, opened the bonnet appearing to discuss the problem. Jumper cables were stretched from the lorry's engine to the Renault. The sound of the bonnet being slammed shut would be O'Donovan's signal that Heddly was within a hundred feet of his car. If O'Donovan missed, Thompson and Dixon would try to finish the job.

It was seven-fifteen. Heddly's partner had not appeared. Thompson then saw Heddly leave his flat and start to cross the street. At this angle, Heddly would cross into the parking lot then walk down behind several other parked cars before coming to his own. As planned, he would pass the car O'Donovan was hiding under.

O'Donovan was cold laying on the damp pavement for this long. He kept flexing his fingers. There was a certain anxiety being under the car, different from the first time with the bomb. He had no sense of what situation was unfolding. There would be no warning except for the signal.

Heddly looked critically at Thompson and Dixon. Both had their backs to him. He continued to walk toward his car, looking back at the lorry once again. He was a cautious man. The bonnet slammed down on the Renault. A car came down the street, pulled into the parking lot and continued past the service lorry toward Heddly.

As Heddly passed the car O'Donovan was under, O'Donovan slid from underneath. He stood upright, saw Heddly's back.

"Heddly! Behind you!" The car had stopped some fifty feet away, the driver, obviously another officer, seeing what was about to happen jumped out and yelled.

For an instant, time seemed in slow motion for O'Donovan as he took in the scene. The R.U.C. officer from the car was pulling a weapon. He could see Thompson and Dixon running towards him, guns drawn. Heddly reached inside his coat for his weapon.

O'Donovan kept his head, knew the mission. He turned from the police officer shouting a warning, back to Heddly. He sighted down at Heddly's chest and squeezed the trigger. The first, then a second round, caught Heddly square on, knocking him to the pavement.

Thompson and Dixon fired at the officer in the car. Being shielded by his vehicle, their shots did not hit him.

As a part of an anti-terrorist unit, the officer had been equipped with an automatic machine pistol, the equivalent of a short-range machine gun. From over the top of his car, the officer fired a burst at Thompson and Dixon. Thompson was struck once in the midsection, and once in the throat. Dixon caught two rounds in the chest and was dead as he hit the pavement.

Paddy McCullough had parked the car and came running to add firepower. He knelt on the grassy knoll in front of the parking lot, taking aim on the officer at the car. Several nine-millimeter rounds hit the officer in the chest and head.

O'Donovan approached the fallen Heddly. His breathing was labored, his eyes closed.

"Finish him, Garrett. Now!" McCullough ordered, having run up to him.

O'Donovan leveled his weapon at Heddly. This should be hard, but it really wasn't. He'd killed before. All that remained was the detail of finishing it. O'Donovan squeezed the trigger. A round hole showed in Heddly's forehead. Blood leaked in mass from the exit wound in the back of the R.U.C. officer's head.

McCullough pulled O'Donovan away. "See to the other copper," he ordered, while he went to check on Thompson and Dixon.

A quick check of John Dixon by McCullough confirmed he was dead. Thompson was rising to one knee, attempting to get up. He was trying to speak. There was no sound. Blood gushed from between his fingers clasping his throat.

The R.U.C. officer was dead. At least O'Donovan thought so. He felt for a pulse at the neck. With his own heart pounding and the adrenaline surge, it was hard to be certain.

"Help me, Garrett" McCullough shouted.

Between them, they carried a bleeding Brian Thompson to the getaway car. McCullough got behind the wheel. O'Donovan cradled Brian Thompson's head on his lap in the back seat. He could feel the warm blood soaking through his trousers, and running down his leg. Christ, the man must be dying. Nobody can lose that amount of blood.

Within a few minutes they reached the market where Seamus Devlin was waiting in a van in the parking lot. There were no other vehicles in the lot. The market was not yet open for business. McCullough jumped out of the car and yelled at Seamus to give them a hand. Seamus went to the car and opened the rear door.

"Holy Mother Mary!" He exclaimed, sickened by the sight of Brian Thompson's head resting on the lap of O'Donovan, whose trousers were soaked in blood. It took substantial will for him to touch the bloody body of Brian Thompson.

Thompson was dragged from the car to the floor of the van. He had died several minutes before from loss of blood.

McCullough dropped Seamus Devlin at his home. He lived with his parents. They were staunch Republicans. They would testify that he was home at the time of the murders.

McCullough stopped at a petrol station to allow O'Donovan to use the restrooms. He was able to sneak out the back of the van without the attendant noticing him. They had had the foresight to bring changes of clothing. Even at that, the restroom floor was a mess with blood that O'Donovan did not have the time to clean up.

"Will Mary Catherine and your mother lie about you being home, Garrett?" McCullough asked.

"Of course they will, Paddy. My mum may not like what the I.R.A. does, but she's part of it. She'll do the right thing," O'Donovan said.

"And Mary Catherine?"

"Jesus, Paddy. She's my wife. A good Catholic wife. She'll do the right thing, too."

Inwardly he was not as confident.

McCullough then deposited O'Donovan at the rear entrance to the pub. He hoped that Mary Catherine would vouch for O'Donovan being home at the time of the killing. He had heard rumors about things not being good between them. Rumors about other women. He could ill afford to lose O'Donovan who was proving to be a most able man.

McCullough dumped the van in a remote rural area near the border. He made the sign of the cross over the body of Brian Thompson, then wiped the van clean of any fingerprints.

Chapter Five

It was a cold December morning in 1973. The sky was low and gray. The rain had stopped, but the sharp wind coming out of the North Atlantic drove the damp through even the warmest overcoat. Two cars pulled up to the curb on a downtown Belfast street. It was 9:00am exactly. Two large glass doors were being unlocked from the inside. Over the door a sign identified the building as the Commerce Bank of Ulster.

Three men exited the lead car and proceeded to the bank entrance. Another two men exited the second car but stayed on the sidewalk. A driver stayed behind the wheel of each vehicle.

A short man with a slight build in his mid-thirties pulled a nylon stocking over his head, withdrew a handgun from under his coat, then entered the bank. Two other men followed behind him.

Ten minutes later the three bank robbers rushed out of the bank. Both cars sped away at high speed as the bank security alarm sounded. Dropping to the speed of other traffic, the two cars headed south out of the city on Lisburn Road intending to pick up the M1 motorway further south.

Five miles south of the city, traffic slowed, eventually coming to a full stop. A few hundred meters ahead there was a roadblock supported by a British Saracen armored personnel carrier. Clearly, they would never pass scrutiny by the security forces.

Both cars swung out of the line of waiting vehicles and proceeded back north, turning east, and then south again after a few blocks. They hoped to wend their way through the urban areas that stretched almost continuously from Belfast south to the city of Lisburn. The security forces could not block all the streets and highways.

They hoped to pick up the A3 Motorway in Lisburn, then travel southwest through Armagh, eventually crossing the border into the Republic near Monaghan. Thirty minutes later they had picked up the A3 and were heading out of Lisburn, the countryside turning more rural.

"How'd we do, Patrick?" the slight man asked one of the men in the back seat.

The man started to remove the bank notes from the satchel. "Don't know exactly, Michael, but it looks pretty good. I'd say well over five thousand, maybe ten," he said, referring to an amount in British pounds sterling, while he felt through the satchel.

"Piece of cake. You had it planned perfectly, Michael," one of the other men said.

"Michael, behind us! There's a copper with his lights on coming up fast!" the driver said. "Looks like maybe two cars."

"What do we do, Michael?" the driver asked anxiously.

"Nothing yet. Keep your speed. Can't out run them. Could be they're not after us. At any rate, we let them close then we'll have it out with the bastards if that's what it's to be. Patrick, you and Tim get down low so they can't see you," Michael Flynn said.

"Jesus, look at that! They've fucking panicked!" the driver exclaimed, referring to their companions in the car ahead.

The lead car with the other three men had apparently seen the police coming up behind and decided to make a run for it.

"What do you want me to do?" the driver asked.

"Keep your speed," Flynn ordered.

The police cars pulled along side. The officer in the passenger seat looked the I.R.A. driver over intently. The driver, to his credit as an actor, smiled and made a brief gesture of a wave. The lead police car accelerated, followed by the second.

"God damn it. I don't think the bastards even knew it was us," Flynn said. "Stay behind them, but don't get too close."

Flynn's driver accelerated, keeping the flashing lights of the police vehicles in sight a kilometer ahead. The chase went on for ten minutes.

Rounding a curve, Flynn's driver suddenly braked hard. A few hundred meters ahead the two police vehicles had apparently stopped. Lights were still flashing.

All four police officers were out of their vehicles. Flynn could see them moving off the road down a gentle slope with their guns drawn. Pulling up behind the police vehicles, Flynn saw the overturned I.R.A. car.

"Patrick—you and Tim get ready, get your weapons" Flynn said. The two men in the back seat grabbed their automatic weapons, American made Armalite AR-18, 5.56mm assault rifles. Flynn pulled his own handgun, a Colt .45 automatic, from his shoulder holster.

The driver proceeded slowly, stopping just behind the police vehicles. Flynn and the two men from the back seat exited the car in a crouched position. They observed the R.U.C. officers approaching the overturned I.R.A. car cautiously.

"Now, lads, kill them!" Flynn shouted.

Patrick and Tim fired several short bursts, just as Flynn had drilled them. Two of the R.U.C. officers went down immediately. A third fell to Flynn's own fire. The fourth was hit in the legs.

Flynn's group reached the wrecked car. Two of their comrades were still alive. The driver was obviously dead. The man in the front passenger seat was also dead from hitting the windscreen. Patrick and Tim helped their injured comrades back to the car.

Flynn approached the only surviving R.U.C. officer.

"Christ, don't kill me. I was only doing my duty. I've got family — a wife, two kids. I'm not political," the officer pleaded, looking into Flynn's face. He was young, perhaps in his late twenties.

"You can identify me. No way around that, lad," Flynn said, then shot the R.U.C. police officer in the forehead.

The six I.R.A men drove off.

The security forces were now on full alert. A second bank robbery had occurred in Derry that same morning. Main highways were blocked. Highways leading across the border into the Republic were manned with bolstered security. Flynn had the driver stop in the village of Killmore, just north of the A3, six kilometers out of Armagh. Flynn placed a call from a public telephone.

His call brought three different vehicles to a remote spot along a country road north of Killmore. The six men transferred to the various vehicles, abandoning the car used in the robbery. During the next twenty-four hours, all of Michael Flynn's group would be smuggled south across the border into the Republic of Ireland.

Three weeks later, Flynn was again mounting another mission. This time he had twelve men, all well armed. If the truth were known, they possessed a significant percentage of the total automatic weapons arsenal of the Provincial Irish Republican Army. Flynn was the boldest field commander in the Army and thus got the best available weaponry.

Contrary to newspaper stories, the I.R.A. had limited weapons resources. British security forces in Northern Ireland were very effective in intercepting weapons smuggling into the north. Likewise, the Irish Republic also was aggressive in preventing arming of the I.R.A. from bases of support across the border.

Flynn's next mission was to mount an attack on British Army personnel near the border village of Crossmaglen. Crossmaglen was at the front line of the battle between the security forces and the I.R.A. During a recent night patrol, British troops stationed in the area had been responsible for the deaths of four I.R.A. men smuggling explosives into the north.

Flynn did not like the plan. He did not think that the I.R.A. should risk men and resources in openly confronting a superior armed enemy under circumstances that did not offer any equalizing advantage. The I.R.A. was a guerrilla force. Flynn understood the tactics that made such a force effective. A force to be used in a war of attrition on the enemy's will to continue. An open confrontation, no matter the element of surprise, left many possibilities for disaster for the inferior force.

His commander pointed out that it was necessary to show the I.R.A. as a real rebel force with strength to bring off a direct attack on the British Army in a show of strength.

Flynn felt however there were less risky targets. Not that he was afraid. But failure in such a direct confrontation could diminish public impression of the I.R.A.'s strength. Regardless, Flynn would obey orders. He also knew that he was the best suited to plan and execute this raid.

The weather was bitter. The men were terribly cold. All were veterans. All had seen action before. All were still anxious. It was at a time like this with a black moonless night, the damp and the biting cold, the loneliness and the fear, that one questioned what he was doing. Only Flynn did not. Such hardships only served to define his sense of purpose.

They were waiting, concealed along a narrow, unpaved road that wound through a wooded area. Half of the unit was distributed on either side of the road, positioned to avoid hitting each other in a crossfire. Information had been fed to a suspected informer about a shipment of arms moving across the border. If the intelligence was correct, they would not only ambush a British army unit, but also confirm and eliminate an informer.

They had been concealed in the wet thicket bordering the road for several hours. It was two o'clock in the morning. Flynn reacted at a noise. A branch breaking? Hard to tell with the damp. Then again—someone was moving about behind them. Flynn swung around to face in the direction of the sounds. He was armed with an AR-18 assault rifle.

Within moments all hell broke loose. Automatic fire erupted from behind the men on one side of the road. Several were hit during the initial bursts. Flynn could see the muzzle flashes. He fired short bursts at two such flashes, hearing a response from at least one man being hit, then dropping to the ground and rolling to a new position after each burst.

The I.R.A. men on the near side of the road to the attacking force returned fire. Those situated on the opposite side of the road were forced to hold their fire. There was no way to distinguish the attackers from their own comrades.

Flynn knew he must get to the other side of the road and lead an escape. They had become the victims of an ambush themselves. He suspected the attackers may be an S.A.S. search and destroy operation. The S.A.S., the British Army's Special Air Service, an elite special forces unit, would be armed with the latest technology, including infrared, or light enhancement optical instruments. They would locate and pick off each I.R.A. man one by one.

The S.A.S. had the earned reputation for preferring to kill the enemy, rather than taking prisoners. They were not only highly trained and critically selected, but entirely ruthless from the command structure down to the soldier.

Flynn crawled across the road. Firing continued behind him. These were good lads. They'd hold their ground, hopefully take some casualties. But he knew they had little chance of survival against the resources of the enemy.

"Patrick? Gerry? Brian? Terry?" Flynn called out in a loud whisper. "It's me, Michael."

In a moment, one of his men responded, "Michael, over here."

Flynn found him. "Gerry, we've been ambushed. Got to get out of here. Everyone's to go in a separate direction. Stick low. Look for cover. They've probably got night glasses. Now go!"

The man crawled away frantically using the dense brush for concealment.

Flynn moved on down the side of the road to warn the others. Within a few minutes he had contacted three of his men. The last I.R.A. man on that side of the road was firing across the road. Flynn reached him just as the man was hit in the upper arm.

"Holy Mother, Michael, I'm hit right bad," the man yelled. It was Terry Fergus, a likable chap and good soldier.

The bullet had hit a major artery. Blood spurted from the wound, but neither could see the effect in the dark. Flynn felt the warm wetness soak through his jacket. Using his belt, he was able to get above the wound and tourniquet the arm.

Flynn fired a burst then quickly pulled away from the position, half dragging the wounded man with him. If Fergus succumbed to shock, he would be forced to leave him. As it was, they both had poor chances.

Frequently stumbling, crawling as best they could, they made several hundred meters progress in a few minutes. It was pitch black. Unseen branches scratched their faces as they crawled through the thicket. There was only one incidence of automatic weapons fire in the distance, then silence.

If the attacking force had infrared optics, Flynn and Fergus would soon be found. Even at a considerable distance, the signature of their body heat would stand out vividly against the comparatively cold background. Light enhancement technology on the other hand, did only that—amplify what little light did exist at night. On this dark night, that was mercifully very little. Escape might come down to the technology employed by the attacking force.

Terry Fergus was almost at his end. The loss of blood, the exhaustion after the dissipation of the adrenaline surge, the pain of his shattered arm had all taken a terrible toll. They had traveled perhaps three kilometers with Flynn half carrying Fergus. Locating a depression, a little ravine surrounded by a few trees, he laid the wounded Fergus down.

"We'll rest here, Terry," Flynn said.

"It's so fucking cold, Michael." The ground was wet. Fergus was shivering uncontrollably. "Am I to die, Michael?"

"Not yet, lad. I think we got away. You need to hang on just a while longer though. I'll be getting you out of here." But he was not confident that Fergus would survive the next few hours.

"Go to sleep, lad. I'm goin' to be a short distance away. Anybody comes close I'll catch them unawares."

Fergus grabbed Flynn's arm, "Michael, don't let me die out here."

"I'm with you, Terry. I know it's tough but you're up to it. You hang on and I'll be getting us out of here. We need to wait it out until first light. I'll be close by. Don't worry now."

Flynn situated himself twenty meters away, looking in the direction of his wounded companion through a fork in a double-trunked tree. If a patrol happen upon them, it would be tactically better to be separated. Flynn was armed with only his .45, having abandoned his assault rifle to make his escape and help his wounded companion. Terry Fergus was armed only with a 9mm pistol.

Dawn broke. Flynn castigated himself for falling asleep. After first checking the area, he crawled down to his wounded companion. The sight was horrific. A good portion of Fergus' clothing was soaked in blood, now mostly dried. The man was cold. He thought that maybe Fergus was even dead. Flynn first rubbed the man's cheeks, then slapped him gently. Eventually, the man woke from his stupor.

Looking at his arm, then his blood-soaked clothes, Fergus said, "I'm scared, Michael, I'm come-to-Jesus scared. I'll be dyin' without a priest. You've got to get yourself out of here, Michael. I can't go any further. Don't think I could even stand. You know they're lookin' for us."

"You stay here, I'm going to reconnoiter. There should be some farms in that direction," Flynn said, pointing. "I'll look for shelter. Then we'll find some way to communicate with our people."

Flynn dragged Fergus to a clump of bushes offering better concealment and draped his own coat over him. He then left, moving cautiously in a crouch through the high grass in the meadow.

After moving off only a few hundred meters, Flynn saw several men emerge from a thicket, moving in the general direction to where his wounded companion was concealed. He knew it must be an army patrol pursuing the remnants of his attack force.

Fucking hell. This was a major disaster. Good men had died. It was his fault. Bad strategy. Poor planning. He hadn't planned for such a contingency, one that would place them in ambush. How did the Brits know? Still, he should have covered for such an eventuality. He was to blame. He had been in command. He could not let Terry Fergus die in that lonely field at the hands of the bloody British army. They'd kill him for sure. Maybe this was the time he himself should die. For sure he would take some of the bastards with him.

He started back in the direction where he had left Fergus. Gauging the probable direction of the advancing security forces, he moved in a circular pattern that would hopefully bring him up behind them. He would have to get in close. With only the .45 pistol, his range was limited.

It was a regular British army patrol, not the S.A.S. Appeared to be four men. They were headed directly toward where Terry Fergus was concealed, probably following the beaten down grass and the muddy tracks. Half carrying his wounded friend, and pushing hard for distance through the night, there had been little time to be delicate about leaving signs.

Flynn crawled on his stomach to within fifty meters behind the soldiers who were advancing cautiously and spread out at ten-meter intervals. Suddenly there came the report of several shots in quick succession. Sounded like a handgun. Automatic weapons fire erupted from the army patrol.

The firing stopped after several moments.

"Henderson?" someone yelled, probably the platoon sergeant.

"Here. OK," came a reply.

"Smith?"

"Here"

"Hodges?"

No reply.

"Hodges?"

"Kirby?"

"Here"

"Hodges?"

One of the soldiers found Corporal Hodges. He had taken a round in the chest. He was barely conscious, spitting up blood from a damaged lung. The other soldier frantically put a field dressing on the wound to try to stem the flow of blood.

The two other soldiers joined the third. Soon, more automatic fire erupted. From Flynn's position, he could see the kneeling soldiers firing at what must be Fergus' position. The soldiers quickly moved down the slight slope to the clump of bushes. Two of them each grabbed an arm, and dragged the body of Terry Fergus from the underbrush.

"Fucking I.R.A. pig!" one soldier screamed, kicking the life-less Fergus in the head.

"Enough of that. See to Hodges," the sergeant ordered.

"Kirby, radio our position. Tell them we got one," the sergeant said.

Flynn crawled to within fifteen meters of the scene. Flynn took the opportunity. All three of the soldiers had diverted their attention. Kneeling, with a two-handed stance with his weapon, he fired two shots into the back of the radioman. He then hit the sergeant before he could fix on the direction of the attack. The third soldier ran back toward his other downed companions. He had not yet spotted Flynn, but sprayed a burst of automatic fire in a broad 180-degree arc.

Flynn emptied his remaining rounds from the clip, hitting the soldier twice. He reloaded a new clip.

His waist was on fire. He could feel the blood running down his leg. He rose slowly. The pain was awful, worse when he took steps, but he could walk.

He moved carefully down to the killing ground. With his weapon ready, he checked the radioman first. Dead. The sergeant was not yet dead. One shot had hit him in the lower abdomen. He was writhing in pain. With no hesitation, Flynn held his weapon close to the soldier's head and fired a single round. The third soldier was also dead. The fourth, wounded by Fergus, was also dispatched by a bullet in the head.

Flynn quickly took the few personal belongings from the body of Terry Fergus; a wedding band, a watch, a rosary, several photographs. Small remembrances that would eventually find their way to his widow.

Flynn rummaged through the soldiers' field packs for first aid supplies. Loosening the belt of his own trousers, he emptied a packet of sulfur powder on his own wound then applied a field dressing. Fortunately, the bleeding was not profuse but the wound must have damaged his pelvis. The ampoules of morphine were pocketed. They were for later. Escape was now essential and he could not afford to be drugged.

Taking one of the assault rifles, he started out across the meadow. He had to make a dense hedgerow quickly, expecting additional British troops at any time. The pain was excruciating but he could move reasonably well if he kept his left leg stiff.

Flynn made the hedgerow then kept up a slow but steady pace putting a good distance between him and the recent battle-ground. Once the bodies were found, the search area would widen. British patrols would be moving along every road. He would have to locate a safe place and go into hiding.

Flynn knew the location of many staunch republican sup-porters in this area near the border, several probably willing to take a risk to help an I.R.A. soldier. None would turn him in. The problem was he was not sure of his exact location. It took until mid-day to locate a road sign. He had seen unusual numbers of army and police vehicles that morning.

Flynn knew of a farm only a couple of kilometers from here. The owner was an old farmer by the name of Callum O'Neill. Flynn had never met him, but he was known to have aided the I.R.A. in the past. O'Neill himself had been actively involved as a volunteer in the forties.

Reaching the farm proved an enormous test of strength and will. Flynn was near collapse from exhaustion and pain when he caught sight of what he hoped was O'Neill's place. The location seemed correct, but he knew he was not thinking clearly. The breeze seemed to confirm the location. Callum O'Neill raised hogs.

Flynn crawled his way to the small stone barn some distance from the house. He would wait for dark to approach the house and Callum O'Neill.

Flynn came awake abruptly with the creak of the barn door hinges. O'Neill slapped the flank of an old dairy cow as he moved her into the barn for the night. A pail full of milk hung from his arm.

"O'Neill," Flynn called out in a loud whisper. He was back in a corner in the shadows.

"Aye! What the fuck!" O'Neill exclaimed. He dropped the milk and reach for a pitchfork.

"Easy with that fork friend. I need your help, I'm hurt. Don't even think I can get up," Flynn had his gun trained on O'Neill who was clearly visible with the fading light coming through the barn door, while Flynn was in the shadows.

"Who the fuck are you?" That was the closest translation to the ancient Gaelic spoken by O'Neill. O'Neill held the pitchfork threateningly.

"Better for both of us, you don't know my name," Flynn responded in his broken Gaelic.

"You don't speak Irish worth a damn, boy. How'd you get hurt? And how'd you know my name?"

"Shot. I'm hurt right badly. Shot by a British soldier. As to who you are, you're Callum O'Neill. You were one of us. You're I.R.A. Fought in the forties and fifties I'm told. Still one of us. Known to have helped a man or two find his way back across the border."

"Holy Mother," O'Neill sighed. "You'll be one of those that got into it with those soldiers last night near here. Word is you lads didn't do too well. Killed some of you. Army patrols are all over the countryside. One stopped here couple of hours back. Told me anyone helping the I.R.A. terrorists would go to prison. Bloody stupid thing to say. Where are you hurt? I can't see you," O'Neill said.

Flynn stuck his .45 into his coat pocket, then eased his way out into the light, half crawling, propped up on one arm and the knee of his good leg.

O'Neill dropped the fork. "Can you walk if I help you?"

"Shouldn't take me into the house. The Brits might search there."

"Well, if they do, don't you think they'd be checkin' the barn too?"

Flynn didn't argue. He was near collapse, not thinking clearly. He needed help. With O'Neill's assistance, he hobbled painfully to the door of the small farm cottage. Lying in the barn had stiffened the use of his damaged hip. O'Neill shoved the door open with a foot. "Emily, I need your help, woman."

A short, plump woman came from the kitchen. After an understandable exclamation, she helped her husband take Flynn into their own bed. Flynn collapsed into sleep from exhaustion immediately. Emily O'Neill cleaned the wound. Flynn did not even stir. As much blood as was soaked into his trousers, Flynn had been fortunate. No major blood vessels had been severed or he would have bled to death. Emily O'Neill shook her head. It was a nasty wound. She could see shattered bone. The pain must be terrible she thought.

"He's in a bad way, Callum. Could die if there's infection. If he doesn't die, he'll not be walking right ever again," she said to her husband.

O'Neill woke Flynn at dawn, offering him a hot cup of tea with sugar. Emily brought a hot bowl of oatmeal. Flynn was barely able to hold a cup or spoon. Emily fed him.

"You lads did a right number on the Brits. They say you killed six British soldiers. Rumor is that some were executed. Shot in the head close-up." O'Neill said to Flynn. The old man sat on a rough-hewn stool, sipping his own tea. "That true?"

"It was combat, Mr. O'Neill. We were ambushed. We fought back. A soldier's job is to kill the enemy," Flynn answered, avoiding the question. "How many of my people were killed?"

"Five, they say. Four more captured," O'Neill told him.

"I'm afraid you can't be stayin' here in the house for long, lad. Patrols are getting heavier. No tellin' when they might be back."

"I'll be leaving soon, but I'll need your help. I'll tell you how to get word to my people. They'll send someone to get me off your hands."

"I didn't say we'd turn you out, only you can't stay here in the house or barn, that's for sure. Never seen patrols this thick. We could be searched at any time. Sure to happen sooner or later with my past and all. Got to move you to some place safer," O'Neill said. "Best place I can think of won't be pleasant I'm afraid."

"Where's that?" Flynn asked, still exhausted. He knew he was still close to total collapse.

"The cellar I call it. Different from most. Hidden well, it is. The authorities have never found it out. Searched the house a few times, they did. Kept guns and explosives there in the old days. Now we only use it for keepin' food. The Misses does a lot of canning."

"Trouble is, it's no place for a person to stay, especially wounded and all. It's damp and cold."

This cellar was far worse than even O'Neill's description. It was located under the floor of the kitchen. Three boards could be removed, accessing a ladder. O'Neill had done a clever job to conceal the entrance. Even a close inspection would not easily reveal that the boards were removable. Beyond that, however, it was nothing more than a hole in the ground.

O'Neill and his wife had suspended several planks over some wooden crates, creating what would serve as a makeshift bed. The floor was earth. Shelves of canned goods lined the walls. It was maybe two by three meters. The size of a cell. It was exceedingly difficult getting Flynn down the ladder with his injured hip and reduced strength. Clearly, he would not be moving up and down regularly.

Flynn gave O'Neill someone to contact in Monaghan, south of the border in the Republic of Ireland.

By the following day Flynn knew he had a fever. The last of the morphine had been consumed. He wondered if his wound was infected. Within hours, he started to question his ability to endure. His "cell" was pitch dark. He had the use of a kerosene lantern, which he found could be used only sparingly. The fumes from the lantern soon turned the air noxious. Flynn alternated between this and the deprivations of hours without light. In the near absolute darkness, his was often in delirium with the effects of the fever.

By the time O'Neill descended the ladder that evening, Flynn was in a bad way. Even with several blankets, chills racked his body from the growing fever. The damp and cold could soon contribute to pneumonia. Flynn's eyes did not focus well.

"I got to your people in Monaghan today. They say they'll be here day after tomorrow to get you out. Didn't say how, though. I told them you were wounded. Had me wait 'til they got me some medicine. Antibiotics your man said. Supposed to take four of 'em every few hours. Gave me some medicine for the pain, too," O'Neill said.

He spooned some soup and tea into Flynn, then gave him a heavy dose of the antibiotics and a couple of pain tablets.

The narcotic brought some relief from the pain for a couple of hours, but there was no real sleep, only fitful bouts of semi-consciousness, mixed with fever distorted dreams. Flynn alternated between sweating, then uncontrollable shivering. His wound generated continuous pain. The hard planks that served as his bed, added torment to his whole body.

The next day was spent in a haze of drug-sedated relief. O'Neill left the floorboards off, giving Flynn precious light. There was nothing worse than the absolute dark. As he sealed Flynn in the hole for the night, O'Neill gave him a maximum dose of painkiller. With luck, Flynn's people would be here within the day.

Fortunately, it was the next morning when a lorry pulled up. Two men assisted O'Neill in lifting Flynn from his premature grave and quickly maneuvered him into the truck. The truck, a two-ton affair, purposely larger than necessary, was covered with a wooden wall at the front behind the cab. The interior wall was false, affording a space sufficient to conceal Flynn. Flynn was placed on a bed of blankets in the narrow space.

In the rear of the lorry, the men manhandled O'Neill's prize boar hog, an unpleasant, aggressive animal, weighing close to four hundred kilos. The pig resisted the efforts of all three men to get him up the planks into the bed of the lorry.

"Leave some slack in those ropes tied to that snout ring. Some free play with this sonofabitch will discourage anyone from getting' too close," O'Neill instructed.

Within two hours, Flynn was across the border into Monaghan County, in the Republic of Ireland. The lorry off-loaded both the boar and Flynn at a farm. Flynn was running a high fever, moving in and out of delirium.

Flynn could not be taken to a hospital. He would most certainly be arrested. A sympathetic doctor brought the necessary instruments to perform surgery on Flynn in the kitchen of the farmhouse. In reality, the surgery was not complicated. There was little the doctor could do other than remove the bullet and do basic repairs to clean out the bone splinters and suture the wound. The doctor pronounced that he would live, but he would not walk well ever again.

Twenty-three years later, Michael Flynn again found himself in a farmhouse in Monaghan County in the Republic of Ireland. It was a meeting of the I.R.A. army council. Flynn himself was a ranking member, Chief of Staff and in charge of operations. Operations meant that he was in charge of all military actions, or what the rest of the world referred to as acts of terrorism.

Heavily armed men guarded approaches to the farm. Appropriate escape routes had been established in the event that police were to raid the gathering. The South was not exactly a safe haven for the I.R.A. since the Irish Republic had also outlawed the I.R.A. Arrests had been made on occasion, but compared with the North, there existed none of the sectarian antagonisms that pit the government against the I.R.A.

"Gentlemen, the purpose of this meeting is to establish new strategies," Terrance Dolan announced. He was a veteran since the sixties and now Commander-In-Chief of the Provincial Irish Republican Army.

He continued. "New membership is flagging. Dissident factions have taken unauthorized actions. Discipline has become lax. While Mr. Adams has made some inroads with the British, it has come at some expense. A reduction in military actions has changed how we are perceived by not only the people, but many of the rank and file. We are less visible. Some sentiment suggests that the I.R.A. is less of a force to be reckoned with."

"Therefore, gentlemen, we need to explore a new focus, backed with new strategy. The meeting is now open to discussion," Dolan said.

There was little new in what most of the men had to say. They were all hard men, dedicated, having sacrificed much in their lives for the Cause. Most were firmly entrenched in their ideas of how to carry the fight forward. Most had aligned themselves with the three most influential I.R.A. leaders, Terrance Dolan, Commander-In-Chief, Gerry Adams, President of Sinn Fein, and Michael Flynn, Operations Chief of Staff.

All three had substantially different strategies for conducting the war. They were united only by their common cause. The three were not friendly. Each had a strong following among the Army's senior members.

Adams, the youngest of the three, was the only publicly known figure of the leadership. He was a natural politician, good-looking, with a low-key, persuasive style, and a natural charisma.

Adams had a presence on radio and television that in itself lent a degree of legitimacy to the I.R.A. When necessary, Adams could distance himself from I.R.A. violence. As head of the political party, Sinn Fein, he could publicly support all of the I.R.A. objectives, yet express disagreement with certain actions. He avowed that Sinn Fein spoke for the I.R.A., but had no control over that organization.

Dolan privately resented Adam's public recognition. He also felt him to be too much enamored with his own public role. Adams was less ardent a republican than he was a politician. Now he talked of negotiation. There was no blood on Gerry Adams hands any longer.

For Adams part, Dolan more and more resented the blind, entrenched, sometimes unthinking, frequently unrealistic positions of much of the leadership. There was no appreciation for the possibility of achieving many republican objectives with only minimal compromise. If only the others could see the possibilities, see the changes in the circumstances, changes in the opposition, and then seize these new opportunities. Flynn was even further beyond Dolan.

Adams, like the others, could see the division between Dolan and Flynn. They were quite open about their philosophical differences. Odd, since both represented what Adams thought to be the old school thinking of the seventies. Dolan still harbored socialist concepts, Flynn unrelenting warfare.

Adam's own activism had started in 1969, but he had found the prevailing Marxist concepts of the time naive. He had also progressed from the martyr mentality, and the almost religious fervor of the struggle that still dominated I.R.A. thinking.

Adams was more wary about Michael Flynn. Flynn was certainly a dinosaur. Unlike Dolan however, Flynn could care less about economic social systems. Ireland was his cause. He was a staunch advocate of violence. He was a classic warrior. In war, the overriding objective is the destruction of the enemy. Flynn was a super fanatic.

Flynn was a formidable influence in the I.R.A. with his legendary exploits in the early years. He also had a charisma. Where Adams conveyed sincerity and logic in a low-key style, Flynn would sell his position with fiery Irish passion and a keen intellect.

For Dolan's part, Flynn alone continued to give the I.R.A. a violent face. Flynn was both his and Adams' major obstacle on issues where they could both agree. However, Flynn's reputation could not be denied. What irked Dolan the most was that Flynn had never been imprisoned, never even been arrested. Dolan had. He had suffered terribly, the memories of which could still make him shudder. Even Adams had been interned. But it was Flynn that had been a gunman. It was Flynn that had killed so many times that the legend was now as important as the man himself.

Flynn's exploits in the field were still the subject of I.R.A. lore. Even the failed ambush that eventually lead to Flynn's crippling wound and cost the lives of a good many men, had become a Flynn triumph in the succeeding decades.

Flynn was from County Monaghan, part of the Republic of Ireland. Monaghan was part of the ancient Irish province of Ulster. Strong ties existed with the northern six counties that constituted Northern Ireland. Dolan always harbored resentment for Flynn who could fight his war, than return to a comparatively safe haven. Now he lived even further south in Dublin. Most, like Dolan lived in the northern six counties, subject to constant risk.

Most of the debate at this meeting would focus on the three principle leaders. Adams spoke first. Adams was the ranking contact with the 'unofficial' negotiations being conducted with the British.

"Gentlemen. The pace of these negotiations is agonizingly slow. However, we continue to make progress. Short of curtailing military operations we have conceded nothing. Yet the British have conceded much," Adams said.

"I do not share Mr. Dolan's concerns about erosion of our ranks. Those that are falling away do not have sufficient conviction for the Cause. I am more concerned about unauthorized military actions. These can seriously damage what we are seeking to gain at the negotiation table. The British are desperate to achieve a resolution to the conflict. However, they cannot be seen as caving in to violence."

Adams continued. "My strategy is simple; use this time of relative peace to strengthen the I.R.A. by amassing resources and developing international support. Any military actions should be carefully planned and used only to support negotiation strategies. If we plan well and are disciplined, we can achieve disproportionate concessions."

"Our objective of a free and united Ireland will not come in one great leap. It will come at the end of a process that continually moves closer to that goal," Adams concluded. As usual, he was low-keyed and brief.

Dolan turned to Flynn to speak next.

Flynn said, "Everyone knows where I stand. I'd like to hear first what you are proposing, Terrance."

"Very well," Dolan said. "I am afraid I do not share Mr. Adam's confidence in the negotiating process, unless there is continuing pressure applied to the other side. Otherwise I fear we shall be at this same position years from now. By then, our base of power will have seriously declined."

"Let me first say that I fully support the negotiation process. We voted some time ago to move in that direction, and I have not changed my mind. However, we simply are not applying enough pressure."

Dolan continued. "What I propose is similar to Mr. Adams, but more aggressive. Actions should be considered as to how they will effect negotiations. I propose that we use our resources to continually attack the economic structure of Northern Ireland and Britain."

"This means military actions, but of a sort that does not provoke negative responses internationally. The toll of innocent victims repulses a good segment of the Catholic populace, not to mention the rest of the world. These killings have hurt our support and the flow of money from America."

"We must avoid attacks that risk civilian lives. We should also avoid direct attacks on paramilitary personnel, the police, or the army. In short, we should focus our military actions on things not people."

Dolan looked directly at Flynn but received no indication as to Flynn's reaction. This was clearly a challenge to Flynn's management of operations.

Dolan continued. "I propose we focus on generating strikes and boycotts. We should disrupt government services. Military operations should be directed at economic targets."

Dolan talked for some time, going into specific details. Although much of what he outlined was operational, Flynn had never been consulted.

Having waited to hear all the others, Flynn finally rose from his chair with the help of his cane. He walked with a heavy limp to a table set out with whisky and glasses. Adams and Dolan had addressed the group sitting down. For effect, he slowly poured whiskey into a glass.

Flynn took a healthy swig of his whiskey.

"Gentlemen. Like all of you, I too am frustrated. But not in the same way that Mr. Dolan is."

"This reduction in military action is taking a toll. We are a fighting force contrary to Mr. Adams view from his Sinn Fein position. I voted against any concessions in order to enter into negotiations with the British. Negotiations were premature."

"Sure it is that we're tired. Tired of this fight that is at our very soul. Those that came before us experienced the same weariness. Will it be said that it was this generation that tired of the fight and surrendered with victory in sight? Yes, in sight. The British government is no longer wedded to an inflexible policy of dominion over the northern six counties. But let's not talk, let's increase our negotiating strength."

Flynn continued. "What are we fighting for? We're fighting for the same thing all Irishmen have always fought for — a united Ireland, free from the British. Partition in the twenties was a clever maneuver by the British. Placate a good segment of the Irish populace, look progressive in the eyes of the world, and yet retain the industry and the wealth of Ireland. There were those, even great patriots that chose to compromise. It may have been the best move then, but not today."

"You men, you Irishmen, you leaders of the Provincial Irish Republican Army, do not need reminding that this is a war. We broke from the original I.R.A. twenty years ago because that leadership had no stomach for the fight."

Flynn paused and took a drink of water.

"We're not a political movement. We are an armed resistance force fighting an occupying power. We do not want to change any social order. We do not want to change any laws. We want our country back. We want the fucking British out! We want their Protestant puppet government in the North out! We want freedom for all Irish men and women. We want an end to discrimination against Catholics! And, we want a united Ireland!" Flynn uttered the last sentence in Gaelic.

Flynn looked at each of the assembled men in turn.

"I would welcome any tactics that would push the British out. Boycotts and strikes sound like grand talk. And who will suffer the worse from strikes and boycotts? The Catholic poor as always. How long will their resolve be maintained? How are we to sustain that resolve?"

Flynn paused again. As he continued, he moved about the room, his limp made evident for effect. Dolan glared at him. Adams was passive in expression.

"Mr. Dolan does an outstanding job in raising funds abroad. I for one do not know how he does it," Flynn said.

"But gentlemen, this is a war. We need to focus our efforts on destroying the enemy. I do agree with Mr. Dolan that we might do more in the area of striking at economic targets. I shall begin a study immediately to develop plans along those lines."

"We have already refocused on targets that are more directed at British commerce. Flynn said. "I think the most recent missions support that strategy. But in any war, civilian casualties cannot be avoided."

"Christ, Michael, you don't seem to appreciate the fact that we cannot continue to conduct a guerrilla war indefinitely," Dolan interrupted. Flynn was too much. This lecturing was particularly irritating.

"We must engage new tactics, tactics consistent with changing circumstances. The British are close to agreeing to a withdrawal. We need to be careful not to give the Unionists new reasons to tie the hands of the British."

"Close? Why then is Mr. Adams having such a struggle?" Flynn responded. "I don't see them as close. And their army leaving will not insure a united Ireland."

"Our ultimate objective has always been the uniting of the thirty-two counties. This is the reason for the existence of the Irish Republican Army. It was the reason for countless other organizations that have preceded us in history."

Flynn continued. "Obviously the British must leave Ireland. But if only the British army leaves, then we're no better off than twenty-five years ago when we started this rising. Can we honestly hope to achieve anything if we do not oppose the British and the Protestant paramilitaries with the gun?"

"Gentlemen, if we were to agree to easing military operations, we have nothing to fight with. We have no court where we can plead our case. Civil protests will never accomplish the changes we strive for. We cannot inflict enough economic damage. Violence. Violence against an occupying enemy power is and always has been necessary to effect change," Flynn said, the passion increasing in his voice.

"I suggest, gentlemen, that the only pressure the British understand is violence. Palestine, Egypt, South Africa, Kenya. Only India was somewhat different, and violence there was still the compelling catalyst. Would Mr. Dolan have us practice Gandhi-like non-violence to free us from the British?"

"To bargain away our most effective leverage will never achieve our ultimate goal of a united Ireland. Historically, the British have always caved in. We must have the courage and will to sustain the fight. Mr. Adams must find a way to get to the negotiating table with no prior conditions." Flynn concluded.

After two more hours of discussion, a compromise strategy was reached that would only marginally alter the tactics of the I.R.A.

First, Military actions would continue. There would be no consideration for a cessation of violence. Adams was not yet advocating such a move, but would have hoped for more freedom of action in his secret negotiations with the British. Adams did win a victory by the council suspending any large-scale bombings, unless approved by a majority of the council.

Secondly, Flynn's Active Service Units were to begin a strategy of inflicting damage on Protestant economic targets. Targets such as factories employing predominately Protestant workers, trucking firms, warehouses, port facilities, ships, communications were suggested.

Thirdly, Dolan's call for a campaign of organized civil disobedience, boycotts and strikes met with little enthusiasm. These were hardened men. Generally men who had practiced violence. Men who had violence committed on them. Such tactics were too passive. They could not emotionally embrace Gandhi's concept of non-violence.

Flynn left with a bad feeling. On the surface, things had changed very little. But he knew that it would be increasingly difficult to maintain the war as he saw it.

Terrance Dolan wanted to take the I.R.A. in a different direction. Acceptance to negotiation and compromise would continue to grow amongst the leadership. All it would take would be the catalyst of an offer by the British that would be publicly and politically unpopular to reject.

Flynn thought about how often those before him had faced the same crisis in this struggle that was Irish history. He walked now in their shoes. He could not compromise the Irish blood that had been shed for these hundreds of years.

Chapter Six

Garrett O'Donovan walked through the security gate out of Long Kesh Prison located to the south of Belfast. This was where the British held suspected I.R.A. It had been six months almost to the day since he and Paddy McCullough were arrested for the murder of the R.U.C. police officer, Matthew Heddley.

Long Kesh was erected on the site of an old airfield soon after the *troubles* began. It became infamous for the internment of suspected I.R.A. without trial under the emergency powers. It was a dismal place lacking in adequate facilities. There were recurring prisoner protests. One such protest in 1978 resulted in the prisoners' refusal to empty their chamber pots, giving one an idea of the quality of the facility. In 1981, a hunger strike lead to the deaths of ten Republican prisoners within Long Kesh.

Even though Long Kesh was a pesthole of a place, at least there were no interrogations for O'Donovan after the first few weeks. It was the few days at the R.U.C. barracks after being arrested that were the roughest.

His previous experience with interrogation had somewhat prepared O'Donovan. At least knowing was better than the stark fear of that first time. Neither he nor Paddy McCullough had broken under intense interrogations. McCullough had taught O'Donovan how to develop a counter to the psychological torture. Once that was accomplished, the physical abuse and deprivations were manageable.

However, enduring was not always enough to insure survival. McCullough was in the prison infirmary. Something about kidney failure. O'Donovan had seen him only once after they were brought to Long Kesh Prison, and that was two weeks ago. He had complained of severe pains before they hospitalized him.

"Jesus, Paddy, you look somethin' awful," O'Donovan said.

"I'm feeling pretty bad, Garrett. Worse time they've ever given me. Been usin' a rubber truncheon. Doesn't break bones, but does real damage. Look here." McCullough raised his shirt.

O'Donovan winced at the sight. "Fuck, Paddy. How bad is that?" From his front to his back, he was swollen and the skin was a deep purple.

"Bad enough, but look here," McCullough said and tried to raise from his cot. O'Donovan needed to help him.

McCullough lowered his pants. His testicles were each swollen to the size of a large apple.

"Been peein' blood regularly. Almost pass out with the pain."

"Christ Almighty, Paddy that looks real bad. You need a doctor."

"Doctor? You think the bastards 'll go to all of this trouble just to have a doctor fix me up.? How you been fairin,' Garrett?"

"Lot better than you. Wasn't allowed any water or toilet facilities until the second day. They don't let you sleep. Hard to anyway in that cold. Least it's warmer here."

It was winter and the police barracks cells were no more than fifty-five degrees. No blankets were provided.

"I know. Think I got a fever there in the cold. Hope it's not pneumonia."

If it was, O'Donovan feared McCullough might not make it. "Anyway, they slapped me around and kicked me pretty good for a few days. Kicked me in the nuts. Vomited each time. Not as bad as what they did to you though. Burned me. That was the worst. See here." O'Donovan showed him a half dozen burn wounds on his chest. "Guess they decided I wasn't goin' to tell them anything, so they finally sent me here."

For several months, a vigorous defense had been mounted on behalf of O'Donovan. Fellow I.R.A. prisoners commented, some enviously, that O'Donovan must have friends in high places. If he did, O'Donovan did not know them. Two solicitors were working on his case aggressively.

O'Donovan enjoyed their frequent visits to Long Kesh, particularly when it involved the woman barrister named Reilly. Brigid Reilly was something to look at, even with her conservative business attire. She was tall, with long legs, a narrow waist, full breasts, and long auburn hair pulled up in a conservative style. Her face was somewhat angular, with high cheekbones and a nose that probably was a slight bit too long.

O'Donovan knew that women found him attractive, but Reilly was a difficult sell. He was even more aroused by her assertiveness and obvious intelligence. O'Donovan would fantasize about what it would be like to have sex with her.

After a time, Reilly became more personable even laughing at O'Donovan's jokes. He could be charming to women, and even a woman like Reilly was not immune.

"Let's go over this one more time, Garrett. These are questions I will ask when you testify in court," Reilly said.

"Do you belong to the Provincial Irish Republican Army?"

"No, mam."

"What do you do, Mr. O'Donovan?"

"I run a pub."

"Were your father and brother involved with the I.R.A.?"

"Yes."

"Why do you think you were arrested for suspicion of the murder of Police Officer Heddley?"

"Cause of me family history. The R.U.C. think that anyone with relatives in the I.R.A. must be one too."

"Where were you on the morning of the murder of Police Officer Heddley, Mr. O'Donovan?"

"I was at mass, at St. Vincent's. "

"Do you go to mass regularly?"

"No, mam."

"And why were you there that morning?"

"I was upset. I had a bad argument with my wife the night before. We been havin' a good many arguments lately. Thought I might talk to a priest."

"You were going to confession?"

"Well I don't know 'bout that. Probably just talk to the priest."

"And did you?"

"No."

"Why not?"

"Well – I don't go to church. Felt odd talkin' to a stranger about personal problems, even if he was a priest."

"Did anyone see you at the church?"

"I don't know. Probably not. I sat in the back and left before mass was over."

"Well, Garrett, you are consistent. Just stay with your story and don't let the prosecution get you angry," Reilly said.

"What are my chances, Brigid?"

"Good I'd say."

"What with you defending me, I shant worry. How did someone as beautiful as you get into law?"

"Are you flirting with me, Garrett?"

"A wee bit. Can't help myself. Any woman as smart and good looking as you can't be resisted."

"Easy, Garrett. I don't get involved with clients, particularly married ones."

Reilly had become more personable over the weeks she had seen O'Donovan. O'Donovan could charm, and he was good looking.

O'Donovan had rehearsed the story with McCullough. Reilly and her colleague knew it was a fabrication. They knew O'Donovan was I.R.A. but never challenged his story. Bottom line was the government had no real evidence so they just interned a number of potential suspects.

Within a couple of weeks they told O'Donovan that a hearing had been scheduled to review his arrest. There were apparently several witnesses after all to his being in the church at the time Heddley was being murdered.

At the hearing, O'Donovan heard for the first time the testimony of two middle-aged women and an elderly man, apparently the church sexton. All testified that they saw the man in the prisoner's dock at mass that morning. The prosecution knew what was going on, but could offer little in rebuttal. They had no physical evidence, nor any witnesses that could identify O'Donovan as being involved with the Heddley killing. The magistrate adjourned the proceedings, indicating he would render his decision within one week.

To O'Donovan, Reilly's smile suggested more than just her pleasure with the outcome of the hearing, and more than mere friendliness to the client. She shook hands with O'Donovan, and said, "call me when you're out." From the gallery, Mary Catherine noticed O'Donovan's attention following Reilly as she left the courtroom.

And so it was a week later that a release order was issued by the magistrate on grounds of insufficient evidence. An old time patron of the pub drove O'Donovan's mother and Mary Catherine to pick him up from Long Kesh the following day. Tears rolled down his mother's cheeks as she hugged him. Mary Catherine's display was more reserved.

Within a day of his release, O'Donovan was summoned to a meeting across the border in Monaghan. Something was happening. Now he would perhaps learn why all the interest in him by the I.R.A leadership. Besides, a journey to Monaghan would take him through Armagh. It would be an opportunity to see his woman friend there and make up for the last few months. Mary Catherine had been less than enthusiastic sexually since his return.

O'Donovan left the following day. As instructed, he made contact with the I.R.A. in Armagh. They would secret him across the border somewhere south of the city, not a feat to be taken lightly in that area. News media had labeled this area as Bandit Country, or the Killing Fields. It was laced with electronic barriers and patrolled by both the British army and the R.U.C. The I.R.A. had waged a constant war against Protestant landholders in the area for some time.

A single I.R.A. man guided O'Donovan into the Republic of Ireland over a precise three-mile route. It was a pitch-black night in the early hours of the morning. O'Donovan marveled at the man's intimate knowledge of the terrain. The trek was without incident. His guide stopped frequently to use a hand held transmitter/receiver. No words were spoken, only short bursts of noise in a code.

Once over the border, they linked up with another man for another half-mile walk to a lorry loaded with produce for market. To the Irish police, the Garda, they were only farmers on their way to sell their produce in the predawn hours. The I.R.A. was also outlawed in the Republic, but the Garda was less vigilant than the R.U.C. and British Army.

The truck pulled up at a farm to the south of Monaghan. Dawn was just breaking. It was cold with a heavy fog. O'Donovan was escorted into the house and to a large kitchen. A middle-aged woman acknowledged his presence and served him a large breakfast of eggs, sausage, and bread. Half way through his meal, a slight man, middle-aged, with a decided limp, entered the kitchen and sat down. The woman left the kitchen.

"I'm Michael Flynn. Thank you for coming."

O'Donovan paused with a forkful of food to his mouth. Holy Jesus, Michael Flynn in the flesh. Flynn was a legend. O'Donovan knew him only as that. He knew nothing of Flynn's present involvement with the I.R.A. O'Donovan stumbled to his feet, accepting Flynn's hand.

"Sit down and finish your breakfast, lad. You've been through a lot." Flynn poured himself a cup of coffee.

O'Donovan wolfed down the remnants of his breakfast, eager for Flynn to tell him what was going on.

"We've been hearin' good things about you, Garrett. Paddy McCullough thinks you're one of the best he's seen. We were impressed with the Webster bombing, more impressed with the Heddley hit. I know good men that would have shied from that task. Takes a special man to go toe-to-toe, eye-to-eye so to speak, then do what he has to."

O'Donovan was dumbfounded. Such praise coming from the greatest legend in the I.R.A. since the *troubles* started, sent his ego soaring.

"There's something else," Flynn said, "Your unit, what's left of it, is being disbanded and reassigned."

O'Donovan didn't understand what Flynn was saying. "I thought you said we were doing a good job?"

"You are. You were. But the unit has been inactive since you and McCullough were jailed. And I'm afraid it soon will be without their commander. Paddy McCullough has been taken to a regular hospital. I'm afraid he's not going to make it. The bastards destroyed his kidneys. Doctors give him maybe a couple of months at most."

Flynn poured them more coffee. "Whiskey?" Flynn brought a bottle of Bushmills over to the table, pouring a splash in each coffee. "Take the chill out of the morning damp."

Flynn sipped his coffee then asked, "What do you think about all this talk of cease fire and negotiations with the British. Do ya think there's a peaceful solution in the North?"

O'Donovan was still shaken about Paddy McCullough and not sure what Flynn wanted to hear. It was clear though that Flynn hadn't gone to all this trouble to get him out of prison, then meet with him here in the Republic for the purpose of discussing peace.

"If you ask me, I'm against it. Don't sound like the British have done what we want, so why back off? Sooner or later the Brits will get sick and tired of pissing away money fighting us. They'll get sick of their boys dying in Northern Ireland for a bunch of wealthy Protestant bastards. I'd say I was for continuin' the fight. It's too early for a truce."

"Would you be willing to go up against those in the I.R.A. Command if they choose to cave in to a cease fire and negotiations?"

O'Donovan didn't know what to say to such a question. He didn't like the corner he was being forced into.

Flynn preempted his answer. "Listen, lad, this isn't the first time that good Irishmen like you have been asked to choose. Remember, we broke from the old so-called Official I.R.A. back in the late sixties to form our Provisional I.R.A. They were a bunch of Marxist intellectuals with naive objectives to overthrow governments in both the north and the Republic, then set up some sort of workers society. They forgot about the great struggle for independence back in the twenties. They forgot what the

I.R.A. was about. Military uprising was called for then, and real patriots chose to fight rather than debate. It's coming to that again, Garrett."

O'Donovan took a drink of his whiskey-laced coffee and looked into Flynn's fiery eyes.

"I fear that's the situation we have come to. Many in the leadership are tired of the fight. There are those that favor negotiating with the British. They think it enough to gain only small concessions. For this we are to stop military operations? Stop the pressure? And for what? To face endless years of debate while nothing changes?"

"Are you fighting Gerry Adams on this?" O'Donovan asked, not sure whether it was his place to ask such a question.

"You're damn right! That self-serving asshole is in it only for his own aggrandizement. He'll sell us out for sure. He has the public's eye now throughout the world. He's the one that supposedly speaks for the I.R.A., disguised as Sinn Fein. Adams is the darling of the media."

Calming, Flynn continued, "But it's not just Adams, it's others in the leadership, not the least of which is our commander, Terrance Dolan." O'Donovan had not known the name of the I.R.A. Commander-in-Chief until now.

"I've known Terry Dolan for many a year. He's getting old, cautious, and too tired to carry on the fight. His idea of a new strategy includes things like boycotts and civil disobedience. Unfortunately, he's not alone. We've got a bunch of tired old men that call themselves leaders. They no longer have the will to carry the fight to the enemy."

"What is it you want me to do, Sir?"

"I want to know if you'll follow me in continuing the fight. I want your commitment to continue the war against British occupation of Ireland."

"You know of me, Garrett. What you don't know is that I'm Chief of Staff of the Provisional I.R.A. And I am telling you that I will not give up the fight to the politicians that have invaded our ranks. I'm prepared to split with the other leadership and continue the war just like we did back in the sixties."

"I now put that same question to you, Garrett O'Donovan, because I fear that we are again at that point."

Flynn was giving him no way out. If he refused, or was maybe even unconvincing in his commitment, he guessed that someone would see that he did not return to Belfast. But the answer was easy anyway. He had found his niche, and peace was not it. He was good at operations, good with weapons. He could kill and most of all he liked the adventure.

"I joined the I.R.A. to fight to get the British out of Ireland. My father and brother were I.R.A. It's long enough we've been shit on. Sure it is that I will continue to fight. If you'll lead us, Mr. Flynn, I'll carry the gun."

"That's what I'd hope you say, Garrett. You are key to my planning. I want you to head up a new unit. This will be a unit of specialists, selected for their expertise in field operations."

O'Donovan was flattered by the offer but equally uneasy about the implications. "Why me, Sir? There must be others with more experience."

"Many I should say. But you have what is required. You've executed two successful missions. The leader of your first mission said you had no nerves. Calm as could be after you set off the bomb. Paddy McCullough said you shot Heddley straight on without blinking an eye. You've been an intelligence officer. You know security. You know how things work."

"I don't pretend to know your motivations, lad, but you're born to this. I don't think you could do without it. I don't think you'd be happy being a barkeep."

Flynn continued, "Now, I want you to go back to Belfast. Go back to your pub and wait for orders. Only my orders. The others of your old unit will be informed not to come around anymore, or contact you. Security reasons."

"There's one more thing, Garrett. Can you be away for a couple of months? Can your family get along?"

O'Donovan's curiosity and excitement were barely contained. "I guess so."

"Good. You, and members of your new unit will receive special training in America. All of you will be there with various reasons to explain your absences that will preclude suspicion back home. But you've got to create a plausible cover with your family."

"Why America for training, Mr. Flynn?"

"Simple. We have powerful friends there, friends with resources. It's also easier to hide training maneuvers there and discharge firearms. Americans won't at all be alarmed with gunfire in a rural area. In short, the security's easier."

"Now, I must be leaving," Flynn continued. He stood abruptly and put his coat on. O'Donovan was standing looking slightly down at the shorter Flynn. "I'm counting on you, Garrett."

Flynn shook hands, then left. The man that had guided him across the border entered the farmhouse and told him he would come for him that night to make their way back across the border. Sorry for the wait said the man.

O'Donovan would spend a restless day waiting for nightfall and trying to sort out what had just happened. But no matter. He was full of himself. Within the last few days he was released from prison, been given command of a unit, and let in on the highest level of politics and secrets in the I.R.A. He was going places. No telling where it might lead. Gerry Adams himself started out as a barkeeper.

Even the marathon sex with the Armagh woman had not sated his desire. Besides, she was still just common. Brigid Reilly was uncommon. It took several calls to her office to finally get put through to her.

"Brigid Reilly, you're hard to get hold of."

"Busy day. Who's this?"

"Garrett O'Donovan."

"Well, Garrett. Are you in trouble again?"

"No. This is like a social call. Need to be thankin' you for the work you did."

"Well I have been paid, Garrett. What did you have in mind?"

"A couple of drinks and a lovely dinner."

Reilly hesitated briefly then accepted and agreed to meet at a trendy pub downtown. She had no illusions about what would happen after dinner. O'Donovan's good looks and charm during their work on his release had sexually aroused her. She wanted to take him to bed. Nothing more, just a good one-night stand with a handsome man, and maybe a dangerous man for added spice. Men did that sort of thing all the time. It was only mildly troubling that he was married.

Reilly was not disappointed with the prospects after seeing O'Donovan. He wore a leather jacket over a turtleneck knit shirt. He was over six feet, apparently very fit, with dark blue eyes and an infectious smile. She had not been with a man for weeks, and the last was nowhere near as good looking as O'Donovan was.

Conversation was light at best. Both shied away from politics. He talked about football, she about past cases. At the end of dinner, O'Donovan said, "An after dinner drink?"

Reilly looked directly at him, "I have some very old brandy at my flat."

O'Donovan smiled in reply, and hurriedly paid the bill. He hoped Reilly would be worth what the dinner had cost.

She closed the door to the flat and turned to face O'Donovan in the semi-dark. He moved against her, crushing his mouth against hers. They embraced for several minutes, each rubbing their hands over the other. She led him to the bedroom.

He sat on the bed, she stood in front of him. She pulled her sweater over her head. He undid her skirt. She helped pull his shirt off, then bent down and pulled his shoes off. He stood to remove his trousers, but she took over, unbuckling the belt and unzipping his fly. He sat back on the bed as she pulled trousers and underwear off together.

In the pale light she could see his fully erect penis. She unfastened her bra, letting it come away slowly revealing her full breasts.

She removed her heels and pantyhose, and came to him on the bed. She bent down, rubbing his cock with her hand, letting him move his head between her breasts. He kissed her nipples.

"Like my cock?"

"It looks very good."

"Take it then," O'Donovan said. With his hands on her waist, he gently, but firmly guided her to her knees on the floor, between his legs.

Reilly didn't like his assertiveness, or presumptuousness. But she was hot - very hot. She could feel herself getting wet. And she did want him. She lowered her mouth over his erect member, forcing a gasp of pleasure from him.

Reilly pleasured him with her mouth for several minutes. Pulling away from him, she said, "Let's get on the bed."

O'Donovan obliged and pushed Reilly down on the bed. She wanted more foreplay, but his hard cock caused her also to gasp in pleasure as he entered her. His long slow strokes sent waves of pleasure through her. Her back arched as his penetrations became deeper.

She could sense his impending release. She wasn't ready yet, and she wanted more. He brought both hands under her buttocks and pulled himself inside her as deeply as possible as he let loose. She could feel his hot fluid empty into her.

"I'm not through," Reilly said. O'Donovan looked quizzically into her face.

"Turn over," she said.

O'Donovan pulled out as Reilly rolled over and got up on all fours, guiding O'Donovan's into her again from the back. He got harder as she exerted more friction on his cock. She liked it this way. Penetration was deeper. At least he had good stamina. Following her lead, his thrusts were rhythmic and forceful as she grabbed him ever tighter and escalated to her own orgasm. He pulled out immediately afterwards.

Laying on his back, O'Donovan said, "Damn, Brigid — you are some woman. I like the fact you wanted it, then did something about it. Most women wouldn't ever tell a man."

Reilly went to the lavatory to clean up. Most of the time she wanted to stay in bed with the man, hold and caress after lovemaking. But this was just a lay. Probably exactly what O'Donovan thought it was.

Reilly put a robe on and went back into the bedroom. O'Donovan was not there. She found him in the kitchen. He had his shirt on and his underwear.

He turned. "There you are, Luv. Found that old brandy you talked about. French, huh?" He poured each a drink into two snifters he located in the cupboard.

They took chairs opposite each other in the living room.

"Jesus, you're some good lookin' woman, Brigid Reilly."

Stupid sight she thought. She in her robe and bare feet, he in his underwear, drinking brandy. Didn't know the bloke. Probably an I.R.A. killer like the police charged. Just handsome with a charming smile. Just a fuck.

"Thank you, Garrett." She absolutely could not think of anything to say to make conversation. What if he wants to spend the night? Dinner had not been intellectually stimulating, but then again it was only a means to a physical end. Now it was a different matter.

He satisfied her dilemma. "Listen, Brigid, I can't stay, but I would like to see you again. What about Wednesday? You free?"

Reilly needed to dodge a 'next time.' This had probably been a mistake. As sex it was only mediocre. As lovemaking, it wasn't. Garrett O'Donovan was not a prospect for any sort of relationship. "I don't think so, Garrett. I have several new cases that are keeping me working all sorts of hours this week. Perhaps you could call me in a week or so."

Bitch, O'Donovan thought to himself. Probably just wanted to get laid by a real man. Maybe she liked the idea of fucking an I.R.A. gunman. She'll see him again. Women always did. And next time, he would come in her mouth.

He did call a week later. She was polite and apologized for suggesting they get together. He was married, and she just didn't feel right about getting involved.

"Bullshit. You just wanted to get fucked, and I was an adventure. You knew I was married and you didn't give a shit then. So why's it bother you now, Luv?"

Jesus, she could kick herself for being so stupid. This was probably not the type of man to get on the wrong side of. But he was right about what he was accusing her of. "Garrett, I made a mistake. We had a good time that night. We both needed it, but we lead different lives."

"Both needed it? You listen, Luv. You may have needed it, but not me. Getting screwed is not something I have to work at. I took you to bed because you came on to me and you've a good body. But your pussy's no different than any I've had."

"Bugger off, O'Donovan, I don't need this shit," Reilly said, then rung off. She made a mental note to have her number changed.

The rage O'Donovan felt was soon replaced by news that he would leave for the United States in two weeks.

His mother said little when he told her. She knew it was I.R.A. business. Business that had brought so much sorrow into her life. Mary Catherine was more concerned about the added work at the pub without his help. She was somewhat appeased when he told her that she could take on a temporary person to help while he was away. The I.R.A. had given him several hundred pounds to help with expenses during his absence.

O'Donovan left for the United States within the week. It was his first flight. He was met at Boston's Logan Airport by a young man who drove him to a farm ninety minutes west of Boston. It was late summer and the evening was still warm. Entering the farm required unlocking a steel gate, then proceeding up a winding road for a quarter mile.

The young man let O'Donovan into the large house, and showed him upstairs to a small bedroom. It was one a.m. No one else was about. The man left without saying anything.

O'Donovan woke at daylight, did a quick wash-up and left the room for downstairs.

"Mr. O'Donovan. Glad to meet you. I'm Murphy, Master Sergeant Murphy. Late of the United States Army, Special Forces, Special Operations. I'll be in charge of your training." Murphy extended his hand. "Come meet the others. They all arrived earlier. I understand that none of you know each other."

Five men were gathered around a large dining room table.

"This here is Garrett O'Donovan," Murphy announced. "I'll let you introduce yourselves."

O'Donovan made his way around the table. Each man stood and shook hands.

"Erskine Colbert. Glad to met you."

"Jack Burns."

"Martin Kelly. Glad to meet you."

"I'm Peter Sullivan."

"Brennan Magee."

O'Donovan sat down and poured himself a cup of coffee from the pot in the middle of the table.

"All right gentlemen. Here's the deal," Murphy said. "I've been hired to train you in weapons, explosives, close-in combat, and small unit tactics. You'll be here for ten weeks. You'll train hard, you'll go nowhere. No one leaves the farm. You need a woman - use your hand." A couple of the men chuckled.

"I know you're I.R.A. But don't let my being Irish fool you. I'm a soldier - not political. I don't give a shit about your cause. I've trained troops all over the world; Africa, South America, Asia. Been hired by leftists, rightists; worked for democracies, dictators, and rebels. Don't give a shit about the politics."

"How well you learn is a reflection on my skills. It's how I make my living. Don't screw up. If you think you're tough, I'm tougher. Fuck with me and I'll hand you your head. Obey my orders precisely. So, if you leave the farm, it is a breach of security. I'm licensed to sanction you in such a case. For those of you who don't know the term, 'sanction' is intelligence jargon for blowing your fucking brains out."

O'Donovan and the others were not raw recruits. All had been on missions. Yet Murphy commanded attention. He was tall and lean, obviously fit, somewhere around fifty, with a close-cropped military haircut. Dark, cold eyes suggested that he could back up anything he threatened.

"Now to routine. We're it - there's nobody else here, except security on the perimeter. We cook our own meals, clean up after ourselves. The first two weeks will be physical conditioning, and weapons familiarity. The next two are in weapons proficiency. Throughout the remaining six weeks, we'll continue a regular routine devoted to these areas. Next, you'll become proficient in various close-in combat techniques. Lastly, we'll work on small unit tactics. In the end, I expect you to be a crack combat team, or I'll kill you in the process of trying."

"O'Donovan, I understand you'll be in command once this unit becomes operational," Murphy said. O'Donovan nodded.

"Good. Then you can take charge organizing how the kitchen is managed during your stay here. As for now, you've got one hour to eat, then fall out outside. You'll find fatigues upstairs. From now on, you'll wear them. This is your last morning of leisure gentleman," Murphy said, then left.

"Jesus, they told me it was training not prison. I fear this is going to be no picnic," Erskine Colbert said.

"So you're our new commander, O'Donovan," Jack Burns said. The comment held no warmth. Burns was a short, stocky man with a chip on his shoulder.

"That's what I'm told, Burns. I get my orders just like you. Any problem with that?" O'Donovan asked.

"No. At least not yet," Burns answered.

Ignoring Burns, "Erskine is it?" O'Donovan asked the man introduced as Colbert. Like most, he was around twenty-five, tall and slender, with longish brown hair with a bookish look, probably because of his glasses.

"Yes. That's right," Colbert answered.

"How about you and I fix all of us breakfast?" O'Donovan said.

"Sure enough. I'm a right fair cook if I do say so."

Sergeant Murphy immediately started their training in earnest. The first several days consisted of a five-mile morning run through the hilly Massachusetts countryside, followed by calisthenics and basic marshal arts training. After lunch they worked through an obstacle course, more marshal arts, finishing with another five-mile run to end the day.

Routine had settled in by the fourth day. The fatigue they all felt from the physical exertion lessened. The evenings were theirs. Television was the only real diversion.

"God, will ya look at her. There's a fine set of breasts if I ever saw one," Martin Kelly remarked at a prime time television program.

"Better be getting your mind off women, Kelly. It's going to be a while before you get close to one," Colbert chided.

"How well I know. It's worse even than all this runnin' and jumpin' and gettin'' filthy as a swine every day. Not to mention having to look at all you ugly fuckers," Kelly responded good-naturedly.

"Christ, what are you two so happy about. You're like a couple of fucking schoolboys. Didn't the last few days take some of that cheer out of you? What I want to know is when we get to do some real training? We haven't even used weapons yet," Jack Burns said.

Burns was the shortest of the team, with a muscular build. Murphy's initial training regimen included a lot of running. Burns shorter legs and heavier build made a grueling day even more difficult.

"Jack, ease up. I hurt, just like you do, just like all of us hurt. The training's hard, but we know it's what's necessary. None of us are new to this game. We've all handled weapons. We're here for advanced training," O'Donovan said.

Burns got to his feet. "And who the hell are you anyway to be put in charge, O'Donovan. You famous or something?"

O'Donovan rose to his feet. "That's enough Burns. If you keep it up, I'll have to do something about that mouth of yours."

"What the fuck did you say?" Burns shouted.

O'Donovan moved menacingly toward Burns, standing only two feet away. "I said, sit down, Jack - now."

Burns backed down uttering a grudging acknowledgment.

After a week, the training started to include the technical areas of weapons and explosives.

"See here, lads, this here is the famous Israeli designed Uzi submachine gun" Murphy said, holding up the short compact weapon. "It's distinct from an assault rifle like the AR-18s you boys of the I.R.A. are so fond of. The distinction of course is in the range and size of the weapon. Each having its own combat application."

"Your AR-18 fires a .223 Remington cartridge which is a 5.56 millimeter with a one-in-twelve rifling twist. This gives the bullet a tumbling action, and a muzzle velocity over three thousand feet per second. It's good for reaching out to a couple of hundred yards, and the tumbling action of the smaller caliber projectile gives good knock-down power at that range."

"This little baby here fires a nine millimeter pistol cartridge, but with a much lower muzzle velocity. It's good for knocking people down at close ranges. It's short, especially with the stock folded, therefore maneuverable in close quarters. It's also highly reliable. Most think it the best submachine gun design ever developed."

"This afternoon we'll start with the basics. You'll do some target shooting to get a feel for the weapon, then we'll field strip and reassemble until you know it like your lover. We'll also do training as well with the AR-18 and 9 millimeter hand guns," Murphy concluded.

"Don't see as why some of us need more training with weapons we already know, Mr. Murphy. Dare say I'm as good as any I've seen with an AR-18," Brennan Magee said sarcastically.

"That a fact Magee? So you can probably handle an Uzi with no problem?"

"Sure. Function's the same for any automatic weapon."

"Fine. Then show us. Take the weapon and hit that target. It's less than thirty yards out," Murphy said pointing to a row of cardboard man-sized targets. He handed Magee a Uzi and a magazine.

Magee inserted the magazine. He checked the function of the Uzi and unfolded the stock. Taking aim on the target, he fired a burst of ten rounds. Only two hit the target, neither was centered.

Murphy took the weapon from Magee. With a quick motion he raised the weapon, firing several two and three round bursts at another target. All shots hit the silhouette target.

"Just what I've been talking about. It's a wonder you people haven't shot each other or lost some toes. That's why we'll start with the basics."

All the I.R.A. men had received some training in the use of weapons, but not in the formal, detailed way pursued by Murphy. Murphy told them to forget anything they had been taught before.

The weeks passed. O'Donovan was assuming the role as commander. Part of Murphy's training was to help establish O'Donovan's authority. It was an easy task. O'Donovan was a natural leader. He was confident. He could out-perform any of the others. He knew when and how to apply pressure, who needed praise, who needed reprimand. Murphy had seen it before. O'Donovan was one of those whose natural abilities and inclinations for combat came together to make a superb soldier.

One evening, Murphy pulled O'Donovan aside. They strolled outside. The night air was brisk. It was now autumn. All the men had remarked on the spectacular colors of the trees.

"Training is almost over, O'Donovan," Murphy said. He offered O'Donovan a cigarette and lit up himself. "You and your people have done well. As a unit, you should fair well in any combat situation, at least from a technical standpoint. My scope of involvement and the time permitted, limit what I can do in making your people a real unit. And that's where the real difference in combat effectiveness comes from. So I'll give you the benefit of my assessment."

"First, Colbert. He's intelligent, probably your natural second in command, or at least someone you could delegate to where some latitude of decision is called for. Maybe too intellectual though. May not be up to some of things you lads might be planning."

"I'm not worried, Sergeant. I understand Colbert's proven himself in the past. That's why he was selected," O'Donovan said.

"Just the same, remember my comments," Murphy responded.

"Kelly and Sullivan are good soldiers. They're proficient, they obey orders. They take their hardships and their pleasures like soldiers, not like Burns and Magee."

Murphy continued, "Burns. I'll give him credit for being tough. With that physique, a lot of the training was tougher on him than the rest of you. But I don't need to tell you about his personality. He's a bitcher. Blames his misfortunes on everything but himself."

"He's obviously not real sharp. The best way to handle him is be strong, direct, and don't put up with any of his shit. Don't give him an inch. If he gets out of line, kick the shit out of him. In short, he's got to fear you."

"Probably the same goes for Magee, too," Murphy continued. "But Magee is different than Burns. For one thing, he's a lot smarter. Secondly, he's the most aggressive of the group. Probably likes violence, probably likes the idea of killing. Not uncommon among soldiers, not even necessarily undesirable. After all, that's what we're about. It's a question of motivation. The thing to watch out for in Magee is a threat to your unit. He's the one that could be disruptive. He could challenge your leadership in a way Burns couldn't."

"I appreciate your comments, Sergeant. I appreciate what you've done for us, too," O'Donovan said. He shook Murphy's hand.

"Just doin' what I get paid for, O'Donovan. Tell me something though. I'm curious why you people have been waging what amounts to a half-ass guerrilla war for over twenty years, and getting nowhere? Your strategy, if you've got one, sucks. Christ, you could do this for another twenty years and be no further ahead."

"Ah, now that's the question, Sergeant. I'll be telling you that I don't have an answer. We all feel different. We all have different reasons, at least that's what we tell ourselves. But it's something you feel, not something you think. You've got to live in Ireland, in the North I mean, to know what it's like. It makes your life. You don't always make it. Besides, the I.R.A. is a helluva lot more exciting life than working in a factory. Isn't that why you became a soldier, Sergeant?" O'Donovan said. They walked back to the house.

It was the first of November and the weather had turned cold. Their training had concluded. Murphy had departed earlier in the day. After dinner, the men celebrated with beer and whiskey.

"Easy on the whiskey lads. Some of you are leaving in the next few hours," O'Donovan announced. "Just like you arrived, you'll be leaving in intervals. Your routes back home are varied from different U.S. airports. Here're your tickets. Your individual times of departure from the farm here are written on the envelope. And like instructed before, those driving you are to be told nothing."

"We have never discussed why this unit was formed and why we were sent for special training here in America. I am instructed to tell you now," O'Donovan paused a moment for effect. "We all know about talk of negotiations with the British. Word is a cease-fire might not be far off. I have that on good authority. It's obvious that Adams has the upper hand in the way things are going. The public stuff is pretty much what is really happening."

He continued. "Way I see it, we stand down, things drag on with the politicians, the Army falls apart, and the enemy wins. What I want to know, lads, is how each of you feel about layin' down the gun?" O'Donovan threw it out as a challenge.

"Fuck them pussies. I didn't join to negotiate," Brennan Magee shouted angrily. "The fucking Protestants shit on us and the British kill us. What do we get out of negotiation?"

"I'm with Magee," Martin Kelly said, "that ain't what I joined up for."

"What about you, Peter?" O'Donovan asked.

Peter Sullivan considered his thoughts for several moments before answering. "I'm an I.R.A. man true enough. So was me Da and his Da. Before them, there were others in the family that fought for the Cause. My grandfather was killed by the 'Black and Tans' in the twenties. Me own Da was killed in seventy-six by a British army patrol. I was only a lad just like he was when his Da was killed. I've two cousins that are in prison. They're I.R.A., too." Sullivan paused. "I take orders. I'm a soldier. But I can't say that stoppin' the fight is the way I feel. I'm dead against it."

"Burns how about you?" O'Donovan asked.

"How about what? Nothing I can do if these spineless assholes decide to call a cease fire," Burns answered in his usual antagonistic manner.

"What's this all about, Garrett," Erskine Colbert asked.

"It's important I know where you all stand on this question," O'Donovan answered.

"Well let's just say I'm against a cease fire. Like the others, that's not what I'm here for," Colbert said. "I assume you're going to tell us what's going on?"

"You were selected to form a new unit. That much you know," O'Donovan responded. "Now I'll tell you the why. Have you all heard of an I.R.A. man named Michael Flynn?"

"Of course. Everyone knows the name. Helluva gunman in the seventies. Killed a lot of security forces. Died in some major shoot-out with the British, I think" Colbert said.

The others all nodded.

"Not exactly. Flynn was not killed. He actually lives in the south. He's a ranking member of the Army Council. Only others in the Council know this. That information must not go beyond this room. I hope you all understand the consequences of such a leak," O'Donovan said. They all understood the threat of personal consequences of any breach of security. O'Donovan had everyone's attention.

"Flynn is committed to the fight. If the Council votes to accept a cease fire, Flynn is prepared to break with the Provisional I.R.A.," O'Donovan said. "I take my orders directly from Flynn."

"Jesus," someone said in low tones.

"It's happened before. After all, that's how our Provisional I.R.A. happened. The original I.R.A. leadership didn't have the stomach for the fight either," O'Donovan said. "The question is, are each of you willing to keep to the gun? To follow Michael Flynn?"

Their answers were more crucial than most could imagine. If O'Donovan were to have any doubts about anyone, he would have to act by killing that individual. That possibility was not lost on any of the men. All acknowledged they would follow Flynn's orders.

"I'll see all of you in Belfast." O'Donovan shook the hands of each of the men, heartened by the fact he would not have to kill any of them.

Chapter Seven

Devereux had been back in Belfast for two days since his trip to Derry with Kevin Flanagan. He had been holed up in the Europa Hotel mostly reading and making notes. The weather had turned for the worst. Rain continued. Temperatures were colder than normal. The locals all said he should have been here this past summer. It was marvelous weather. Devereux guessed that Ireland probably had only two or three months of habitable weather. Working here in the winter was not an encouraging prospect.

He was seriously considering leaving Northern Ireland. It was not likely that he would be able to develop a project here. Belfast only hinted at opportunities for an intriguing photographic project. It would be difficult to get real compelling shots and new material. Not only difficult, maybe even unrealistic to be able to dig deep enough. He did not know the extent of Flanagan's connections with the I.R.A. Even so, it was not likely that the I.R.A. would find it in their interest to assist him. And if they did, what kind of shots could he expect?

A conversation with Larry Neuson, his literary agent, was not particularly encouraging. "I'll make some calls. Jackie's pretty excited about the way your last project is coming together," Neuson had said.

Jackie was his editor at the publishing house that bought his last book and they could be expected to put up a significant advance for his next project.

"They're debating format alternatives. Now about this Northern Ireland thing. You haven't given me much. Lots of stuff's been done there before. And you yourself say that things are not as violent as they used to be. With all the hell going on elsewhere, what's the interest there, Mason?"

"I told you, Larry, it's the fact that this is a western industrialized nation, an English speaking nation. These people have been at it for all of the twentieth century. It's not Eastern Europe. It's not some third world country. It's not Muslims, it's not African blacks. You've got white Christians on both sides, organized into paramilitary camps, engaged in urban sectarian warfare."

"Nice speech, Mason. I'll try it out on the publisher. They probably won't have much choice since they've got an option on your next book. Right now you're their darling. Not likely they would balk at an advance and risk pissing you off. How much might be the question, though."

"Well, just feel them out. Like I said, unless I can get myself inside what's going on, I'll dump the project myself. I've been trying to talk myself out of it for days, but something still intrigues me. I'll probably make up my mind in the next couple of days."

The next day, Flanagan called. He had found the someone who knew someone. They were to have lunch tomorrow at a pub in Andersonstown. He would pick Devereux up at the Europa at noon.

"Kevin - I haven't heard from you in months. Sorry to hear about John Malone getting killed," Brigid Reilly said, taking the call from Kevin Flanagan. Kevin acknowledged the condolences and made some brief small talk.

"Listen, Brigid, I've got someone you might want to talk to. He's an old friend of John Malone's brother. An American. A journalist, or more accurately, a photojournalist. Freelance guy. Wants to consider doing a piece on Northern Ireland. He's looking for fresh material. Might be sympathetic to the Catholic view. Seems to do pieces focusing on those that suffer in wars."

"Sounds like he's interested you, Kevin. So what makes him any different from just anybody else looking for a story?"

"His name's Devereux, Mason Devereux He's done some really interesting work. I've got one of his books. John's brother

Eagan is a good friend of his. That's how I met him. I think Egan got him interested in doing a book on Northern Ireland. From what I know, he does his own thing. Not afraid to piss off the establishment. I've spent some time with him. He's hard to figure, but he could be of use."

Flanagan knew of Reilly's political work on behalf of Catholic rights. She was a force in Catholic politics. She was an unwelcome irritant to bureaucrats at City Hall, using her legal knowledge to pressure and otherwise do all manner of mischief. She had assisted in organizing several moderately successful boycotts.

"Of use? In what way?"

"PR. God knows the Cause could do with some," Flanagan answered.

"So what do you want from me, Kevin?"

"Just to meet with him. See what you think."

"To do what, Kevin? What's he want? What's he looking for?" Reilly responded, her annoyance evident at what Flanagan was seemingly holding back.

"Brigid, he's looking for candid shots, photographs that will depict the situation here in the North. He'd be looking for things that others haven't captured. The guy's no lightweight. If he's assisted by the right people, his work could be biased to the Catholic cause. Could put the struggle back into the world news."

Reilly agreed to meet for lunch with Kevin Flanagan and Devereux the next day. Flanagan told her he would drop off a copy of Devereux's book on El Salvador at her flat that evening.

She would not bother if it was not for Kevin Flanagan asking. This was a bad time for her and this Devereux was probably a waste of time. She was frustrated with her job, frustrated with the Cause, frustrated with her life in general. Right now she didn't know where her career was headed, or for that matter, what her career actually was. There was talk of running her for a parliamentary seat, but she found herself less than enthusiastic.

As for her personal life, it too was a major frustration. After that stupid mistake of a one-night stand with that I.R.A. chap, O'Donovan, she had become wary of sexual liaisons. The casual

relationship with Harry, another solicitor, was becoming difficult. She liked sex and he was a reasonably good lover. He was
also good looking, dressed well, and was educated. The trouble
was he did not arouse any passion within her. Disagreements
were increasingly frequent.

Flanagan picked Devereux up at the Europa the following
day a little before noon. Devereux had mixed expectations after
his conversation with Flanagan the previous day.

"So what's this woman lawyer Reilly like?" Devereux had
asked.

"She's a tough one, she is. Some would say she is a real bitch.
Guess you'd say she was pretty aggressive. Smart. Knows what
she wants. Staunch republican. First rate barrister I'm told,"
Flanagan answered.

"That's fine, Kevin, but what I really meant was why should
she be interested in helping me do a project? And how is she
connected?

"Because I've convinced her that helping you with a successful photographic book could be beneficial to the Catholic cause
here in the Six Counties. She's a strong Catholics rights advocate.
Pushes for strong actions such as boycotts. She's an activist that
carries political clout."

"That's not what I had in mind," Devereux responded.

"Mason, her law firm is the one primarily used by the I.R.A.
in Belfast. She regularly defends accused I.R.A. defendants.
More than that, she's well connected into the I.R.A. Believe me,
she knows the right people, or the people that do. Besides,
there's something else that should make it a fine lunch. Brigid
Reilly is quite a looker."

"Well that never hurts. Where are we meeting Ms. Reilly,
Kevin?"

"At another pub over in Andersonstown. Been there a couple
of times. She set the place," Flanagan said.

Entering the pub, Flanagan looked around for Reilly. Not
seeing her, he asked the barkeeper.

"Friends of Miss Reilly are yuh? She hasn't been in yet. Tell
you what. I'll clean up that table over there where those lads just

left. Best table in the house. Little quieter. You can see it gets a bit noisy in here at lunch time," the barkeeper said. "How about a couple of pints while you wait?"

Devereux and Flanagan had just been served their beers when Reilly entered the pub. Devereux knew immediately it must be Reilly. She was more than a just a 'looker.' She drew the eyes of all the men in the pub. It was not only her beauty and her figure; it was the commanding style of her movement and expression. She was one of those people that took over attention when they entered a group.

Devereux and Flanagan stood.

"Hello, Kevin," Reilly said, giving Flanagan a hug then turning to Devereux. She smiled and extended her hand. "So you are the famous photographer, Mason Devereux."

Devereux shook Reilly's hand. "Moderately successful, but I wouldn't say famous."

After ordering a glass of red wine and exchanging pleasantries, Reilly got down to business.

"Kevin here tells me you want to do some kind of piece on the violence, the so-called *troubles* going on here in the Six Counties. Something like you did in your book about El Salvador," Reilly said, digging out of her handbag Devereux's book that Flanagan had brought to her the evening before. "I understand you've done other books about war. What goes on here would seem a little tame by comparison with your previous exploits, Mr. Devereux. Why here rather than some other place that is having a real shooting war?"

It was disconcerting looking at Reilly. Her stare was direct into your eyes and her face drew you into her. She had an angular face with high cheekbones, a large mouth, and a nose slightly too long. There was the suggestion of similarity in appearance to Sophia Loren.

"Most of the world thinks you're having a shooting war. The numbers just aren't as extreme. But the West pays more attention than other places such as in the East or in Africa," Devereux answered.

"But doing a project on Northern Ireland would be different. It would also be more difficult to capture dramatic shots. Why am I interested? Why does an artist fix on any topic when there are so many options to choose from? The answer to that is because for some reason that's what intrigues him at the moment. I like to think of myself more an artist than a photojournalist. The sectarian warfare in Northern Ireland intrigues me."

Devereux continued, "Kevin probably told you that I came here because an old friend lost his brother to the violence. I never had any idea to do any work here. It was only after Egan, that's my friend, brought up the idea and Kevin here pushed it, that I've seriously considered the project. As I said, I'm intrigued but frankly I don't know if it's possible."

"What do you mean possible?" Reilly asked.

"Whether it's possible to get the kind of shots that would distinguish my photographs from those news photos that we've seen of Northern Ireland for years. Shots showing only backgrounds and aftermaths."

"It sounds like you're looking for what journalists call an exclusive, Mr. Devereux."

"Perhaps. But I'm not looking for any particular prospective. I am looking for exclusive and unique material. I'm looking for material that tells its own story. Photographs that evoke emotion in the viewer. I'm looking for shots that provoke a response."

Reilly stared at Devereux over a sip of her wine. "Just what has Kevin told you about what I could possibly do for you in that regard, Mr. Devereux?"

Devereux paused to take a large swallow of his beer before responding. "Kevin told me you were 'connected,' meaning you had contacts to the I.R.A., knew people you could perhaps recommend I talk to. But that's crap," Devereux said, then paused for effect. Kevin Flanagan's head snapped back as if slapped. "You're more than connected. I believe you've got direct access to the I.R.A. leadership. You're here to feel me out and make a recommendation to someone."

"That's quite a speculation, Mr. Devereux," Reilly said. She decided to deflect the issue for the moment. "Regardless what you think my influence to be, why do you think the Republican cause would be interested in assisting you?"

"I bet you're a very good lawyer, or rather barrister, Ms. Reilly. So, let's not waste time fencing,

"The world doesn't see Northern Ireland as a major issue anymore. The I.R.A. is nothing more than bad guys from the seventies. These are the nineties. Corrupt regimes, revolutions, guerrilla actions, civil wars now kill people in the tens of thousands. Displaced refugees number in the hundreds of thousands. Accounts of human rights atrocities rival the horrors of the Nazis."

"And the struggle for Irish nationalism? Your cause is lost among the clutter of such conflicts all over the world. You've got a public relations problem. You know that. That's why you're interested in what I might do."

"And just what is it that you might do, Mr. Devereux?"

"Depends. Depends on how good your people are, how good their intelligence is."

Clearly, this Devereux was not a dilettante. "What do you mean exactly, Mr. Devereux?"

"Shots of Protestant violence. Shots of Protestant paramilitaries training. Police and military excesses. Maybe even some I.R.A. training operations, identities obscured of course. I'm sure if it suits the I.R.A.'s purpose, they could be creative," Devereux said.

Reilly was taken back by the boldness of Devereux's suggestion. "That's a tall order, Mr. Devereux. Interesting prospects I'll admit. But why come to the I.R.A. for assistance in photographing violence in the Six Counties?"

"Look. There are four warring factions here in Northern Ireland, or the Six Counties as you republicans prefer to call it. The R.U.C., the British, the Provisional I.R.A., and the Protestant paramilitaries. The R.U.C. and British wouldn't or couldn't give the kind of support to the shots I'm looking for, and I don't have an 'in' with the Protestants. Since the I.R.A. is opposing all three of the others, and I find myself sitting here, it's the most logical approach. It does not reflect any political sympathy on my part, however."

"Won't your photos be biased in favor of the I.R.A.?"

Devereux knew Reilly was probing, maybe even goading. "No. The shots will be real. I just won't have shots of the I.R.A. committing acts in kind. And I'll acknowledge that in my book. From your perspective however, the photographs will illustrate the other side as a warring opponent. Ask anybody right now and they'll tell you the I.R.A. are terrorists and killers. Most of the world knows nothing of these Protestant paramilitaries."

"And all this to bring the Republican struggle into the forefront of world attention," Reilly said. "The world doesn't give a twit about Irish suffering."

"You're not concerned about the world, Ms. Reilly. There are more people of Irish descent in the United States than there are in Ireland. There are significant populations also in Canada and Australia. According to what I've read, I.R.A. financing is largely from U.S. Irish organizations. Increased publicity means increased donations. And money is the lifeblood of any movement. You are only trying to convince certain interested people. It's not unlike the Israeli appeal to Jews of the rest of the world for funding, particularly from the United States."

Reilly looked hard into Devereux's eyes attempting to get confirmation of this foreigner's intentions. After several moments she averting her own eyes and smiled.

"You make an interesting argument, Mr. Devereux, but you may have exaggerated on a couple of points."

"Perhaps, but I don't think so, Ms. Reilly. First of all, you people should have done what I'm proposing some time ago. By all accounts, the Protestant paramilitaries are just as bloody as your I.R.A., yet everyone identifies the killings and terrorist acts only with the I.R.A."

"Secondly, the way the political winds are blowing, a cessation of hostilities is likely in the near future. If you don't do something different your fight will end up a truce and no net gain for all the years of fighting."

"Thirdly, you're interested or you wouldn't be here. The sort of thing I'm suggesting compliments the type of things you yourself have been involved in. Political activity, boycotts, civil disobedience, that sort of thing. Things that change awareness, Ms. Reilly."

"Lastly, I do think you have connections into the I.R.A. leadership. You're their lawyer, Ms. Reilly. And Kevin here wouldn't have set up this meet if it wasn't with someone with pull," Devereux concluded.

Flanagan had intently listened to Devereux and Reilly without comment up to now. "Now listen here, Mason, I never said — —"

"Of course you didn't, Kevin, but it's obvious. Besides, so what. My speculation doesn't change anything, or even jeopardize Ms. Reilly."

Devereux turned to Reilly with a warm smile, "Look, I'm not going to try to persuade you anymore, Ms. Reilly. I don't think I could anyway. There's nothing I said that you didn't already know. So, you think about the idea, not too long though, and let me know. Right now how about some lunch?"

Reilly wasn't smiling. She didn't like being dismissed. This Devereux was irritatingly arrogant. But she was certainly interested in the idea. She was intrigued with what Devereux specifically had in mind. Anxious to discuss specifics. Devereux himself might be interesting. She'd be damned if she would make it easy, however.

"I'll do that, Mr. Devereux. I'll think about your proposal and I'll let you know," Reilly said. There was no smile only that beautiful mask that revealed nothing. "As for lunch, I'm afraid I have an appointment. Perhaps another time."

Reilly rose from her chair. Devereux and Flanagan got up in response. "Mr. Devereux, I'll be in touch. Kevin, good to see you." She shook their hands and abruptly left the pub.

Devereux allowed himself to appreciate her excellent figure as she strode briskly away.

"Jesus, Mason, you didn't have to piss her off," Flanagan said.

"Come on, Kevin. As you Irish say, 'I shouldn't worry.' Your Ms. Reilly will pass on the information and give her own recommendation based on the merits. That is if she's the person you think she is."

"She is, Mason."

The following day, Devereux picked up a message at the front desk of his hotel after returning from lunch. It was from Brigid Reilly. The message requested simply that he call her at her office.

He rang through to her office. After brief greetings, Reilly got right to the point. "There is interest in your proposal, Mr. Devereux. I'm instructed to discuss specifics with you further. Would tomorrow be convenient?"

"What about this evening? Perhaps over dinner?

Reilly wasn't prepared for the offer.

"I don't think so, Mr. Devereux. I'm really rather busy. I've a lot of paperwork I must work on this evening."

"I wish you would reconsider, Ms. Reilly. I've spent a lot of my life in societies that place a high regard on developing relationships as a basis for doing business. The relationship we are negotiating certainly demands that we both know each other. Besides, on a more personal note, I'm getting weary of dining alone."

This was certainly a more charming side to Devereux than their first meeting. Dinner with this man did hold more promise than scrambled eggs in her flat, curled up with a particularly dull legal brief she was attempting to finish.

"Very well, Mr. Devereux. I'll meet you at your hotel at seven," she answered in a businesslike manner and rung off abruptly.

Reilly entered the lobby of the Europa Hotel right at seven. She wore a simple cream-colored suit and gold necklace. Her auburn hair cascaded over her shoulders contrasting with the lighter fabric. The well-tailored suit emphasized her body.

No matter how sophisticated and worldly Devereux may have thought himself, this woman's style and looks were riveting. "Good evening, Ms. Reilly," Devereux said, rising from a chair in the lobby and walking over to her. He refrained from commenting on how beautiful she looked. "Thank you for coming."

They exchanged brief pleasantries. He told her he had made reservations at the La Belle Epoque, a French restaurant not far. Reilly said she knew of it, but had never eaten there. She offered to drive, but Devereux suggested they take a cab so as not to hassle with parking.

They were seated at a table allowing for discrete conversation. Reilly ordered a gin and tonic, Devereux a Bushmills Black Bush neat. He was beginning to take a real liking to Irish whisky.

"I'll get right to the point, Mr. Devereux. There is considerable interest in you doing a book about the situation here in the North. Someone with your publishing credentials could give an important boost to the Republican cause. But only if it can be clearly shown that the violence stems from the repression of the Catholic minority."

"Ms. Reilly, let's be candid here. If the I.R.A. likes this idea, then they are going to get me photo opportunities to show the other side pushing Catholics, pushing suspected I.R.A. sympathizers, committing human rights abuses, and maybe even violence if they're clever enough. Show the face of the other side, the Protestant paras, the R.U.C., the British, as they have not been shown before. This is the opportunity for the I.R.A. to quit being political neophytes."

Reilly took a sip of her gin, continuing to look into Devereux's eyes. "Mr. Devereux. There is— —"

"Mason, we're past Mr. Devereux, aren't we, Brigid?"

"Very well, Mason. I'm still having trouble with why you want to help the I.R.A."

"Help the I.R.A.? I don't give a damn about the I.R.A. My guess is that most Catholics disavow most everything the I.R.A. does. The average person does not condone the bombings and the murders. The average person doesn't see this as a war. The average person just wants to get on with his or her life. If you want to do the kind of work I do, get the shots I do, you're going to have to get inside one opposing faction or the other. If you felt compelled to give 'equal time' to each side, you would never publish. You can only question yourself from the prospective, 'have you depicted the truth?,' not the only truth, but at least a truth."

Devereux continued, "Insofar as truth, it seems pretty clear that there is repressive discrimination against Catholics here in Northern Ireland. Sure, if there was no I.R.A. violence, there would be no need for Protestant retaliation. As long as all Catholics lived like good 'niggers,' things would be just fine. It goes on everywhere like this, Brigid. So exposing repression and violence against only the Catholics may not be the whole truth, but neither is it a lie. So you see, I'm not unsympathetic, but neither am I out to justify the I.R.A."

"One must dance with the Devil in my profession, Brigid. In that regard, it's somewhat like your profession isn't it?"

"Like being a barrister? I could hardly compare what I do with your adventures, Mr. — -, Mason."

Devereux was certainly an interesting man. More than most and more than she had been acquainted with in a very long time. For a soldier of fortune type used to living in the worst of conditions, he was most sophisticated in his appearance and habits.

"How is it you got into law, Brigid?"

"That's simple. It was my father. He was a barrister. Just natural I should follow in his footsteps."

"From what I hear about discrimination against women here, that couldn't have been all that simple. What's your father like, Brigid?"

"I'm afraid he died some time ago, Mason. Ah, but he was a grand man. Everything a man should be. He had this way about him. This way in which he would cause you to think, really think. Sloppy answers were not accepted. Oh, he wouldn't criticize you, he would just respond with a more probing question. When you were stuck for an answer, or gave a stupid response out of frustration, he would give you an alternative concept to consider. It was never the answer. It was never preaching. It was alternative perspective, followed by some in-depth argument and annotation of facts. He gave you information, rarely instruction. Sometimes he was truly exasperating when all you wanted was a direct answer."

With her eyes slightly tearing at the memory of her father, Reilly continued, "He was a great teacher, Mason. He taught me more about law, about history, more about life than I ever learned at university."

"Your mother, what was she like?"

Devereux sat with his elbows on the table, hands under his chin, intent to Reilly's comments.

"My mother?" Reilly responded, a little taken back. "She's a dear. Family matriarch since my father passed on. Strong lady. I see her every week."

Reilly paused. She had no other comment that came to mind. She felt slightly embarrassed with her inability to say more about her mother.

"Seems you were maybe closer to your father."

"That's not true. It's just that my father and I had more in common intellectually than my mother and I."

"Well that's what I meant. As an adult, it's those intellectual bonds that will stand out."

The waiter came. Devereux asked his recommendation for the evening. Reilly choose the salmon, as did Devereux, thinking it a welcome alternative to the typical heavy Irish fare. Devereux chose a white wine after consulting Reilly's preference.

After dinner, Devereux ordered coffee and cognac. He encouraged Reilly to talk about her career. There was no ulterior motive, just interest. This woman made him want to know her. To know what she was about.

Reilly was feeling relaxed with Devereux. She realized that he had talked little about himself and that he had manipulated it that way. He was handsome, tanned, with a rugged, weathered look to his face. He was trim and fit. She realized that she was intently focused on how attractive he was.

Devereux settled the check. Holding her arm, he shepherded Reilly out of the restaurant. She felt his closeness and did not pull away. Neither said anything on the short ride back to the Europa. Their eyes communicated a mutual intensity.

They walked into the lobby of the Europa. Devereux turned to Reilly, "I don't want you to leave."

Reilly acknowledged nothing in her eyes, but let Devereux direct her to the elevators.

Once inside the room, Reilly pulled Devereux to her, kissing him hard, holding his face in both hands. Devereux responded by wrapping Reilly tightly against him. His hands slowly explored her body.

Reilly eventually pulled away, towing Devereux to the bed. She quickly removed his coat and shirt. Unfastening his belt, she pulled his trousers and undershorts down to his ankles. Her hands moved around his scrotum, cupping his balls and moving up around his now erect penis.

As Devereux removed his trousers, Reilly removed her suit jacket, then her blouse, then her bra. Devereux kissed her breasts as he removed her skirt and panties, then guided her to the bed.

"I want you, Mason."

To her delight, instead of entering her, he moved his face between her legs. She gasped as his lips touched her delicately. He licked and probed her with deliberate attention to her responses. Soon, Reilly's hips were rising with Devereux's manipulations. She was soon in that place of feeling, that feeling of being on the edge of orgasm, beyond reason, beyond anything but the pleasure.

Reilly came in Devereux's mouth in convulsive waves of orgasm. Not yet through, Reilly pulled Devereux up to her, guiding his cock between her legs. As he entered her, his erection and thrusts brought on continued waves of her orgasm. Devereux himself came with an intensity that he had forgotten was possible.

Both lay spent, saying nothing. Exhausted, they both fell asleep within minutes. For some short time of peace, there were no politics, no careers, no egos.

Chapter Eight

It was six P.M. on a Monday. Quinn McLeash's usual time to show up at the pub. Actually, for the past year, he was stopping in most everyday after work. Couple of pints, then home by around eight. The wife had dinner waiting. But Monday night was different. The wife knew not to expect him for dinner. Not to wait up. Monday night was his end to a workweek. His drinking night. An unusual schedule, but the theater where he was maintenance superintendent was busiest on the conventional weekend days of Saturday and Sunday.

As usual, there was only a small crowd in McLeash's favorite pub on a Monday night. He took a stool at the bar and ordered his first pint. He recognized the few patrons there, but they were not his usual drinking acquaintances. He actually had very few acquaintances. McLeash usually forced himself on various regulars in the establishment. He was tolerated to the point where he became overly aggressive with his anti-Catholic rhetoric. This came after he crossed some threshold of alcohol intake, which typically happened on his weekending Monday nights.

On this night, McLeash had invited himself to join a table with two patrons he knew by name. Around eight o'clock, a man and woman entered the pub. The all male clientele drew their attention to the woman. She wore a tight fitting outfit showcasing a full figure. The couple seated themselves at a table and proceeded to engage in what seemed to be a heated discussion.

McLeash and his companions returned to their own conversation and drinking. As much as they would like to have continued to take in the form of the woman, they were obliged to return to their own company, taking only furtive glimpses at the woman's table.

"Holy, shit. Can you think of yourself with the likes of that?" One of the men at McLeash's table said, looking over to the woman.

"You're right on that. My old lady never looked anywhere near that good even before the kids. That's sure some piece of ass, lads, the likes of which we don't see often around this shit hole," McLeash said.

An hour passed. McLeash and his acquaintances observed that the woman's companion was proceeding to get drunk. His voice was rising as he continued to appear to argue with the woman.

Feeling the call, McLeash rose and went off to the lavatory. Within a moment, the man at the woman's table rose and made his way unsteadily to the lavatory. The lavatory was small and cramped with only one urinal, a stall, and a sink. McLeash was using the urinal. The man entered the commode stall. As McLeash was putting himself back into his pants there was a thud followed by a groan from within the swinging door to the commode cubicle. McLeash saw the man's feet jutting out.

"You all right in there?" McLeash asked.

Getting no response, McLeash cautiously pushed open the door to the cubicle, which was not latched. The man was sitting in the corner, wedged between the wall and the commode. His head slumped forward.

"Shit," McLeash muttered. "All right lad, looks like you've had one too many. Let me give you a hand."

McLeash leaned down and grabbed the man by both arms and attempted to pull him to his feet. The man groaned but co-operated with McLeash's efforts to get him to his feet. Slurring his words, the man mumbled, "Leave me 'lone. I can make it."

"Sure you can. No problem. I'll just give you a little hand," McLeash said, still wrestling the man to his feet.

He steadied the man as they walked out of the lavatory. With some effort, McLeash navigated the man to the table where the woman was seated. The woman jumped up at the sight of

McLeash assisting her companion who was having difficulty walking even with help.

"Aw, Patrick, what a mess you are. I thank you kindly, Sir," the woman said as she helped McLeash in lowering the man into his chair.

McLeash noticed that the woman was older than the man, maybe by ten years or so. He was captivated by her figure. She was not slender, but her breasts and hips would draw any man's eye. "If you'll forgive me suggesting, Miss, your boyfriend here has had about all he can handle. Anymore and you'll not be getting him out of here easily."

"Boyfriend? Lord help me. You put up with the likes of him only because he's family. My brother he is. My younger brother. My younger brother the drunk, hey, Patrick?" the woman said looking at her brother whose head rested on his forearms on the table.

"And you are right, Sir, I'll be getting him out of here right now. Maybe you could continue your kindness and help me outside with him."

"Sure. Be glad to, Miss," McLeash responded eagerly.

McLeash and the woman helped the man outside. The woman indicated a beat-up lorry in the parking lot. They hefted the man into the passenger seat and closed the door.

"Lord I appreciate your kindness, Sir. But could I be asking another great favor?"

"What would that be, Miss?" He was sure he would agree to anything reasonable. Any excuse to get closer to this woman.

"I don't think I'll be able to drive his lorry back to his flat. It's one of those shifting jobs, and I've never done that before. I favor those automatics without all that need to shift and push clutches. It's not far either. I'll bring us back in a cab. I'll pay of course. I don't know what else to do and I'd be ever so grateful."

"Sure. Be glad to, Miss. But I'll tell you what. Why don't you drive my car and I'll take you home after we drop your brother at his home. Mine's an automatic. You'll have no trouble handling it." McLeash said.

"You are such a kind man. What is your name?"

"McLeash. Quinn McLeash. Call me Quinn."

"Mary Jamison. Please call me Mary, Quinn," she said, offering her hand.

The woman led the way in McLeash's small sedan. Twenty minutes later they arrived at the man's flat. There was a brief exchange with a plain looking woman at the door, the uncomfortable scene of returning a drunken husband and the relief of escaping what must be a recurring domestic problem.

Once inside McLeash's car, the woman rushed to explain, "He's a real problem, but what can I do? He's my brother. His drinking is getting worse. Cost him a real good job. Problems at home. I was tryin' to talk some sense into him. That's what I was tryin' to do tonight, but he was pretty well into his drink when we got here."

"No need to explain, Mary. By the way, where should I take you?"

"What I'd like, Quinn, is to buy you a drink. You've been so kind to go out of your way. And selfishly, this has been a difficult night and I could use some pleasant company."

"I'd like that too, Mary. I know a place that's nice,"

This was too good to be true. The woman was enticing. Starting to show a little age in the face and neck, but not in her body. A touch too heavy on the makeup perhaps. Probably pushing fifty. Her legs were long and the muscles alluringly articulated with heels.

McLeash took her to a pub that was outside of his usual haunts, one that he had been to only once before. He remembered the intimate atmosphere, the dark booths, and a more mixed crowd. Although comparatively busy for a Monday night, they found an unoccupied booth.

Mary ordered a gin and tonic, McLeash a whiskey and pint of Guinness.

"I took you away from your friends, Quinn. I didn't mean to disrupt your evening. Here's to you for being such a kind man."

She lifted her glass and took a large drink.

"It's nothing really, Mary. I was glad to be of help."

"You know, my brother Patrick's an ass, but that wife of his is something else. You can almost forgive him his drinking being married to the likes of that woman. Nags something terrible.

Makes him small. I know he could be better if she'd just be more understanding. Do you know what I mean, Quinn?"

"Yes, I know what you mean," McLeash said, thinking about his own relationship with his wife. It mattered little that his wife was subservient and long-suffering, and never given to condemning his own actions. He held her in contempt and resented her more by simply being in the presence of this alluring woman.

"I was married for six years myself. Been divorced for twelve," Mary said. "I should have gotten a divorce six months after I was married. The man wanted children right away. I wanted to live a little first. Can't do much livin' with children under foot and all the money gone. It was a fight all the time."

"You married, Quinn?"

McLeash hesitated then answered, "Yes."

"Do you love her?"

McLeash hesitated. "That's hard —- I —- I don't really know. Never had that asked before."

"I'm sorry, Quinn. I've no right to ask something like that. Don't mind me. I guess I've been alone so long I've gotten too nosy. So since I'm nosy, tell me what you do."

McLeash took a stout drink and looked at Mary, pride evident in his manner, "I manage all the facilities operations of the Grand Opera House. I'm superintendent of maintenance."

"Lord no. You manage the opera house? I've never been there, only passed by it."

"Well, I don't really manage the opera house, just the building. The heating, the plumbing, the electrical systems, all the stage equipment. Got a staff of seven men. Place needs constant attending. Gets pretty hectic when we're doing performances."

McLeash talked on about his responsibilities at the Opera House. Time passed quickly. The pub was closing. McLeash had learned that Mary Jamison was from Ballymena to the north of Belfast. She was of course Protestant like McLeash. Took a week off her from her job to look for a better position in Belfast. Her brother had told her there were more opportunities here than back in Ballymena.

"I guess I should be taking you home, Mary," McLeash said reluctantly.

"That would be awfully nice, Quinn. You are a dear man. Why couldn't I have found someone like you," she said, taking his arm as they left the pub and giving it an affectionate squeeze.

It took twenty minutes to drive to a small modest hotel in a Protestant area of West Belfast. McLeash escorted Mary Jamison to the front door. It was two o'clock in the morning.

"I shouldn't be sayin' this, Quinn, but I will anyway. I would like to see you again. Is that too bold? Please don't think badly of me." She averted his eyes as if embarrassed by her own brazenness.

McLeash could hardly believe what she had said.

"Of course not—I mean of course I don't think badly of you. I would like to see you again too, Mary. You're—a charming woman, and a beautiful woman," McLeash said, blushing at his own boldness. "Tomorrow. Could I see you tomorrow? It's my day off."

"That would be nice. What time, Quinn?"

"Noon? We'll have lunch?"

"That would be grand, Quinn. Noon it is."

She then kissed McLeash on the cheek and entered the hotel.

Feigning an excuse to his wife for needing to be out for the day, McLeash arrived at the hotel promptly at noon the following day. The desk clerk told him he had instructions from the lady in room two-twelve to send a Mr. McLeash up when he arrived.

Mary Jamison opened the door. Her makeup was on and she was dressed in a robe. She ushered McLeash into the room. "I am running a bit behind, Quinn. My brother was here this morning. Tells me how badly things are at home. No wonder I says to him, with his drinking. Gave him hell I did for last night. He left not too long ago. Anyway, enough of that," she said. She moved close to McLeash.

"I'm glad you came, Quinn. I didn't know if you would or not."

She moved closer to McLeash.

McLeash didn't know what to say. He could smell her perfume. Her robe exposed the deep cleavage between her breasts.

"Kiss me, Quinn. I want that," she said as she put her hands on his face and drew him to her mouth. Her ardor rose as she kissed him. He in turn was aroused beyond anything he had felt for years. Nonetheless, it was she that was the most aggressive.

"I want you, Quinn. Make love to me. Make love to me right now."

She let McLeash help her remove her clothing knowing that it would arose him even more. His eyes fairly bulged as her bra fell away revealing her large breasts. As much as Jamison tried to prolong the intercourse, McLeash spent himself quickly. She feigned her own orgasm as she squeezed and pulled at his erection, increasing his sensation.

McLeash was flushed with post-coital relaxation. After an hour of laying in bed and talking, Jamison suggested they shower and get dressed. She showered first and put her robe back on.

McLeash came out of the bathroom, a towel wrapped around his waist. Out of shape, but not really fat. She had been with much worse. She let her robe gape open as she sat on the bed. She knew McLeash was enthralled by her body. Looking at her he became aroused, evident by a rising of the towel with his growing erection.

"My, Quinn, that is a real compliment pointing to his erection. Come here."

McLeash went obediently to her. She rose and pushed him down on the bed and pulled the towel loose. She took his semierect member into her mouth. Several minutes later Quinn McLeash spent himself again as she worked her mouth on his sensitive cock. His wife had never done any such thing to pleasure him like that.

For Quinn McLeash, the rest of the day was a fantasy. They said good-bye late that night, with McLeash promising to call her the next day. Mary Jamison did not doubt that he would.

Jamison placed a call from a pay phone in the cheap hotel. There was barely an acknowledgment on the other end as her call was answered.

"He took the bait. He's to call me tomorrow," Mary Jamison said.

"You're sure you have him––have him compromised?" the person on the other end asked, searching for an appropriate way in which to phrase the question.

"Listen laddie, if you'd been fucked like that, you'd be eating out of my hand, or should I say out of my pussy, too. He'll be seeing me again. Soon, very soon. Now the money. Two hundred quid I believe."

"Of course, as was promised. Don't forget though, there's much more you must do. Remember, the pay's good, but failure would be most costly, Mary Jamison," the voice said. There was no emotion, only the hard professionalism of the type she knew only too well. Several seconds of silence was broken by the tone of the disconnected line.

McLeash did of course call the next day. He came to the hotel twice more by the end of the week. She let McLeash think he had convinced her to stay in Belfast and look for a new job. He would pay for her hotel.

Within two weeks McLeash had set up Jamison in a small flat he was able to locate after extensive work and calling in a favor. Jamison ostensibly got a position as a receptionist in an insurance firm. She actually worked there for the last four years.

Mary Jamison had lived in Derry most of her life. Born Catholic, she was a widow of an I.R.A. man. After his death she moved to Belfast, professing to be a Protestant, even to the extent of joining a congregation. Liking the company of men, she found she could augment her modest salary by taking money in exchange for sexual favors.

Her life had changed two weeks ago when see met Garrett O'Donovan at a pub. Flattered by the attentions of this handsome younger man, she thought maybe she would not even take his money. At her apartment she was anticipating being with this man when O'Donovan stunned her by reciting her background.

"So what do you want?" Jamison asked.

"Just for you to do what you do best — fuck. And get paid very well for it of course."

"Why should I?"

"Well if you don't, Mary, all manner of terrible things will happen to you. First, your employer will be told of your past association with the I.R.A., and your masquerading as a Protestant. I should imagine you'll get the boot. Then there's a certain successful widowed businessman by the name of Parker. Perhaps you're hoping for matrimony? Not likely he'd marry a Catholic whore is it, Mary?" O'Donovan said.

Jamison was crushed. Her world could be torn apart. She knew this man was I.R.A. If she didn't do what he wanted, he would do all that he threatened, maybe worse. After the initial shock and tears, she rationalized what she was being required to do. It wouldn't be that difficult and the promised pay was pretty good. What the I.R.A. was up to was probably terrible, but there was really nothing she could do about that. They'd do what they would with or without her.

Weeks later she had settled into a comfortable routine. She entertained her would-be fiancée at her own flat, and spent two nights or so a week at the small flat McLeash paid for. Her absence from either place was explained by frequent visits to a friend with cancer in the former circumstance, and time spent with her brother and sister-in-law in the latter case.

At the office one day, Jamison received a call from a distraught McLeash. "Mary, I'm afraid I can't see you tonight. Something terrible has happened. Two of my men were killed last night in an accident. Leastwise it appears to be them. Seems they'd been drinking. A lorry struck their auto. Must have been a real bad collision. Anyway, it burned with them inside. They can't make positive identification 'cause they're burned too bad, but it's them all right. It was Colin's car. I need to see to their families. I'll call you tomorrow, Luv."

O'Donovan visited Jamison at her flat that evening. "You heard about the accident with McLeash's staff?"

"Yes," she answered flatly.

"McLeash will be looking for replacements soon. You're to convince him to take on two of your 'cousins.' Their names are Donald and Clarence. Don't worry, they're both well qualified. One's an electrician, the other experienced in factory maintenance. The story is that they're looking to come to Belfast from Ballymena. Both are working at menial jobs having been laid off from a plant closing. The point is to convince McLeash to hire them, Mary."

"You fuckin' murderin' bastards. You've had them men killed, now you want me to do whatever to probably kill some more," Jamison shouted. The rush of anger overcame her fear. "I've enough of you. I won't help you kill others."

O'Donovan moved close to Jamison and pulled a nine millimeter automatic from his waist. His left hand closed around her cheeks and with his right, the gun was inches from her face. "Listen you old whore. You'll do as you're told. You'll fuck him till he can't stand if that's what it takes, but you'll get him to hire these two 'cousins' of yours. If you fail, Mary, it won't be disgrace and a sacking from your job, or your rich boyfriend dumping you that'll be the real problem. If you don't accomplish what is required I'll see that you're killed. How that's done could be very unpleasant. Do you understand?"

She sunk to her knees and wept with great shaking sobs.

"Did you weep like this over your dead husband, Mary?"

O'Donovan released her and opened the door to leave. "I expect this done within the week. I'll call again. Don't disappoint me, Mary."

Mary Jamison slumped onto her bed. She cried herself to sleep.

Jamison was a survivor, however. The day after the funeral, she convinced herself to proceed as O'Donovan had requested. She was in this far. The sins already piled deeply. Easy to remove one more piece from her soul. Why get hurt. These were hard men. They would do her badly.

It was not an easy sell to McLeash though. He was not about to hire a couple of her relatives who he didn't know. He sure as hell didn't want to be saddled with a couple of incompetents just because this woman fucked like a bitch dog in heat. Jamison mellowed his position over a couple of days with furious lovemaking, the likes of which McLeash had never experienced. In a pliable state, McLeash eventually agreed to try them out for a week.

Mary Jamison's 'cousins' reported to McLeash two days later. Donald and Clarence Fell they told McLeash. Actually they were Peter Sullivan and Brennan Magee respectively. Both men could claim experience and skills to replace the two men that had been killed. Sullivan was a former electrician, Magee was a mechanic with a short term of employment in maintenance on the docks.

On the surface, the two men looked all right to McLeash. They answered his questions satisfactorily. "Hope you lads know how to work. We're busy as hell here always, busier than hell many times. Don't mind telling you I'm a bit leery of hiring based on being a relative of — —," McLeash paused, searching for the word, "a friend. Your cousin Mary's a nice lady. Made a strong case as to how good you lads were. Don't be letting her down, you hear?"

"We certainly appreciate the opportunity, Mr. McLeash. Things have been hard for us in Ballymena. Laid off we was. Plant closed. Taken work wherever we could these past months. Clarence and I are no strangers to hard work. We'll do right by you, Mr. McLeash," Sullivan said.

McLeash was pleasantly surprised after a week. Both men worked hard and competently. Donald, the electrician, seemed to work well with the other men. The one called Clarence he wasn't as sure about. There was something underneath his outward manner as if he were trying to control himself. But he also did good work, and even though he was not too friendly, neither was he a troublemaker. On the whole, it had turned out well. Best of all, Mary Jamison had been particularly appreciative.

Chapter Nine

Devereux awoke with the pale light of a gray Belfast morning working hard to penetrate through the hotel room curtains. He felt the lethargy of a hangover, but without the effects of a pounding head or rebellious stomach. Maybe it was the lovemaking. Next to him, covered only with a sheet with one bare leg exposed, Brigid Reilly breathed heavily, still deeply asleep. Devereux had a sudden urge to kiss her face and embrace her, but refrained for fear of waking her from such peace.

This was not at all what he usually experienced. The morning after was frequently awkward. The previous night's pleasure too often was just that. There were times when he had hoped for more. With Reilly it had been more than the lovemaking.

Devereux's introspection was abbreviated by Reilly's awakening. He was sitting up with his legs crossed. She turned on her side and looked at him.

"I must look like hell," Reilly said.

Devereux touched Reilly's cheek gently with his hand. "On the contrary, you look lovely. Perhaps just a little disheveled from intense lovemaking. Coffee?"

"Not yet."

She reached over to touch him, the sheet falling away from her breasts. He came erect in her hand. After a few moments she moved on top of him, rubbing his cock against her mound.

"Need to get us both wet, luv."

Devereux laid back and enjoyed the sight of looking up at her breasts and abdomen as she worked both of them to climax.

Still inside her, he kissed and hugged her as she lay on top of him. He felt a rare joy making love to her.

"Is there some man in your life?"

"Not anymore. And if there was, would you think badly of me?"

"No. But since I'd like to spend more time with you I was just curious."

"And you? No special woman?"

"No one."

They spent the day driving in the countryside enjoying each other's company. Reilly wanted to know more about Devereux, but his tendency toward privacy made it fairly an interrogation. After several hours, all she had really learned was that he had a graduate degree in journalism, had worked for a newspaper, traveled throughout the world working for a news service, and photographed wars and wrote a couple of books. His parents had died in an accident when he was young, as did a wife of three years. He had no brothers or sisters.

"Damn it, Mason, I've spilled my whole life out to you, had more sex with you than newlyweds on their wedding night, yet I know nothing about you."

Devereux laughed. He felt freer than he could remember with this woman. "But I've told you about my life."

"Bullshit. A bunch of facts. Few at that. I want to know about you."

"Very well, Brigid. I'll tell you my life. What do you want to know?" he said smiling.

"Tell me about your wife, Mason."

Devereux gave it a few moments before answering.

"Her name was Angela. We met in graduate school at U.C.L.A. I was working for the Los Angeles Times as a staff photographer going to school in the evenings. She was working at an advertising firm. We knew we were attracted to each other, but she was involved with someone else at the time."

"I guess I was too focused on my career to have noticed deeper feelings, both with her and with me. At any rate, I hit on what I thought was a unique idea for my master's thesis." As a kid I had fantasized about the mystique and romance of the

French Foreign Legion. What if I could do my thesis on the life of the typical legionnaire, viewed first hand, and photographed?"

"And did you?"

"Yes."

"You mean you were in the French Foreign Legion?" Reilly asked, truly intrigued.

"Yes, but only for six months. I didn't really enlist. It took months of negotiation with the French Army command to get them to accept the proposal of doing a series of articles on the Legion. They eventually allowed me to go through training just the same as any recruit. Thanks to my editor, they thought I was a full-fledged reporter with a byline, with a potential for a wide syndication. As it turned out, the paper did print a series of articles, and *LIFE* magazine picked it up. The Legion probably got a good deal out of it after all."

"What was it like?" Reilly asked.

"A real test of your will and endurance. Pure hell really. Learned a lot about what you can do. Met some real interesting types. Taught me to speak French. Taught me how to kill."

"Tell me about the Legion later. Back to your wife."

"Well, when I got back from France, I found that Angela was no longer engaged. We started seeing each other and were married a few months later."

Devereux turned quiet.

"And?"

"Well I loved her very much. We were good for each other. We were happy. She made me happy. We connected intellectually and emotionally. She changed how I experienced life. Then she was killed. Traffic accident like my parents. She was coming home late in the evening from a business dinner. Drunk driver ran a red light. She was killed instantly. I was waiting up for her. Police came to the door. I knew immediately by the looks on their faces that something had happened."

"I only knew her three years, but I still think of her often."

Much to his dismay, tears formed causing Devereux to rub his eyes. Reilly noticed and changed the subject to less emotional ground.

After a few moments Devereux continued.

"I developed a real interest in photography at the Times. I was good at it. Found that I liked the fluidity of a news scene. You could not construct the photo opportunities, but the challenge allowed for its own range of creativity."

"I liked the combination of technical elements and art. But I wanted to get away, maybe lose myself. So I left the Times and joined Reuters, the international news service, as a correspondent and photographer. I could write pretty well too."

"I discovered I had a skill for capturing the emotion of a scene in photographs. After receiving a Pulitzer Prize for a series in Afghanistan I had the opportunity to turn freelance. "

"I still don't see what Northern Ireland holds for the kind of work you have done, Mason. I know what you want, but you know that this is not the same type of war as those you've covered elsewhere. You're not likely to get photos of people shooting at each other," Reilly said.

"Take a real look at my work, Brigid. It's the rare shot where there is the actual perpetration of violence. If you cover enough ground, if you're always close to the conflict, and if you're lucky enough a few times in your career, you'll get those opportunities. But that isn't what my work relies on."

Devereux continued, "There are two things I try to achieve to distinguish the work from just 'pictures.' First, the photographs must convey a real sense of the situation. Photographs of troop movements and aftermaths of destruction convey little feeling, much less understanding of an issue. Whereas, the classic photo of the running Vietnamese young girl, naked and burned with napalm, conveys in itself a depth of perhaps many stories and many levels of perspective. The really great photographs cause each viewer to react in a fundamental way unique to that individual. All good photography extends the story beyond what the viewer sees. And second, since such photo opportunities are exceedingly rare, I use a series of less dramatic photographs to paint what I see and build a story."

Devereux continued. "In my research, I came across just such a photograph that made me feel more about the violence here in Northern Ireland than all of what I have been told or read. The picture was of a young boy riding a bicycle with a burning lorry in the background, obviously set ablaze by rioting or some confrontation with the police. What struck me was the boy's expression. It may have been excitement, maybe adventure. But not fear. To this kid, such violence was just part of his life. For me it suggested many profound questions about what was going on here."

"Northern Ireland just isn't like all the other places you read about, like in Africa or Bosnia. It's nowhere near as bad as those places. Why do a book about violence here?" Reilly asked.

"You live here, Brigid. Maybe you're used to it. You're I.R.A., or at least sympathize with them. But to the rest of the West, Northern Ireland is a terribly violent place. It doesn't matter that countless other places in the world are far more violent. But it's the type of violence. Northern Ireland is political violence in a setting like in America or Western Europe. There's also a common social background. It's the same as a multiple homicide in London or New York attracting more attention than thousands killed in Africa."

"Goddamn it, don't pack me up with the I.R.A. I hate their methods. I'm a republican true enough, but I'm not one of them," Reilly said angrily.

"Come on, Brigid, you defend them in court. I bet that not too many law firms do that."

"Sure I do. Just like your A.C.L.U. in America. We defend the law, not the defendant's view. And why shouldn't we use the legal system to attack institutionalized discrimination and abuse of power?"

Devereux considered Reilly's argument and responded, "I see your point. I shouldn't bundle you as part of the I.R.A.'s position. Guess I'm learning just how complex the issues are here."

"I love a man who can admit when he's wrong," Reilly said and kissed Devereux on the cheek.

"Angela was never this difficult," Devereux said with a smile.

Reilly had not expected such a comment. She took it as an expression of intimacy. "And I'm not Angela. I couldn't ever compete with her."

They just looked at each other for several moments. Devereux finally smiled and said, "It is terribly distracting to attempt serious political debate with a beautiful woman baring her breasts."

"Well, male pig that you are, I shall rearrange myself to allow your full attentions to be directed back to the matter at hand," Reilly said jokingly and drew the sheet around her.

After breakfast, Reilly said, "I understand what you are after, Mason. But the reality is that getting the kind of photographs you want is going to be much more difficult in this environment compared to the literal war zones you have covered."

"You're right, it will be difficult, Brigid. But understand that it will be a different approach, a different story than those that I've done before."

Reilly left Devereux after breakfast, promising to explore his proposed project further. She told him it would be a matter of some days before she had anything to tell him. In the mean time she said she intended to spend as much time as she could with him.

She was sure Devereux was genuine. She told 'Uncle Terry' as much. Terrance Dolan was Commander-In-Chief of the Provisional Irish Republican Army. Reilly argued passionately that Devereux offered an opportunity to add measurably to their public relations effort. If peace was in truth coming, then tactics such as using the likes of Devereux would be more viable than military action.

"This Devereux checked out as what he appears to be. What you're asking' though, Dear, is to let an outsider get close with some of our lads. Don't know if that's wise. Don't know that I could get anyone to cooperate. Don't know that I would order anybody to," Terrance Dolan said to Reilly.

"Look, Uncle Terry, this could be as important to the Cause as any other mission. You can't tell me you haven't risked men's lives before. Besides, this has never really been done before. Devereux is right. We have been lousy at public relations. Here's a chance to balance the world's view and keep the struggle in the world's eye."

Dolan looked at the daughter of his old friend. She was as much a niece as his actual relations, perhaps more the daughter he never had. She was smart, a competent barrister, and a staunch supporter of the Republican cause. She condemned the violence, but faithfully defended I.R.A. soldiers.

"All right. Tell you what, My Dear, I'll authorize it if you can convince Michael Flynn. After all, it will be his people that would have to assist this Devereux," Dolan said.

"Jesus, Uncle, that miserable sonofabitch won't agree. He'd sooner kill people. And besides, I know how you two—-"

"Now watch your language. I know you can out curse a sailor, but it doesn't become you. I know what Flynn is. I know he sees things differently than we do. But nonetheless, he's still in charge of operations," Dolan said to her.

Reilly did not know the actual depth of animosity between Flynn and Dolan.

In truth, Dolan himself was at best lukewarm on Reilly's project. He doubted it would yield anything of real benefit. He assumed Flynn would deny any help to Reilly, particularly since she was close to him. Let it end like that rather than he take the responsibility.

"If that's what's necessary, then I'll go see him in Dublin. Can I take Devereux if I don't reveal who Flynn is?" She asked.

"Who will you say he is?"

"I'll tell Devereux he's an academic with substantial influence in the republican movement. Devereux will interpret that to mean he's a ranking member in Sinn Fein. No reason for him to connect him with operations of the Provincial I.R.A."

"Very well. I'll contact Flynn. If he agrees, I'll call you. He may not wish to be introduced to Devereux," Dolan told her. She kissed his cheek and left, admonishing him to contact Flynn as soon as possible.

Two days later, Reilly got her answer—directly from Flynn himself by telephone. He told her he was interested in the idea and would agree to meet with both her and Devereux in Dublin. Dolan was surprised when she told him. This was not in character for Michael Flynn.

Devereux was becoming a very agreeable habit to Reilly. She was intrigued by his inconsistencies. He was well educated, well read, seemingly cultured, yet he seemed to revel not only in the danger, but in the extreme hardships often imposed by his profession. It was maybe something like an anthropologist or archeologist who liked to work in the field. Devereux however, seemed to like the finer things offered by more conventional surroundings. He dressed well, took her to see King Lear, and introduced her to fine red wine. What was he? A journalist, a photographer, a writer? The French Foreign Legion? He was impossible to categorize.

Of all the men she could have called lovers, Devereux was the most considerate and intense. He seemed intent on giving her pleasure. He could read her signals already, knew what she liked and responded instinctively.

She could love this man. Maybe she was already in love with him. For the first time in her life, Brigid Reilly worried about how a man felt about her.

Devereux and Reilly took the express train to Dublin the day after hearing word from Flynn. Reilly was like a schoolgirl, rambling on about all sorts of things. She felt uncommonly free. Devereux was relaxed too, captivated by the beauty of the countryside and by Brigid Reilly, but still focused on the task ahead.

"Tell me more about this Michael Flynn. What's his real influence in the 'movement,' if that's the right word?" Devereux asked. "Are there a lot of people in the I.R.A. leadership living in the south?"

Reilly had rehearsed her cover story. "Mason, I told you, I didn't think Flynn is in the I.R.A. leadership. He's an influential intellectual. A professor of history at University College. Highly respected in the republican movement. He's something like one of your presidential advisors in the United States."

"That's bullshit, Brigid. I think he's more than just connected. The republican movement is the I.R.A. and Sinn Fein. I think he's part of the leadership," Devereux responded.

"Leadership? What leadership?" Reilly asked.

"At the least, Sinn Fein. Maybe even the Provincial I.R.A. itself. Do you know?"

Reilly hesitated before answering Devereux. It was uncomfortable having to lie to him. "No, he's not in any leadership position that I'm aware of. I was told only to set a meeting with him. All I know is that he is a highly respected advisor. He's not secretive, Mason. His political leanings are well known both in the south and the north. Hates the British. Wants to see a united Ireland. Makes those views clearly known publicly."

Devereux did not push the point. Obviously Flynn was in some position of influence. More than that, Devereux had contacted Egan Malone in Dublin. Malone was well acquainted with Flynn's politics. He also told Devereux that it was fairly well established that Flynn had himself once been in the I.R.A. back in the seventies. Wanted by the British, but there had been insufficient evidence to extradite him from the Republic. In some quarters, there are rumors that he was an old-time gunman of some legend.

Reilly must at least know the rumors. Devereux of course assumed Reilly was more intimate with the I.R.A. than she would admit to him. But that was business not personal.

Understanding Flynn's position was not really important to Devereux as long as Flynn approved the project. The project was taking on a life of its own by now. Devereux wanted to get started.

They arrived at Connolly Station. They would be meeting with Flynn tomorrow noon. Reilly had suggested they take a day and see Dublin. Not the tourist sights she said, but from the historical perspective of the struggle against British domination in the twentieth century.

Reilly looked intently at Devereux. "I want to show you the places where the events of the 1916 Rising took place. You know about it from your research, but I want you to feel that history. I made these same rounds with my father ten years ago. It moved me like nothing else since. It gave me a connection with the past. There's also a personal factor with me." She paused, then continued. "My great-uncle, Eamonn Kent, was part of the 1916 Easter Rising. I'm not sure you'd actually consider him my great-uncle, but my grandmother, my father's mother, was the sister of his wife Aine. He was one of those executed at Kilmain-ham Jail."

"We'll see the jail. It's a museum now. Grim place. I can re-member the chills it gave me when I was there ten years ago. You could feel the presence of those patriots that had been im-prisoned there. After visiting the jail I became interested in the historical roots of the modern day struggle. I read volumes. The accounts of the executions of the leaders would bring tears to your eyes. These were extraordinary men, Mason."

"All fanatics seem that way - super patriots, especially the leaders. They make their way into the history books and the folklore," Devereux responded. He could see Brigid's reaction developing and sought to appease her.

"Listen, Brigid - all I'm saying is that their greatness, their patriotism is a matter of perspective. Read a book about the his-tory of the Japanese Kamikaze pilots once. To me as the occiden-tal and a product of the enemy so to speak, I didn't see patriot-ism. Chilling stuff though. I read about the 1916 Rising in my research. Same kinds of justifications."

"God damnit, Mason, that's not the same thing at all," Reilly responded with some irritation. Devereux interrupted her.

"It's clear isn't it that the rising was ill-conceived, and almost assuredly doomed to failure before they started? Even the Irish population of Dublin at the time reviled them. They sure as hell didn't view them as 'liberators.' Thousands of Irish men were fighting World War One in British regiments in the trenches in France and Belgium at the time. There was no sympathy for the revolt. They became martyrs simply because the British were incredibly stupid."

Devereux continued. "Convince me on this, Brigid; how are these so-called patriots of 1916 different from Palestinian terror-ists in the West Bank area of Israel?"

"I don't suppose they are," Reilly answered.

"Jesus Christ. Are you arguing the justification of Palestinian terrorism? What about Bader Meinhoff, the SDS, the Japanese Red Army faction in the seventies? Were they patriots? Because you have a point of view, is there some moral justification to take violent action against noncombatants?" Devereux asked without rancor.

"Come on, Mason. Those analogies aren't the same." Reilly said. "I mean the Palestinian issue has lots of similarities, but those others are outlaws. With the Palestinians, their historic homeland is occupied by a foreign power. The British again made that problem. Economic disenfranchisement. Cultural disenfranchisement. Yeah, the Palestinians have the same issues as the Irish," Reilly said forcefully.

"Mason, Ireland's struggle to rid itself of British rule is no different than America's war for independence in the eighteenth century, except for one basic difference. The people doing the fighting in America were predominately English. They had already subdued or killed the native population. They fought the government of England, not the English. We Irish are more like those native Americans."

"What about all the innocent people killed by I.R.A. bombings? How do you rationalize that as acts of patriotism?"

"What were Dresden, Hamburg, not to mention Hiroshima and Nagasaki during the Second World War? Noncombatants will be killed during any war. For my thinking, I don't condone all that the I.R.A. does. But with few exceptions, I.R.A. attacks have legitimate targets," Reilly answered.

Devereux was about to remark about the I.R.A. recent history of bombings in England. Few could be considered 'legitimate' targets. But before Devereux could respond to her last comments, Reilly continued. "Let me tell you about the events that spring in 1916, and show you where it happened. It wasn't terrorism. The insurrectionists killed no innocent people. They attacked British troops and institutions only. It's at the heart of how I feel, Mason, and I want to try to share that with you."

She grabbed his arm and drew him to her.

Devereux looked at the longing in Reilly's eyes. She wanted desperately to have him understand her feelings. This was more than an intellectual issue with Reilly.

"Show me 1916 then, Brigid."

Reilly hailed a taxi. "O'Connell Street, the General Post Office please."

It was a short ride from Connolly Station, less than a half mile. Reilly had the driver detour a few blocks south, then come up the boulevard. Anything of historical interest had long since been removed from O'Connell Street. Neon lights and fast food joints, occupying decidedly ugly architecture, now prevailed along the wide historic boulevard. But she wanted Devereux to see the statues lining a paved stretch from the southern bridge end of the boulevard. The General Post Office building was the one notable exception to modern urbanism.

"This is where it all started. On the Monday following Easter in 1916." Reilly said.

They had exited the taxi to stand in front of the old building, or at least its facade with an Ionic portico of six fluted columns.

"The original building was destroyed in the battle and re-built some years later. That's the original facade you see. It was an awful battle. A siege really. Many of the leaders of the rebellion were captured here. Those scars you see were left by the bullets from 1916. The only visible reminder from that time."

Reilly continued. "O'Connell Street was always the grandest boulevard in Dublin. The leaders of the rebellion, Pearse, Connolly, Clarke, and MacDonagh, marched their hundred or so men to take over the Post Office as their headquarters. Most of the buildings in this area were destroyed by British artillery during the revolt. It suffered again later in the Civil War in the early twenties."

"Doesn't look very grand now," Devereux commented.

"It's terrible what it's become."

"I remember reading about a statue of Lord Nelson that was blown up by the I.R.A. Was that near here?"

"Yes, right over there," Reilly said, pointing to a spot at the corner of Henry and O'Connell Streets. "More than a statue. It was a tall pillar over a hundred feet tall with steps up to the top to an observation balcony. Must have been a hell of a vantage point for anyone up there that Monday morning in 1916. It was destroyed on the fiftieth anniversary of the rising in 1966."

"Sounds like draft card and bra burning in the U.S. during the sixties," Devereux said flippantly.

"Damn it, Mason, don't trivialize it. The Irish have hundreds of years of repression to fight. It's not like your Vietnam," Reilly answered angrily. Devereux held up his hand to signal submission.

"It was here that Padraig Pearse delivered the proclamation of a free and independent Irish republic. It has much in common with your own declaration of independence. My great-uncle signed that document, Mason."

They took a brief tour through the reconstructed marble halls of the GPO, then hailed a taxi. The taxi took them south over the O'Connell Bridge, then west for a mile and half. They passed the Guinness Brewery's tower with its green oxidized copper roof. The taxi deposited them at a grim building Reilly told him was the Kilmainham Jail, now a museum.

"This is where the 1916 insurrection ended, but where Irish independence really began, Mason," Reilly said. "It's an awful place. Imagining what it must have been like makes you shudder."

Devereux paid the admission price, then queued up with other visitors for the guided tour. They entered through the main gate over which was a bas-relief of a serpent in chains. Reilly had been correct about the strong impressions the place gave off. Devereux had once been to Alcatraz and had felt some of the same sensation. But this was stronger and the place even more oppressive with the suggested brutality of an earlier time.

The tour guide told them it was constructed in 1792. At one time or another, it had interned most of the great Irish patriots that rebelled against the British. The cells were smaller than those of Alcatraz, and windowless. The guide informed them that candles were used for lighting. Devereux tried to imagine the place lit only by candles. It could have been a medieval dungeon.

They were lead down a narrow corridor then up steep iron steps. "This is the chapel where Joseph Plunkett and Grace Gifford were married," the tour guide said as the group of visitors cramped into the small room. "Imagine the scene lit by only a single candle. Twenty British soldiers with fixed bayonets lined these walls. They were married at one-thirty a.m. on May fourth, nineteen-sixteen. They were allowed only ten minutes in each other's company. Joseph Plunkett was then executed two hours later at three-thirty a.m."

The tour guide brought us down once more through the prison and out into a high walled courtyard. "This was known as the Stonebreakers' Yard. The executions took place here. Sixteen of the leaders of the nineteen-sixteen so-called Easter Rising were shot by firing squad. The first to die was the most militant of the leadership, Tom Clarke. Clarke's life was devoted to fighting the British, and he was a veteran of British prisons and torture. His was the first signature on the independence proclamation. He was grateful for the honor of being the first to die, and also not to suffer incarceration. Clarke was followed by Thomas MacDonagh, then by Padraig Pearse, the President of the newly proclaimed Provisional Government."

The courtyard was in the shape of an ellipse with a gate at the far end.

"The prisoners came through the same corridor we just did. Some were brought down to wait in the dim recesses of that corridor for a fellow prisoner to first meet his death. A crate was placed there for the prisoner to sit who may have difficulty standing as the volley from the firing squad outside rang through the stone walls."

The tour guide continued. "The last to die was James Connolly. Connolly had been badly wounded in the leg during the fighting. One can only imagine the pathetic sight of the wounded Connolly, unable to walk, propped up in a chair, then roped to the back to prevent him from falling over. Fresh from his sickbed, he wore pajamas. A priest asked him if he would pray for the men who were about to shoot him. Connolly replied, 'I will say a prayer for all brave men who do their duty.'"

"Sadly, in nineteen twenty-two, the first executions of the Civil War also took place in this courtyard," the tour guide continued, "thus concluding the bloody history of this place until its closure in 1924."

Devereux and Reilly exited Kilmainham Jail, welcoming escape from the depressive atmosphere of the place. It was early in the afternoon. The sun had started to peer out from the cloud cover. Devereux suggested lunch. Reilly said she knew a pub less than a mile away and they could walk.

"Your great-uncle, this Eamonn Kent, what was his part in the rebellion?" Devereux asked as they walked.

"My grandmother said he was a handsome man. A very proper man that showed little emotion. A man with an iron resolve. But he loved all things Irish," Reilly said. Although not what Devereux had asked, he listened attentively to Reilly recount stories told by her grandmother of her famous brother-in-law. Eventually she returned to the subject of his involvement with the Easter Rising.

"He commanded one of the four Dublin battalions of the Irish Republican Brotherhood. His men seized what was known as the South Dublin Union west of here. It was a collection of buildings for the poor and elderly covering fifty acres. It was a strategic position intended to cut off reinforcing British troops streaming in by rail through Kingsbridge Station."

Reilly continued. "His battalion saw fierce action. But like all the rest they ultimately were forced to surrender. They were marched off to Richmond Barracks. Most were sent to prison in England. My uncle was tried before a military tribunal like all the other leaders. The tribunal had clear instructions by the British commander, General Sir John Maxwell, to convict all the ringleaders. And Maxwell had the backing of London, even to the extent of executions. My uncle was the last of four to be executed on that particular spring morning."

Tears flowed down Brigid Reilly's cheeks. "I remember my father reading the brave words from Eamonn Kent's last letters to his wife before his execution. It was part of our family history."

"Why did they shoot them in the cold and dark of the pre-dawn morning? Just to be more cruel?" Reilly asked rhetorically.

Devereux said nothing but took her arm. They arrived at the Brazen Head pub on Lower Bridge Street, south of the Liffey River. Devereux told Reilly about his friend Egan who lived outside Dublin. Reilly welcomed his idea to invite Egan and Jenny Malone to dinner. It was a chance to feel part of Devereux's life, part of his experience, and perhaps share some of his feelings he so jealously guarded.

The afternoon was spent seeing the less personally emotional sights of Dublin. Devereux called Egan Malone at the newspaper. Delighted at the prospect, Malone suggested dinner at the King Sitric restaurant in the fishing village of Howth. Howth was to the north and east of the city, and south from the Malones' home in the village of Malahide.

Howth is located at the end of a promontory that represents the northern definition of Dublin Bay. There is a magnificent scenic view from the cliff that overlooks the fishing harbor. The congenial and enterprising taxi driver offered a leisurely drive to take in the view. He took them by Howth Castle with its beautiful gardens, too late for the rhododendrons to be in flower though. The area was a fashionable place to live on the north side of Dublin. According to the driver, H.G. Wells had called the view from the head of the promontory the most beautiful in the world.

"I just realized, Mason, the only photographs you took today were of the General Post Office and the Jail. Why not take pictures here? Just fun pictures," Reilly asked.

"Sure," Devereux said with a matter of fact tone.

"I don't think you cherish memories the way most people do, Mason. You live in the present and the future. Am I right?"

Devereux hesitated. Such probing him made him slightly defensive. All the women he had known had always wanted to explore and analyze. Seemed a female trait. Never content to just accept things as they are.

"That's a complex question, or at least any answer is. I suppose I do focus more on the future. You Irish should do more of that." He immediately regretted the remark.

"You are a miserably stubborn and argumentative bastard, but I refuse to be angry with you," Reilly responded, kissing Devereux on the cheek and taking his arm.

Dinner was a success for everyone. As much as Devereux might resist, Brigid learned more of his past as he and Egan Malone shared past experiences. Devereux captivated everyone with stories of his experience with the French Foreign Legion.

Jenny Malone and Brigid liked each other instantly. Egan Malone was delighted to see Devereux under these happier circumstances. It was also obvious to him that Devereux thought much of this striking and intelligent woman.

After dinner, they walked from the East Pier to the Abbey Tavern, internationally known for its traditional folk music. Being a weekday, they were able to find a place in the authentic old stone walled bar room with its flagstone floor.

The Malones dropped Devereux and Reilly at the Howth Lodge Hotel, where they had had the foresight to reserve a room. Too tired and slightly drunk, they fumbled out of their clothes and fell asleep within minutes.

The view from their room overlooking the sea was spectacular in the morning. Without any verbal acknowledgment, both wished they could leisurely enjoy the beauty of this place and each other's company. But they both knew they must get on with the reason they came to Dublin.

They took a taxi to University College in the Dublin suburb of Donnybrook. It was the second oldest university in Ireland, and the Catholic answer to the strong Protestant bias of the venerable Trinity College. University College marked as famous graduates, Padraig Pearse the rebel leader in 1916, Eamon de Valera the only surviving leader of the 1916 rebellion and the first president of a separate Irish Republic, as well as the writer James Joyce. Michael Flynn had taken degrees here and now held a chair in history.

"Flynn is a real piece of work. I don't mind telling you I don't like his kind," Reilly said. "His type is what's wrong with the movement," Reilly told Devereux in the taxi.

"Why's that?"

"It's his rabid, uncompromising, unyielding rhetoric, his call to violence. He's the counterpart to the Protestants' Ian Paisley," Reilly said. "Both cut from the same cloth."

"Every ethnic group seems to produce such a spokesman," Devereux said. "So do you think he will go for our proposal?"

"I don't know. I've never met him. I know Flynn only from what he writes," Reilly replied. "He may. He's criticized non-violent methods in the past. This is something different, though.

He might agree that we have done a poor PR job in world opinion. He also knows that this kind of attention helps in raising funds for the Cause internationally."

"Don't remind me. Helping the I.R.A. is not what I intend," Devereux said.

"Fine. But don't put it like that to Flynn," Reilly cautioned. She knew the truth of the rumor about Flynn's past in the I.R.A. Terrance Dolan had told her.

Over twenty years ago, and after a year of convalescing from his wounds in the failed ambush, Michael Flynn wanted to continue an active operational role in the I.R.A. But he soon learned that he could only be a liability with his limited mobility that required the assistance of a cane.

Michael Flynn's father ran a successful cartage business out of Monaghan. Most of his freight hauls were between the counties that were part of Northern Ireland and the Republic where Monaghan served as a hub. His father was a staunch Republican with an active conviction to drive the British from Ireland. He developed a vital smuggling operation to move men and materiel over the border for the I.R.A.

His father worshipped education, and having the means, sent his only son, Michael off to University College in Dublin. Michael Flynn returned home with a degree in history and a desire to enter the fight to free the northern six counties from British domination. His father supported his son's feelings and made the necessary introductions.

The elder Flynn could not have been more proud of the exploits of his son. There was many a night he sat up knowing that his son was out there somewhere in the North on a mission. Those were lonely nights. He had lost his wife years before and it was only he and Michael. It was his books that kept him going by providing some diversion to his worried thoughts. He had only a limited education himself but was an avid reader from his early years. He loved words and knowledge.

It was he who persuaded Michael to return to university for postgraduate studies after his wounding. Within four years, Michael Flynn had earned both masters and Ph.D. degrees, and was offered a position on the faculty as an instructor. Several years later he was an associate professor with tenure. By the time rumors circulated as to his involvement with the I.R.A., it was too late for the University to do anything, even if the Board of Regents had been so inclined.

With Flynn's operational exploits as credentials, he quickly earned a place among the I.R.A. operational leadership that directed the Active Service Units. With his field experience and intellect, he was a natural. By the late eighties, he had risen to the position of Chief of Staff of the Provisional I.R.A., and in direct command of operations. Publicly, Flynn was an intellectual that was vocal in his condemnation of continued British control of the northern six counties. Many at the University shared similar views. Flynn was by no means viewed as a pariah.

Both Devereux and Reilly were somewhat taken back by the physical presence of Michael Flynn. He was a short man with a slight build and thinning hair that was heavily salted with gray. His face suggested his age to be in his late fifties, but the total impression was of someone older. Exceptionally dark eyes suggested intensity. He wore a crisply starched white shirt and a stylish tie. He rose with the aide of a cane.

"Miss Reilly, it's good to meet you. I've heard excellent things about you," Flynn said, extending his hand to Reilly. "And you must be Mr. Devereux, the photographer, or is it photojournalist?"

Devereux shook Flynn's hand. "Either way. It's just a label anyway."

Flynn offered them coffee. After some minutes of small talk directed mostly to Reilly, Flynn turned his attention to Devereux. "Upon hearing of your idea to do, what shall I call it, a piece? A project? I looked at your past work myself. No offense, but I was not familiar with your name. At any rate, I was impressed. Most of the photographs were compelling. Many were remarkable. I can see why you received a Pulitzer. I've heard the reasoning for why certain interests might wish to cooperate with you, but I want to hear your argument first hand."

Devereux spent the next twenty minutes outlining the project. He made the case for the I.R.A. interest in what might be achieved, with Reilly interjecting supporting comments. He was candid about his apolitical stance of the situation in Northern Ireland, and direct about his personal and professional interest in the project. Flynn listened without comment, but his eyes rarely left contact with Devereux.

"I appreciate your forthrightness, Mr. Devereux. I harbor no delusions that this is anything other than an opportunity with potential benefit to your personal interests," Flynn said after Devereux had concluded his pitch. Devereux made no gesture to counter Flynn's comment.

Flynn continued. "Anything less and I would be skeptical of your motivations. You're not Irish, and you're certainly not the kind of person looking for a cause. After all, the best deals are struck when both parties understand what the benefits are to the other."

"It is no secret as to my sentiments concerning the British. This is not a philosophical debate, or a political science debate. In fact, it is no debate whatsoever. The situation in Northern Ireland is a throwback to the nineteenth century. It is imperialism in its most onerous form. Ireland is the first colonial acquisition of the so-called British Empire, and the northern Six Counties are its last hold to that concept. The British have dominated Irish life, have taken from it all the fruits of a hard working, proud people, and continue to treat its citizens as second class. And Ulster was always its seat of power."

"Long before there was a British Empire, the Anglo was subjugating the Irish. Under the Tudors and Stuarts, English and Scotch colonists dispossessed the Irish. Cromwell's massacres at Drogheda and Wexford in the seventeenth century defined the oppressor. The enacting of the so-called Penal Laws at the end of that century effectively established a system of apartheid. Catholics rights to education were restricted and land holding was virtually prohibited. Ireland became a land of tenant farmers, little better than slaves to the plantation landholders. Even as late as the nineteen sixties, most Catholics were not allowed the vote in Northern Ireland."

"The British continued their strategy of empire to dominate with a colonial minority in South Africa in the last century and Rhodesia in this century. Even Palestine illustrates the British arrogance to impose their laws and culture on other peoples. Peoples throughout the world have struggled against the oppression of the British colonial empire. America was not the first. Ireland was. In granting independence to the southern Twenty-six Counties, the British cut their losses and retained their bastion of power in the northern Six Counties. By defining the counties thus, rather than the actual nine counties that comprised the ancient province of Ulster, they retained a Protestant majority, a majority with ties and loyalties to Britain. And the Catholic minority there continues to be denied rights."

Flynn stopped what was becoming an emotional diatribe on his obsessive topic. "Excuse my lecturing. Occupational inclination," he said, sighed, then smiled. "My sentiments and motivations are obvious, Mr. Devereux. I want the British out of Northern Ireland. Their entrenched colonial presence and control over the most economical vital area of Ireland must end. Ireland belongs as a whole, not artificially partitioned. It is no secret that I have advocated any means, including armed revolt, to rest control for the Irish people."

Flynn stopped talking for a moment and stared intently at Devereux as if trying to make up his mind. He had actually decided before Devereux and Reilly arrived to approve the venture. It would show a willingness to seek new methods and surprise Terrance Dolan.

"Very well Mr. Devereux. I'll recommend to certain parties that your project be approved. If they agree, I'll see what I can do to arrange for assistance to your work. The Protestant paramilitaries are a violent lot, but I don't know how to capture that in photos."

"Well that's my area of expertise, Mr. Flynn. Everyone assumes that photographic coverage of violent conflicts means capturing violent situations as they are happening. Yet if you look at any body of work, you'll find only rare shots of this. The photographer is looking to communicate the feeling of the situation to his audience. Even in a hot war zone, actual opportunities for dramatic action shots are rare."

Devereux continued. "What I need are candid shots. Not necessarily of actual violent acts, but shots that paint the picture.

Photos that generate strong emotions in the viewer. News photos are not what I'm after. I need to get deeper."

"I assume you realize that there may, and probably will be, some personal risk in what you're proposing?" Flynn asked.

"Of course. If there isn't, then I'm not getting the kind of material that's important," Devereux answered. "And I must warn you and Brigid, and anyone else, that I'm not developing PR materials for the I.R.A. If I thought I could get better cooperation and material from the Protestants against the I.R.A. I might have taken that route. My motivation is to capture the essence of the struggle in Northern Ireland. No one has looked at it from the Catholic, much less the I.R.A. perspective, so that's new. As it stands, the I.R.A. has the most to gain from offering me assistance."

"Very well, Mr. Devereux. As they say, I know certain people. I will convey your request, as well as my own recommendation that you be provided with all necessary assistance," Flynn said.

Reilly had been silent throughout Devereux's pitch for the project and the ensuing exchange with Flynn. She had learned much. Her opinion about Flynn had been substantially revised. He was not the vicious revolutionary espousing violence she thought him to be. Single minded, intractable, yes, but with intellect and leadership. Flynn was different than her uncle. She could see how the Cause needed both. Her uncle the pragmatist, the politician, the consensus builder, and Flynn the emotional fire that any movement required.

As for Mason Devereux, this was yet another dimension of his personality. She could sense his confidence in the negotiation with Flynn. He was self-assured. He had done this sort of thing before.

Signaling an end to the meeting, Flynn rose slowly from his chair, using the desk for assistance because of his infirmity. "I have enjoyed talking with you, Mr. Devereux. Good luck in your project. I suspect you will be contacted soon."

Flynn shook Devereux's hand.

"And you, Miss Reilly. This has been a real pleasure. As I said, I have heard many good things about your involvement

with the Cause. I am told that you provide excellent legal counsel for those accused of anti-government acts in the North. Keep
up the good work," Flynn said, extending his hand to Reilly.

Once outside the university offices, Reilly said, "So what do
you think, Mason?"

"I think he likes the possibilities. I think he already had his
mind made up. The guy's a shark, but a real charmer. He's no
consultant to Sinn Fein or the I.R.A. He doesn't advise, he makes
decisions, probably even policy. If he's inclined, he'll make it
happen."

Chapter Ten

It had been three days since Devereux's meeting with Flynn. He and Reilly had returned to Belfast. He had stayed close to the hotel. Reilly had stayed over the night of their return, but returned to her own flat and pressing business the next day. The call he was waiting for came in the mid-morning. The caller said little except to set a meeting place at noon at a pub once again in Andersonstown in West Belfast.

Devereux took a taxi to the pub. He seated himself at a vacant table as instructed and ordered a pint of Guinness. A few minutes later two men in their twenties acknowledged him by name and sat down at the table. Confirming his identity, they offered their hands and introduced themselves as Liam and Sean Mullins. There were few people in the pub, and after seating themselves, the two men confirmed they would not be overheard before talking.

The one called Liam, the older of the two brothers spoke. "Been told you're interested in photographing certain things. Could be dangerous, Mr. Devereux. Know that do ya?"

Devereux looked intently at Liam Mullins. "What do you know about me, Mr. Mullins?"

Mullins appeared puzzled by the question. "What'ya mean?"

"I mean, what have you been instructed to do?"

"Been asked, not ordered, Mr. Devereux. We're not I.R.A. Just sympathetic to the movement is all we are," Mullins responded.

"Let's cut the bullshit, Liam. Of course you're I.R.A. or you wouldn't be here. They wouldn't trust what I'm about to do to some outsiders. You've been given specific instructions. I just want to make sure we have the same understanding," Devereux said.

Liam Mullins smiled. "As you say, Mr. Devereux, let's cut the bullshit. We've been told to provide you with 'special' shots of Protestant paramilitary people, them training, or anything else you might suggest. Which brings me back to the risk, Mr. Devereux. This is a war going on, and these people you want to photograph are mean buggers. People die regular here."

Liam was of average height and build. Sean on the other hand was over six feet with a strong upper body. Sean had a youthful, round face with a ruddy complexion and red hair. Liam's face was angular, his hair dark brown. No brotherly resemblance here. Sean had said nothing since they had sat down. He was constantly checking the other clientele in the pub, obviously leaving the talking to his brother.

"First of all gentlemen, I'm aware of the danger. I've been in wars all over the world. Been shot at, been taken prisoner. I've seen people killed. Seen people executed. I've smelled the stench of rotting bodies. Fact is, if you're not taking me onto dangerous ground, you're not doing what needs to be done. Question is, are you lads up to this? Do you have the sand?" Devereux countered.

Liam bristled at Devereux's remark. "Listen, Mr. Devereux, my brother and me are up to whatever it takes. If you're thinking us some sort of newcomers, you're wrong. We've seen our share of tough circumstances, if you get my meaning."

"Then when do we start?" Devereux asked, smiling to solidify the arrangement.

"Tomorrow, Mr. Devereux. We'll pick you up at five in the morning. We need to be somewhere while it's still dark. Be on the sidewalk on the opposite side of the street from the Opera House," Liam Mullins said. He stood up along with his brother and offered his hand.

Devereux shook their hands. "Just one thing - since we'll be working together, call me, Mason. See you tomorrow."

After returning to the hotel, Devereux phoned Reilly and told her he had been contacted. Perhaps from prior circumstances, or simply paranoia, Devereux declined to talk specifics with Reilly over the telephone. He agreed to call her the following evening.

The Mullins brothers picked Devereux up as planned the next morning. Winter was setting in. Devereux wore a sweater and ski jacket to ward off the chilling morning damp.

The Mullins brothers were driving a nondescript van with a deteriorated olive green color. It fit the character of the their destination, a working class commercial district in a Protestant section of East Belfast. After a twenty-minute drive through the early morning darkness, they parked the van across the street from what appeared to be a service garage for large lorries. Using the small parking lot of a market that was not yet open for business, the van joined one other parked vehicle. The brothers had placed one empty and one half full bottle of whiskey on the floor of the van.

"If the coppers should come about, we'll make as if we was drunk last night and parked here to sleep it off. You're a photographer up here to do pictures of Belfast. We're just two fun loving fellows you bumped into at a pub. You should make like you're kind of fucked, ready to puke if you know what I mean, Mister Dev —-, Mason," Liam Mullins said.

"I understand, Liam. Now tell me what we're up to."

Liam left his front passenger seat and sat next to Devereux in the back seat. Sean left the driver's seat and went to the rear of the van behind Devereux and Liam. They could see the front of the garage clearly through the windscreen. From the outside, the van would appear empty as they would be obscured by the dark interior.

"I guess you'd call this background work, Mason. The lads that work at this garage, four of them, are members of a U.F.F. unit. That stands for Ulster Freedom Fighters. There're a fucking bad lot. Rumor has it that this group has killed a number of Catholics. Even the fucking British have outlawed them, but they do shit about stopping them. Prods don't get arrested, only Catholics," Liam Mullins said.

"These fellows arrive for work around seven. Thought you might want to get photographs."

Devereux took two Nikon 35mm cameras out of his bag. Each was motor driven for rapid shots and fitted with a large lens. A gray, damp dawn was breaking at a quarter to seven. A man drove up in a battered lorry. Devereux caught a series of shots as the man exited the vehicle and proceeded to unlock the garage. Ten minutes later, another man arrived in an old sedan, followed shortly by another who was dropped off by a woman. Liam Mullins identified each by name.

Each of Devereux's two cameras was fitted with a different focal length lens. In this case both were long distance lens, one a 200mm, the other a 105mm, both with f2.8 apertures. The alternative was to use a zoom lens to vary the size of the subject. While the zoom lens offered the ability to change the focal length, or size of the subject with a turn of the lens, the aperture setting was not equivalent to the fixed lens.

The aperture setting was the size of the lens opening that dictated the amount of light received by the lens. The maximum aperture of a zoom lens was never as great as that of the equivalent fixed lens, thereby diminishing the sharpness of the subject. Devereux had developed a technique to change cameras quickly to photograph a dynamically changing scene from different degrees of magnification by switching cameras.

The light was poor, but adequate. Devereux had taken a light meter reading and made the necessary camera settings to compensate. At ten minutes after the hour, a late model sedan drove into the parking area adjacent to the garage. A tall, well-built man in his mid-thirties exited.

"That's Krill, John Krill. Prominent in the U.F.F. Some sort of unit commander. Word is that he's a real fuck. Been known to do some real nasty shit, if you know what I mean," Liam Mullins said. Devereux grunted his understanding as he captured Krill on film.

Sean Mullins moved back into the driver's seat after half an hour then maneuvered the van out of its parking lot.

Liam explained, "That's part of the group. The rest work at various other places. This being Friday, we expect them to gather tonight as usual at the Maiden Head. It's a pub on the eastside. We'll get together tonight. Light's goin' to be poor at best that time of day and this time of year. Shant think you'll be able to get any good photos in the dark."

"What kind of light is there?"

"Only light is a street lamp near the parking lot behind the pub, and a light at the back door."

They left the area within minutes after Krill's arrival at the garage. No purpose in extending the risk. Mullins dropped Devereux off two blocks from the Europa. He would ring him later to arrange for picking him up and explain the plan for surveillance of the Maiden Head Pub. Mullins also told him from now on they would meet him at different locations, to be determined each time he called to avoid any pattern.

At five in the afternoon Devereux was picked up five blocks from the hotel. It was a fifteen-minute drive to the east side of Belfast.

Sean Mullins parked the van in a parking lot behind a pub. A poorly constructed chain-link fence insured that the closest vehicle in the lot was still some distance from the establishment. The threat of a car bomb from the I.R.A. was a real concern here just like the Catholic pub that feared the Protestant militancy.

Dusk was settling abruptly due to a totally cloud covered day. They used the same tactic of moving to the recess of the darkened van to remain unseen. Liam told Devereux they would also use the same cover story if confronted.

After an hour, Sean Mullins said to his brother, "I've got to go. There's a vacant lot down a bit. Shant be long."

After Sean Mullins had left the van, Devereux said to Liam Mullins, "Your brother doesn't say much. What's his problem? Doesn't like your orders? Doesn't like me? What's the situation?"

"Nothing to do with you, Mason. Me brother's had some hard times. He's as loyal to the Cause as any true Irishman. He's quiet because he doesn't hear well. Deaf in one ear, he is. From when he was fourteen. A gang of Prods jumped him on the way home from school. Beat the shit out of him. Fuckers used clubs. Spent some time in the hospital he did. Damaged his hearing. Damaged more too."

Liam Mullins, pulled a large set of field glasses from under the seat.

"There's a light over the back door. I'll spot the lads we're interested in. Maybe it'll be enough for some kind of shots. Can you get pictures under these conditions?"

"Not the best, that's for sure. But there's ways to work it."

Devereux was familiar with the challenges of extremes in lighting conditions. This was the nature of photography in his line of work. He had experimented extensively with combinations of aperture setting, focal length of lens, depth of field, and film speed. He had perfected the use of various filters to enhance details by manipulating the effect of the light. Because of his skill, many of his photographs had the quality of art that comes from more constructed and predictable compositions.

Not knowing the conditions and covering for change, Devereux always carried several cameras and lens in the field. From his bag, he choose the large 200mm lens at an aperture setting of f2.8, and set the shutter speed at 1/500 second. He was using high-speed, black and white film to optimize the sharpness of detail. The harsh, directed glare from the outside light next to the door would be mitigated by a lens filter. The filter would sharpen the contrast on the subject's face when developed on the black and white film.

"There, that Fiat pulling in the lot. That'll be Fenner," Mullins said.

The man parked his car and made for the back door to the pub. Mullins had positioned the van to achieve as much angle as possible for capturing the faces of the targets as they entered the pub. Devereux was impressed with Mullins' planning. At best however, a slightly less than profile shot from the rear was all Devereux would get unless the subject turned his head. He had set the motor drive trigger on the camera to take three frames per second to capture any fleeting shot opportunity.

"I wonder what the fuck's keeping Sean? If somethin's gone wrong, remember what I told you," he reminded Devereux while intently looking toward the corner of the lot from which his brother had departed.

Devereux recognized the arrival of Krill, and two others he had seen from the garage and captured a dozen photographs.

After another fifteen minutes, Liam said, "That's it. We're getting out of here. Something's happened to Sean."

"Hold on Liam. Give it some more time. Your brother knows what to do if he gets in trouble. Besides, we don't want to leave him here in the middle of Protestant land do we?"

Mullins looked at Devereux. The pale light filtering into the van revealed the fear on Mullin's face.

"You're right."

Devereux didn't know that he was right. If Sean Mullins had been picked up, the natural assumption for the police would be that there were others in the area. He wondered if the Mullins brothers had weapons in the van. He supposed they did, just as he supposed they would be more of a liability than a defense if arrested.

"How about this group walking to the door," Devereux asked.

"Yeah, two of them. The short guy with the longish hair, and the big guy with the belly. Names are Davidson and Caldridge."

To distract Mullins, Devereux asked, "How is it that you have such good intelligence on these people?"

"Afraid I can't tell you that, Mason. What they call classified."

The truth was, every movement of Krill's U.F.F. group was known to the I.R.A. The one called Davidson had a young pretty wife. She was of course a Protestant, the daughter of a businessman and staunch Orangeman, with a mother equally firm in her anti-Catholic leanings. The woman became involved with a young man who was Catholic. Knowing he was Catholic, she kept their affair secret. However, she did not know he was I.R.A. What turned out as adventure turned to love. That love resulted in a pregnancy.

The reality of the situation set in on the young woman. Her father and mother would literally throw her out of the house. Openly living together as unmarried in Belfast was out of the question. With him being Catholic, it might even be dangerous.

As I.R.A., it clearly would be dangerous for him. They did not have the money or the means to leave Ireland.

The boyfriend was appalled by her suggestion of an abortion as the only way out. It was his child. His religion condemned abortion as a mortal sin. Shortly after hearing of the pregnancy, the man was arrested, convicted, and sentenced to a prison term for involvement in an I.R.A. bombing.

The woman managed a trip to London and secured an abortion without her family discovering the truth. For the man, he was cut off from even corresponding with the woman for his own sake as well as hers. His brother contacted the woman some months later. Knowing the truth from his brother, the man learned that she was no longer pregnant. The implication was obvious.

The man's anger at the woman's betrayal lead him to talk of the affair. The information made its way into I.R.A. intelligence. She eventually married a minor customs official by the name of Davidson. Davidson was also the second in command of a Protestant paramilitary U.F.F. unit, and therefore came under I.R.A. intelligence scrutiny. Background investigation revealed the maiden name of his wife. An alert I.R.A. intelligence person recognized the name from an earlier report.

The information moved up the chain of the I.R.A. command. Eventually reaching Michael Flynn himself. The woman represented a significant intelligence asset. The I.R.A. had precious few inside the Protestant paramilitary groups. The woman had only recently been approached. The choice was simple. She was to provide whatever information requested on the U.F.F. unit her husband belonged to. If she failed to cooperate, it was a simple matter to see that her husband and parents learned of her past love affair with a convicted I.R.A. terrorist, and the sordid details of an aborted pregnancy. She would lose everything. Much the same choice she faced upon learning of the pregnancy. She choose the only viable choice — survival.

It had been close to one hour since Sean Mullins had left to relieve himself. Obviously something had gone wrong. Devereux agreed with Liam Mullins that they must leave. Whatever

Sean had got himself into, they could not help him from here. Liam Mullins dropped Devereux two blocks from the Europa Hotel.

"Liam, you call me tonight, whatever time when you learn about Sean. You hear?"

Mullins nodded his acknowledgment without a word and drove off.

Devereux called Reilly and talked for almost an hour. She wanted to know what he had been doing, but he pleaded in indirect language that the hotel telephone was not sufficiently secure. It also relieved him from telling everything to Reilly. It was not that he didn't trust her, but he instinctively wanted to distance their relationship from the details of his work. He promised to see her for lunch the next day.

Around midnight, Liam Mullins called.

"Sean's back. He's okay. There's no danger if you get my meaning?"

They arranged to meet at a restaurant the following morning through a predetermined simple code. The conversation lasted only fifteen seconds.

Over breakfast the next day at a small restaurant, Devereux learned of Sean Mullins adventure of the prior night. Except for their initial introduction, Devereux had not heard the younger brother speak.

"After I took me piss in that lot, I walked back up the sidewalk. Then this car pulls up. It's coppers. They ask me who I was. They look at me license. Address tells them I'm probably Catholic. They ask what the likes of me is doing in this part of town. Then they start to get nasty. Started pushin' me about. I told them I was out drinking with me mates. Didn't know where we was. Went for a piss in that lot over there. Fuckers left me. Some fucking joke I says."

Sean Mullins started to smile.

"They put me up against their car and searched me. When they turned me around, they looked mad as hell. Looked like I was in for it good. I got this idea to tell them I was sick. I was going to puke. They stepped back. Then I did puke."

With that, Sean laughed out loud. His brother and Devereux couldn't help but grin. He continued.

"Wasn't hard to puke. I was scared as hell anyway. With my hand to my mouth I just stuck my finger down my throat and gagged. Pissed them off fierce. Thought I'd made a worse mistake, but they only took me down to the nearest police station. Pushed me around some more, but nothing worse. After a couple of hours they threw me out with nothing more than a cursing."

The next several days were spent photographing other locations used by various Protestant paramilitary groups. It was obvious that I.R.A. intelligence on Krill's group was very good. But the only thing so far that yielded any worthwhile photographs was a field training exercise with live ammunition by Krill's Protestant paramilitary unit. It cost Devereux and the Mullins brothers an uncomfortable night in the cold and damp.

Devereux was told that this was a favored field exercise location for various Ulster Defense Association, or U.D.A., units. Liam explained that Krill's U.F.F. group was a faction which was part of the U.D.A. The U.D.A. was itself officially outlawed, but that was not rigorously enforced.

Even using his largest lens, Devereux did not feel the photographs would be of particularly good quality because of the light and the distance. He hoped to maybe get acceptable definition of several of the men's' faces with enlargements, but that was questionable. None were wearing masks since they thought the area secure from observation.

Two days later, Devereux received a telephone call waking him at six in the morning.

"Mason, this is Liam. Something's come up. Might be of interest. Pick you up in an hour."

The Mullins brothers picked him up on schedule at a prearranged location.

"Where are we going?" Devereux asked.

Sean Mullins was driving, and as usual, Liam Mullins was the one to respond. "Word is there may be something happening at the office of a local political candidate. Catholic fellow. Real pain in the ass to the fuckers who run things. Accusin' those in power of corruption and all sorts of other shit. He's running for some city office, but I forget which."

"What do you mean something is going to happen?"

"Don't know. All we know is that word has it that Krill's bunch of monkeys are going to pay a visit to this guy named Brennan. Probably this morning."

"What do you think will happen?" Devereux asked.

"Don't rightly know," Mullins answered.

"Shouldn't we notify the police?"

"No. First place, we don't know anything. Second place, the R.U.C. wouldn't do shit without more information and some identification. How the fuck do we explain that?"

"And how the fuck do you explain getting this information, Liam?"

"Don't know, Mason, and that's the truth. Me brother and me are at the bottom of the ladder. It's not for us to see over the wall. But it suits what you're lookin' for doesn't it?"

Sean Mullins parked the same van used several days before on the opposite side of the street and fifty meters down from the campaign headquarters of the Catholic politician Brennan's campaign headquarters. The campaign office was formerly a small retail shop with a large window now painted over with the candidate's name. The neighborhood was Catholic West Belfast.

They waited until eight a.m. Two young women arrived to unlock the office. A third arrived soon after. At half past the hour, a young man around thirty, well dressed in a business suit, entered the building. Mullins identified the man as Brennan. There was little traffic in the street at this early hour.

Two cars approached from up the street coming directly toward their parked van. Both vehicles pulled to the curb in front of the campaign office. Eight men exited the two sedans, all had ski masks over their heads. Most carried assault rifles. Devereux started to take photos. He set the motor drive trigger at two shots per second. This time the light was totally adequate. Six men entered the building, two remained to stand watch. Devereux captured thirty-six frames and reloaded the camera.

Five minutes passed, but it seemed like more. Two of the Protestant paramilitaries exited the building and surveyed the street. The three women exited with the appearance of being roughly pushed. One stumbled and fell. Another woman struck one of the men with a strong fist to the face. A second man swiped the butt of his rifle into the lower back of the woman, dropping her to her knees.

The man in the business suit, assumed to be Brennan, soon followed out the door. He was escorted by one of the masked men with an assault rifle pressed to the base of his neck, Another masked man followed closely with a handgun visible.

Devereux had reloaded the camera and continued to take shots. He had a second camera in reserve to act as backup with a different lens.

Brennan was held by each arm by two men. A third man stood in front and appeared to be saying something to Brennan. Devereux assumed it was the leader Krill. The man backhanded Brennan with a blow across his face. Brennan slumped but was supported by the two men holding him. One extracted a length of nylon cord from his pocket and proceeded to tie Brennan's wrists behind his back. Devereux had just loaded a third roll of film into the camera as events escalated rapidly.

Brennan was thrust forward by the man assumed to be Krill, who then tripped him. The politician went down hard onto the pavement. The women made an attempt to move to his assistance. One was brutally struck in the head with the barrel of an assault rifle. The other two were pinned to the wall of the building each by a hooded man.

Brennan was hoisted to his knees. The one assumed to be Krill, moved behind the man. He held what appeared to be a large caliber handgun to the back of the man's head. Devereux knew what was about to happen. So did Liam Mullins.

"Mother of God, the bastards are goin' to do him right here."

And they did.

Devereux had advanced his motor drive trigger to three exposures per second. He was fairly sure he might have captured the spray of tissue and blood as a large portion of Brennan's face tore away with the exiting of the bullet. The man with the handgun then emptied two more shots into the head of the prone victim.

"Jesus Christ," Sean Mullins said in a whisper, then made the sign of the cross.

The eight men hurriedly piled into the two vehicles and sped away passing the van. Devereux continued to shoot pictures as they sped past.

"Let's be out of here," Liam Mullins said.

His brother started the engine of the van.

"Not yet. I want more photos."

Devereux exited the van and continued to shoot.

One woman reached the murdered man. Kneeing at his side, she raised her hands in anguish reminding Devereux of the famous picture of the young woman kneeling over the Kent State student shot down by National Guard troops during the Vietnam War protests. He went to his second camera, taking shots from a variety of depths, capturing a broad repertoire of perspectives.

At the sound of the first sirens, Sean Mullins pulled the van into the street,

"Now! We must leave!"

Devereux got into the vehicle as Sean Mullins gunned the engine and took the first turn to leave the area.

No one in the van said anything for some distance. The Mullins brothers looked not only grim but shaken. Devereux was also upset. He had seen executions before, but such brutality was not something you became used to.

"Did you know that was going to happen?" Devereux shouted at Liam Mullins.

"Fuck, no! Christ, you think we'd let someone get killed like that just to get you fuckin' pictures?"

"The I.R.A. kills like this, too. Why not this? Your intelligence tells you there's going to be a hit. Now you've got someone who can get the kind of photographs to be published internationally. Someone with independence from the I.R.A. to lend credibility."

"Fuck you, Devereux. You think we're some kind of animals don't you. That bloke they killed back there, he was a good man. A fighter he was. Said things that made sense. I ain't much for politicians, but I listened to him a few times. He was for the

Catholics, for the workingman. I for one wouldn't have nothing' to do with lettin' a man like that get murdered just for some fuckin' pictures, for some fuckin' American photographer."

"So it's not you, Liam. But look at the facts. You get this call to take me to this political candidate's office early in the morning. You're told something may happen. I.R.A. intelligence somehow has this information. And it's good enough for them to want me out there to get photos. What did you think was going to happen, Liam?"

Liam Mullins was quiet for several moments before answering Devereux.

"I thought they would come and wreck the place. Maybe rough up Brennan. Doin' murder like that in broad daylight is real unusual."

Nothing more was said until Devereux was deposited at the usual place, several blocks from the Europa Hotel. Before exiting the van, Liam Mullins asked, "What will you be doing with the pictures?"

"That's my affair, Liam. Tell your I.R.A. handlers that. I don't do their calling. Tell'em right now I'm exceedingly pissed."

With that, Devereux slammed the door of the van and walked away.

At the hotel desk he asked where he might find the nearest Federal Express office. The desk clerk said he could arrange for that right there. Devereux thanked him, but said it was urgent and must get there right away. The clerk gave him directions to the office four blocks away.

Chapter Eleven

"Larry, it's Mason," Devereux said loudly. There was music and a lot of people noise in the background. "Can you hear me?"

"Mason? Where are you?"

"Belfast."

"Where?"

"Goddamn it, Larry, get the fuck somewhere where you can hear me."

It was late in the evening in Los Angeles. A few moments later Devereux's literary agent came back on the line, the background noise absent.

"Good party, Mason. Must be getting drunk. Could have sworn this young thing with gorgeous breasts was trying to put the make on me. Dumb broad probably thinks I'm a theatrical agent rather than literary."

"Cut the pleasantries, Larry, and listen. I'm still here in Belfast. I just put some film in transit to you. Two packages, one FedEx, one DHL just in case. Eight rolls. Dynamite stuff, Larry. I want you to get it to Sergio's shop as soon as you get it. Tell him to rush it. Double the price, whatever. Develop all of it into eight by tens. Take care of the negatives. Then call me as soon as you have them."

Neuson became sober and attentive.

"What is it that you've got, Mason?"

"You look at the pictures, Larry, then call me. I'm at the Europa Hotel. Belfast. That's in Northern Ireland. Here's the number ——"

Devereux hung up before Neuson could continue. He didn't want to talk to his agent right now.

It had been several days since he had seen Brigid Reilly, she being away from Belfast on business. He was dressing when there was a knock on the hotel room door. It was Reilly. She moved against him and kissed him hungrily with her eyes open wide. The preoccupation with the morning's events was pushed aside in his mind. This woman could arouse him like no other.

"I couldn't wait till after dinner, Mason. Besides we can make love again later. Mind?"

She had removed her jacket, kicked off her shoes, and was quickly undoing the buttons to her blouse. Devereux stepped back and sat on the bed. She fixed her stare and smile intently on him as she removed her clothes. She knew she looked good, and she liked the pleasure it gave Devereux.

She removed her blouse, then her bra, baring her upper body before removing her skirt and nylons. Her eyes and smile never left Devereux. Totally naked, Reilly stepped in front of Devereux. He tipped his head back and took the nipple of her breast in his mouth. It was hard and erect. He pulled her close to him. From behind, he reached one hand between her legs. Her pubic hair was wet. She gasp slightly at his touch.

"Take your clothes off, " she said.

Instead, he pushed her onto the bed and moved his head between her legs. She was so aroused that she arched her back immediately as his mouth touched her.

"God that's good!"

The last word came drawn out in guttural tones, followed by subtle noises of pleasure.

Devereux gently explored with his lips and tongue, becoming lost in his own preoccupation at giving her pleasure. After several minutes, Reilly's abdominal muscles involuntarily flexed at his every manipulation. Devereux gently inserted a finger into the rear of her vagina as he continued to lick her clitoris.

"Oh my God, take it, take it!" Reilly said in a throaty guttural voice. She came in increasing waves, culminating in a convulsing scenario.

Reilly pulled Devereux up from between her legs. They both pulled frantically to remove his trousers and shorts. She maneuvered his cock inside of her and the penetration caused another spasm of release. Devereux maintained a slow rhythm of thrusts. The pleasure was exquisite for both. Sensing Devereux's approach to climax, Reilly turned over and rose to her knees. She wanted to feel maximum penetration.

Devereux thrust only a few times before the tightened grip of Reilly's vaginal muscles around his cock drew him over the edge. Like Reilly, he spent himself in a long sustained ejaculation that built to a blinding peak. Uncoupled, both lay spent. Ten minutes later, both were drifting in a sated state of relaxation close to sleep.

"Hungry?" Reilly eventually asked.

"Yeah, I'm hungry. I need the strength."

He kissed an exposed breast.

"I was hungry before you ravished me. Now get your ass moving."

"I'm going to shower. Otherwise, with all these juices they'll be able to tell what we've been up to by the smell."

Reilly swung out of bed and stood looking at Devereux. She bent down and kissed him.

"I think I might be in love with you."

Not waiting for a response, she went into the bathroom and ran the shower.

Devereux sat in the chair. He savored the lovemaking as he listened to Reilly shower. The events of the morning progressively intruded into his thoughts, however. The horror of the murder did not effect him as it might a normal person. A normal person had not seen the brutality, the butchery that he had seen in his years covering violence in the world. He was more than a little troubled though. This was not a war zone. He had witnessed a brutal murder. He had seen many others but always in some pesthole, in a real war, never in a Western city. And he had just made love. Not just any lovemaking, but one of those rare life-moment lovemaking sessions. He would remember this day forever for its extremes.

Reilly had not yet had the opportunity to ask Devereux what he had accomplished in the last few days. After being seated in the restaurant, Devereux ordered drinks and finally broached the subject of what had happened that morning.

"Did you hear on the news about the murder today?"

"What murder? I haven't heard the news today, or even been in the office for that matter."

"Some political candidate named Brennan. He was killed at his office."

"Paul Brennan? Oh my God! I knew him. What happened?"

"I was there, Brigid. I got the whole event in photographs. Probably can identify the killers. Your friends and I have been surveilling this Protestant paramilitary group. Good chance it was them that did the killing."

"Will it ever end? Brennan was a good man. Real pain in the ass to the Government. Now you see what this is about, Mason."

"The troubling thing, Brigid, is that I think the I.R.A. knew what was going down and let it happen so I could get pictures."

Reilly looked at Devereux for several moments measuring what she wanted to say. She didn't want to argue and ruin this magnificent evening. For a while, the never-ending struggle and the violence seemed distant. But there was never any respite. It was always with you.

"Why do you say that, Mason?"

"Too convenient. First we surveil this Protestant group. The intelligence is too good to come from surveillance alone unless the I.R.A. has committed significant resources over a long time. Then I asked Liam Mullins how the I.R.A. came by such good intelligence, he told me he couldn't tell me. Liam Mullins and his brother Sean are my I.R.A. 'guides.' After the murder, Mullins said to me that he thought they were only going to beat up this Brennan guy. My guess is that someone in the I.R.A. leadership knew something might be going to happen."

Reilly decided not to pursue the issue of I.R.A. culpability in Brennan's murder.

"Where's the film now, Mason?"

"On its way to the U.S. In a few days I should have proofs, or at least my agent will. I'll see then about getting them to the police."

"The police? You can't go to the police, Mason. You could get arrested for your involvement with the I.R.A., or for withholding evidence. You also couldn't do any more work here. The project would be ended."

"Of course I'm not going to the police, at least not straight away and identify myself. I came here to get these kinds of pictures. I wouldn't abandon that at the first sign of violence. If I did provide the police with information, it would be at a distance."

He did have a real ethical dilemma here, though. Should he withhold information which might convict murderers in order to gather more evidence? What good was that serving other than his own purposes? Why was this more problematical than the countless other acts of murder and torture he had photographed over the years?

His answer was that here in Northern Ireland, he actually had a real alternative. There was a legitimate governmental body that would prosecute and likely convict the murderers. In the war zones he had covered there had rarely been any constituted legal mechanism to deal with criminal acts. Even if there was a specter of bias against Catholics, the Northern Ireland government would prosecute such crimes if they had the evidence. Protestant terrorists were also imprisoned here. When he had the pictures he would deal with what to do.

Devereux went on to tell Reilly about the surveillance and the details of the murder throughout dinner. He fell into a monotone recital of the events, much like a reporter delivering facts without injecting personal emotion. While having after-dinner drinks, Reilly said,

"You're a hard man to figure, Mason Devereux. You witness a murder, make love the same day and then enjoy dinner and drinks."

She did not mean it in a judgmental way. It was an observation of how difficult he was to understand.

"I'm sorry, I didn't mean that the way it sounded, Mason."

Devereux said nothing in reply, only giving Reilly a quick reassuring smile of acceptance.

"I'd like to spend the night," Reilly said.

Back at the hotel, they made love again, quietly and slowly. Both were tired, but both craved the intimacy. They fell asleep still embracing.

Three days later, Devereux had a message at the desk to call a Mr. Neuson. There were actually three messages noted an hour apart, all marked urgent.

"Larry, I assume you've seen the proofs."

"Jesus Christ, Mason, this stuff is dynamite! How in the hell did you get these shots anyway?"

"That's what I'm still trying to figure out, Larry. It might have been planned."

"Planned? You mean someone planned this murder — this execution, so you could get photographs? A murder photo opportunity?"

"A crude way to put it, Larry, but maybe. More likely the murder was planned by the other side and the I.R.A. found out about it. It was convenient for their purpose to get me to photograph the event."

"Wait a minute. Who is 'they'?, and for that matter, who was murdered and by whom?"

"The guy that was killed was a Catholic political candidate. Rebel-rouser. Pain in the ass to the Government. He was killed by Protestant paramilitaries. The 'they' I referred to was the I.R.A. I've been working with them. Looks like they knew the hit was going down and let it happen so I could get the shots."

"Working with the I.R.A.? Hope you know what you're doing, Mason. So what do you want done with these photos? I'll tell you, when we're ready to use them in your next book, we can also cut side deals with magazines. We'll consider that when negotiating the book deal. Should be able to take in a six-figure advance with material like this. This is great stuff, Mason."

"Forget your commission for a moment, Larry. Right now I've got to decide what to do with this evidence. I've got proof of who the killers are. I've got to get that to the authorities in some way."

"I'll tell you, Larry, from the time I've spent here I think I have a feel for what's going on. Covering wars you see the average people as the victims. They're the refugees. But we don't know them. There're just those 'other people,' those that are doomed to be shit on. Here you can see what it really means. These are people like us. Belfast looks like any Western city."

"So what are you telling me, Mason?"

Devereux hesitated for some moments. "Well, we've got to pass the information to the Northern Ireland government, or the British. Right now, I don't want them to know where it came from. Got any ideas, Larry?"

Neuson hesitated before responding.

"I know someone in New York who'll re-send a package to whoever you want. They'll not only cut out the trail, but also add some misleading clues. Who do you want them sent to?"

"Send copies to the Royal Ulster Constabulary in Belfast. Get the address from the British consulate. Address it to the chief inspector, nothing more."

"Maybe they can identify this face," Neuson said.

"What do you mean, Larry, they all had ski masks on."

"One of them didn't. Picture's grainy and there's a reflection in the windshield. Might be some way to get sophisticated technology to enhance it."

"Shit. Listen, Larry. Talk to Sergio. He must know somebody who can enhance that shot. I need to ID this guy, and I need it quickly before the police do."

"I'll talk to Sergio right away. I take it you're staying on there?"

"Of course, Larry. It's not done yet. Probably only beginning. I haven't got a book with just these shots."

Two days later Neuson called him. Sergio had enhanced the photograph to where you could clearly distinguish the face. A friend at Cal Tech did the work-up. Not really high tech anymore he was told. The photograph was being faxed to the hotel while he talked with Neuson.

Devereux stared at the enhanced enlargement of the man in the windshield of the van. Even with the added imperfections of the fax transmission, it was unmistakably one of Krill's men he had observed at the garage.

Soon after talking to Neuson, Devereux purchased working clothes typical to the city, and rented a small compact car. He used a false U.S. driver's license carried for such purposes. It was backed up by a U.S. passport in the same name. The pair of credentials had cost him two thousand dollars several years ago in Los Angeles.

Before dawn the next day, he had parked the van up the street from Krill's garage. After identifying Krill's car, Devereux left, returning later that afternoon. He could not maintain a surveillance throughout the day without attracting attention. He would assume Krill would stay at the garage the entire day. Devereux parked more than a block away and used high-powered binoculars. Nothing out of the ordinary happened over three days of surveillance. Krill either went home or to his favorite pub.

At five o'clock on the fourth afternoon, Krill's car left the garage. Devereux followed at some distance. He allowed two vehicles to pull in front between Krill's car and his own. They proceeded west on the Shankill Road. This was the working class Protestant area. The signs of hard times were just as prevalent here as in the Catholic neighborhoods to the south. Poverty was not sectarian. They stopped at a red signal light. Devereux saw a man with his head covered by a ski mask exit the car two up from in front of his. A handgun was plainly visible. Instinctively, Devereux reached for his camera on the seat.

The man with the gun ran up to Krill's car. There were three loud reports that Devereux assumed were gunshots, but it didn't seem to come from the man now pointing his weapon toward Krill. Devereux got out of his car, camera in hand.

A second man then joined the first. Devereux shot with the camera on motor drive. Krill was pulled from his car and pushed roughly into the back of the car stopped behind his.

Devereux was able to get a role of exceptional shots. Neither of the gunmen looked his way, occupied as they were with Krill. With the light now green, the two cars in front of Devereux pulled out from behind Krill's now abandoned car, and sped down the street, taking the first turn available at high speed. The event lasted less than forty seconds.

Devereux left his car and approached the passenger side of Krill's car. He reloaded the camera. What he had heard were shots. Apparently out of view from Devereux, another gunman had gone to the other side of the car. The side windscreen was shattered. A body of a man lay at an angle on the front seat. His upper chest was covered in blood from two wounds. The left eye was gone, now a dark hole where a third bullet had entered. Devereux reloaded and took most of a role of shots in less than another minute.

A lorry pulled to a stop behind Devereux's car and leaned on the horn. He rushed back to his car and drove away. Hopefully the lorry driver would not have the presence of mind to observe him or his car too closely. In all likelihood, the driver would think that Krill's car was simply disabled and maybe drive on as well.

For the second time in only several days, Devereux had been witness to a murder. Would these new shots be of any value as evidence to the police? Should he make that judgment? Would these photos expose him? Was he obstructing justice? What made this different than any project?

To do what he did, he had to violate laws. Usually it was easy to rationalize, since the governments typically involved were fundamentally flawed, almost always corrupt. He could only follow his own concept of ethics. Things were more difficult here in Northern Ireland. This was not the alien landscape of warfare typical to some third world country.

Back at the Europa, Devereux again prepared FedEx and DHL envelops to his agent, tipping the concierge generously to send them off immediately. He ordered a room service dinner with a bottle of Bushmills. Working on his third drink, he returned Brigid Reilly's message late in the evening.

"What have you been doing?" Reilly asked.

"Difficult to say, at least over the phone."

"I think you're being paranoid, Mason."

"Maybe, but let's say that I'm the most experienced in such affairs."

"Speaking of affairs, are we having one, Mason?"

"Don't know. What is the definition of an affair?"

"No absolute, agreed upon definition I know of. But repeatedly fucking a handsome, foreign man, with an exotic profession must certainly qualify. Can I see you?"

"Not tonight, I'm exhausted. I'm going straight to bed. Tomorrow? Lunch?"

"Lunch? Tell you what. I'll knock at your room at twelve sharp. We'll have lunch later if you're up to it," Reilly said seductively.

Devereux could not help but to laugh.

"Twelve it is. Don't worry about lunch, I'll eat a late breakfast. Good night, Brigid."

Brigid Reilly was promptly at his door at twelve the next day. Devereux had taken the initiative to order a cold lunch and bottle of wine before her arrival. They were exceedingly hungry by two o'clock.

Devereux brought the conversation around to business. "The Mullins brothers haven't been back in contact since the Brennan murder. Probably told their superiors how pissed I was. At any rate, I need to push forward, assuming the I.R.A.'s still interested. Get them the word?"

"I will," Reilly replied. "But what have you been doing since then? I haven't seen you."

"I've been working. But tell them I'm impatient. I don't intend to wait much longer. I suggest Liam Mullins get in touch with me within the next two days."

Reilly sensed that Devereux was not telling her everything. But she had come to realize that this man was secretive by nature.

"You still sound pissed at them."

"Pissed? That's not the right word for what I feel. Contempt. That would be closer. Just another bunch of fucking murderers as far as I can see."

"And the Protestant paramilitaries? What the hell are they? Are they the good guys?" Reilly retorted, her voice rising.

"They're the same."

"Then what's your problem, Mason? You're a reporter of sorts aren't you? You photograph violence. Do you always get this emotionally involved?"

Devereux hesitated before lashing out. In the first place she was right. He was always effected by the suffering, but emotionally detached from the perpetrators. He was getting too involved here.

"You're right, Brigid. I guess it's because I care for you and I cannot reconcile your involvement with these assholes."

"Who the fuck are you to judge us? We've been through this argument before. You don't understand our fight. You think we're a bunch a brawling, drunken Irish."

"I'm not judging the Irish. I'm talking about the I.R.A. and their Protestant paramilitary counterparts."

"But a Catholic gets killed by these Protestant paramilitaries and you blame the I.R.A. Some logic that is."

"I thought they were just your clients. Seems they're something more," Devereux said, instantly regretting it.

"I don't need your view on politics here. I thought you of all people could appreciate something of the situation. You've been around, seen what oppression is like. But I was wrong."

"All I'm saying is that the I.R.A. and their Protestant counterparts are nothing new. They're zealots and thugs that kill in the name of their cause."

"I don't want to argue over this, especially now. Besides, I've got to get back to the office."

Reilly gathered her clothes and dressed with her back turned to Devereux. Devereux sat on the bed and brooded.

"Call me later," Reilly said and kissed him on the cheek making a hasty exit from his room.

She was a monstrous pain in the ass, and he knew he was in love with her. This was the first woman to whom he cared to make amends to. Damn, he was pissed at himself for not controlling things better. Love didn't make you blind, just stupid. He would call her later that evening. He would say he was sorry. Emotions aside, he also wondered if she would pass the word to the I.R.A. about contacting him.

It took an hour on the telephone later that night to straighten things out with Brigid. She ended the conversation by telling him how much she enjoyed their 'lunch.' She also told him she had made a call regarding his other matter. He ended by telling her for the first time that he loved her.

Devereux spent the next several days on his laptop computer typing not only his notes, but also text he would use in the book. He sent off disks with file copies to his agent in the event that things went wrong here on his end.

The murder of Krill made the front page three days after his abduction. The lead read:

'The body of John Krill, owner of a service garage, and suspected member of an illegal paramilitary group, was found this morning in front of his home just north of Crumlin Road. Krill had apparently died of strangulation. An unnamed police source suggested that the strangulation appeared to have resulted from hanging. The source also confirmed that there was evidence of apparent torture before the victim was killed. This source indicated that Krill had apparently been the victim of kneecapping, the shooting of the victim through the knees, thereby destroying the joint and crippling the victim. The victim also suffered removal of all ten of his fingernails.'

The article went on to recount the events of several days ago where Krill had apparently been abducted and a colleague murdered while stopped at a traffic signal.

The I.R.A. had apparently exacted revenge for the murder of Paul Brennan.

Larry Neuson called the same day as Krill's murder made the news.

"Un-fucking believable, Mason. Over here, we read on page eight, a four-inch column of these murders, then you send me photos beyond any reporter's wildest dreams of a scoop. You are truly a genius, Mason, and one gutsy fucker, and undoubtedly one lucky bastard. You're the Indiana Jones of photojournalism."

They talked about the book. Neuson told him that he had enough material with these two spectacular murder sequences. With some more background photos to expand certain areas, he told Devereux that it was time to do the writing. This would be a great opportunity to establish himself as more than a photographer. Devereux told Neuson that he was doing just that.

"I'm not done yet, though, Larry. I've got an idea to take this further. I think I can burn this I.R.A. group. That would put a real cap on the book."

"I'm telling you, Mason, you don't need any more. Why risk it?"

"Larry, the name of the game is risk. You don't say that's just good enough and wrap it. There's more here. I've got this feeling that there's a better story than what I have so far."

Devereux called Kevin Flanagan at the newspaper. They arranged to meet for drinks at five. Devereux was circumspect about what he had been doing for the past weeks. He implied to Flanagan that he had made contact with certain I.R.A. types. Some interesting results had been produced, but he was not specific. He then made his request to Flanagan.

"Don't be playin' that game, Mason. Take what they're givin' you and leave it at that. These bastards play rough. Sure and you'll be killed you mess around like you're thinkin.' I ain't goin' to help you with this foolishness."

"Come on Kevin, you're a journalist. Journalists take risks. These I.R.A. goons are bad asses, but they're not always the brightest people in the world. All I'm asking is to nose around and recommend somebody qualified to do surveillance. Somebody not squeamish about shitting on the I.R.A."

Kevin took a long pull on his glass of stout.

"All right, Mason, I'll see what I can do, only because I know you'll try it anyway on your own."

Two days later, Flanagan called back. He may have found someone. The man came recommended through inquiries to people he knew in the Royal Ulster Constabulary.

"What's the pretext you used, Kevin? What's the guy expecting?"

"I implied something about a friend and a messy divorce. Needed someone who could blend in, take pictures. Must be dependable."

Flanagan told Devereux he had set a meeting at a certain pub that evening. Flanagan had a description of the man.

Devereux and Flanagan arrived at the pub fifteen minutes ahead of the appointed time. At fifteen minutes past that time, both were assuming they had been stood up. It was then that a gray haired man with a decided limp approached their table.

"My name is William Larkin. I believe you were expecting me."

The man extended his hand and sat down.

Devereux was apprehensive. The guy seemed too old, probably sixty at least, with sparse gray hair. He had a bad limp. After ordering the man a pint, Devereux asked the man to expand on his background and qualifications.

"Born here in Belfast. R.U.C., eighteen years, retired with a disability pension as a result of a wound received in the line of duty. The limp if you will, gentlemen. I.R.A. sniper. Prior to that, I was in the army, retired as a master sergeant after twenty years. Served all over the world in the military police," Larkin concluded in his concise, clipped manner.

They chatted about his past. Larkin was not particularly expansive, but both Devereux and Flanagan were fascinated when they asked questions about his career. Larkin told his stories with remarkable detail and did not at all make himself out to be the centerpiece of each event. All the same, Devereux got the impression of a clear-eyed, objective professional.

"Very impressive career, Mr. Larkin," Devereux concluded.

He was initially hesitant about the guy's age, but his credentials were ideal, and he was genuinely impressed. He would do. But would he want the job?

"But we haven't been completely honest about the job, Mr. Larkin. It's not a divorce situation. It's a surveillance assignment alright, but on the I.R.A."

Larkin jolted back as if slapped across the face.

"Who the fuck are you blokes?"

"The names are right enough, Mr. Larkin. This is Kevin Flanagan. He's a newspaper reporter out of the Belfast office of the *Times*. I'm a freelance photojournalist."

Larkin stared at Devereux and said nothing.

Devereux pushed forward, "I don't assume your sympathies are such that you would have any problem with going against the I.R.A."

"Obviously I wouldn't. Like to see the lot of them hung. Thugs, murderers, cheap scum. The average Catholic wants nothing to do with them. But I'm not interested, gentlemen."

"Why's that, Mr. Larkin?" Devereux asked.

Larkin drained his glass and prepared to leave.

"Because, you gentlemen know nothing about what you're getting into."

Looking at Flanagan, "You — you from Belfast?" Flanagan nodded.

"And you, you're American?"

Devereux also nodded.

"My God. Mr. Flanagan you should know better. Mr. Devereux, you are unbelievably naive. I give you credit for getting this far. At any rate, I'm not interested. Thank you for the drink, and —-"

"I would have thought you a more thorough interrogator Mr. Larkin. You're saying 'no' prematurely," Devereux responded.

"In the first place, Mr. Flanagan is an acquaintance and associate. He's not in favor of the idea. I'm the principle doing the hiring. I'm the one you'd be working for. I won't go into my credentials, but suffice it to say that I have been involved with photographing wars all over the world. Nasty little wars, with nasty assholes like your I.R.A. I've been shot at, imprisoned, and threatened with death more than once. In short, Mr. Larkin, I'm no virgin."

"Well, that may be, Mr. Devereux, but I still don't think I'm interested. Thank you all the same."

"Aren't you interested in what the assignment pays, Mr. Larkin?" Devereux replied as Larkin was about to rise from his seat.

According to Kevin Flanagan's sources, Larkin had retired from the R.U.C. five years ago as a result of the hip injury becoming more debilitating. His wife had died of cancer ten years ago. There was a grown daughter now living in the United

States. He lived alone. He drank too much. He gambled heavily, football matches and local card games. Unfortunately, he was unlucky, and un-talented respectively. There was rumor of debt and even problems with loan sharks.

Larkin took pause. Pride would not allow him to ask what was being offered. Devereux understood and did not wait for a response.

"The pay is five hundred pounds a week."

Larkin settled back into his chair.

"That's serious money I'll admit, Mr. Devereux. But it's my life I'll be risking."

"I'll make it six hundred, Mr. Larkin. And if we get lucky with some real interesting stuff, there could be a bonus in it for you."

This was stupid Larkin thought to himself. He was out of this warfare. The I.R.A. was now only something he read about. But the question was why not. He was in debt up to his eyeballs. The pension was good for the rent, food, but didn't cover the bar tabs. Why not get back into it. This had been where he felt alive. Life wasn't worth much lately anyway. The money really made the choice easy.

"Because I need the money, you have a deal, Mr. Devereux."

Over the next several days, there were news reports of two other killings of Protestants. Devereux recognized the newspaper pictures as two men he photographed at Krill's garage.

Chapter Twelve

Devereux spent the following day briefing Larkin. He filled him in on the background of his involvement and the motivation for doing this book on the *troubles*. He told him about his I.R.A. 'guides.' He told him about photographing the Brennan murder, and Krill's abduction. He told Larkin about meeting Michael Flynn, but did not tell him about Reilly.

"Christ Almighty. I'm truly impressed, Mr. Devereux. You're no amateur. But I still think you may have a death wish. Michael Flynn, you say? You actually met the bastard? That's interesting. We, the R.U.C. I mean, always thought he was an old dinosaur. Thought him out of the fight being a professor and all. Now you tell me you think he's maybe a big shot callin' the shots in the IRA? A real killer he was. At least in the old days."

Devereux raised his eyebrows, "Are we talking about the same Flynn? This guy's a professor in Dublin. Little guy with a bad limp, worse than yours. Looks the academic type to me."

"Know how he got that limp? Took a bullet just like me. Ended his career in the field. That was a long time ago, in the early years of the *troubles*. A right nasty bastard he was."

"Then how is it that he ended up as a professor at University College in Dublin?" Devereux asked.

"I don't really know. I do know that he was a legend in the I.R.A. Credited with a fair number of murders. Never arrested. But I don't think it would be wise for him to ever set foot in Northern Ireland again. I had heard there were still old murder warrants outstanding," Larkin said.

"There was a long standing argument with Dublin over ex-tradition years ago, back in the seventies. Dublin never relented. They said the case was superficial. Word had it that they didn't like the pressure being applied by Whitehall."

"Does the R.U.C. know what he does for the I.R.A. today?" Devereux asked.

"I was just an ordinary copper, Mr. Devereux. Michael Flynn's common knowledge but the brass didn't confide in me. They may know. British intelligence probably does. Hard to imagine a fanatic like Flynn not being involved somehow."

"I was only told he was an advisor. I suspected some leader-ship with Sinn Fein. What do you think?"

"I donno. Could be. Wouldn't think someone the likes of him would turn to politics. But you wouldn't think him a professor either," Larkin responded.

As if on schedule, Devereux received a call from Liam Mul-lins the next day. He was given an address of a pub some dis-tance to the west. He called Larkin immediately. Larkin would arrive early. Before ringing off, Devereux asked Larkin if could blend in with a working class Catholic neighborhood.

"What you mean is, will I be able to respond to the type of questions that will properly categorize me? What neighborhood I live in, what newspaper I read, what football club do I like. You never asked, Mr. Devereux, but I am a Catholic. Not all R.U.C. are Protestants. Won't be a problem."

Devereux met with the Mullins brothers. Liam said that he had been instructed to cooperate by attempting to get Devereux more photographs.

"Some other Protestant paramilitary group I assume. From the newspaper accounts, Krill's U.F.F. must not really exist any-more, what with Krill and two of his men murdered," Devereux said sarcastically.

"This is a war, Mr. Devereux. On one side are the Protestants like Krill, the government, and the British. On the other side there is only the I.R.A."

"Too bad I can only see it from the I.R.A. side."

"Isn't that a problem you've had in other wars, Mr. Deve-reux?" Liam Mullins said with a broad smile.

"Fair enough, Liam. So what's next?"

"We've got a line on a possible shipment of arms for the U.F.F. that's coming in sometime within the next few days. It'll mean another stakeout. Hear it's also going to turn colder. Interested?"

"Of course, Liam."

The Mullins brothers would pick him up. They would phone tomorrow a half hour before the set time and tell Devereux where to meet them. They left the pub shortly after Devereux. Larkin followed them in his old nondescript compact sedan. The Mullins brothers were not experienced. Larkin was. He was able to stay well back. Liam dropped Sean off at his flat, then drove on to his own.

For the next three nights, Devereux suffered the damp, cold winter weather coming in off the North Atlantic. He was situated in the loft of a warehouse overlooking an unoccupied berth in the Pollock Dock area of the harbor. Larkin on the other hand had the easier time of following Liam Mullins during the afternoon before he joined Devereux in the late morning.

Larkin called Devereux on the third day. He had some information. They met for dinner before Devereux would again go to the docks with the Mullins.

After two whiskeys, Larkin said, "The Mullins brothers don't have a record according to my sources on the force. They're I.R.A. of course, but apparently in a low level capacity. Their files indicate they're cousins of the wife of a known I.R.A. man by the name of O'Donovan. O'Donovan runs a pub in a Catholic working class neighborhood here in Belfast. Seems your friends currently associate with their cousin's husband. Followed them there yesterday."

"Can you find out about this O'Donovan?"

"Already have. Name's Garrett O'Donovan. My contact on the force showed me a picture so I can recognize him. Good-looking guy, late twenties. Father was a known I.R.A. sympathizer. His older brother was an I.R.A. gunman. The brother was killed in a getaway after a bombing. Shot by British troops at a roadblock."

Larkin continued, "O'Donovan himself is suspected of I.R.A. involvement as part of an active service unit, but he's never been convicted. He was suspected as being part of a unit commanded by a bloke named Paddy McCullough. But since McCullough's death, they're not sure what O'Donovan has been up to. Arrested a couple of times. Spent a few months in Long Kesh on a murder charge along with McCullough, but the charges were eventually dropped for lack of evidence."

"So what do you want me to do?" Larkin asked.

Devereux asked Larkin if there was a way to set up a surveillance on O'Donovan's pub. Something that could be sustained over a period of time. Larkin said he would see what he could do and report back the next day.

Devereux spent a third uneventful and bitterly cold night at the docks with the Mullins brothers. The next day, Larkin reported that there was a vacant flat that faced into the alley running behind O'Donovan's pub. The landlady had shown him the room. The rear entrance of the pub could be viewed from a distance of less than a hundred meters.

"If you rent the flat, what's your cover?" Devereux asked.

"Retired factory worker. Disability pension. Industrial accident. I assume I can become a patron at the pub. Check out the inside from time to time. Watch the rear door from the flat window. I'll need a long-range lens. I assume you'll want pictures?"

Devereux told him to go ahead and rent the flat. He would set him up with camera equipment tomorrow and show him the basics.

The meeting of the Provincial Irish Republican Army leadership counsel took place at a typical rural location just over the border between Northern Ireland and the Republic. This time the location was in County Donegal to the west.

What amounted to an insurgency war, had been waged for over twenty-five years in Northern Ireland. Little had changed politically. The people were exhausted, the economy perhaps irreparably stunted by a quarter century of sectarian violence. Sympathy from both the Protestant and Catholic populations was almost nonexistent. Views had not changed, only the resolve to continue this collective bloodletting. Only the political forces and the active combatants in the northern six counties had the will to continue the fight. In the Republic to the south, any strong support for a union of the entire island had long since disappeared.

As with the Catholic population as a whole, so too was the leadership of the Provincial I.R.A. divided and exhausted with the continued struggle. On the one extreme were Terrance Dolan and Gerry Adams that were increasingly moving toward some sort of settlement with the British and the government in Northern Ireland. Dolan was highly respected, and as Commander-In-Chief, he exercised considerable influence. Adams was President of Sinn Fein, ostensibly a political party, but what had become the public face of the I.R.A. It was Adams that had engineered the original contacts with the British. Credit was generally given to Adams for also engineering the removal of British troops from an active policing role on the streets of Belfast and Derry. It was perhaps the only evidence of achievement the I.R.A. could claim in the twenty-five years of war.

To the opposite extreme was Michael Flynn. Flynn was cut from the mold of the old patriots. Single minded. Willing to give one's life. Spoke of Ireland as if it was one's flesh and blood mother. In Flynn there was a living legend, a figure larger than life. On the one hand he was a soldier, a leader in the field, someone who had taken more than one life of the enemy and been wounded himself in combat. Educated and articulate, his leadership carried considerable weight.

In between these extremes were seemingly average men with strong senses of history, purpose, ideology, and sectarian identification. These men mirrored the toll the war had taken on the populace. To these men, Dolan's and Adams recommendations for continuing negotiations with the British held the prospect of a return to some sort of normality to life. But they could also not ignore what seemed a voice of their collective conscience as proclaimed by Michael Flynn.

This meeting was to discuss the possible declaration of a broader cessation of hostilities by the I.R.A. As Gerry Adams explained, he had already broached the idea to the British. The

British implied that increased restraint and commitment from the I.R.A. would soon lead to a gradual reduction in British troops from Northern Ireland. They also implied that subsequent agreements could lead to the total withdrawal of British troops. The meeting quickly proved contentious. Adams spoke first. As usual, he was brief, direct, low key, and persuasive. He argued that this was the first opportunity of real gain in the struggle. The British were looking for a way out of the dilemma of Northern Ireland.

Dolan contributed his wholehearted support to pursuing a cease-fire. He added the more pragmatic reason that it was becoming more financially difficult to sustain operations. The war was increasing yielding negative support from the Catholic population and producing no tangible results.

"There is increasing concern about control of field operations. This latest unauthorized incident of the killing of this U.F.F. bunch is a prime example," Dolan said. "I am assuming it was unauthorized since the action was inconsistent with any directive from this council. Most assuredly some of our lads did the killings. That means there are factions operating out there that could upset any progress."

With that parting comment he turned the floor over to Michael Flynn. As Chief of Staff, Flynn was the senior person responsible for field operations.

"My, my, Terrance, don't play the politician on us. I expect that from Adams, but not you. Are you accusing me of something? Are you specifically accusing me of ordering the killing of this John Krill and his U.F.F. gunmen?"

Flynn rose from the table as was his style when embarking on a tirade.

"The truth is that someone took unauthorized initiative in the reprisal against Krill. I said reprisal. You didn't mention that, but as we all know, Terrance, Krill's bunch murdered that politician Brennan in Belfast. I might add, murdered him in broad daylight with his staff as witnesses. Executed him with a bullet to the head right in front of several women. Wanted to make a statement they did. Well, some of our lads made their own statement. Weren't going to wait till we here debated action."

Dolan seethed. This sonofabitch Flynn had almost assuredly ordered the attack. Men in the active service units would never take such independent action, and all at the table knew it.

Flynn continued, "The question gentlemen, is would we have directed, or even approved such a request for reprisal? I wonder. I suspect we'd debate how it would effect these so-called negotiations. What have we become? We've become old and tired of the fight. The fight to rid us of British rule has been going on for centuries. It's not our right to give it up because we're tired. Shall it be said that hundreds of years of struggle for Irish independence ended in the late twentieth century out of exhaustion?"

"Don't you think those before us suffered the same feelings of despair? Nothing was achieved prior to the twentieth century. In all the hundreds of years of resisting the British, there has been only one real achievement — the creation of the Republic of Ireland. The last major achievement will be the inclusion of the remaining six counties in that Republic, making Ireland whole. If it is not to be in the twentieth, then let it be in the twenty-first century."

Flynn's oratory could bring forth tears from a corpse, but his associates had heard this too many times. To the priest that preached an over zealous sermon, one accorded respect for his position but did not change how he lived. To Flynn, several of the governing Army Counsel felt that a termination of hostilities was the only possibility of a future for the six counties. Continued warfare would leave the province behind in economic opportunity. The Catholics represented the majority of the poor, so they and their subsequent generations would suffer the most. The international business community would simply write them off. That process was already evident.

Dolan called a vote of the counsel as to pursuing broadened elements of the cease-fire and furthering peace negotiations under the direction of Gerry Adams. It was the most eventful moment in the life of the Provincial Irish Republican Army. Only Flynn and two others voted nay.

Dolan proclaimed the official result of the vote. He then officially instructed Gerry Adams to proceed with negotiations with the British. Adams was given authority to offer further concessions as bargaining leverage. As he was about to adjourn the meeting, Flynn rose to speak.

"Mr. Dolan. I wish to make a statement to this counsel."

Everyone resumed their seats.

"There was a similar situation to this many years ago that gave rise to this Provincial Irish Republican Army. We sometimes forget that we developed out of frustration with that earlier movement that seemingly sought independence from the British, but did not deliver. That movement, the original Irish Republican Army, turned to a political ideology that was both irrelevant to the Irish people and impotent in achieving the results of uniting with the South. Regrettably, I feel we are again at such a cross roads."

The room was absolutely quiet.

"Gentlemen, I have great respect for all within this room. We have fought Ireland's enemies together. We have sacrificed and suffered together, and that must count for something. But I am ashamed with the lack of resolve of this Council. Irish patriots before us endured. Countless numbers of them died for Ireland. You cannot in good conscience call yourself patriots if you get in bed with the British."

There were several angry responses, and some rose from their chairs.

Flynn ignored them and continued, "What have we tangibly accomplished? Adams and Dolan here talk of gains to be solidified. What gains? Because the British no longer patrol Belfast streets? That's because we curtailed operations. No gentlemen, this is surrender pure and simple. It has always been our tactic to fight a war of attrition. We are a guerrilla force. It is our mission to harass the enemy until they lose the will to continue. In that regard we have been winning. Mr. Adams acknowledges that himself. Pressure by the British populous has steadily increased with continued demands to resolve the Northern Ireland problem. Whitehall has shown far less support for union with Northern Ireland in the last several years. Yet here we are throwing in the towel when our opponent is reeling on the ropes."

Everyone sensed that some momentous confrontation was occurring. All eyes held on Michael Flynn.

"I cannot in participate in this cooperation with the British enemy that this counsel has just voted to condone. I will not surrender. I love Ireland too much. Therefore, I, Michael Flynn, do declare my resignation from this body, and from the position of its command of operations. May God and true Irishmen forgive all of you."

Most of the table rose with expressions of disbelief. Other than Dolan and Adams, most tried to engage Flynn as he limped his way out of the room waving away attempts to dissuade him.

Flynn left the farmhouse for his waiting car.

The remainder of the meeting degenerated into factional bickering. On the one hand, Dolan and Adams argued that Flynn was a dinosaur, an obstacle to progress, and his resignation was for the best. Dolan said he knew that Flynn had ordered the Krill reprisal without the Counsel's approval. On the other side of the argument, lead by a couple of other 'dinosaurs,' there was concern about the loss of someone of Flynn's stature. Several were equally repelled to any compromise with the British government even though they voted to proceed with negotiations.

No successor to Flynn's position was appointed.

Peter Sullivan and Brennan Magee had been working for two months at the Opera House. Posing as Protestants required constant vigilance. Sullivan had become used to the routine, plying his trade as an electrician. Magee was getting restless. Most of all he hated the maintenance superintendent, Quinn McLeash. To Magee, McLeash was just another fat-assed boss who did nothing himself, but liked to tell other people what to do. He was therefore encouraged to hear that O'Donovan had ordered them to find a place within the Opera House to secure a cache of weapons.

This was a bullshit assignment so far. He felt just like any other working shit. Shouldn't have gotten mixed up with this O'Donovan. This wasn't a regular active service unit. With this peace thing quieting things down, it had seemed the best opportunity to see some real action. Magee was expecting something big after that special training in America. Instead, he was fixing stage equipment and repairing toilets. To make matters worse, he was left out of the hit on that Krill and his bunch. Whatever was being planned, he hoped he'd at least have a chance to pop that fuck McLeash.

Devereux joined Larkin the following day at the newly leased flat. It was a dreary room with well-worn furniture, a stained and chipped kitchen sink, and a gas stove that looked pre-world war two vintage. Two windows looked out onto a trash-strewn alleyway.

Devereux was however impressed with the view afforded to the rear of the pub. From the window, excellent close-ups could be obtained with a 300mm lens. Devereux set up a tripod with the big lens mounted on a camera. He then gave Larkin a crash course in the basics of photography and the mechanics of the equipment. A table of camera settings would provide Larkin adjustments for varying light conditions.

Devereux felt the rush of things happening. He sensed he was on to something here. There was always a point on any project where events started to come together in an ever-quickening sequence. Even the surveillance on the docks had paid off. Using infrared film, Devereux had captured shots of what were purported to be arms being off-loaded from a small boat. Some markings on the crates could actually be read in the photographs.

Returning to the car after getting the photos, Devereux confronted Liam Mullins. "Liam, tell the I.R.A. that I want to see their hit on this arms cache."

"What?"

"You heard me. Either this arms shipment is bogus, or the I.R.A. will plan an attack to capture or destroy the weapons. They wouldn't have this kind of intel and use it just for PR photographs. Assuming I'm right, I want to photograph it. If this was staged, I'm done with the project."

"You can't threaten the I.R.A., Devereux," Liam Mullins said indignantly.

"The fuck I can't. I just did in fact. I'm not impressed with its reputation. I've seen much better. Just give whoever you report to the message," Devereux said. He was less in need of their continued help at this point.

Devereux got back to his room at five in the morning. He took a shot of whiskey to warm up. The bed was inviting. The telephone rang. It was Larkin calling to tell him that Liam Mullins showed up at the rear door of the pub a short time ago. Spent half an hour inside and left.

Garrett O'Donovan appeared to be their contact.

Flynn called the pub. Assuming always the possibility of a tap, the message was only a signal for O'Donovan to call from a public telephone to a prearranged public telephone in Dublin at a precise time.

"Mr. Flynn. I was about to contact you," O'Donovan said.

"About what, Garrett?" Flynn asked.

"About this photographer, Devereux. The bastard's getting bloody pushy. That shipment of arms came in. He got the pictures. Now he says he wants to photograph us goin' to get 'em," O'Donovan answered. "Says it was either a set-up, or he expects that we'll stage a raid."

"Cheeky bastard," Flynn said, "But we'll deal with him later. Right now I need to meet with you. The matter's urgent. I'll meet you in Armagh. You know the town?"

O'Donovan smiled, "Know it well, Mr. Flynn."

"Meet me at six tonight at the Raven's Tavern. You'll be needin' certain items."

Flynn instructed him to bring certain weapons.

At one o'clock in the afternoon, O'Donovan left through the rear door of his pub carrying a small satchel. Larkin left hurriedly in time to follow O'Donovan's car as it pulled out into the street. O'Donovan was soon on the motorway traveling south out of Belfast with Larkin following.

An hour later, O'Donovan pulled to the curb in front of a tract of flats in the city of Armagh and entered the building. Larkin parked a short distance away.

Larkin waited for an hour. O'Donovan was still inside the apartment building. He decided to chance getting to a telephone and calling Devereux. He was back within fifteen minutes. O'Donovan's car was still parked in the same place.

After a brief conversation with Larkin, Devereux decided to drive south to join in the surveillance. Larkin gave directions, and the name of a local pub he had passed to rendezvous at later if O'Donovan moved before Devereux arrived.

Devereux arrived in Armagh. Following Larkin's instructions, he drove past Larkin's parked car, swung around, then parked behind him. He took his cameras packed in a shoulder bag and joined Larkin in his car.

Devereux and Larkin had been watching the building for over two hours. It was cold and boring, the routine broken only by moving the car to a new vantage points twice to avoid attention. Making small talk, Larkin learned about some of Devereux's previous work. Devereux likewise learned something of Larkin and life as a cop in Northern Ireland.

Several hours later, with sunlight fading, O'Donovan left the apartment building alone. They did not know that he was only with his woman friend, called from her place of employment to return to her flat for a few of hours of afternoon sex. They followed O'Donovan at a considerable distance. O'Donovan soon parked his car and entered a small pub in the center of Armagh. Larkin parked across the street at a spot from which he could watch the entrance. After a few minutes, Larkin suggested he go inside to see what O'Donovan was up to. Devereux suspected he wanted a drink, but the tactic made sense. He couldn't go himself without causing some attention as a foreigner.

This project was becoming one continual surveillance on cold nights in front of Irish pubs, trying to get photographs in the poorest of light conditions. In this case there was almost no light, only what came from a single, curtained window. Equipped as usual for night work, one camera was loaded with very fast film in order to enhance the effect of what little light must exist. The camera was fitted with the 200mm lens. Devereux assumed a reclined position that put his eyes just above the top of the door. From almost any distance, the car would appear unoccupied.

To be thorough, Devereux took shots of everyone entering the pub. At a quarter to seven, a short man with a limp entered. Ten minutes later, Larkin exited, obviously hurrying to the car.

"Did you see that man, the one with the limp, that entered a little bit ago?" Larkin asked Devereux.

"Yeah. Couldn't see his face, though. Recognize him?"

"Could be Michael Flynn from your description. Never seen a picture of him myself. Limp's far worse than mine, just like you said. At any rate, he sat with O'Donovan. Just the two of them," Larkin then proceeded to describe the man he saw in the pub in more detail.

"Sounds like him. Hell of a chance he's taken coming across the border into Northern Ireland," Devereux responded.

Thirty minutes later, O'Donovan and the man they assumed to be Flynn, left the pub. They both got into O'Donovan's car and drove off. Larkin followed O'Donovan southeast out of Armagh.

After only a couple of miles, O'Donovan turned onto a side road. Larkin turned off the headlamps and drove at a crawl. The sky was unusually clear, and there was a three quarter moon to help. They passed a small cottage that was dark. Ahead they could see O'Donovan's headlights stop at another farmhouse that was well lit outside, maybe a few hundred meters down the road.

Larkin pulled to the side of the road and stopped the car.

"What do you want to do?"

"Back up and park well up the drive from the cottage and off the road if you can," Devereux said, grabbing his cameras.

"Are you armed, Bill?"

"You bet your arse I am."

Devereux and Larkin worked their way up the road toward the house where O'Donovan had stopped. Close to the house, they left the road and crawled on all fours through some high, wet grass, concealing themselves behind a low stone fence. They were no more than forty meters from the house. O'Donovan's car along with two others was parked in front of the house, lit clearly by a bright porch light.

Devereux took a number of shots of the house and the license tags on the automobiles. After some minutes, Larkin pulled a flask and took a stiff shot of whiskey.

"Chase away the cold," Larkin said and offered Devereux a drink.

Minutes later Devereux had no question about the identity of the man with the limp as he caught Flynn's face through the lens emerging from the house and walking toward the car. O'Donovan seemed to back out of the door cautiously, closing it slowly behind him. He was also carrying a long barreled handgun.

O'Donovan joined Flynn and pulled the car back onto the road, accelerating rapidly.

"What the fuck do you make of that?" Devereux asked rhetorically. "Any idea who lives here?"

"Not a clue. Thank God they didn't stay long, though. Laying in cold wet grass with some crazy photographer is not a pleasant night,"

"One hell of a night, Bill. Do you realize what we got. I've got pictures of the legendary Michael Flynn, consorting with a known I.R.A. man, and carrying a gun. But even more interesting, he was here in Northern Ireland where he's still a wanted man."

"And by the way, Bill, the word's photojournalist. That's why we freeze our ass off and lay in wet grass and other shit. Just lookin' for the shot. Photographers are pussies who do their work in nice warm studios shooting naked women and such. Photojournalists shoot people getting fucked over."

Devereux was feeling uncommonly good. Larkin was just feeling wet and cold.

O'Donovan saw Flynn enter the pub. He was short and slight, wearing a trench coat and hunting cap. The limp was pronounced, giving him a left to right gait as he walked. It was hard to believe that this man was once a killer, and still ordered others to kill.

Inside the small pub, Flynn and O'Donovan huddled in a far corner. O'Donovan wondered what Flynn wanted. Flynn was like a magnet, you couldn't get away from him. He was at the heart of what was Irish. But he was also dangerous. Siding with Flynn could be very dangerous. He had talked of going against the I.R.A. He had forced O'Donovan to choose. Either way was dangerous. At least with Flynn there wouldn't be any cease-fire and quitting. With Flynn there would always be war.

"You and your boys have been doin' grand work, Garrett. Taking care of that bastard Krill and his henchmen was a professional piece of work," Flynn said to O'Donovan. "Fitting deaths for the murderers of that young man, Brennan."

"Did we know that Krill was goin' to kill Brennan?" O'Donovan asked Flynn.

"No, lad. Intelligence had it that they intended to break things up at Brendan's office. Supposed to have been only a couple of Krill's people," Flynn answered, then moved away from the subject.

"How are your two people at the Opera House getting along, Garrett?" Flynn continued.

"Fine. Restless, at least Magee is, but they'll be doin' okay, Sir."

"Good. See to it though, Garrett. Make sure this Magee understands orders, Magee's a heady bastard. Needs a firm hand."

"What are we up to, Sir?"

"We are about larger business, Garrett. The time for decisive action has come. Effective right now, we are no longer under orders from the Provincial Irish Republican Army. I have resigned my position so that I can take up the fight without the constraints of those weaklings that have betrayed Ireland."

"Garrett, yesterday the Counsel voted to continue with the cease fire and to enter into serious negotiations. Those negotiations mean giving up the armed struggle. Without waging war, Irish independence will forever die, and Ireland will never be made whole."

Flynn continued, "We cannot betray our history, Garrett. Among the many without the will, there must always stand a few that carry the fight. We are those chosen few, Garrett. Are you and your men with me?"

Garrett hesitated before answering yes.

Yes, because he could not deny the likes of Flynn. *Yes,* because a life without the recognition and authority, without the excitement of the violence, was not imaginable. And *yes* because it might be more dangerous to say *no.*

"I knew I had made the right choice in you, Garrett," Flynn said. "Now, did you bring the weapon?"

"Yes, Sir. It's in the car."

Flynn laid down money to cover the drinks and told O'Donovan they were leaving. O'Donovan made brief eye contact with an older man seated at the bar. Something bothered O'Donovan about the man. Had the man been watching them?

During the short drive, Flynn told O'Donovan where they were going and what was to be done. O'Donovan was visibly shaken by the enormity of what Flynn intended to do. They arrived at the farmhouse fifteen minutes later. Flynn told O'Donovan that Terrance Dolan was expecting them as a result of an earlier call.

A bodyguard answered the door at the farmhouse. His hand rested on his weapon in a shoulder holster as he scrutinized Flynn and O'Donovan. They were escorted into a sitting room where there was another young man standing, also with a shoulder holster weapon. Dolan entered moments after.

"Well, Michael. I hardly thought there would be anything more to say after your surprise yesterday. Change of heart perhaps?" Dolan said with some sarcasm.

"There are certain things to resolve and things to transition, Terrance. We should probably discuss this privately," Flynn said, nodding to Dolan's two men and O'Donovan.

"You two take Mr. Flynn's associate to the kitchen. There's fresh coffee there,"

He closed twin sliding doors leading to the entry vestibule. Dolan assumed Flynn needed to hand over certain sensitive information related to operations.

"Whisky, Michael?"

"No thank you, Terrance, but you go ahead."

Dolan poured himself a drink from an array of bottles on an armoire. "I'll tell you, Michael, I hate to see you leave, but you have been a major problem lately." Dolan took a seat across the small room.

"Then why do you hate to see me leave?"

"For one thing, your stature among the commanders. Everyone has you as a bloody legend. Your position as Chief of Staff makes it look bad that the top leadership is split. Most of all, however, I wonder what you're going to do. Are you going to openly oppose us?" Dolan said.

"Of course I'm going to oppose you. More than that, I'm going to actively oppose you, Terrance, and Adams as well, and any of the others that will sell out Ireland." Flynn opened the flap on his well-worn briefcase. He extracted a nine-millimeter Czech-made automatic, fitted with a silencer.

Dolan made to rise. "Remain seated, Terrance."

"You're a fucking coward, Terrance. You sold out to that political shit Adams. Fact is you've become something of the politician yourself. You've lost your Irish soul, Terrance."

"What do you intend — —" Dolan was cut short by two rounds in his chest. Flynn fired a third into Terrance Dolan's forehead. The silenced rounds still made a frightfully loud popping noise.

Opening the sliding doors slowly, Flynn could hear the voices of the men in the kitchen. They had obviously not heard the gunshots. He walked down the hallway to the kitchen as quickly as his limp permitted.

Upon entering the kitchen all three men looked toward him. Flynn's first shot took one man down still holding a mug of coffee. The second attempted to unholster his weapon as Flynn let loose a series of shots. Two found their mark. Flynn then finished both with shots to the head.

Flynn handed the weapon to O'Donovan. "See if there is anyone else in the house." He assumed O'Donovan knew what he must do.

O'Donovan was overwhelmed by the murders. Flynn was everything everyone said he was. And he still was a monstrous force. The killings made O'Donovan feel more confident that he had chosen sides correctly. He took the weapon and ascended the staircase.

Moments later, Flynn heard a telltale pop, like compressed air escaping. There had been someone else, and O'Donovan had shot that person with the silenced weapon. Flynn and O'Donovan gathered their coats and left the house. They had touched nothing, leaving no fingerprints. O'Donovan pulled the front door shut behind him using a handkerchief.

Chapter Thirteen

Devereux wanted to determine who lived in the farm-house that Flynn had visited. Since they had two cars, he sent Larkin back to Belfast. He then took a room at a small inn in Armagh. He would see what he could find out in the morning, perhaps get some daylight photographs.

Devereux did get photographs, but not what he had intended. After a hearty Irish breakfast, he arrived at the farm-house early in the morning. That is to say, he got no closer than a quarter mile. The entire lane was cordoned off by the police. Devereux parked his car and took his cameras.

"Excuse me, but do you know what's going on?" Devereux asked a middle-aged man dressed in work clothes.

"Can't say that I do. Rumor is it's got somethin' to do with Terrance Dolan's house," the man said.

"Who's Dolan?"

"Mister Dolan's an important man hereabouts. A solicitor. Owns a farm a wee piece down that road."

Devereux got long distance photos of covered bodies being carried out on gurneys.

Two hours later, O'Donovan was back in his room at the Europa. Devereux called Flanagan at the newspaper office. "Kevin? This is Mason."

Before Devereux could continue, Flanagan interrupted him, "I tried to reach you earlier. Seen the papers yet?"

"No. Why?"

"Just get a paper and call me back. I've got to meet a dead-line. Talk to you in a little while."

Flanagan had been up all night working on the lead story for the early editions. He was still busy on putting together material to run in the next day's edition. He'd see Devereux later.

Devereux went to the lobby and purchased a copy of the *Times*. The headline read 'IRA LEADER MURDERED, ADAMS ESCAPES.' It was Kevin Flanagan's byline:

'COUNTY ARMAGH, NORTHERN IRELAND — The increase in sectarian violence during the last few weeks continued last night and perhaps reached new heights. In Armagh, the bodies of four people were discovered in a farmhouse a short distance outside of that town. The bodies have been identified as those of Terrance Dolan, his wife Emily, John MacManus, and Patrick Dillon.

Preliminary police reports indicate that all four victims were shot at close range in an execution style. All had wounds to the head. Emily Dolan was apparently murdered in her bed. The bodies were discovered at nine p.m. last night after police received an anonymous call to investigate the residence. An unnamed police source said that two of the dead were armed, but that there was no indication that they had used their weapons.

Terrance Dolan was a local solicitor in Armagh, but widely rumored to occupy a leadership role in the Provincial Irish Republican Army. MacManus and Dillon had known I.R.A. associations according to police.

In a potentially related incident, Sinn Fein President, Gerry Adams, escaped injury from an attempted assassination in East Belfast. Adams was apparently leaving a restaurant when unidentified assailants attacked with automatic weapons. Bodyguards with Adams allegedly returned fire although police made no arrests of Adam's group. An associate of Adams was seriously wounded.

The murder of Terrance Dolan and the attempted murder of Gerry Adams follow recent incidents of escalating violence in Northern Ireland. Several weeks ago, Paul Brennan, a militant Catholics rights activist, and candidate for the Belfast City Counsel, was brutally murdered in broad daylight by masked assailants. A week later, John Krill, an alleged leader of an Ulster Freedom Fighter's group, an illegal Protestant paramilitary organization, was murdered. An autopsy reportedly revealed evidence of torture. Two others, known to be associates of Krill, were also murdered within a few days.'

The rest of Flanagan's article held no further information.

"Sonofabitch," thought Devereux. He and Larkin must have been there close to the time of the murders. Did Flynn narrowly escape the same fate as Dolan, or did he kill Dolan himself? O'Donovan's presence with a gun suggested the later. He needed to talk to Larkin.

He did not have to wait long. Larkin had also read the newspaper. "What the fuck's going on, Mr. Devereux? You're into some real shit. And I'm in it too now."

"Tell me this, Bill, you're an ex-cop. Could Flynn and O'Donovan have killed those people? Would we have heard a silenced weapon?"

"Had the same thought myself. And no, we probably wouldn't have heard a silenced weapon from where we were. They could have done it. We were there at about seven-thirty. The papers said the police discovered the bodies at nine," Larkin said in a manner as if thinking out loud.

Larkin continued his thoughts. "The most interesting fact is the victims were shot at close range. There was no indication of a gunfight. If it wasn't Flynn and O'Donovan, how'd anybody get close enough to do 'em without them shooting back? I can tell you this though, it wasn't some Protestant paramilitary group. It was I.R.A. It was someone who Dolan knew. There was some reason for letting his guard down."

"So do you think it was Flynn and O'Donovan?"

"Must have been. But it would have been one hell of thing to pull off. Just the two of them. Flynn is way past such things at his age. With a bad leg and all. And two of the guys they took out were apparently bodyguards. I'd say this O'Donovan is the shooter. Must be one bad fucker to do this kind of work."

"So what you goin' to do?" Larkin asked.

"What do you mean?"

"Goin' to give the police those pictures you took? Place Flynn and O'Donovan at the scene?"

"Eventually, but not yet. I want you to stay on O'Donovan's ass. Any problem with that, Bill?"

As an ex-cop with the R.U.C., Larkin did have a problem with not turning over the evidence on the I.R.A., especially these two. But it was Devereux's show and he was paying.

"Right you are, Mr. Devereux," Larkin answered curtly.

Devereux prepared another shipment of film for his agent, Larry Neuson. He would give the I.R.A. another few days to see if they would take him up on the idea of filming the expected raid to recover or destroy the Protestant weapons he had photographed previously. One way or the other, he had plenty of material for the book.

He knew this time would come, and so did Brigid. Neither had any idea what to do. Both were in love. Both had lives that would be difficult to reconcile together. Maybe not, though. The adventure of his work was losing its edge. The thought of dying in some remote war still did not provoke a fear, but the idea of being away from Brigid was uncomfortable. He wondered what else he could do well. Something more conventional?

Where would they live? Brigid's career was in Belfast. The thought of living in Belfast would be an ultimate sacrifice. Ugly climate, ugly city. Nice enough people, but they live their lives through this shroud of sectarian hatred that permeates everything.

He tried Reilly all that day, but did not reach her until the following day. She sounded upset when she answered.

"Oh, Mason. I'm glad it's you. I'm so sorry I haven't called," Reilly blurted out, then started crying. "It's my uncle. He was killed a couple of days ago."

"Jesus, Brigid, killed? What happened?" Devereux asked.

"Murdered, both he and my Aunt Emily. It was in the papers today. My uncle was Terrance Dolan."

So that was Brigid's connection into the I.R.A. Family. And from the sounds of it, highly placed. "I need to see you, Brigid. I'll come to your flat."

After some time of hugging, followed by tears, both sat down at her small kitchen table. Brigid busied herself with making a pot of tea.

"No need anymore to hide what my connection was with the I.R.A. Terrance Dolan was my father's close friend. He was a true uncle to me. We became very close after my father died."

Devereux let her talk on without interrupting.

"He was a lawyer too. A solicitor. Small town stuff, deeds, wills, contracts. Born around the town of Armagh. Lived there all his life. Studied the law. Became an activist for Catholic rights. His family had always held strong republican views. The country thereabouts was the place for it alright. So it was natural that he eventually became involved with the Provincial I.R.A."

"Was your father I.R.A.?"

"No. My father and Uncle Terry agreed on most things, including a united Irish Republic that included all of Eire. So he was a republican but not I.R.A. My father was his own man. He did not condone the violent methods of the I.R.A. Intellectually, he understood that armed struggle was probably the only way that Irish independence would ultimately be achieved. Everywhere in history this has been true, including this century. But my father could not participate in this violence that always took unwilling victims. But he respected his friend Terrance Dolan for his sacrifices and his soldier's courage."

"And you? Where do you stand, Brigid?" Devereux asked, hoping he did not sound condemning. He did not want a repeat of their last argument. He sensed that Brigid was having her own crisis with reconciling her sympathies.

Brigid thought for a moment before answering. Her attack on Mason last time was foolish. How could he feel what being Irish meant? "I guess I side with my father's views. There was a time when I was much more militant. But I could never really reconcile myself to the violence. Ultimately I found a middle ground by working for the defense of accused I.R.A. defendants."

"Right now I'm not so sure. I wish the I.R.A. would rise up and kill everyone connected with the goddamn Ulster Defense Association, the Ulster Freedom Fighters, and every other Ulster whatever Protestant bastard paramilitary organization."

Tears welled in her eyes. "They murdered Emily as she laid in bed. Holy Mother, only criminals do that."

Brigid wept. Devereux took her hand. "It wasn't some Protestant paramilitary group that killed your uncle. It was Michael Flynn."

Brigid reared back in her chair as if slapped. "What are you talking about. Flynn is some sort of advisor and a professor in Dublin. He's also an old cripple for Christsakes. And why would he want to do such a thing? And how would he do it? Terrance Dolan was well protected. Christ, he wasn't just on the Army Council, he was the Commander-In-Chief of the Provincial I.R.A."

Devereux was visibly surprised. "Your uncle was the head of the I.R.A.?"

"That's what I said. That's why he was a target. That's why they tried to kill Gerry Adams as well. It's not the first attempt on either of them. What's this nonsense about Michael Flynn, Mason?"

Devereux wasn't sure he wanted to divulge everything to Brigid. No telling what she might do. There was an element of danger for her in even knowing. But she had a right to know. If he loved her he must trust her.

"Listen, Brigid. A lot has been going on that you don't know about. I haven't just been lead around by the Mullins brothers getting shots the I.R.A. would like. I've been looking at some things the I.R.A. has been up to. Using my own methods."

"What do you mean?"

"I was following John Krill by myself when the I.R.A. abducted him. I got some unusual shots. Shots of the murder of the man with Krill when he was kidnapped. It will help balance out the book against the Brennan murder."

"Mason, what the hell have you gotten into? You don't know these people. They're a real bad lot."

"Oh, I know them, Brigid, I've seen their work. But what you need to know, Brigid, and believe me on this, is that Flynn and somebody with him went to your uncle's home in Armagh. I followed them too. Saw them leave at seven-thirty. The bodies were discovered at nine. This was not a Protestant thing. This was a power struggle, a palace coup d'état. Flynn and another man killed your uncle."

Brigid felt as if in one of those dreams where you could not make sense of the circumstances. Everything was out of context. "Why were you there? How did you know to go there?"

"I told you, Brigid, I've developed my own intelligence on an I.R.A. group. I have someone in my employ to do surveillance. I believe this other man is part of an Active Service Unit, apparently taking orders from Flynn. The group probably was involved with the attempt on Adams too."

Brigid shook her head and rubbed her forehead. "You come to Northern Ireland. You want to do one of your great photographic works on our famous *troubles*. You're tired of the little brown and black people killing each other. Let's show some white westerners killing each other. You choose one side, the I.R.A., because you think you can best sell your idea to them. They agree and give you special cooperation. But from the onset, you think they're the bad guys. Now you're spying on them. What would you do if you were them and found you out?"

"If I were I.R.A.? Kill me of course," Devereux responded vehemently. "But I don't think they're any more the bad guys than the Protestant paramilitary thugs. Remember that I've seen what they did to that guy Brennan. My point is, the I.R.A. are the same. They're both the bad guys, Brigid. Christ, we've been over this same argument over and over."

Devereux tried to calm his frustration. "As a matter of course, I always deal with assholes, riffraff, and even sadists. After all, they're the ones that carry out the killings for those that hold power. You make it sound like I've somehow betrayed the I.R.A.'s trust."

"Well haven't you? And what about my trust?"

"You tell me you're not I.R.A. And I made it very clear to you, and to Flynn himself, that I would not bias my work in favor of the I.R.A."

Devereux continued, "You make it sound like I violated some ethic by spying on a bunch of murders."

Brigid was hurt, angry, and confused. "And what the fuck makes you so sure that it wasn't the Protestants? Or maybe even an S.A.S hit squad? The British wouldn't be above such things you know. Maybe even made it look like your theory of an internal power struggle."

"Jesus, Brigid, how would any Protestants, or the S.A.S. get that close to your uncle? His bodyguards didn't even get off any shots. It had to be someone he knew," he retorted in exasperation.

"And all you know is what the government, the Protestant government wants you to know. And what the fuck is so important about convincing me of your theory anyway?" Brigid lashed back angrily.

"You forget, I was there. Or maybe you don't believe me," Devereux shot back. "And I love you and I think you should know the truth. That's why!"

"Fuck off, just fuck off, Mason. I don't know if I believe you. But I do know I'm tired of arguing and defending my politics to you. You can never feel what I feel, and you can't understand. You're not Irish!"

Devereux had had enough. He was as angry with himself as he was with her. He should never have gotten this emotionally involved. He calmed the tone down as much as possible and left with a vague commitment to call her. She did not argue for him to stay. After he left, she cried for what felt like a new loss in her life.

Devereux spent the next three days trying to occupy himself. He must come to terms with himself about Brigid. Maybe this latest rift was for the best. There was no future for them. She would never leave Ireland, and he doubted if he could stay. Even if the violence ever ceased, the hostilities would never go away. And there was the god-awful weather. And what would he do? He had never thought about that before.

Devereux prowled Belfast to kill time. There were no further photographs to take. He had taken all the background shots necessary to portray the effects of the *troubles*. He also had a full compliment of background shots of the 'normal' side of Belfast. There was nothing left here. He decided to give the I.R.A. two more days. If they did not contact him he would leave Belfast to work on the text and finished the project. It would mean spending a couple months in the United States. It would test his feelings about Brigid. Maybe she would fly over for a couple of weeks. Maybe — if she thought they had a future.

The next day there was a message from Liam Mullins. Devereux was to meet him early that evening. Mullins did not say why. After picking up Devereux a mile from the Europa, Sean Mullins drove the van around for twenty minutes to insure there was no tail on Devereux.

"Where're we going, Liam?" Devereux asked. Liam Mullins had taken a seat in the rear with Devereux. His brother Sean drove.

"South. Toward Lisburn. You got what you wanted Mr. Devereux. The I.R.A. is going to recover those weapons you photographed being smuggled. Just like you demanded," Liam Mullins answered. There was an unfriendly edge to his tone.

"Where do they have the weapons?"

"What do'ya mean?"

"I mean, what kind of place is the I.R.A. going to attack? A home, an industrial building, what?"

Mullins hesitated before answering. Devereux could see he was very nervous. He had not been like this even at the Brennan murder. Sean Mullins also seemed jumpy, checking his rearview mirror frequently to look at him.

"Factory area. It's a warehouse I think. We were just told where to go. Won't take long to get there," Liam Mullins answered.

There was no further conversation. It was hard to tell how far they had gone, or where they were with Sean Mullins making frequent turns and doubling back. Liam Mullins was sweating now. He rolled down the window even though it was quite cold outside.

"Why're you so nervous, Liam. What's going on?"

Liam Mullins stared at him with a clear expression of hatred. Devereux knew something was wrong an instant before Liam Mullins pulled a gun from inside his jacket. It appeared to be a thirty-eight revolver, now pointed at his head.

"You been fucking around where you shouldn't have, Devereux. You think the I.R.A. are stupid fools?"

"Yeah, I do, Liam. The I.R.A. are stupid fools. You're also assholes," Devereux said.

He did not know what had gone wrong, but there was no way he was going to allow himself to be taken somewhere to be 'interrogated' by the I.R.A.

"Shut the fuck up, Devereux."

Devereux knew he had little time. There might never be a good opportunity. If he assumed correctly that Liam Mullins was not an experienced I.R.A. gunman, he might hesitate before shooting. If he did not, then let it end here making a fight rather than later be led like a sheep to the slaughter.

Devereux looked straight at Liam Mullins, then turned his head abruptly to the front as if startled by something. The maneuver worked. Liam Mullins instinctively turned his eyes away from Devereux. Devereux then swung his arm at the weapon, Forcing Mullins' arm upward, the weapon discharged through the roof of the van.

Devereux lunged from his seat and drove the heel of his left hand into Liam Mullins' nose. The crushing of cartilage made an audible noise. Blood gushed profusely.

Devereux grasped Mullins' right wrist. In a fit of desperate strength, he wrenched Mullins' right arm across his neck pushing Mullins' forearm under his chin. By now, Devereux was on top of Mullins, hammering his face with his own left forearm. Mullins struggled but the pain and shock of his damaged nose hampered his defense of Devereux's blows.

Sean Mullins turned at the sound of Devereux's attack on his brother. They were doing maybe seventy-five kilometers per hour. He felt helpless, but did not slacken speed. He could only see snatches of the fight going on behind him. Sean Mullins did not see the stop sign or the large lorry that crossed in front. The impact was taken just behind the cab of the lorry, spinning it around ninety degrees.

Moments later, Devereux realized that they had been in an accident. He was crumpled against the rear of the driver's seat. His left arm hurt like hell and did not respond well. He felt warm liquid running down his cheek. Liam Mullins body was crumpled under him and sandwiched against the broken back of the driver's seat.

Sean Mullins' head had shattered the windscreen. His chest had collapsed the steering column. The effect had been increased by the added inertia of the weight of both Liam and Devereux's bodies being propelled forward against the driver's seat.

Dazed and in shock, Devereux scrambled out the door then fell to the pavement.

Someone helped him to his feet. The man tried to calm what he thought was someone in shock. There were the effects of shock but Devereux was lucid enough to understand that he had to leave the scene as soon as possible. He did not want to stand questioning for being with two suspected I.R.A. people with guns. He had no idea what kind of story he would have to fabricate, then try to substantiate. It was imperative to leave the area quickly.

He went back into the van, and checked for a pulse at Liam Mullins' neck. There seemed to be none, but then the sound of his own heartbeat pounding in his ear made it hard to tell. Liam Mullins looked dead. As for Sean Mullins, Devereux could only assume he was also dead with the massive damage to his head. From the back seat floor he picked up his camera bag and Mullins' thirty-eight, stuffing it into the waistband of his trousers.

Pushing the man away, he walked unsteadily down the street, then quickened his pace to a jog once out of sight of the accident and the gathering crowd. It was cold and dark. A factory district shut down for the night. Devereux's legs were weak, his breathing labored.

Devereux traveled for what he thought must be more than a mile. He could still hear sirens in the distance. There was no telling where he was. His thinking was still fussy but improving with the cold and the exertion of walking. By his watch it was a full hour before he came across a pub. It was a run-down hole in the wall. Heads turned as he entered. He was not a local and something was obviously wrong with him. He located the public phone and called for a taxi. Devereux sat down at the bar.

"What'll it be friend?" The bartender asked.

"Whiskey. A double."

The bartender brought his drink. He could see the wound on Devereux's cheek. "Had some trouble friend?"

"Just an auto collision. Called a taxi."

"Foreigner? American?" The bartender asked. He had now stationed himself directly in front of Devereux.

"French actually," Devereux answered, then took the last of his drink in one gulp. "Got to go. Taxi will be along soon." He stuck out in here like a whore in church.

Devereux escaped the bartender's inquisition, and the taxi arrived minutes after he had stepped outside. He gave the driver a destination of a restaurant several blocks from the Europa Hotel. He did not want to leave a direct trail.

Thirty minutes later, Devereux was back in his room at the Europa. He washed the wound on his face. The skin under the left eye had been torn badly. Probably should have stitches. Devereux made do with some adhesive tape. The adrenaline had slowed. Thinking was clearer.

He was blown. The I.R.A. was trying to kill him. The attempted abduction would have lead to his disappearance. That meant they knew that he had turned on them. Larkin too would be in danger. He had to warn the old man.

Devereux changed clothes and packed hurriedly. He called the desk and told them he was leaving and to bill any outstanding charges to his American Express. He would not be returning.

The project was over. He had good material. Understatement. It was outstanding material. He should have called it quits days ago. He would warn Bill Larkin, then he would see Brigid. Then he would take the next plane out.

Devereux rushed from the hotel and loaded his bags and equipment into his rental car. Devereux knew the city by now. It was fifteen minutes to the surveillance flat located behind O'Donovan's pub. Devereux found a parking spot on the street in front of a row of flats a block away from the building. He changed clothes in the car, dressing in local working class clothing he had previously used; pea coat, brimmed cap, and scuffed heavy shoes. There was no one about, but Devereux kept his hand inside his coat with a hold on Mullins' revolver as he walked to the building entrance of Larkin's flat.

A dim, bare bulb lit the entrance. The wooden stairs made noise as he ascended to the second floor. The hallway was clear. Larkin's room was halfway down. Devereux knocked as softly as possible and still raise awareness inside. He kept this up for over a minute. There was no response. He had a note prepared. It read simply, 'Get out. We're blown! Signed D.' He slipped it under the door. As a formality, he tried the door. It was not locked.

Devereux looked down the hall both ways. There was no one. He pulled the revolver and entered the flat. The only light in the room came through the window from the entrance lamps at the rear of the establishments along the alleyway. He whispered Larkin's name repeatedly in the semi-darkness. There was no response. He switched on the light.

Twenty-four hours earlier, Bill Larkin had been in the flat. He was now bound at the wrists, and gagged. Two men had abducted him outside as he entered the building. A large caliber handgun persuaded him to follow their commands. Once inside the flat, the two gunmen forced Larkin into one of the kitchen chairs. The first thing they noticed was the camera mounted on a tripod at the window. While Jack Burns manhandled Larkin, Erskine Colbert sat at the chair Larkin had placed at the window. He looked through the viewfinder of the camera with a long distance lens mounted on a tripod. The rear entrance of O'Donovan's pub filled the field of view.

Colbert looked back at Larkin. "Who are you?"

"Fuck you," Larkin responded. Burns responded with a swipe to the head with the barrel of his revolver. Larkin was knocked from his chair. Blood streamed from a ragged cut below his left eye.

"We mean business. We mean to know who you are, who you're working for. There will be an end to this. How it ends, what you will endure, is up to you," Colbert said. "Now once again, who are you?"

Larkin simply shook his head, no. Burns was about to strike him again, when Colbert stopped him. "Very well. You'll come with us then. I warn you, one move to escape, and we'll shoot you. We'll also shoot anyone you warn. It's a matter of security, so don't test us."

While Burns manhandled Larkin, Colbert gathered the cameras and all the film they had found in Larkin's flat. Colbert had cut short the abuse to Larkin. He had killed before, but torture was contrary to his nature. He would leave such things to others. Once they were outside at the car, Burns bound Larkin's wrists behind his back and forced him into the rear seat. Burns drove, with Colbert in the rear with Larkin.

Larkin knew he was doomed. You didn't fuck the I.R.A. and live. God he was scared. He knew they wanted information. The one man looked like he could be a decent sort. The other was clearly a thug. Experiences of years on the police force flashed through his mind. It didn't matter who these two were, it was who he was being taken to. There was no way to prepare for torture. He knew what the I.R.A. was capable of. Would he tell them what they wanted to know? Could he not? What would he first endure? His own sweat chilled him. Jesus Christ he was scared.

Larkin was driven to a rural location some distance to the south of Belfast. Before leaving the city, the car had stopped at a public phone booth. The driver had made a brief call. The car eventually turned off a paved highway unto a dirt lane. Half a mile further, the car stopped in a secluded swale, populated by a few trees. Larkin was hauled from the car.

It was thirty minutes later when Garrett O'Donovan and Martin Kelly arrived. They approached Colbert and Burns covering Larkin with their weapons. Larkin was on his knees. Larkin, without a jacket, was shivering with the cold mixed with fear. He had no illusions. He was in for a bad time of it.

O'Donovan approached and stood in front of Larkin. "Mr. Larkin, if that's your real name, you will tell us what you've been about. I can promise you that if you don't you will suffer. In the end you'll tell us anyway. I suggest you avoid the pain."

Larkin looked at O'Donovan with contempt. "And if I tell you what you want to know you'll kill me anyway, right?

O'Donovan looked Larkin square in the eye, "Of course you will die, Larkin. It's simply a matter of how, and how soon."

With little hesitation, he turned to Burns, "Get on with it."

Burns went to the boot of the car, retrieved a rope and tire iron, then returned to the group huddled around Larkin.

Colbert and Kelly maneuvered Larkin against the trunk of a tree, then secured him with the rope. Both men were breathing heavily with anxiety. Larkin seemed like a small old man. He was trembling.

"For the last time, Larkin, who are you working for?" O'Donovan asked. Larkin said nothing. He looked at O'Donovan with an empty expression. The clash of fear and thoughts produced a moment of blank emotion.

O'Donovan nodded to Burns. Burns struck a sweeping blow to Larkin's lower left leg with the tire iron. Everyone winced at the sound of bone breaking. Larkin screamed.

"Holy Jesus," Colbert muttered to himself.

O'Donovan waited for a full minute. Larkin groaned repeatedly with the intense pain. Sweat poured down his face. Tell them what they want. Be done with this, Larkin told himself. But he couldn't. Couldn't give in to these assholes. He was more than that. Larkin's thoughts ceased abruptly with a blow to his right shin. He slumped, held semi-upright against the tree by the ropes that bound him.

O'Donovan asked his question again.

Burns was breathing heavily. Colbert's face was ashen. Kelly was physically ill, fighting not to vomit.

Larkin held out for twenty minutes, suffering additional blows that shattered both knees and then both elbows. The pain was unbearable. His limits reached, he told O'Donovan everything.

With nothing more to get from Larkin, O'Donovan drew his nine-millimeter automatic. Larkin looked straight into O'Donovan's eyes and said, "You bloody fucking animals. I spit on you and the —-" O'Donovan's bullet to his forehead cut Larkin's curse short.

O'Donovan could not make contact with Flynn but rendez-voused at a prearranged location in the rear of a small local market in the Falls Road area the following day. O'Donovan told Flynn about Larkin, and this photographer Devereux.

"We will deal with this Devereux tomorrow. We have more pressing work tonight. These cousins of yours, can they be relied upon?" Flynn asked O'Donovan.

"They're good lads, Liam and Sean. They obey orders. What are we to have them do? Don't think they're up to any nasty work if that's what you have in mind," O'Donovan said.

"No nasty work. I want to talk with this Devereux chap personally. Could be that he's something more than what he seems. We need to know what he knows, what sort of pictures does he have? Is he working for British intelligence? Lots of questions we have for Mr. Devereux. Can these cousins of yours secure this Devereux until we're done with our business?"

O'Donovan considered Flynn's question. Liam and Sean were capable, and dedicated to the Cause. They could easily get close to Devereux. They could do it. They would do it after he told them of Devereux's betrayal. "I think they can handle the job."

"Good. Get word to them. Have them tell Devereux that a raid on that U.F.F. arms cache is planned. Tell him that the I.R.A. leadership has agreed to allow him to witness and photograph the raid. Hold him until tomorrow. You and I will settle with him then," Flynn said.

"Wouldn't it be better if I had Colbert and Burns nab Devereux?" O'Donovan asked.

"Probably, but we can't spare them now."

The flat was cold. Devereux turned on a light. Obviously Larkin had been away for some time. A cursory look revealed that the camera equipment was missing. Larkin migh have taken it, but not likely the tripod he had positioned at the window.

Devereux continued to look around. Larkin had obviously not made this place home. Either that or he lived a very spartan existence. There were only a few can goods in the pantry and a bottle of Irish whiskey. A coffeepot with cold grounds was on the gas range. A half a cup of coffee and a stale loaf of bread were on the Formica kitchen table. The closet revealed only a couple of shirts and a jacket. Dirty clothes were piled underneath. A chest of drawers held only gray underwear and a few pairs of socks. The bed was unmade.

There was no sign of a struggle, but the front door had been unlocked. He could not believe that Larkin, an ex-cop, would leave his door open. Devereux suspected the worse, but he would give it an hour. After that, he would leave the note and be out of here and then out of Northern Ireland.

Devereux switched off the lights in the flat, then sat himself in one of the kitchen chairs at the window, the revolver in his lap. Even though it was cold, he opened the window. He looked down the dirty alleyway, populated with all manner of trash containers. The rear of O'Donovan's pub was lit by a dim yellow light. The thought of O'Donovan learning of the death of the Mullins brothers brought some satisfaction.

Twenty minutes later, Devereux saw a black taxi moving up the alleyway away from the flat window. It stopped behind the rear entrance to O'Donovan's pub. The door of the taxi opened, and a diminutive figure emerged. He was wearing a black coat with a black cap. There was some difficulty as he exited the vehicle.

Devereux sighted through a 200mm lens. At this distance, it was the same as being twenty feet away. The taxi driver knocked at the door to O'Donovan's pub. Seconds later the door was opened cautiously until the taxi driver was recognized. Before entering, the taxi driver turned his head to check the alleyway.

"Jesus Christ," Devereux said to himself while getting at least three head shots. "It's Flynn!"

Chapter Fourteen

Peter Sullivan and Brennan Magee reported for duty at three in the afternoon on a Saturday. This was typical for performance nights at the Grand Opera House. Tonight however, was not a typical performance night. In the audience would be the Prince of Wales, the Prime Minister of the Republic of Ireland, the British Home Secretary, and the Lord Mayor of Belfast, along with influential businessmen and lesser government types.

All access to the Opera House was secured. To get to the rear entrance, Sullivan and Magee passed through two security checkpoints to even get to the rear door of the building. There, another R.U.C. constable searched them while another held an automatic weapon at the ready. Once inside, they reported to Superintendent McLeash.

"Never seen nothin' like this," Sullivan said.

"Neither have I in all my years here," McLeash said. "Sign of the times. Great target for the fuckin' I.R.A. No choice but to lay on security heavy."

McLeash continued, "Let's look sharp tonight. No fucking off. You lads'll take stage right tonight. Harris and Smithson will take the left. Everything checked out yesterday like I told you?"

"Right you are, boss. Everything's fine. Replaced a couple of lights. That's all that was wrong," Sullivan said.

Magee was so agitated at listening to Sullivan suck up to McLeash that he stomped away towards the stairs leading down to the building basement.

McLeash turned to Sullivan, "Your brother's becoming a surly fucker lately. Somethin' he doesn't like about the job?"

"Don't be paying any mind to him. It's woman problems he's havin.'"

McLeash grunted as if to acknowledge his understanding. "Know how that can be." As Sullivan was leaving, McLeash added, "In a couple of hours we got some more security types want to go through the place with these dogs that can smell explosives. I want to stay around the stage in case there are any last minute problems. You take these fellows through the place."

Sullivan acknowledged McLeash's instructions, then moved off quickly to join Magee. He found him coming out of the toilet in the basement next to the maintenance storage area.

"Fuck that Protestant shithead. Last of his crap we take. I'm going to love doin' him. You know, we could get him down here right now and take care of business. Nobody'd miss him," Magee said.

"Shut up, Magee. Somethin' more important we've got to attend to. The police'll be sendin' dogs in here soon. Lookin' for explosives."

Magee did not like being talked to like that. "So what. We've got no explosives."

"No, but we've got all that ammunition. It's got explosives in the cartridges."

"Can the dogs be smellin' that?" Magee asked.

"Don't know what they can smell out. But do you want to chance it? We've got to find some place out of their reach."

Sullivan and Magee had stashed two Armalite AR-18 assault rifles, and two Sterling L34A1 submachine guns, along with ample magazines for each. The weapons were placed in an old oil soaked cardboard box in the back of the maintenance storeroom in the Opera House basement. The box was concealed amid a clutter of miscellaneous debris typical of a maintenance department. Well concealed from probing eyes, but uncertain against the probing olfactory capability of a trained dog.

"I've an idea," Sullivan said. "We'll put the ammunition in the paint locker. The smell of the solvents in there should overpower any other smells the dogs could pick up."

A few hours later, Sullivan escorted two R.U.C. officers and a German shepherd throughout the Opera House. At the paint locker, the dog winced at the pungent smells but made no indication of contraband. One officer opened the cabinet, but made only a cursory examination.

It was two hours before the start of the evening's performance, a celebration of Irish music. Several world-renowned opera tenors from the United States, Italy, and Ireland would be performing classic Irish music.

Forty-five minutes after spotting Flynn going into the rear of O'Donovan's pub, Devereux observed Flynn coming out. Two men followed after him. One was O'Donovan. To Devereux's surprise, O'Donovan and the other man were dressed in formal evening attire. Standing beside the taxi, they engaged in a conversation with Flynn.

Devereux assumed they would be leaving in the taxi that Flynn had driven. He fairly ran out of the flat, descending the stairs three at a time. He was breathing heavily by the time he reached his car. Luck had placed him a couple of hundred meters down the street from the alley running behind O'Donovan's pub. The taxi was pulling out of the alley onto the street as Devereux fumbled with the lock.

By the time Devereux started the engine, the taxi was almost out of sight. Shifting through the gears as rapidly as possible, he closed the gap in time to see the taxi make a turn onto another street. Stopping at a signal light, Devereux confirmed he had the right taxi ahead of him by the license tag. Fortunately for Devereux, they got on the M1 Motorway, making it less likely to spot that they were being followed.

Ten minutes later Flynn exited the Motorway at Grosvenor Road, traveling east. Within a few more minutes, they stopped at Great Victoria Street and turned right. Fifty meters ahead was a roadblock manned by four R.U.C. officers. Flynn's taxi was third in line at the roadblock. Devereux was three cars behind Flynn. Whatever was going on, Flynn was apparently allowed to pass.

Once Devereux's car moved up to the roadblock, a police officer inquired, "May I see your invitation or pass, Sir?"

"My what? What's going on?" Devereux asked.

"The opera performance, Sir. I assume then you're not a guest. 'Fraid you'll have to turnabout here, Sir. Security you know."

"But I'm a photographer," Devereux said as he picked up a camera from the front passenger seat.

"Not without a press pass, mate. Now you'll have to be moving on. You're holding up traffic," the officer replied more sternly.

Devereux turned his car around and tried to find a way to the Europa Hotel to park since he was a recent guest there. The Europa was located on the opposite corner of Glengall Street across from the Opera house. It was no use. All access had been blocked and there were security personnel in evidence. The Europa itself had been the scene of many an I.R.A. attack. It had the dubious distinction of being the most bombed hotel in Europe.

Devereux turned his car around and began circling the area in an ever-expanding radius looking for a place to park. He ended up many blocks away from the Opera House.

So that was it. They were going to do something at the Opera House. Of course, how stupid could he be not to realize it sooner. It had been in the newspaper all week. The Prince of Wales, the Taoiseach, or Prime Minister of the Republic of Ireland, the Mayor of Belfast, and God only knows how many other dignitaries. Devereux remembered now the fuss with the celebrity performers checking in the day before at the Europa.

Devereux jogged back toward the Opera House with his camera bag over his shoulder. He wondered if he would be able to get any closer on foot. The roadblocks at some distance from the Opera House and the Europa Hotel would mainly be to guard against the obvious threat of a car bomb.

Devereux had no idea what he would do. For that matter, what could he do? If he tried to alert the police there was the likely possibility that he would be taken into custody and his warnings probably ignored. Worse yet, when something then did happen, he would be the only one the police had. He might actually be charged as an accessory.

What were Flynn and O'Donovan going to do? Dressed in evening wear, he could only assume that O'Donovan and the other man had gained entrance into the Opera House. They could not smuggle weapons in with this security. A car bomb did not make sense. Or did it? They did get past the checkpoint. Maybe the tuxedos were only to get the taxi close to the building, then leave the area. Jesus, it could be!

As he hoped, Devereux was able to move about quite freely, except for the area directly in front of the Opera House entrance. He put a camera around his neck, and appeared to take photographs like a number of other photographers. He must locate the taxi.

Devereux moved down Great Victoria Street in front of the Opera House and the Europa. Looking down Glengall Street, he could see taxis had queued up in a long line on the north side of the street. If Flynn's taxi was a car bomb, it was well away from inflicting direct damage on the Opera House.

He moved down the opposite side of Glengall Street where police and other official vehicles had parked for some distance. Midway among the row of taxis and limousines, Devereux spotted Flynn's taxi by the license tag. Someone was sitting in the driver's seat. He assumed it must be Flynn.

Devereux found a spot behind a police car that gave him an observation point to the taxi. The idea of the taxi being rigged with a bomb no longer made sense. For the moment, he would wait.

Inside the Opera House, and behind the curtains, the flurry of activity seemed like chaos. Technicians and grips moved equipment and wiring. Musicians were starting to take their seats. Security personnel only added to the crowded wings off to the sides of the stage. McLeash was moving about checking things and barking orders at his staff.

Sullivan looked at his watch. It was twenty minutes before the curtain was to be raised. He was sweating profusely from the tension. Catching Magee's attention, he nodded his head. Both men walked toward the front of the Opera House, opposite to the stage. Sullivan opened a service door leading to the foyer a crack. Garrett O'Donovan and Erskine Colbert moved through the door quickly.

The four men went quickly down the stairs to the basement.

Sullivan and Magee lead O'Donovan to the weapons and Colbert to the ammunition. They then went to their personal lockers and took out tuxedos and dress shoes. Both men stripped to their underwear then fumbled with the unfamiliar garments.

O'Donovan removed the wrappings of towels and plastic bags covering the weapons. He unfolded the stock, then checked the barrel of one of the Sterlings. Made for just this type of use. O'Donovan smiled at the thought that it was a standard weapon for the I.R.A.'s most aggressive enemy, the British S.A.S. He wondered how the I.R.A. had laid hands on these. Shame to have to leave them behind.

The Sterling was classed as a submachine gun. The submachine gun fired larger caliber ammunition than a so-called assault rifle, but at a considerably lower muzzle velocity. The L34A1 Sterling was fitted with an integral silencer. The silencer reduces the velocity of the bullet thereby eliminating the sonic boom of the projectile breaking the sound barrier.

The Sterlings were for the close-in work. Neutralize security and get the other shooters to the targets. The silenced rounds would serve to not alert other security outside the immediate vicinity. The assault rifles would do the real work of the mission.

While the assault rifle used only a 5.56mm projectile, less than two-thirds the diameter of the submachine gun's 9mm, it packed a more deadly impact. The velocity was more than double the submachine gun's, with the impact of the bullet carrying three times the energy force of the larger 9mm slug. The smaller, faster bullet is the more lethal. When it hits tissue it expands, shatters, and tumbles, leaving greater damage than the heavier caliber round.

Colbert returned with the ammunition magazines. O'Donovan installed a magazine in one of the Sterlings. He hefted the weapon to gage its feel.

Sullivan and Magee came into the storage room dressed in their tuxedos. O'Donovan tossed the loaded Sterling to Magee.

Magee examined the weapon, chambered a round, then set the safety to off. "I hope the fuck it's McLeash who I see first."

O'Donovan handed the other Sterling to Sullivan. Colbert handed him two loaded magazines, and tossed a spare to Magee. Responding to Magee, O'Donovan said, "You'll do the fuck as planned, Magee. McLeash's not your fucking target. You hit the coppers and the plain clothes security as you've been told."

The plan called for Sullivan and Magee to reconnoiter how security was dispersed since they would be on the scene hours ahead of the performance. They would use the Sterlings to first neutralize security personnel for O'Donovan and Colbert to gain a vantage point to set up an assault position on the real targets. The targets would be the boxes, particularly the Royal Box and the first rows of guests seated toward the center of the lower seats. This should be where the most prominent guests would be clustered. Sullivan and Magee would provide cover by attempting to shoot security personnel entering the fight.

O'Donovan and Colbert picked up the AR-18 assault rifles. They extended the folded stocks and inserted forty round magazines into each weapon. Both put an additional loaded magazine into their trouser waists.

The AR-18 was a favorite weapon of the I.R.A. It weighed less than seven pounds. It fired the 5.56mm round at a maximum rate of fire of over seven hundred rounds per minute. It was reliable. It would be remarkably deadly within the confines of the Opera House.

They had reviewed the plan repeatedly. It was Flynn's plan, but O'Donovan could not add anything to improve upon it. It was simple and direct. It gave them access. It gave them surprise. It gave them potentially equal firepower to that of the enemy. And most of all, it gave a plausible means of escape, although a chancy one with no better than fifty-fifty odds of success by O'Donovan's estimation.

But it would be a grand stroke. Kill the fucking heir to the British monarchy. Stick it up the British arse. Not since the killing of Lord Montbatten had the I.R.A. struck with such impact. This was the fight. This wasn't the politics. This wasn't those

Sinn Fein pussies and their talk of truce. This was Ireland against the British. This would put the situation back on a war footing.

Flynn was the only one to have kept the faith. O'Donovan knew he had made the right choice. He checked his watch. The performance had begun two minutes ago. Ireland's most celebrated tenor was opening with *Danny Boy*, sure to bring a tear to the eye of all with its evocation of all things Irish, and the perfect vehicle for a tenor to exhibit his range. He could hear the faint strains of the song. Few songs could move the spirit of the Irish like melancholy strains of *Danny Boy*. O'Donovan thought it fitting for what they were about. They would move at the start of the second song. All of the men were ready. Weapons checked and loaded.

Looking for his staff, McLeash opened the door to the maintenance area. He then stood there stunned as he looked upon four men dressed in tuxedos in the dingy maintenance basement.

"What the fuck— —-" McLeash started to say before Magee exercised his wish with a three round burst that caught McLeash in the midsection.

"Not yet. Another minute. When the applause stops," O'Donovan cautioned, ignoring the shooting. He was the only one appearing calm. Magee's blood was up. His eyes were alive with the rush. Sullivan and Colbert were only barely controlling their anxiety. They were both quiet men given only to the killing through a zealot's devotion. Colbert repeatedly dried his sweating palms on his trousers.

The seconds seemed like minutes. O'Donovan visualized the forthcoming attack. He was anything but calm. Every nerve was taunt. He was simply focused and under control. It was a singular gift that had served him well in the past.

"Now," O'Donovan said as he heard the next song start. All four men left the basement maintenance room, with Sullivan and Magee out in front.   O'Donovan hoped that the tenors would not be killed. That would be a shame.

Devereux had been keeping watch on the taxi for almost thirty minutes when the driver got out and stood beside the vehicle. There was good light provided by a street lamp. The 200mm lens clearly revealed that the taxi driver, even with his brimmed cap, was Michael Flynn. Devereux took several photographs, then moved for a different angle that captured not only Flynn's taxi license tag, but that of the taxi directly behind. He wanted to place Flynn at this scene.

Scene of what? That was still the question. But Devereux knew something was imminent and he must attempt some warning. It was not a car bomb. Since O'Donovan was not with Flynn, then he must be inside. It must be an assassination attempt. Devereux moved briskly back down Glengall Street towards the Opera House.

O'Donovan and the other three men moved purposefully down the basement corridor, then ascended the stairs. Sullivan opened the door at the top a crack. Two uniformed officers could be observed. They had not been there earlier. Sullivan guessed they might have come in from the outside by the rear door nearby. Sullivan motioned Magee up to the door. O'Donovan followed with Colbert behind him. It was Sullivan's and Magee's job to neutralize security personnel.

Sullivan looked back at O'Donovan. With less than conviction, he nodded ever so slightly. O'Donovan did not hesitate. He had made his choice some time ago. He was committed. This was what he was about. This would acknowledge him as the best. At this point he could not fail. Die perhaps, but not fail. They could not help but to deliver a spectacular attack. He nodded affirmatively to Sullivan.

Sullivan opened the door quietly. All the security personnel had their backs to the I.R.A. men. Sullivan had the Sterling on semi-automatic. With the stock raised to his shoulder, he aimed at the back of one officer, squeezing off two rounds. The silencer reduced the noise of the shots to heavy thuds caused by the expelled gases of the ammunition. It was by no means silent, but the noise would not be heard beyond the immediate area.

Both rounds hit the officer in the back, knocking him down. The noise turned the other officer around. He attempted to pull his own weapon. Both Sullivan and Magee opened up with bursts that devastated him.

The four men moved down the corridor leading to stage right. They encountered no one for some distance, which suggested the possibility that the silenced weapons fire had not yet alerted other security people. Unfortunately, there was no cover as they approached the backstage area. An alert security plain clothed officer was doing his job rather than listening to the performance like most of his colleagues. He fairly choked as he saw the four I.R.A. men running down the corridor toward him, obviously armed with automatic weapons. He also knew that he was about to die.

Magee fired two, three round bursts that took the man down before he could remove his own weapon from his shoulder holster. Several people turned at the sound of the loud burps from Magee's silenced Sterling. Two were security. Both knew they had made a fatal mistake in alertness. Sullivan and Magee fired bursts, dropping the two before they could even unholster their weapons and return fire. Three other people in the stage wings were also felled in the firing.

Hearing nothing with the attenuated shots, the orchestra played on. The Irish tenor continued his song. Two flutists, awaiting their cue in the score, were distracted by the commotion off stage. There were a couple of seconds of recognition to absorb the situation, then they dropped to the floor.

Within a matter of seconds, all four I.R.A. men stormed unto the stage and moved toward the front of the orchestra. Now running, Sullivan and Magee attacked across the stage to the opposite wing. Facing the stage, the entire orchestra dropped to the floor as firing began. People, chairs, and instruments tumbled in panicked disarray.

Security officers on the other side of the stage assessed the situation and pulled their own weapons. Sullivan and Magee unleashed repeated bursts into the right wing of the stage. Several people were hit including two security officers. Others scattered away. A third security officer dropped to one knee and drew his own weapon. He was armed with an automatic machine pistol, actually a reduced length Israeli Uzi submachine gun. He was able to fire two short bursts before taking a round that exploded through his forehead.

Sullivan's and Magee's fire suppressed the minimal opposition fire coming from stage left. Sullivan had fallen to one knee, hit by a round to the midsection, but continued to fire bursts. O'Donovan and Colbert ran to center stage. To their shock, the audience was difficult to see due to the glare of the stage lights into their faces.

The Prince of Wales was in the Royal Box, the first box to stage right. The I.R.A. assumed that one or more dignitaries would be seated with his Royal Highness. However, even the lowest box was elevated some twelve feet above the stage, presenting a poor angle of fire. The plan was for O'Donovan to fire at the Royal Box, then fire a burst into each of the other prestige boxes on that side of the theater. Colbert would fire into the boxes on the other side.

O'Donovan fired two long bursts from his assault rifle into the Royal Box, then fired into two other boxes. He questioned the effectiveness because of the angle. Colbert was firing to the opposite side of the theater. O'Donovan then trained his fire to the front lower rows where people were now attempting to escape in panic. Colbert followed suit.

The effectivity of their firing into the box seats could not be determined. But there was little question about their attack directed into the lower seats. Most of the high velocity rounds found a target within the crowd. Wounds to the abdomen and muscled areas absorbed the energy of the projectile leaving devastating damage. Wounds to the extremities exploded blood and tissue, and sometimes passed beyond to claim another victim.

To those in the audience directly in front of the stage, there was the terror of being trapped. People began to scramble in panic. Those seated near the aisles poured into a clogged mass of people. Those in the middle tried to climb over seats to distance themselves from the deadly source of firing coming from the stage. Men tried to help women in evening dresses. Women tried to help wounded spouses. Many survived with evidence of others blood on their clothes.

For those not in the front seats and targets of fire, the scene was equally horrific. There was much pushing. The best and the worst came out in many people. Many injuries occurred on the stairs as people descended down from the balcony levels and box seats. The carnage was awesome. O'Donovan and Colbert each emptied forty round clips, reloaded, and again emptied their weapons.

Sullivan and Magee had successfully suppressed opposition fire from the other side of the stage, but Sullivan was down on the stage on his knees. He had laid down his weapon and was breathing in measured breaths.

O'Donovan and Colbert dropped their empty weapons and ran toward the downed Peter Sullivan. Each grabbed an arm, hoisting him to his feet. Sullivan let out a cry of pain. Magee stood with his weapon, out of targets to shoot at.

"Drop it, Magee. We're to be out of here," O'Donovan shouted. The place was a bedlam of screaming.

Magee complied reluctantly. Four men in tuxedos moved quickly toward the exit, two helping a wounded victim. At a side door, the four I.R.A. men became part of a surging crowd that overwhelmed security personnel outside. It would be several minutes later before security could regroup and enter the Opera House with an assault team. All they would find would be a surreal scene of countless bodies with blood pooling all over and the sound of agony from the wounded.

Devereux ran down Glengall Street toward the Opera House. This was useless. This was desperation but he had to try to signal some alert. He spotted an R.U.C. uniformed officer.

"Officer. Listen. There's something going to happen. I have reason to believe that the I.R.A. is planning some sort of attack at the Opera House. You need to alert security."

The officer looked Devereux over with obvious suspicion. "Easy now, lad. Now what the hell are you saying?"

"Goddamn it, there's an I.R.A. attack going down. Do you know of a Michael Flynn? He's wanted by the British," Devereux said.

The officer now looked at Devereux with greater concern. This was no place that anyone would joke about I.R.A. violence. "What are you saying? What about the I.R.A.?"

"Michael Flynn. Do you know the name?" Devereux asked.

"No, I don't know this Flynn. Now what is it you're tryin' to tell me?"

This was not going to work. He would not be able to convince them. Of what, he himself did not know. There was no credible way to explain how he would know of a pending I.R.A. attack. And most assuredly he would be taken into custody. From there it would only get worse. He had to try, though. Devereux knew the I.R.A. was going to launch some sort of attack. Why else would Michael Flynn himself be taking the personal risk. Undoubtedly the intent was to kill the dignitaries. They would take countless others with them in the process.

"I am a reporter. I've been following certain people undercover. They're Provincial I.R.A. They're led by a Michael Flynn. Old time bad guy. Wanted by you chaps. The sonofabitch is right over there in one of those taxis," Devereux paused, still breathing hard, and pointing back up Glengall Street.

Devereux had the officer's attention now. Also suspicious, his hand rested on his holstered weapon.

"This Flynn just dropped two guys off. They were dressed in tuxes. My guess is they got tickets somehow. Must be inside," Devereux said.

"What newspaper you with?" The R.U.C. officer asked.

Shit. The cop wanted to establish his bonafides. "I'm not with a paper. I'm freelance," Devereux said with exasperation.

"May I see some ID, Sir?"

"Goddamn it, officer, if you don't get on the stick and warn security you'll have a fucking blood bath on your conscience!" Devereux shouted.

At this point, the conversation was interrupted with the sounds of panic as people poured out the doors of the Opera House. Both Devereux and the officer turned at the sound. With the doors open, they could clearly hear sounds of automatic weapons fire from within.

Both Devereux and the officer started to run toward the Opera House, perhaps two hundred meters away. Outside the building the officer stopped, bewildered as to what to do. Other police had the same problem.

Devereux started to take photographs. Elegantly dressed people, mostly middle aged, poured from the Opera House. Many fell in their rush to escape. Some were bloodied. One man collapsed and blood formed in a pool from the wound to his abdomen. A woman with a massive wound to her upper arm was assisted by a police officer. Others looked as if they had been splattered with the blood and tissue of others. Devereux loaded another roll of film and continued to shoot. Within less than a minute, the firing stopped. People continued to pour out of the Opera House.

Devereux rushed into the Opera House. Cries of pain punctuated the air. Security personnel were shouting, some with orders, others with questions. One officer was screaming curses out of sheer frustration.

Once into the performance hall, Devereux ran down the aisle. It would be only a short time before he would be ejected from the scene. It was in the front rows that the carnage was concentrated. Devereux guessed the gunmen had come from near the stage or the stage area itself.

The I.R.A. had probably achieved their mission gauged by the concentration of casualties in the first few rows near center stage. Devereux hurriedly attached a flash and adjusted his camera settings accordingly. He was in a hurry and needed the full benefit of adequate lighting on the subject. He took an entire roll of film before a plain-clothes security officer intervened. "Who the fuck are you?" The man said, brandishing a machine pistol version of the Uzi. "Well?"

"Just a photographer, officer," Devereux answered. At this point he wanted only to exit without being detained. It could be a matter of only minutes before the R.U.C. police officer he tried to warn would pass the word to be looking for a photographer fitting his description.

"Get the fuck out of here. This is a fucking crime scene, arsehole."

Devereux did as he was told immediately. He then proceeded to run down Glengall Street away from the Opera House toward the string of taxis. The drivers had for the most part rushed on foot toward the Opera House. Flynn's taxi was of course gone. So were the I.R.A. gunmen unless they were among the dead and wounded inside.

It was now clear to Devereux. The tuxedos allowed both entry and escape. Cease the firing, drop the weapons, then run out just like they were part of the rest of the crowd. Simple and elegant.

The mixed tones of a chorus of sirens could be heard in the distance. Devereux continued to walk east on Glengall Street away from the Opera House. He turned north on Sandy Row, eventually getting to his rental car parked on a side street. He had to assume that someone fitting his description was now being sought. He needed to leave immediately. Not only the area, but Belfast and Northern Ireland. He found a public telephone and got through to Brigid Reilly. Her reception sounded cold.

"Brigid. I must see you. Right now in fact," Devereux said.

Brigid had not heard from Devereux since their argument days ago. She was still angry. The hurt from the loss of missing him and the hurt from the fact that they were probably lost to each other. Too many obstacles. "Mason, I've had a really hard day. I just got home from the office. Not tonight. Besides, I'm not sure I want to see you."

"Brigid, you must see me. I need your help. I've got to leave Belfast, tonight in fact. More than that, I must see you," Devereux said.

Concerned now, Brigid responded, "What's happened, Mason?"

"Not on the phone. When I see you. Okay?" He asked.

Brigid agreed. Devereux said he would be there in twenty minutes. Apprehensively, she removed her robe and dressed in sweater and jeans.

Brigid opened the door to Devereux's knock. "Your face? What happened?" Brigid exclaimed seeing the bandaged wound on his cheek now that he was in the light. Her concern overrode her other feelings.

"Auto accident. I'm ok. Long story." He responded.

For a moment they stood looking at each other. Brigid made the first move by grabbing his face in both hands and kissing him full on the lips. He responded by hugging her tightly. After some moments, they awkwardly separated and Devereux brought his suitcases and camera equipment into the flat.

Without a word, Brigid turned and went to the kitchen. She returned moments later with two glasses of whiskey. It was a mechanism to regain control over her feelings. Something was wrong but she was so glad to see him.

Brigid seated herself on the sofa. "Now what's this about an accident? And why the bags?"

"That's not important right now, Brigid." Devereux took the glass from her and seated himself on the coffee table directly in front of her.

"I didn't want to do that, Mason. Kiss you like that I mean. You're not good for me."

Brigid continued, "I'm very physical and you arouse me like no man before. You're a great fuck. Every time we make love it seems to be the best time. But every time we're together we end up fighting."

She took a sip of her drink. "You're an exciting man. You're intelligent, handsome, and whatever it is that makes you do what you do. But we don't get along well. Maybe it's me. Probably is mostly. I'm a great bitch. Never have done well with relationships."

Devereux drank his drink in two large gulps. He placed his hands on her knees. "Brigid, I love you. I loved my wife in the same way. I know what I feel. But I don't know if we could live together either. I do think we should try."

"Come with me for a couple of weeks. A vacation, a holiday. A chance to be together in our own environment. Not working, either of us. None of the things around us that have spurred our past arguments. We can go anywhere you want. What do you say, Brigid?"

She held both hands to his face. It was a great thought. Get away with this man. This man who made her feel new things. This man she wanted to be with, share things with. This man she did not want to hurt, yet always ended up doing so. She was bloody stupid if she did not give them this chance.

She looked at him, tears welling in her eyes, "I love you, Mason. And I would love to have it work between us."

Brigid kissed him full on the mouth. Tears streamed freely down her face.

"Brigid, there's something else we need to talk about," Devereux said, "I have to leave Ireland immediately. Tonight in fact. I want you to leave with me."

Reilly pushed back from him, "What's happened, Mason?"

"Didn't you hear yet? The Opera House. The I.R.A. hit it. I was there. I followed Flynn there. A real slaughter. I tried to warn the police before it happened, but it was too late. Prince of Wales was there, lot of other big players. Don't know if any big shots got killed. But now they're going to be looking for this photographer that seemed to know that an attack was about to take place," Devereux told her.

"Jesus, it'll never end," Reilly said.

"There's something else. The I.R.A. group who did this tried to kill me earlier. At least I assumed that was the plan," Devereux added.

"What happened, Mason? Is that how you hurt your face?"

"My two friends, the Mullins brothers tried to snatch me. Liam pulled a gun on me. We were in a van. I jumped him and we struggled. Sean was driving. Probably distracted, he hit a lorry at an intersection. Killed both of them. I was lucky. A few bruises and this," he said pointing to his cheek.

"Then I went to this place where I had this guy I hired holed up to watch the back of this pub. He was gone. Door to the flat was open. My guess is they found out about him. Maybe made him tell them about me. I don't want to think about that part."

"Anyway, I stayed at the flat for a while in case my guy were to show up. I needed to warn him. Know what I saw? Who I got photographs of? Flynn. Michael Flynn himself. The bastard's driving a fucking taxi. Now mind you, this is at the rear of this pub owned by a guy named O'Donovan."

"So Flynn —-" Devereux said, but Brigid interrupted with a question.

"O'Donovan you say? Garrett O'Donovan?" She asked.

"Yeah. You know him?" Devereux asked, hoping she was not that close to these assholes.

"In a way. Defended him once, that's all," she said, recalling her stupid tryst with the handsome I.R.A. gunman.

Devereux then recounted the details of the rest of the events that evening.

"Puzzling thing is Flynn's personal involvement. Guy's too old to be out in the field. Besides, he's got a cushy academic job in safe Dublin. Why is he coming to Northern Ireland? There's still old murder warrants out for him from the early seventies."

"Either he's split with the I.R.A., or there's some sort of power struggle going on. Either way, I'm more convinced then ever that Flynn killed your uncle."

Brigid did not argue. She in fact said nothing. Too many events happening. Too many conflicting thoughts and feelings.

"Oh God, Mason. What is happening? This will change everything that may have been accomplished. There will never be an end to this violence."

"Can you leave with me tonight?" Devereux asked.

"Tonight? I want to go away with you for our vacation like you said. But it will take me the week to clear up things at the office. I can't just drop all the things I am working on. Too many people depend on me. Can you understand, Mason?"

"I understand. Just hoped it were otherwise. But I've got to leave tonight. Not sure it's a good idea to even try to catch a flight out of Belfast. Bus or ferry's probably no safer if they're looking for me. I need you to drive me to Dublin, tonight. Now that's a hell of thing to ask."

"I love you, Mason. And that means getting you out of Belfast. You're not safe here and there's no escaping these people if you stay. We'll leave now," Reilly said.

Devereux convinced her to spend the night in Dublin, then drive back in the morning. He wrote down the address and telephone number where he could be reached in California.

Devereux parked his rental car in a supermarket parking lot. He would call the rental agency later and report it stolen. There was no problem at the border. Devereux showed his Monaco passport and spoke broken English with a heavy French accent. They were not looking for a Frenchman, accompanied by a woman. There was a midnight flight to New York's JFK Airport.

"Antigua," Devereux said.

"What?"

"Antigua. The island in the Caribbean. That's where we'll meet," Devereux said as they called his flight.

"Why there? Is it nice?" Brigid asked. It felt good to be free and innocent, not always in control. Was that love?

"Very. But I've never been there. Only pictures," Devereux said. "Small and quiet. Simple people. Great beaches."

"Have you been to the Caribbean, Mason?" Brigid asked.

"Many times. St. Martins and Martinique," Devereux answered, conscious that he must board.

"With who?"

"With Angela," Devereux answered. Angela defined the capacity for Devereux's love.

"Why Antigua?"

"Because it's new to both of us. We'll make our own memories there," he answered.

Final boarding was called. They kissed.

"Call me tomorrow?" Devereux asked.

"Yes, of course. I love you, Mason" Brigid said as Devereux boarded the aircraft.

Chapter Fifteen

Garrett O'Donovan and Erskine Colbert helped the wounded Peter Sullivan out of the Opera House. Sullivan groaned with the pain from the wound in his midsection as they hustled him along. Brennan Magee, after reluctantly dropping his weapon, followed close behind. With their tuxedos, they blended with the crowd escaping the carnage. Once out onto the street, they proceeded west up Glengall Street. To security personnel, they were just part of the surging crowd helping a victim of some as yet undetermined terrorist attack.

Flynn was the only driver standing next to his taxi. The other drivers had run toward the Opera House as they saw people running and screaming. The wounded Sullivan was helped into the rear. O'Donovan sat in the front seat next to Flynn.

Flynn pulled out of the row of parked taxis. "Tell me the details," he demanded.

O'Donovan's adrenaline was high from the killing, higher yet because they got away. He was breathing hard.

"It was bloody grand. Right as planned. Fucking police never knew what hit them. Killed the security around the stage with no problem," O'Donovan said.

"Casualties? The Prince?" Flynn asked.

"Killed a lot of big shots we did. People falling everywhere. People in the best seats."

"Did you get the Prince, man?"

"Don't know, sir. I fired at his box but I never saw him. Hard to gauge from the angle. It was a bad angle into the box seats."

For the next fifteen minutes, he recited the chain of events, and responded to Flynn's frequent questions.

"Well done, lads. This has been a masterstroke. But there are a few loose ends to conclude yet this night. This Jamison woman and this photographer Devereux. Better not to leave the matter 'til tomorrow," Flynn said.

"Burns should have already taken care of the Jamison woman. The Mullins brothers should have Devereux waiting for us," O'Donovan reported.

"We must first find out who this Mr. Devereux is and what does he know," Flynn said. "And we must take care of this matter tonight."

Flynn needed to get to a safe house and make his plan for getting back south into the Republic the next day.

As the attack on the Opera House was proceeding, there was a knock on the door of Mary Jamison's flat. She was dressed in an old comfortable cotton robe. Wary of late callers, she asked who it was.

"I'm a patron of the opera," Jack Burns said, repeating the code phrase.

Jamison hated these men. Hated their cause. Hated her Catholic background. Hated being blackmailed and controlled to do God only knew what. She opened the door a crack. It was someone she had not seen before. A short, powerful looking man. He had thinning hair, a large nose, crooked teeth, and was in need of a shave. Even with the code phrase, she was uneasy about letting him in. "I have instructions. May I come in?" The man asked in a not particularly polite tone.

"Yes, come in," she answered. She wondered what new information she would be ordered to obtain.

The man entered and Jamison closed the door. Turning toward the man, she found a gun pointed to her face. Before she could utter a word, Burns fired two small caliber, twenty-two caliber slugs into her face. He then completed the killing by firing three more rounds into her head. As instructed, he dropped a note that had been pasted together from newsprint letters that read, "Catholic whore."

Flynn drove the taxi to a prearranged parking lot outside a movie theater. At this hour, the lot was still full of vehicles. Each man had previously parked his own vehicles at the location. Each had been instructed to set up an alibi for the evening with their wife or girlfriend. The three men retrieved regular clothing from the boot of the taxi, then removed the tuxedos and patent leather shoes. Colbert asked O'Donovan what were they to do about Sullivan. He was bleeding badly and suffering intense pain from his stomach wound.

"We'll call the police and get medical help. No other choice. We can trust Peter. He won't tell the fuckers a thing. Man's got to get medical help, though," O'Donovan said. "I'll stay around long enough to see that he gets help. Now you lads get back home. And don't be coming around to the pub until I contact you."

Flynn said to them, "I'm proud of you lads. You are true Irish patriots. It is men the likes of you that will always keep Irish independence alive. I am honored to fight at your side. This attack is only our first."

Flynn shook hands with Colbert and Magee who then left for their cars. He turned back to O'Donovan and asked in a low voice out of earshot of the wounded Peter Sullivan. "How bad is he?"

"Looks real bad. The bleeding hasn't stopped by the looks of the floor. I'd think as how he'll be dead soon if he don't get help. But I'm no doctor, Sir."

"Let's wipe the car down," Flynn said, meaning they would wipe all surfaces that could hold any of their prints. Flynn produced rags from under the seat, placed there for just this purpose.

With the task completed, Flynn said to O'Donovan, "Sullivan could be a problem. All of our lives could be in jeopardy. The future of our fighting the British could be in jeopardy. One man's life is not worth that, Garrett."

"I don't believe that Peter would ever tell anything to the coppers," O'Donovan said in a weak attempt to avoid the inevitable.

"I'm sure that would be unlikely. But even the slightest risk cannot be taken. He's dying anyway you say. Can you take care of this, Garrett?" Flynn asked as he looked hard into O'Donovan's eyes.

Flynn then removed a Smith & Weston 9mm automatic pistol from a shoulder holster. The pistol was modified to accept a silencer. It had been a gift from someone in the United States, an Irishman and veteran of the U.S. Navy's elite commando force known as SEALs. It was a standard issue weapon for that combat unit. Flynn kept the weapon handy at all times.

Flynn had no qualms about taking care of Sullivan himself, but he wanted to see the depth of O'Donovan's commitment to his leadership. He screwed the eight-inch silencer to the barrel and offered the weapon to O'Donovan.

O'Donovan had no problem killing. He had no special feelings toward Peter Sullivan either. Still, this was different. This was different than anything he had had to do before. Killing Sullivan made for him the realization that he was still an instrument of others bidding. He too could be expendable. This was something he always had known, but killing Sullivan made it real and immediate.

Once again there was no choice here. Ever since Flynn made him the offer to join with him, there were no real choices. He received orders and he obeyed. So Garrett O'Donovan took the weapon from Flynn and went straight away to the taxi. He opened the rear door and with only a moments hesitation shot Peter Sullivan twice in the head.

O'Donovan returned to Flynn and handed over the weapon. Flynn said, "Garrett, you are destined for great things. You have my complete confidence. Now we must take care of this photographer. Bad idea on my part to let him get this close to us. It's what I get for playing along with the softness of my colleagues on the army council."

Flynn continued as they walked to O'Donovan's car. "We've got to determine who this Devereux is. Was he working with anybody else besides this Larkin? What kind of pictures did he take? Where are the photographs? Can you and I be identified?"

"Is Burns, going to be there?" Flynn asked.

"Yes, Sir. He was to have taken care of the Jamison woman then gone straight away to join the Mullins brothers holding Devereux. They're at a garage in the Andersonstown area. Won't take long to get there."

They left the parking lot with O'Donovan driving. Flynn asked, "Is Burns up to interrogating this Devereux?"

O'Donovan responded, "No question there. Worked on that man Larkin with real pleasure. Burn's a mean bugger. Likes to hurt people. Doesn't get along with anybody. Pissed off about not going on the mission. Killing the woman should have been a real pleasure for him. Can't say as I trust him like the others. Wished it had been him rather than Sullivan that took the bullet."

Fifteen minutes later, O'Donovan parked his car next to a row of three other parked vehicles. He and Flynn had no sooner gotten out of the car, then Burns approached them from out of the shadows of the building.

"Everything all right, Burns?" O'Donovan asked.

"Fuck no. Been here three fucking hours. Door's locked. No one's here," Burns said angrily.

"The Jamison woman?" O'Donovan asked.

"She's dead. I do my job. Not like those fucking Mullins arseholes. Shouldn't have given them —-"

"Shut up, Burns," O'Donovan said angrily.

"You need to find out what happened, Garrett. And do it fast. I'll be getting myself to somewhere safe, but I'll not be leaving Belfast until this Devereux situation is resolved," Flynn said. "I'll contact you in the morning."

O'Donovan dropped Flynn at a location where another car had been previously parked for Flynn's escape. He dropped Burns off a few blocks from his flat. Told him to go home, but to stay ready when he heard from him. It was too risky to continue being out on the street in the aftermath of the attack at the Grand Opera House.

It was eleven at night when O'Donovan returned to the pub. O'Donovan's mother was behind the bar. There was a time when she would have asked where he had been. But not now. He would not be telling her the truth, and he knew she did not want to hear that truth anyway. O'Donovan slapped the backs of two patrons. Both of them, as well as several others in the pub, would testify that O'Donovan had been at the pub at the time of the attack at the Opera House.

"That's quite a ruckus I hear happened at the Opera House tonight. Been on the radio. Looks like the I.R.A.'s back in action," one of the men said to O'Donovan, hoping to get some glimmer of inside comment. Most in the pub suspected that O'Donovan was somehow involved with the I.R.A.

"Just heard about it on the radio myself. Not much details though. Only a lot of people killed," O'Donovan replied non-committally. "Helluva thing if it was the I.R.A."

His mother had come over to him and led him away from the table before he was drawn into further conversation.

"Garrett, I've got bad news. Mary Catherine's cousins, Liam and Sean were killed in a car accident earlier this evening. We only learned about it an hour ago. Mary Catherine went to be with her aunt."

O'Donovan left in a hurry for his wife's relatives home not far away. There were many people gathered at the house. O'Donovan was able to learn only that the two brothers had been killed as their van struck a lorry as they went through an intersection. The police had told them that it appeared that Sean, the driver, had ignored the stop sign. They did not know exactly where the accident had taken place, much less the direction the brothers were headed. Several thought O'Donovan's questions not only lacked concern but were terribly odd.

Watching O'Donovan, Mary Catherine suspected that he may have involved her cousins in some sort of I.R.A. activity. He was clearly trying to get information. What with the killings at the Opera House, the death of her cousins, and O'Donovan being away tonight, she could only suspect the worse.

She thought again about what she would do if she too were to be arrested. Would she lie for O'Donovan? Tell the police he was with her like a faithful I.R.A. man's wife? Yes, in all probability she would. The consequences of retribution from the I.R.A. were worse than threats from the police, or the threats of her own conscience. I.R.A. justice was like the Mafia portrayed in the American movies. She did not know how real the Mafia was, but she knew the reality of the I.R.A.

"Is everything all right, Garrett?"

"Not to worry, Mary Catherine."

O'Donovan kissed his wife on the cheek and left.

Had the accident occurred prior to the Mullins' abducting Devereux? Had they failed to entice him? Was Devereux warned off? Or had the Mullins made contact and something went wrong?

Returning to the pub, O'Donovan went upstairs and called the Europa Hotel, asking for Devereux's room. He was informed that Mr. Devereux had checked out that evening. There was nothing he could do until tomorrow when Flynn would call. He thought about getting out of Belfast. The police could be arriving anytime now. Devereux could identify the pub. Perhaps he should go to Armagh. But there was no way he could leave. Flynn would be making contact tomorrow. He must be here. If he left, and was wrong about the police being after him, he would be finished. No choice once again. So O'Donovan did the only thing he could do. He pulled a .357 magnum revolver from a false panel in the wall under the bathroom sink, then sat up in bed to await the police, or the dawn.

The first rays of light woke O'Donovan. Nothing had happened. He was still dressed from the night before. Mary Catherine had not returned, probably staying the night at her aunt and uncle's home. Needing to take some action, he went out to get a newspaper, the London Times, the revolver stuck into the waist of his trousers. He returned to the bedroom and read of the Opera House attack. The oversized headline read:

'ATTEMPT ON LIFE OF PRINCE OF WALES: BELFAST, NORTHERN IRELAND: Last night, gunmen staged a daring attack on a gala performance at the Grand Opera House in Belfast, Northern Ireland. The scheduled performance of Irish music to be performed by such internationally acclaimed artists as Placido Domingo, Albert Duvac, and Jonathan Finny, was interrupted by gunmen attacking with automatic weapons shortly after the opening of the performance. Casualties are unofficially estimated at thirty-five dead and over fifty injured, many seriously.

The performance was attended by His Majesty Prince Charles, the Prime Minister of Ireland, Mr. Eion Dunmore, the British Home Secretary, Mr. Nigel Smith, and the Mayor of Belfast, Mr. Clarence McDonald. The distinguished guests were seated with His Majesty in the Royal Box. Only Mr. Smith sustained wounds, the extent of which are not yet known, however hospital sources said that he is expected to recover. His Majesty, Mr. Dunmore, and Mr. McDonald were not injured. None of the performers has been reported injured, although reports are still sketchy.

His Majesty and the other dignitaries were quickly evacuated from the scene by British Royal Marine helicopters which landed on the grounds of the City Hall building. It is believed that His Majesty and Mr. Dunmore have now left Northern Ireland for security reasons. Mr. McDonald remained on the scene to assess this latest attack on his troubled city.

Reports are still fragmented at this time, but unnamed sources within the security services state that at least two gunmen entered onto the stage shortly after the start of the performance. Armed with assault rifles, they directed their fire first into the box seats then into the front rows of the theater seating. Police sources speculate that fire directed at the Royal Box was thwarted by the angle from the stage. Authorities believe that several other accomplices who directed automatic weapons fire against armed security personnel supported the two gunmen. Reports indicate heavy casualties among security personnel, suggesting a well-planned attack that was intended to neutralize opposition. It is uncertain as to how many security personnel were among the victims of the assault.

Names of the dead and injured have not yet been released. The event was well attended however by many prominent business and political leaders of Northern Ireland. All emergency hospital services were fully activated to transport and care for the large numbers of causalities.

Superintendent Brian Carpenter of Scotland Yard confirmed earlier reports that no bodies of any of the perpetrators has yet been identified among the casualties. Superintendent Carpenter refused to speculate further on the status of the investigation. He indicated that there were leads that were being pursued. While there was no warning, nor as yet any claim of responsibility, other British authorities have stated their belief that this is the work of the Provincial Irish Republican Army.

A highly placed source at Whitehall suggested that the Prime Minister was considering increasing the British military presence in Northern Ireland. The Prime Minister, who has been generally conciliatory to the republican movement, and with rumors still abounding as to his government's secret talks with the I.R.A., is said to be in high temper over this renewed act of terrorism. He is tentatively scheduled to speak to the nation in an address tonight over the BBC.'

O'Donovan read the newspaper over coffee downstairs in the pub which was closed at this hour. It was a disappointment in not killing the heir to the British throne. That would have really been something. But it was still a masterful attack. All critical elements of the attack had gone according to plan. It was as much to his credit as to Flynn's. Even if the coppers came for him now, the attack would still be counted as a daring exploit. He would become part of the lore of the great Irish freedom fighters. Famous as Flynn himself. This Devereux spoiled what should be a celebration.

O'Donovan helped his mother open the pub at ten o'clock in the morning. Flynn called shortly after. It was a quick conversation consisting of a prearranged code. O'Donovan then went to a certain public telephone and waited for Flynn's call precisely twenty minutes later.

"What have you learned?" Flynn said sharply.

O'Donovan resented the fact that Flynn was so short with him after the success of the attack on the Opera House. Not even an acknowledgement now that the details were news.

But O'Donovan said nothing to Flynn about these thoughts. He told him that the Mullins brothers had been killed in a crash. No, he did not know if Devereux was with them and then escaped, or if they had their accident before picking him up.

"Garrett, Devereux must be found and silenced. By what that man Larkin revealed, I suspect that Devereux may not yet have gone to the police. He knows he couldn't continue to operate freely if he presented his evidence about I.R.A. activities. More than that, the police might detain him. Might be hard for him to explain his association with the I.R.A. Might even be charged with withholding evidence. What we don't know is if he's just left or if he's bolted because he knows we're on to his game."

Flynn concluded by saying, "I will not be returning south, Garrett. There is something we must pursue here in Belfast in order to locate this Devereux. Devereux must be found and killed."

O'Donovan did not need to be instructed on this fact. Larkin had revealed that he and Devereux had photographed Flynn and himself at Terrance Dolan's farm the night he was killed. If that were to be made known, there were those in the I.R.A. who could be expected to seek a terrible retribution.

Flynn instructed O'Donovan to meet him at a particular bookstore that afternoon. He also instructed O'Donovan to bring Jack Burns with him and to come armed with concealed handguns.

Chief Inspector, Graham Lenox, the ranking operations officer of Scotland Yard in Northern Ireland had just concluded several hours of an exhaustive examination of the Opera House. It was a grisly scene. The bodies of the victims had not yet been removed. Nor would they until forensic technicians had completed their work. Two teams from London had arrived within hours.

Lenox had seen many a dead person in his career. Many from I.R.A. bombs. Several from I.R.A. individual murders. This certainly was worse than anything he had experienced. Blood soaked the carpet in great stains. Human tissue was splattered everywhere. The dead laid in various poses that suggested their final efforts. A man attempting to shield a woman. A woman attempts to take cover by ducking below the seats.

Lenox personally conducted several debriefing sessions of security personnel on site. Accounts varied from as little as three to as many as six assailants. Descriptions varied, but all consistently identified the attackers as wearing tuxedos. Their method of escape was obvious. How they smuggled in the weapons was still unknown.

Before leaving the scene, Lenox waited until all the victims, at least the male victims, had been preliminarily identified by ID found on their person. All had identification indicating that none of the assailants were among the casualties.

A check of the Grand Opera House staff the next day revealed that two maintenance staff could not be accounted for. Their names were not known to any governmental agency. Their backgrounds fake. Their addresses non-existent. Fellow staff could not shed further details beyond their physical descriptions.

Lenox was grudgingly impressed with the boldness and simplicity of the plan. The execution of the attack was disciplined and precise. This was clearly above typical I.R.A. standards. More often as not, the I.R.A. used bombs as their weapon of choice, usually delivered in cars or lorries. Bombing attacks were comparatively easier to execute and easier for the perpetrators to escape. This attack was on a different level of planning and operational expertise. In addition, infiltration was a wholly new tactic never previously employed by the I.R.A. It was not a comforting thought.

Several days later, Lenox was wading through volumes of reports from security personal and witnesses. A report from a police officer outside the Opera House the night of the incident caught his attention. The officer told of a man that had approached him just minutes prior to the attack saying that he believed the I.R.A. was going to attack. The officer lost contact with the man during the ensuing excitement.

What made the report of even more compelling interest to Lenox was the comment about the man claiming to be a photographer and carrying camera equipment. Only his most senior subordinates knew of photographs received of a Catholic politician's murder and the actual abduction of a Protestant paramilitary leader later found murdered. Someone out there was intimately plugged into the sectarian violence and taking pictures.

To get such photographs, this person must have close contact with people the Yard was interested in. This person would be key to the investigation and undoubtedly an important witness. Was it this same man with the cameras at the Opera House?

Lenox immediately made a call to set-up an interrogation of the R.U.C. officer who had made the report.

It was a miserable flight for Mason Devereux. Although exhausted, he slept fitfully. Disjointed dreams full of dangers and frustrating dilemmas passed for sleep between episodes of semi-consciousness. In all the years of being in war zones, Devereux had never felt so uneasy, and perhaps emotionally disoriented. Reilly of course was at the heart of it. This was the first person since the death of his wife to evoke such feelings. He knew he was in love with her.

A sandwich and a beer at JFK International Airport in New York did nothing to alleviate a pounding headache. He resisted the urge to call Brigid, assuming she was at the office at any rate. Better to call her in the evening, Belfast time. He spent the flight to Los Angles working on an agenda for finishing the book and planning the vacation with Brigid.

It was mid-morning in Los Angeles when Devereux's flight landed. Devereux intended to crash for a day before contacting his agent. He called for a room at the Radisson Hotel in Santa Monica. It was only a fifteen-minute taxi ride from LAX, and a place he knew from his days at UCLA.

Devereux was exhausted when he finally got to his room but anticipated talking to Brigid. It was seven P.M. in Belfast when he called.

"Hello,"

"It's, Mason, how are you?"

"I'm fine. A little tired. I left Dublin early. It's good to hear your voice. I miss you, Mason."

"Good. Then the sooner you see me the better. When can you get away?" Once Brigid was out of Northern Ireland, he could rationally assess what they should both do.

"Three days. That's the soonest I can tie things up at the office. I've told them I'll be on holiday for two weeks. And there's another matter I need to attend to."

"What other matter?"

"I'm seeing certain people in the I.R.A. tomorrow. People close to my Uncle Terry. I'll be telling them your story. I want them to kill Michael Flynn and Garrett O'Donovan for killing my uncle. They'll be no place safe for them. You think I could just walk away after what you've told me, Mason?"

"Brigid, you can't do that. It's too dangerous. It's conceivable that Flynn and O'Donovan could come after you in order to get at me. They know I have evidence that could convict them."

Without waiting for his reply, she continued, "I'll be along in three days, Mason. I need to do this. I'll be fine."

Devereux knew he would not be able to change her mind.

"Then do me this favor, Brigid. Stay somewhere else, including tonight. And don't leave the office alone, in fact don't be alone at any time. Will you do that?"

"Very well, Mason. I'll pack tomorrow and go to a hotel for the next couple of days. But not tonight. I'm too tired."

"Brigid, please. Spend the night somewhere else."

"Okay, Mason. But you're worrying unnecessarily. Now, tell me about this Antigua."

"It's pronounced *An-tee-ga*. It's got great beaches all around the whole island. We can sail or go diving. Not many people, but they speak English. Good place to be alone and make love."

"I like the sound of that, Mason."

Devereux and Reilly chatted for a little while longer before saying good-bye. Devereux told her he would be at the Neuson's weekend house in Laguna Beach, south of Los Angeles. He gave her the telephone number. Reilly promised to call him the next day.

Devereux slept fitfully and woke up late that night. After a room service meal, he called his agent, Larry Neuson.

Neuson wanted to come immediately to pick him up. Devereux suggested that he still needed sleep and that he would see him the next day.

"Fine. I'll be at the hotel at ten to pick you up. Marge too of course. No way she would miss seeing you and hearing everything. We'll have lunch in Laguna. Can't wait to hear about this adventure, Mason. The photographs are extraordinary."

"And, Mason—we're damn glad you're safe and out of there."

Devereux woke early and waited for the Neusons in the lobby. He still felt slightly fatigued, but at least rested. He had time to visit a men's shop and buy a suitable ensemble consisting of fashionable slacks, a silk shirt, and Italian loafers. What few clothes he brought from Belfast were either unsuitable or dirty.

Promptly at ten, Larry and Marge Neuson strode across the lobby. Larry and Marge were both in their mid-fifties, both were still trim and elegant. Larry was dressed in a blue blazer, tan slacks, pale blue shirt, and floral print tie. His hair was thinning, but he was still a good-looking man. Marge wore cream-colored slacks and an orange blouse. She knew how to show herself. Her auburn hair was full and long and her body could still turn heads. Marge was not what one could call pretty, but she was elegant and California tanned.

Marge Neuson sighted Devereux, and literally ran to him. Mason Devereux was technically her husband's client, but she closely followed his exploits simply because he was the firm's most interesting client.

"Mason, mon cheri," she exclaimed as she embraced him and kissed him full on the lips. "But what happened to you?" Referring to the bandage and discoloration of his cheek.

"Auto accident, Marge. But I'm okay," Devereux answered as he hugged her in return.

"Damn if you're still not one handsome man. You're the only one to have ever tempted me to have an affair, Mason," she joked as she held him at arms length by his shoulders.

Larry Neuson was equally as effusive in his greeting, hugging Devereux and then grasping his hand. Both Larry and Marge Neuson genuinely liked Devereux. They saw him only rarely, but they had come to know him from a personal perspective. Both knew that Devereux was a solitary sort and made few close relationships. Both felt they had been privileged to gain such a relationship. In return, they felt that Devereux had a similar affection for them, one that transcended business.

The Neusons took Devereux to an oceanfront restaurant for brunch. With small talk out of the way, Larry brought the conversation around to business.

"I tell you, Mason, this stuff on Northern Ireland is dynamite. It's not a matter of who will be interested as it is a matter of how much. With this escalation of violence, it's great timing. That sounds shitty the way I've phrased it, but you know what I mean. This latest attack yesterday at that theater. An attempt to kill the Prince of Wales. Great stuff. The key here is to get to press as soon as possible while it's still front page news."

"Larry, what I have is much bigger than those headlines," Devereux interrupted. "Much bigger than what those previous photographs say. It's a true scoop in the newspaper sense."

"For starters, I was at the Grand Opera House in Belfast the day before yesterday. I was there during the attack. And I also know who planned and executed the attack. I've got more pictures too, Larry."

Larry and Marge Neuson sat stunned as Devereux recounted his activities of the past weeks in Northern Ireland. Larry hurriedly ordered breakfast and more coffee to get rid of the waiter. Three hours later, Devereux had brought them up to the present.

"Fantastic, Mason, truly fantastic. This is real blockbuster stuff. We've got to get at this right away. I will start testing the waters tomorrow. Wait till I show some of the most influential editors a sampling of the photos. They'll cream their pants. A couple might even have a stroke on the spot," Larry Neuson said with delight.

"Listen, Larry. The shit's going to hit the fan when we publish. There's the problem of what I have being declared evidence in criminal charges under British law. More than that, I'll be wanted as a material witness. Probably broke any number of British laws myself."

Devereux continued. "I'm willing to give them what evidence I have, but I'm not willing to go to Northern Ireland and testify in any trial, or for that matter, go to England. But I do want to see is this asshole Flynn captured or killed."

"I don't know the law, but to police types it's going to sound like you were chummy with a lot of the wrong people. World's getting smaller for you, Mason. Can't go back to Mexico. After this book is published, probably not the UK either. Probably means the Commonwealth nations would not be a good bet either."

"Thanks, Larry, but let's skip the levity. Fact is, I'm suddenly concerned about extradition treaties. I think I should have a conversation with an attorney. May want to provide some information about Flynn right away if it will help to catch him. Can you find me someone with the right credentials? International law type?"

Before Larry Neuson could answer, Marge asked Devereux, "Are you in any danger, Mason?"

Devereux was startled by Marge Neuson's question. He had not considered the thought. He had felt safe once he left Ireland.

"I don't think the I.R.A.'s reach extends to Southern California." Marge's next question however mirrored his own sudden concern.

"What about this girl, Brigid. Is she in danger?"

"I don't think so, Marge," Devereux said without conviction. He was probably making too much of a possible threat from Flynn. And Brigid herself was in some way part of the I.R.A. She certainly knew people high up in the I.R.A. Once she talked to them about Flynn, it would be Flynn and O'Donovan who would be in hiding. As soon as he provided information to Scotland Yard, the police would be looking for Flynn also.

"She'll be taking certain precautions. I'll be seeing her in a couple of days. We're going to the Caribbean for a while."

"But, Mason, you can't go off now with all the work —-," Larry Neuson said, but was interrupted by his wife.

"Mason, you're like a younger brother. I won't admit that you could be my son," Marge Neuson said as she grabbed both of Devereux's hands. "You could easily be my lover except that I'm in love with Larry here. So I'll play the sister role. Get your girl out, Mason. I don't like the circumstances. I know nothing of the politics there, only what you've told me. But listening to you, there's danger for her. I can see you feel it too."

Devereux did feel uneasy but he had done all that he could. Brigid Reilly was her own person. If he was to love her, he would have to come to terms with that.

They left the restaurant and drove south to Laguna Beach to the Neuson's house in a place called Monarch Bay. Monarch Bay was an up-scale gated community off the Pacific Coast Highway.

The Neuson's home overlooked the Pacific Ocean from a height of forty feet. Devereux had stayed there to finalize work on his last book. On the way, they stopped at Sergio Valencia's photography shop to drop off Devereux's film. Sergio promised to have proofs by the evening and would deliver them personally.

Devereux and the Neusons spent the rest of the day mapping out the final elements to put the book together. Neuson had brought the proofs of the previous photographs Devereux had taken. He had taken the liberty of having enlargements made of particular shots of all Devereux's photo sequences.

Devereux looked at the shots that had been sent previously to the Northern Ireland police. The sequence of photographs of the Brennan murder and the face of one of Krill's men driving the getaway van. Not much in the way of evidence now, particularly since Krill and the man driving the getaway van were now dead. The evidence Valencia was now processing was a different matter.

The photographs of Flynn and O'Donovan at Dolan's farm the night of Dolan's murder were not conclusive, but could place them at the scene. It would be more condemning in the eyes of the I.R.A. If Flynn escaped justice from the R.U.C. or British, an I.R.A. court martial would most assuredly result in a death sentence. The photographs capturing Flynn at O'Donovan's pub were another matter. Capturing O'Donovan and another man in tuxedos, and the license tags of the bogus taxi, with those same tags and Flynn himself at the Grand Opera House, amounted to evidence that would clearly convict.

The real issue would be Devereux's own testimony. That's what the British would want. He could testify regarding the circumstances that allowed him to be at the scenes of these acts of violence. He could testify that he followed Flynn and O'Donovan to the Grand Opera House the evening of the attack.

Devereux's thoughts were coming together now. His testimony would add substantially to the weight of evidence of the photographs themselves. Any information he could additionally contribute would not only help flesh out the story for the police, but also add weight to the photographic evidence. Anything he could provide he could and would do through deposition. To testify, they would have to grant immunity for any laws he violated.

Sergio delivered the proofs to Laguna Beach at seven o'clock that evening. To the photo developer, these prints did not seem as dramatic as those he had processed previously. But a quick inventory obviously met with Devereux's approval. This would be compelling evidence against Flynn and O'Donovan. Neuson gave Sergio a generous check for his services.

Marge Neuson had Chinese food delivered in as all three worked well into the night. By one A.M. they had selected the preliminary shots and laid out the rough sequencing for the book. Both Larry and Marge Neuson were fascinated and drawn to the dark photographs.

"Jesus, Mason. This is unbelievable stuff. Looking at these pictures I can feel what you have been talking about," Larry Neuson said looking at the many large corkboards on easels arrayed around the large family room. "I'm in the office tomorrow, on a plane to New York the day after. Wait till they see a sampling of photos."

"Larry, I'd feel better with Brigid being out of Belfast before the word got out about what I've been doing. For that matter, I'd feel better talking to a lawyer before you start talking to editors. Besides, I'm obligated to get this evidence to Scotland Yard first."

Larry understood and reluctantly agreed to postpone his negotiations until the following week. He would have a name of a lawyer by tomorrow.

Devereux opened his bedroom window. The sound of the surf was a sedative. Talking to Brigid the following morning would bring the world back into equilibrium.

Chapter Sixteen

Chief Inspector Lenox of Scotland Yard had been in Belfast for over twenty-five years. He had seen the level of sectarian violence rise and fall. This final step toward a cease-fire seemed a very real possibility. Violence had substantially reduced. The government had taken army patrols off the streets. At least that was the situation up to a few weeks ago.

The attack on the Grand Opera House now threatened any possibility of a cease-fire. Too many important people had been killed. Most were Protestants. The attack had been brought off in spite of tight security. Every police and security agency involved was coming under heavy attack, including Scotland Yard, and particularly the Belfast office.

Lenox reread the interrogation report of the R.U.C. officer that reported being approached by a man who claimed there was about to be an I.R.A. attack. Spoke English as if American. No press affiliation given. Two cameras about his neck and what appeared to be an equipment bag. Close to six feet, slender, dark brown hair, tanned face, late thirties, early forties. Details that provided no avenue of pursuit. There was however, one item of riveting interest. The name Michael Flynn. The photographer had told the officer that Michael Flynn was behind this.

Lenox knew the name well. When he first came to Belfast in the mid-seventies, considerable time was spent in researching the history of the I.R.A., and the circumstances surrounding the recent period of violence that started in Londonderry in 1969. Michael Flynn's name was prominent among the lore. He was something of a legend of that time. A real firebrand. Directly responsible for the killing of numerous British soldiers and R.U.C. policemen. A gunmen from the old school.

Lenox leafed though the Yard's file on Michael Flynn. It was comparatively thin for such a famous outlaw. That was largely because Flynn had never been arrested. Apart from a birth certificate, a couple of photos, the file consisted mainly of intelligence reports, and clippings of Flynn's later activities.

The Crown knew of Flynn's whereabouts. Had known for many years. Problem was there had never been sufficient evidence to extradite Flynn from Dublin. They had tried to push the issue in the late seventies and were rebuffed sharply by Dublin. He was a citizen of the Irish Republic and there simply was no concrete evidence of his crimes. He was now a professor at University College in Dublin. If Flynn had truly been in Belfast, it was extraordinary and had to be linked to the attack. There were still murder warrants outstanding for Flynn's arrest. It also meant that Flynn was and always had been active in the I.R.A. It would be a real embarrassment for Dublin if true. A real coup for Scotland Yard.

Right now, there was little more he could do except put out a broad dragnet for this man with the cameras. All border exits had been alerted with the description. All known press in the country at the time were being investigated.

Garrett O'Donovan arrived at the bookstore designated by Michael Flynn as a rendezvous. Jack Burns sat in the car a half block up the street. They were in the Catholic Andersonstown area. O'Donovan felt exposed being about in the aftermath of the attack on the Opera House, not to mention carrying a firearm. He browsed a display of magazines nervously.

The wizened old man at the counter seemed equally wary about O'Donovan. Flynn's arrival was both a relief as well as an added risk. O'Donovan hardly recognized Flynn. He was dressed in a workingman's coat, knit cap, denims, and work shoes. The dress was typical to merchant seamen. There was some subtle recognition between Flynn and the old man as Flynn strode to up to O'Donovan, the only customer in the shop. The old man locked the front door and put a sign in the window indicating that he was closed. He then disappeared into the back room.

In answer to O'Donovan's questioning expression, Flynn said, "Not to worry. Tom's old I.R.A. He was fighting back in the fifties. Served time in a British prison, but that didn't change his ardor for the Cause. I saw his son die at the hands of the British. I.R.A. records don't show him as currently active, but we've kept in touch over the years. Doubt if the Brits or R.U.C. even know that he's alive. He's to be our communications link from hereon. Here's the phone number. Memorize it. To identify yourself, say this is 'Michael's friend, the Michael that knew your son.' He'll get in touch with me."

"We must locate Devereux quickly. My guess is that he has not yet shared his information with the police. Why should he? He's looking to publish and make money. Might be that he could be in trouble himself if he went to the police. So here's where we'll start. There's a newspaper reporter by the name of Flanagan, a Kevin Flanagan. Works out of the Belfast office here for the *Irish Times*. He's the one that introduced Devereux to us."

And a project that you agreed to and now risks bringing us all down, O'Donovan thought to himself.

"You and Burns get to him. Find out where Devereux has gone. And you must be quick about it. We must have answers today. And one other thing, Garrett—-Flanagan cannot live once you're done with him."

O'Donovan nodded his understanding. He regretted the day he had met this old lunatic. To all sides he was now an outlaw, not the least of which might be the I.R.A. itself.

O'Donovan summarized the situation for Burns, then told him of the plan he had just constructed after leaving Flynn. Burns then drove to a telephone booth somewhere in the center of the city.

"Flanagan here,"

"Mr. Flanagan, I've been told by a Mr. Mason Devereux to contact you. He says I'm to be givin' you a package of photographs but he says he doesn't want me to bring them round to your office. Could you suggest a place, Sir?" O'Donovan said.

"And who are you, Friend?" Flanagan asked sharply.

"I work at the Europa Hotel. Mr. Devereux stayed there but he's gone now. He paid me to deliver this package to you." O'Donovan answered. "So where can I deliver this to you, Sir?"

Flanagan thought for a few moments. Knowing what Devereux had been up to, he felt slightly uneasy. "Castle Court. The shopping mall on Royal Avenue. There's a tobacco shop. I'll be in front."

"How will I recognize you," the caller asked.

"I'll be wearing a dark gray raincoat and carrying a copy of the *Irish Times.*"

The Castle Court shopping mall had been pedestrianized some time ago for security reasons. It was public and offered an obstacle to any attempt to kill or abduct him.

"Very well. I'll deliver the package there at one o'clock if that's all right with you, Sir?"

"Fine. I'll be there."

Burns had parked in front of Flanagan's office building. O'Donovan spotted who he assumed was Flanagan as he left his office. Flanagan was looking to hail a taxi. Both O'Donovan and Burns left the car quickly and were on him with drawn weapons within seconds.

"Into the car, Flanagan. If you resist we'll shoot you right here," O'Donovan said.

Flanagan obeyed and entered the rear of the car followed by O'Donovan. Burns drove. Flanagan's questions were met with orders by O'Donovan to be quiet. Fifteen minutes later Burns parked at one of the wharves in the Victoria Channel sector of Belfast harbor. There were a few other vehicles scattered among the docks but no one in sight.

"I'll ask this just once Flanagan. Where can we find Mason Devereux?" O'Donovan asked.

Flanagan knew this must have to do with Larkin. These guys were I.R.A. Why else would they want Devereux? Somehow they found out what Devereux was up to. God, what had he gotten himself into?

"I thought Mason Devereux was still at the Europa until you told me otherwise. So your guess is as good as mine," Flanagan said.

O'Donovan shot Flanagan in the left knee.

Flanagan screamed in horror and pain, "You bloody fucking animal! I don't know where Devereux is. I haven't seen him for weeks. Thought he was still in Belfast."

"Know a man by the name of Larkin?"

Flanagan was breathing heavily with the agony of his damaged knee. Blood gushed between his fingers as he held the wound with both hands. He would tell them whatever they wished.

"Yes. I know him."

"You set him up with Devereux to spy on the I.R.A.?"

Flanagan hesitated before answering. They knew anyway. "Yes."

The question was irrelevant. O'Donovan already knew the answer from Larkin. "I want to know where Devereux lives."

"I don't know where he lives. He's American but lives in Monte Carlo I think. I don't know where, I just met the guy," Flanagan gasped. It was hard to keep down his nausea.

"If you don't know where Devereux has gone, then who would? Answer carefully newspaper man."

"Jesus Christ, I don't know," Flanagan screamed.

O'Donovan shot him in the other knee.

Flanagan writhed in agony. He vomited and continued to retch uncontrollably. After several minutes he said, "Holy Mother, no more."

"Then tell us what we want to know."

Flanagan contemplated his situation for several moments before answering. "Perhaps Brigid Reilly would know where Devereux is. I believe they were close, maybe even lovers."

"Reilly? The barrister?" O'Donovan asked. He remembered the bitch. He remembered her luscious body. "How in the hell is she involved?"

Once he had crossed the line in betrayal, giving out more information became easier. "I knew she was connected with the I.R.A. I introduced Devereux to her. She linked him up with you people. I think they became close. She might know where he is, but I have no idea."

O'Donovan considered what Flanagan had said. Flynn never told him how Devereux had made contact and obtained special privileges. Reilly handled legal work for I.R.A. defendants. She undoubtedly knew people in the I.R.A., perhaps even those in the leadership.

Convinced that Flanagan did not know Devereux's whereabouts, it was time to move on. Flanagan's eyes widened as O'Donovan pointed his weapon at his head. The shot cut short a final plea. Blood and tissue splattered across the windows.

Burns drove the stolen car to a remote section of the docks. O'Donovan pushed Flanagan's body to the floor. O'Donovan and Burns walked several blocks then took a bus to distance themselves from the body. From a pub, O'Donovan called the bookstore then returned to his table to await Flynn's call. It took only twenty minutes.

Flynn told O'Donovan to find Reilly. He gave O'Donovan Reilly's home and office addresses. His orders were the same as for Flanagan, except not to kill her. O'Donovan cringed at the thought of torturing a woman, especially one that looked like Reilly. In the end he would be ordered to kill her. Flynn was running scared. That alone put a new edge to things. Since Flynn knew Reilly's address, O'Donovan knew that Flynn knew of Reilly all along. The old bastard was the cause of all this now he was running amuck.

O'Donovan called Reilly's office and confirmed with the receptionist that she was in the office. It took a half an hour to locate another car for Burns to steal. They spent the rest of the afternoon watching Reilly's office building. Reilly emerged late in the afternoon. She was striking even at a distance. A wave of arousal distracted O'Donovan briefly, followed by anger in remembering the woman's rejection.

Reilly walked to her car and drove off in the direction of her flat. As Devereux had insisted, she would pack some things and stay at a hotel for the next two nights before she left. Reilly felt it was foolish but she had promised. Once home, Reilly packed outfits for the next two days at the office. What was she to pack for the Caribbean? She had little warm weather clothing. No bathing suit even. What was the need here in Northern Ireland?

To hell with it. Devereux seemed to have money. He could buy her whatever she needed. She would take a pair of jeans and a jacket for the flight, and a simple evening dress and heels for dinner.

Reilly had just begun to gather some things when there was a knock at the door. She was about to open it when caution set in. She rarely had anyone come to her door. "Who is it?"

"I've a package for delivery, Mum. A Mr. Flanagan, a Kevin Flanagan sent me round with it. I was to wait until you arrived home was what he told me. Said it was very important and urgent," O'Donovan said.

With little hesitation, Reilly opened the door.

"Remember, me?"

The shock of seeing O'Donovan paralyzed her for a moment before she tried to slam the door shut. O'Donovan easily forced his way through followed by Jack Burns.

"What the fuck do you want you murdering pig!" Reilly screamed.

"My, my, such language, Brigid. Now just who is it that I'm supposed to have been murderin'?"

Reilly's better sense took hold. She was clearly in some sort of danger. It would not do to reveal her knowledge that O'Donovan and Michael Flynn had murdered Terrance Dolan. With as much calm as she could muster, Reilly asked, "What do you want, O'Donovan?"

"A kind word, a little information, Brigid. Sit down now if you will."

Burns pulled a weapon from inside his jacket. It had an exceptionally long barrel, oversized for the last few inches. The man holding it had crooked teeth and needed a shave. She sat down in the single stuffed chair in her living room. She was genuinely scared.

"We've not much time, Luv. Tell us what we need and we'll be out of here. Don't be thinking about tryin' to run. That gun my friend is holding is what they called silenced. Just like in the movies. If he shoots you, your neighbors would never hear it. Now, tell me where we can find this photographer, Mason Devereux."

Graham Lenox reflected upon the task force staff meeting he had just left. The attack had been devilishly well planned. There was a lot of evidence to work with, but nothing showed promise as yet. Several witnesses identified two of the Opera House maintenance staff as being gunmen. Both were unaccounted for and not among the casualties. Personnel records indicated they had been employed at the Opera House for only a few months. They had no useful descriptions of the two other men.

No one had yet claimed credit for the attack. Curiously, several calls claiming to speak for the Provisional Irish Republican Army vigorously disavowed any responsibility for the attack. The task force was evenly split on this being the work of the Provos, or that of a renegade I.R.A. faction. The only avenue of promise seemed to be this photographer that tried to warn of the attack.

With a sad resignation, he picked up today's *London Times* and read that the British army would again commence patrols in the streets of Belfast. The Prime Minister had also announced an increased deployment of two thousand troops in Northern Ireland in the wake of this attack. Political pandering Lenox thought to himself. Troops could not do a damn thing to prevent this type of attack. The PM simply had to show a get-tough approach to counter the fallout of speculation that he had allowed his government to engage in secret talks with terrorists.

Later that day, an aide brought him a report about a body that had just been discovered. The man had been murdered. His body discovered in a stolen car abandoned on the docks. Death resulted from a shot to the head, but the victim had also suffered 'kneecapping' before being killed. The body had been identified as that of Kevin Flanagan, a reporter for the *Irish Times* working out of their Belfast office. Not a photographer, but nonetheless it had the appearance of another I.R.A. attack, and only two days since the attack at the Opera House.

Calling in one of his lead detectives, Lenox ordered him to have a team get over to the *Irish Times* offices. They were to determine if the *Times* had any photographers on staff in Belfast, or if Kevin Flanagan had ever worked with contract or freelance photographers.

"Brigid, Dear, it's to no use for you to keep telling us that you don't know where this Devereux is. You were fucking him regular is the way I hear it. So that being the case, it's not bloody likely he'd leave and not tell you where he was going," O'Donovan said. "If you don't start talking, my friend here is going to get rough with you. I think he might like that, Brigid."

Reilly kept to the same line of denials. Then O'Donovan hit her hard across the cheek with the back of his hand. She cried out, "You fucking bastard."

O'Donovan hit her again, this time with a closed fist. The blow jerked Reilly's head back and to the side. She slumped forward, dazed and only semi-conscience. O'Donovan ordered Burns to help him lift her. Together they half carried her into the kitchen and sat her in a chair. O'Donovan held her up in the chair while Burns went to get some bed sheets. Returning, he ripped the sheets into strips and proceeded to tie Reilly's wrists behind the back of the chair.

Once she realized what was happening it was too late to effectively resist, especially after another blow from O'Donovan. When Burns was through, each leg had been secured to the leg of the chair, and she was bound at the waist as well.

O'Donovan stepped back, and let Burns get to the task. The first step of which was to gag Reilly's mouth with a strip of the sheet.

"What he's going to do will be very unpleasant, Brigid. So one last time, where is Devereux?"

Reilly's heart was pounding violently. Sweat beaded on her forehead. Her eyes were wide with terror. She made no response.

Burns located a long carving knife. He was nearly salivating as he approached Reilly. The pronounced rising of her breasts transfixed his eyes. He slit open her blouse, then her bra. Laying the knife on the table, Burns pulled away Reilly's bra and cupped each breast in his large, coarse hands. He squeezed her breasts roughly and rubbed the nipples.

"I'm sure my friend would like to continue his pleasure with your magnificent body. You might even like it too. But, as I said, we're in a hurry. So I'm afraid he must become a bit more persuasive."

Burns lit a cigarette. He took a deep draw, flicked off the ash, then touched the lit end to the side of Reilly's left breast. Reilly screamed in agony, but only a course guttural sound came through the gag. The tendons on her neck stood out as she clamped down on the gag with her jaw.

Burns removed the cigarette and inhaled again. The end glowed brightly as he brought it in front of Reilly's eyes. He then applied it to the other breast. Reilly struggled violently as Burns held her by the shoulder as he applied the cigarette. She urinated involuntarily. He took another drag, then quickly applied the burning end to a new location.

"Brigid. Brigid. Can you hear me?" O'Donovan asked.

Reilly's eyelids fluttered. Her breathing calmed as she came down from the pain. Her body was drenched in sweat.

"Brigid. I'm going to ask this only once. If you do not answer, my friend will continue. And if the cigarette does not make you talk, then he will move to more advanced methods. Right now, you'll have three small scars. Only your lover might wonder. If he works on your face with that knife, now that's a different matter. So what'll it be, Luv?"

God should curse her, but she could not bear any more of this. She rationalized that Devereux could escape these monsters. After all, this was his life. Flirting with death. She also knew she simply did not have whatever strength or conviction that was necessary to withstand torture. She nodded affirmatively with the briefest of gestures. O'Donovan removed the gag.

"Talk, Brigid. Where is Devereux?"

Tears streamed uncontrollably down her face. "He's in California."

"Where in California?"

"Somewhere near the ocean. His agent's house. Place called Laguna Beach. No address. I have the phone number." She recited the number to O'Donovan.

"What else?"

"What do'ya mean?"

"When did he leave? How did he leave? When is he to contact you?" O'Donovan shouted at her. "Tell me everything, Brigid, or we'll begin again."

Reilly told him everything she knew, after which, O'Donovan left the kitchen and made a call to the bookshop. Fifteen minutes later, Flynn called back. O'Donovan briefed him on the information. Flynn said that he would be at Reilly's flat within two hours.

Flynn arrived as scheduled. He went into the kitchen and was offended with the sight of Reilly's bare breasts. "Burns, get something to make her decent."

"Decency he says. You bloody, fucking hypocrite," Reilly said to Flynn. "A naked woman offends you but not murder. You murdered Terrance Dolan, you fucking pig."

"You've a sharp tongue, lass. See that you control it or the worse you'll be for it," Flynn said.

"I see that our friend Devereux has shared not only his bed, but all his confidences with you, girl. According to what you told Garrett here you're to meet him in a couple of days in the Caribbean. That true?" Flynn asked.

Reilly did not answer.

"Well I'm afraid that will have to wait awhile my dear. Our Mr. Devereux must give up his pictures first, and you're the price. For your sake I hope his feelings for you are strong enough."

Burns returned with a jacket and covered Reilly. O'Donovan telephoned Martin Kelly who arrived within the hour. O'Donovan and Flynn then left, with only Flynn returning two hours later.

Reilly hurt terribly from having been tied to the kitchen chair for hours. The cigarette burns screamed out in constant agony. Burns had dropped the jacket to her waist and scarcely took his eyes from her breasts while Flynn was gone. Kelly was at first slightly embarrassed, but soon fell in with Burns' raunchy comments.

With Flynn's return, Reilly asked, "Are you goin' to be keeping me tied here forever?"

"There's one thing to be done first, my dear," Flynn answered. "We're going to be calling Mr. Devereux."

Flynn dialed the number. It was afternoon in California.

"Hello?"

"Mr. Devereux?"

The accent was Irish but he could not place the voice. "Yes. Who is this?"

"Why it's Michael Flynn, lad. Disappointed you didn't recognize my voice. From what I understand, you're well acquainted with my face. Took pictures and all they say."

Devereux was stunned. Only Brigid knew where he was. "And who is *they*?"

"Why an old fellow by the name of Larkin. An employee of yours I believe. Also a journalist acquaintance, a Mr. Flanagan. And of course, the lovely Miss Brigid Reilly. Miss Reilly's with me right now in fact. But I'm afraid Mr. Larkin and Mr. Flanagan unfortunately met with fatal accidents recently."

Devereux felt defeated. He suspected maybe Larkin, but not Brigid and Kevin Flanagan too. He should have somehow forced Brigid to leave immediately.

"So what is it you want, Flynn?"

"Oh, come on, Mr. Devereux. You know what I want. It's those interesting photographs you have."

"So you want the photographs and of course the negatives in exchange for the woman?"

"Ah, if it were so simple, Mr. Devereux. The problem is how to be sure you give up all the evidence. This call is only to stop you from doing anything further with those photographs, Mr. Devereux."

"Let me speak with Brigid," Devereux said.

"In good time. Now listen to me Mr. Devereux. I don't think I have to convince you that I will have Miss Reilly killed, unpleasantly if necessary, if I do not get what I want. The problem of how we can effect a transfer, and how I'm to be sure that I have all the photographic evidence, is now your problem. You have four days to devise a plan, Mr. Devereux. I'll contact you at the same time, four days from now."

"Let me speak with Brigid, Flynn."

Flynn had Burns and Kelly carry Reilly still strapped to the kitchen chair into the living room close to the telephone.

"Mason, oh God I'm so sorry. I couldn't take it anymore."

Devereux closed his eyes at the thought of what they may have done to her. "What did they do to you, Brigid?"

"They burned me with cigarettes. Then they were going to cut my face. I couldn't, Mason, I couldn't," she said and broke down crying uncontrollably.

"Easy, Brigid. No harm. They'd have found me anyway."

Flynn was back on the line. "You see the position, Devereux. Four days from now. Same time. Be creative my friend." Flynn disconnected the call.

Devereux sat on the deck listening to the surf roll onto the beach for over an hour. Dipping into his reservoir of professional strength, he found a way to isolate the terrible emotions of knowing that Reilly was in imminent danger. A rough course of action was forming. He went inside to call Larry Neuson at his office.

"Miss Reilly. We are going to untie you. You're to clean yourself up, pack a few things, and be ready to leave in fifteen minutes," Flynn said. "Keep the door open. Do not try to escape or call for help. If you do, you'll be killed. It's as simple as that."

Burns and Kelly untied her. The relief in her hands and feet with the flow of blood almost made her faint. She quickly gathered clothing from the bedroom, then went into the bathroom and washed in the sink. She shook with fear. The angry wounds on her breasts brought tears as she gently washed herself.

While Reilly was readying herself, Flynn instructed Burns and Kelly to take her to a farm in County Armagh near the border. He gave them specific directions. They were to hold up in the barn with Reilly. Food and water would be provided.

"Mind you, Burns, you'll not be taking any pleasures with her. Do you hear what I say?" Flynn said. He glared at Burns.

"Yes, Sir," Burns answered grudgingly. This was one old man that would surely put a bullet in his head for disobeying orders. Too bad. Just looking at this woman aroused him.

The team of detectives following up on Kevin Flanagan's murder reported back to Chief inspector Lenox after a couple of hours. From the office staff, they had learned that Flanagan knew a Mason Devereux, a freelance photojournalist with several published books to his credit. Photographic works taken in various war zones. Flanagan had two such books which the investigators brought back. Hotel registration records indicated that a Mason Devereux had stayed a couple of months at the Europa, checking out the day of the attack on the Grand Opera House. Devereux's passport was from Monaco which did not seem to fit with the description of an American.

Lenox decided to take a direct route to track down this Mason Devereux. Interpol was too plodding. He called an old acquaintance at the Surete in Paris. As Monaco was still closely connected with France, the Surete extended its jurisdiction to the tiny principality.

Not waiting to hear back from his French colleagues, Lenox directed an aide to place a call to another contact within the Federal Bureau of Investigation. Old gossip and pleasantries taken care of, Lenox stated his formal request to locate Mason Devereux. To expedite matters, Lenox gave his F.B.I. contact the publisher of the Devereux's last two books, and the editor's name gleaned from the acknowledgments.

Twenty minutes later, the F.B.I. contact called Lenox with the name, address, and telephone number of Devereux's literary agent. Ten minutes after that, Chief Inspector Graham Lenox had bullied his way through a receptionist to Larry Neuson.

"Sir, it is imperative that we speak to Mr. Devereux. I'm sure you are aware of the recent terrorist attack at the Grand Opera House in Belfast. We have reason to believe that Mr. Devereux may possess vital information in that investigation. Do you know how we can contact him?"

Neuson knew how to deal with editors, negotiate contracts, and generally smooze his way around the publishing business. Dealing with heavy weight police types, especially foreign, was another matter.

"I'm only generally aware of the venue in which he has been working. In fact, I'm not sure where he is at the present, Chief

Inspector," Neuson lied. "However, I understand your urgency. If you'll allow me some time, I'll try to locate Mr. Devereux."

"I can't impress upon you how urgent this matter is. I'll call back in two hours, Mr. Neuson." Lenox hung up before Neuson could offer an excuse.

Neuson immediately called Devereux at the beach house. Devereux listened to Neuson's recounting of Graham Lenox's inquiry.

"Larry, they've got Brigid."

"What? What do you mean, Mason?"

Devereux explained the situation to Neuson. He then proceeded to lay out his plan of attack. "Did you locate a lawyer for me, Larry?"

"Yeah. I've got a list of three, all with good credentials in the international area."

"Good. Get one of them here in an hour," Devereux said. "Must be any number of them in L.A. of all places."

"Jesus, Mason. An hour? These guys are not chopped liver."

"Fuck it, Larry. They're lawyers, they're whores. Offer them double their normal billing rates. Sell them that I'm a big ass photojournalist. Tell them this could be high profile publicity. Come on, Larry, sell it. I need the legal representation and the ability to confound any British effort to extradite."

"Time is short, Larry. I need to talk with this Inspector Lenox. I've got to get Brigid out of this."

"You come up here to the office. One hour. I'll see what I can do," Neuson said.

Devereux arrived at Neuson's Santa Monica office in less than hour. Ten minutes later, a lawyer by the name of Banning joined them. Devereux spent the next thirty minutes filling in the background for Banning. Banning made notes furiously, and asked only a few questions. Devereux concluded with the call from Flynn.

"Extraordinary, absolutely extraordinary, Mr. Devereux. I'll be one of the first to buy this book." Banning said. "I can help you on the international legal issues. Afraid I can't advise you on what to do about the woman though. What do you intend to do?"

"Get the police on it. It's the only choice. I'll start with this Scotland Yard chief inspector, Lenox who contacted Larry. Sounds like he needs no convincing about what I might have. I'd intended to send them the pictures anyway but I assume that my offer of testifying should be a powerful inducement. Am I right, counselor?"

"Absolutely. You have first hand testimony that not only backs up the photos but puts the photos in a larger context," Banning said.

"Could the British extradite me on any charges?"

Banning considered Devereux's question for a few moments before responding. "They could try. They could file charges of conspiracy, maybe even charges of being an accessory to murder."

"And if they wished to pursue that tack, what happens?" Devereux asked.

"They would have to file a complaint in U.S. federal court. Since you are a U.S. citizen, they must convince a U.S. federal magistrate of criminal, and I might add, serious criminal activity, before any order of arrest would be given."

"So? What is your assessment?" Devereux asked Banning.

"You obviously broke criminal laws in the U.K. However, they'd have a difficult time arguing for extradition. If they tried, we could tie them up indefinitely. They want to get these guys. So do you. Since you have a mutual interest in cooperating, they should be more interested in your information right now rather than your extradition.""

Devereux considered what Banning had said. He generally disliked lawyers but at least Banning did not equivocate.

"In a few minutes I'm going to have a conversation with Scotland Yard. I may need your advice."

"More than happy to stay, Mr. Devereux," Banning said. He would not miss this for anything.

Chief Inspector Lenox called Neuson a few minutes later. With little preamble, Neuson switched to the speakerphone and introduced Devereux.

"Mr. Devereux. I must tell you that you are in serious legal difficulty here," Lenox said. "What we would like —-"

"What you would like is of little interest to me, Chief Inspector. I know what you want, and you can eventually have it. In fact you can also have my testimony. However, I need something first."

"Which is what, Mr. Devereux?"

"Do you know a barrister by the name of Brigid Reilly?"

"Yes. I.R.A defendants mostly," Lenox answered.

"Well, Chief Inspector, Michael Flynn has her. He wants these pictures too. Says he'll kill her if I don't find a way to return all photographic evidence and find a way to convince him there are no other copies. I know he'll kill her even if I deliver them."

"Do you mean Michael Flynn, the old I.R.A. gunman, the professor in Dublin?"

"Yes. I take it you know him?"

"We know of him, but from the old days. You mean he's directly involved himself and actually here in Northern Ireland?"

"I'll tell you all the details at a later time, Chief Inspector. Right now you've got to concentrate on rescuing Brigid Reilly. My cooperation is dependent upon Reilly's life. So I suggest you get on with it immediately."

Devereux told him the time he received the call from Flynn and spoke with Reilly. He did not know where the call had originated from. Lenox told him he would call back within a couple of hours.

Thirty minutes after talking with Devereux, heavily armed officers of the R.U.C. surrounded the apartment building where Reilly had her flat. Soon after, the officers broke down the door. No one was there.

Chapter Seventeen

Garrett O'Donovan again felt out on a limb. Only this time, he was way out there. What Flynn wanted him to do was an act of desperation.

They had left Brigid Reilly's flat and gone to the bookstore. Flynn made a call to the United States. O'Donovan could understand little of what was said since the conversation was in Gaelic. Concluding the call, Flynn instructed O'Donovan on what was to be done.

"I was speaking with a good friend in Boston. He has offered his help," Flynn said. "You and Magee will fly to New York in the morning. You'll meet two men out of Boston at the airport. I'm told they're former I.R.A. from Derry. Good lads. Handy with weapons."

"From New York, you'll fly to Los Angeles. The men from Boston will go with you but you're in command, Garrett. Your mission is to destroy any pictures this Devereux took and to kill him. You'll have to kill his literary agent too. Arrangements for weapons will be made. You'll pick them up in Los Angeles."

"Remember, Garrett, if the pictures get out, not only the Brits will be looking for us, but friends of Terrance Dolan as well. We'll all wind up living underground in some godforsaken place."

O'Donovan returned to his flat above the pub at three in the morning. Before going upstairs, he called Brennan Magee from the public telephone. Magee was surly at having been woke until O'Donovan told him to be ready to leave within thirty minutes and to bring his passport.

Mary Catherine awoke as he entered the room but said nothing. He turned on the bathroom light and left the door slightly ajar to afford some light to pack a few things.

"Will you be going somewhere, Garrett?" Mary Catherine asked.

"Yes. For a few days."

"And if the police come around, what am I to say?"

"You say that you don't know where I am, which is the truth, woman."

In five minutes, he had packed a small duffel bag.

"Be careful, Garrett." Even through the dark she could sense O'Donovan's anxiety. There was something different about his manner this night.

"I'll be seein' you, Mary Catherine. You tell my Mum ya hear," he said, then left their bedroom without kissing her.

O'Donovan picked up Magee. They were stopped twice by newly instituted British army patrols. Apart from the usual rudeness of the soldiers, they passed without incident. They arrived at Aldergrove International Airport in time to catch a seven a.m. shuttle on British Airways to Heathrow Airport in London. They connected to a nine a.m. flight to JFK International, arriving mid-morning in New York.

They were told to look for two men, both wearing Boston Celtic caps. They were to approach them and ask if they were friends of Michael. 'Michael, who?' was to be their response, confirmed by 'Flynn, of course.'

The two men from Boston were waiting as O'Donovan and Magee arrived at JFK and cleared customs. After the recognition signal, all four had coffee while they waited for their flight to Los Angeles.

The two men from Boston were beside themselves with excitement at the prospect of going on a mission here in the U.S. with two gunmen out of Belfast. Both men were I.R.A. They had been involved with a bombing resulting in the probability of arrest. A well-established relative of one of the men who was active in the Irish republican movement in the U.S., arranged for the two to come to Boston. The relative was closely associated with a long time friend of Michael Flynn, who in turn was a dominant figure in the American Irish community. Many a Provo had found a new home and a new identity in the U.S. to escape arrest in Northern Ireland.

"Do ya know what we're up to in Los Angeles?" One of the Boston men asked O'Donovan, wanting to make conversation.

O'Donovan ignored the question. "So what are your names?"

"I'm Eoin Russell, and this here's Brian Kavanagh."

"I'll be Mr. Smith, and my friend here is Mr. Jones," O'Donovan responded. "Now as to what we're about in Los Angeles, I'll tell you. We're to kill an informer. You lads have any problem with that?"

Russell answered somberly, "No, sir."

Magee asked, "Ever kill anybody?"

Russell and Kavanagh looked at each other. Kavanagh answered, "We done some bombing. Some coppers died. That's why we had to leave and come to America."

"Big fucking deal. I'll tell you what killing is —-" Magee started to respond, but was cut off by O'Donovan.

"Tell us about the arrangements in California. Have you ever been there?" O'Donovan asked.

Russell answered, "No, sir. But one big city is pretty much the same. We learned Boston good. The map we got of Southern California shows the place where you want to go. Looks easy to get to from the airport."

"How do we get the weapons?" O'Donovan asked.

"Easy. They were shipped earlier by airfreight from Boston. We'll pick them up at the United Airlines air freight terminal when we arrive," Russell answered.

"What about a car?"

"We're to rent one. I've a stolen driver's license and credit card. Fresh stolen too," Russell said.

"What's this guy done?" Russell asked.

"Done things against the I.R.A. Can't tell you more. Your job is to get us to the target. My friend and I will do the hit. Then you'll get us out of there," O'Donovan said. "Now let's see the map."

Russell produced two maps, one of Los Angeles County, and one of Orange County. They would arrive in Los Angeles County and drive to the target location in Orange County. Russell outlined the route from Los Angeles international Airport to South Laguna Beach.

"And where is Santa Monica?" O'Donovan asked.

Russell did not know, but found it on the map. "North of the airport. Opposite direction from this South Laguna Beach. Are we to go there too?"

"Depends. At any rate, it doesn't look far. Right along this same main highway called the four-zero-five. We'll go to this South Laguna Beach first. We believe our man is there," O'Donovan said.

Continuing, O'Donovan asked, "I was told your people would get us information on what sort of neighborhood this house was in?"

"This man you're after must be a rich fucker. The address that was given is a place called Monarch Bay. Right on the ocean. The problem's going to be that it's what they call a gated community," Russell said.

"Which is what?" Magee asked sharply.

"Means they've got a guard gate to get into the area. Won't let you in unless you're okayed by whoever you're goin' to see," Russell said.

"We'll just have to figure out a way in then. Not to worry," O'Donovan said with more confidence then he really felt. This was another obstacle adding to the uncertainty.

Little else was said while they waited for their flight. O'Donovan had made it clear that there was to be no further talk about the mission, Ireland, or the I.R.A. The flight was to arrive at three o'clock in the afternoon, California time. Both O'Donovan and Magee spent most of the flight sleeping.

O'Donovan was stirred awake by a flight attendant requesting he return his seat to the upright position in preparation for landing. He was still groggy. It was poor quality sleep and not much of it. He had dreamed a strange confused dream that included his father and Mary Catherine.

As they flew over the vast expanse of greater Los Angeles, both O'Donovan and Magee looked out the window with some awe. O'Donovan felt disoriented and uneasy. He was to rely on people he did not know and who themselves had never even been to Los Angeles. He was in a foreign country of which he knew nothing. When he had been in Massachusetts for training, he saw nothing outside of the training camp. He could have been anywhere.

O'Donovan wondered if Flynn really thought they could recover all the photographs this Devereux took, or did he simply want revenge? If he got back alive, he must find some way to separate from Flynn. Flynn would surely get him killed.

The four men proceeded to the rental car counters. O'Donovan worried about the stolen credit card that Russell was to use and watched the clerk intently. But the clerk did nothing to verify the status of the card, probably because it matched the name on the driver's license. In ten minutes they were out of the terminal, catching a Hertz shuttle bus to the rental car lot.

Picking up the car, Russell drove and followed the instructions of the rental car clerk to the United Airlines Cargo terminal on Century Boulevard. At the counter, Russell showed a copy of the freight bill, and the driver's license as identification. It mattered little that he did not really resemble the picture on the license.

The man returned with a box. Russell signed for it. Returning to the car, Russell opened the trunk and began pulling open the tape sealing the box. The other three men joined around him.

Inside, wrapped in towels to secure them in transit, were four Browning 9mm automatic pistols. Two of the weapons were modified to accept silencers. Eight spare magazines were also included. O'Donovan and Magee took the modified pistols and put the silencers in their jacket pockets. Russell and Kavanagh took the other two pistols and put them under the front seats of the car.

Ten minutes later, they were traveling south on the 405 Freeway. Russell ventured a question to O'Donovan. "Do ya know how we're to get to this man, sir?"

The truth was that O'Donovan had no idea, especially with this new problem of the security gate. "Not until I look at the site first."

"I might have an idea, if you'd care to hear it?" Russell said.

After the conversation with Chief Inspector Lenox in Belfast, Neuson insisted on driving Devereux back to Laguna. He asserted that this was no time to be alone. Neuson advised his secretary to call Lenox's office in Belfast and give them the number in Laguna. He had never seen Devereux like this before. Devereux was scared.

Once at the house in Laguna, Neuson called his wife who was in San Francisco on business. He recapped the day's events, after which she wanted to talk with Devereux.

"I won't give you any motherly crap, dear, but keep your head about you. You live in danger all the time and you survive by your wits. This is no different," Marge Neuson said, knowing this was clearly different.

"Marge, I can't lose her, too."

"I know, Mason. I'll be on the next flight and be there in a few hours, Mason."

Chief Inspector Lenox called only minutes later.

"We entered Miss Reilly's flat. No evidence of forced entry. No evidence of any struggle. Difficult to say if any of her clothes are missing," Lenox said. "Her office confirms only that she left at around five o'clock yesterday."

"Then what would you suggest, Chief Inspector?" Devereux asked.

"Mr. Devereux, the only thing you can do now is string them along. You have to find a way to offer them a solution that is convincing."

"That would do the Crown's case no good, Chief Inspector."

"We're not all bloody animals in this war, Mr. Devereux. I'd rather see your Miss Reilly safe than have those photographs that incriminate Flynn. We'll get Flynn anyway now that we know of his involvement in I.R.A. field operations. Right now I've a team of key people working on trying to figure a plausible plan for you to present to Flynn."

"I appreciate your efforts Chief Inspector, but I really think that Flynn is simply using Brigid as a means to postpone my going to you guys. Probably knows he's blown and this is a way to buy time. He could hold Brigid hostage for weeks. Time to get out of the country. He knows there would be no way to be absolutely sure that he got back all the photographs."

"Perhaps. But he has reason to believe that the police know nothing of his involvement. We wouldn't if you hadn't sent those pictures to us. He might plan to get the pictures back then threaten to kill Reilly, or your friend Egan Malone, or your agent, or somebody else close to you if you ever reneged on the deal. Not really that farfetched of an idea if you think about it. Or, he might simply be looking to kill you in the exchange."

"Maybe you're right, Chief Inspector. Rest assured, if Reilly is rescued safely, I'll do whatever's necessary to help you get Flynn. Too bad you do not still execute in the U.K., Chief Inspector. People like Flynn should die. If I were to get the opportunity, he would not see a courtroom."

"Well I can understand your feelings, Mr. Devereux. Flynn is definitely a species of vermin that needs extermination. I would like to see that old bastard laid out too rather than stand in the dock while lawyers argue legal technicalities. But either way, we have to run him to ground first."

Lenox continued, "You know Mr. Devereux, that whatever plan you devise to return the photographic evidence to Flynn presents a prime opportunity to apprehend Flynn, or at least his key associates."

"That's obvious, Chief Inspector, but I've no intention of compromising the safety of Miss Reilly."

"Come on Mr. Devereux. You know the score. I don't need to tell you that Miss Reilly's chances are very slim."

"Yeah, I know about her chances, Chief Inspector. But I also know she's not your main concern. After all, she's just an I.R.A. lawyer. Good riddance to the bitch I'd think you'd probably feel. So forget any attempt to monitor further calls from Flynn by your colleagues in the FBI."

Devereux felt the anguish of terrible fear for the first time in his life. That anguish responded with anger to Lenox, "I know I can't stop you, but if you screw up anything that causes Reilly's death, you'll get shit from me."

Lenox held his own anger. It was obviously not in his best interest to alienate Devereux. "I assure you, Mr. Devereux, that Miss Reilly's safety is our foremost concern. I merely wish to emphasize the need to provide us with whatever information that may be useful in her rescue."

A few more unproductive exchanges occurred between Devereux and Lenox before they rung off.

Marge Neuson arrived a couple of hours after Lenox called. Larry Neuson was already slightly drunk on his third vodka gimlet. Devereux was quiet and sullen, nursing a scotch. The three of them talked strategy for hours, reaching no conclusion. Devereux participated in the discussion, but in a detached way. Finally at one in the morning, Marge kissed Devereux good-night, then helped her husband navigate unsteadily to the bedroom. Devereux went out onto the balcony, oblivious to the cold night's breeze coming off the ocean.

"So what's your idea?" O'Donovan asked of Russell.

"Well, sir, I'd think we'd be best tryin' to take this house at night. But at night it might be harder still to get in I figured."

"Get to it, man. What are you suggesting'?"

"Gas truck, sir. We lift a gas company service van. Then we tell the guy at the guard gate that we have a report of a gas leak. Gas leak's a big deal. Law even requires the gas company to check such reports immediately. Gives us a reason to enter even after dark."

"Where do we find one of these gas company vans?"

Russell was warming to the attention this big shot I.R.A. gunman was paying him. This could be important for him back in Boston. "Probably the best bet is one of their maintenance yards. They must have trucks leaving all the time." Russell was not at all certain of his last statement. "I'll look up an address in a telephone book."

Russell suggested they get off the freeway and look for a telephone booth. O'Donovan agreed and Russell left the 405 freeway and proceeded down Jamboree Road in Newport Beach to the Pacific Coast Highway.

Before they located a telephone booth, the other man from Boston, Brian Kavanagh, yelled out, "Shit, Eion, there's a bloody gas company truck right there." They all looked at the van parked on the Pacific Coast Highway at a fast food restaurant north of Corona Del Mar.

Eion Russell pulled the rental car to the curb. O'Donovan barked orders, "Russell you stay here. Kavanagh and I will go into the restaurant. Mr. Jones will watch the van."

O'Donovan and Kavanagh entered the restaurant. They quickly spotted the gas company service man's uniform. He appeared to be concluding his meal. O'Donovan and Kavanagh went back outside to wait. Each lit a cigarette.

As the man left, O'Donovan fell in behind him and put the muzzle of his gun into the man's back. O'Donovan and Kavanagh pushed the man into the back of the van.

"Take off your uniform," O'Donovan shouted. The man obeyed. O'Donovan then shot him twice in the chest with his silenced weapon.

Kavanagh was no stranger to violence, but he had never seen a man killed. This close up, he was nearly in shock at the murder. O'Donovan ordered him to put on the gas company uniform. Kavanagh obeyed, making the sign of the cross before putting on the clothes of the murdered man.

They drove south to Laguna. As they approached the entrance of the Monarch Bay community, Kavanagh slowed to allow a look at the guard gate. Magee and Russell followed in the rental car.

"Park over there," O'Donovan told Kavanagh.

Across the Pacific Coast Highway from the Monarch Bay Community was a small shopping plaza. It offered a convenient place to park the rental car. It was not yet six o'clock in the evening.

"We'll wait until after dark," O'Donovan said to the others standing outside the vehicles. "Kavanagh will drive, the rest of us will be in concealed in the back."

"What about the body?" Russell asked.

"What about it? Stays in the van. What else can we do with it?" O'Donovan said.

The men sat and smoked as the minutes crawled by. Clouds moved in off the coast bringing a dark night after the sunset. O'Donovan motioned to Magee and Russell to join him and Kavanagh in the van.

Weapons were checked. O'Donovan gave final instructions. "Kavanagh, you'll drive. You convince the guard at the gate, you hear? If he gets suspicious, I'll shoot him. Problem then will be time. If that happens, you and Russell get out and haul him into the back of the van."

O'Donovan continued, "Best thing is for you to get us through, Kavanagh. So be your charming best."

As the phrase goes, Kavanagh didn't know whether to shit or go blind. This was nothing like anything he had ever done back in Ireland. This O'Donovan was one cold fucker. He'd seen how he did the gas company man. Wouldn't hesitate to do him too he figured. Best not to fuck up.

Kavanagh said nothing, only nodding at O'Donovan.

With O'Donovan, Magee, and Russell in the rear of the van amongst the equipment and fittings shelving, Kavanagh pulled the van onto Pacific Coast Highway then turned into the Monarch Bay Community. Kavanagh stopped the van at the guard building and traffic barrier.

"Can I help, you?" The security guard asked.

"Gas Company. We've got a report of a possible leak. Three calls actually. Let me see," Kavanagh said, then pretended to refer to a clip board, "All three reports from Crown Coast Drive addresses. Three reports, might be something major. Can't take any chances. Even the law says we've got to respond immediately."

"You Irish?"

"Yeah," Kavanagh answered warily.

"Thought so. My wife's Irish. Still has a little accent. Where you from?"

Jesus Christ, Kavanagh thought. There's the potential of a gas leak and this guy's asking where I'm from.

"Dublin. I'm from Dublin originally. Now I really should be checking this leak out."

"Right, right. Hope it's a false alarm. Be careful ya here. This street dead-ends at Crown Coast Drive. What's the address you're looking for?" The security guard asked, but Kavanagh had already accelerated away.

Devereux had spent both a difficult day, and a day of unusual bonding with Marge and Larry Neuson. He had never been under such emotional turmoil since the death of Angela. Fear had never involved anyone else.

The next day, Larry Neuson made himself busy with professional issues, and tried to avoid things that would confront the Reilly issue. Marge, on the other hand, avoided nothing. She asked Devereux direct questions, and offered objective advice. She took control and intuitively managed the situation since her arrival the previous night. Even through the distraction of his stress and fear, Devereux was amazed at Marge's strength and love. He felt guilty for not recognizing her's and Larry's affection before.

Nothing is as bad as waiting. He had not heard from Lenox. He had not heard from Flynn. It was after eight in the evening and Devereux had only picked at his food. Marge had made a simple dinner of grilled sea bass fillets and Caesar salad. She poured Devereux and her husband cognacs and served coffee after dinner.

The door chimes rang, startling all three.

Devereux's war zone instincts kicked in. "Expecting anyone?"

"No," Larry Neuson answered with more than a little anxiety at Devereux's unease.

"Get upstairs, both of you. And do it right now," Devereux ordered.

"Jesus, Mason, I think you're over-reacting," Larry Neuson said, but was moving as he spoke.

"Probably, but don't argue, Larry, just do it."

Larry pushed his slightly protesting wife up the stairs. Once upstairs, he moved quickly for the Smith & Weston .357 magnum in the nightstand next to their bed. He and his wife had twin .357s, one of which he had given to Devereux.

Devereux had thought himself being somewhat paranoid by bringing the gun downstairs during the day. The idea of an I.R.A. attack in Laguna Beach, California even sounded ridiculous. But he had placed the weapon in a drawer of the dining room armoire as a practical matter. He also reminded himself to never underestimate Flynn. Doing so got Bill Larkin murdered.

Devereux retrieved the .357 from the dining room and went to the door. Looking through the small lens in the door, Devereux could see a work uniform with a monogrammed name over the pocket.

Through the door, Devereux asked, "Yes? Who is it?"

"Gas Company. We've a report of a leak in the neighborhood, Sir."

An Irish accent. One of Flynn's fucking gunmen! It was like a preposterous dream coming to reality. Caution was one thing, but he never really believed it could happen.

It was difficult to say what prompted his next actions. Armed as he was, he could probably defend against any attack and wait for the police to arrive. But he was not interested in a defense. There was the welled up hatred for those who had taken Brigid Reilly. For Michael Flynn. For his own failure. Whatever the reason, an irrational Mason Devereux violently pulled open the front door.

Brian Kavanagh stood stunned as Devereux stuck the Smith & Weston into his face. Devereux knew that the guy in the Gas Company uniform was not alone. Seeing the man frozen, Devereux immediately shifted his view to the right. A man with longish brown hair in a beige windbreaker pointed an exceptionally long barreled handgun at him and fired.

Brennan Magee was startled by Devereux's offensive move. He suddenly saw what was to be a victim had a weapon of his own. Magee fired two shots. The first shot missed Devereux, and the second was fired too quickly, missing even wider. Devereux was not distracted by Magee's shots. His own safety was of no concern at this point. Fueled by rage, Devereux shot Magee once in the chest, then a second time in the face. He then turned on the still stunned Kavanagh, and shot him in the forehead from only a foot away.

From off to the left, O'Donovan witnessed the exchange of fire. He saw Magee go down, then Kavanagh. It was this bastard, Devereux. It did not matter that he needed Devereux alive. O'Donovan fired a three round burst from less than twenty feet. The silenced weapon emitted muffled thuds. One round hit Devereux in the abdomen.

Devereux staggered back into the doorway. He resisted firing back since he did not see a target. He also knew he had only limited rounds left. The Smith & Weston held only six shots. He had fired three. Or was it four? Devereux slammed the front door shut and ran toward the rear of the house. His side was on fire.

"Stay upstairs, Larry. Use your gun! Call the police!" Devereux screamed as he ran through the house.

O'Donovan flung open the door to the back deck overlooking the ocean. It was a dead end. There were no stairs from which to exit the deck. The ground sloped sharply down to the sea, not quite a cliff, but not easily descended. Devereux's quandary as to a way to escape was interrupted by the un-silenced report of several shots, with the wooden deck railing exploding next to him.

Devereux fired two shots instinctively in the direction of the shots to the right of deck, then vaulted the railing. The drop was over fifteen feet. Devereux landed feet first, but pummeled end-over-end down the steep embankment. He hit a rock hard going down and lay semi-conscious at the bottom. The incessant pain from his wound brought him around. He did not know if it had been seconds or minutes since his fall from the house. Standing proved barely possible. He knew that the effects of shock were taking hold. Somehow the .357 was still in his hand. He moved deliberately down the beach for no more than twenty feet before collapsing.

"Devereux. Devereux. Don't die yet you fuck. The pictures, where are the pictures? If you don't tell me, the Reilly woman dies," O'Donovan said.

Devereux was face down in the sand. It was hard to concentrate as he fought to stay conscious.

O'Donovan grabbed Devereux's left shoulder and turned him over. He could not see Devereux's face because of the lightless sky out to the sea. Devereux, however, could see the silhouette of O'Donovan's head against the pale lights from the houses on the hill.

As O'Donovan turned him over, Devereux brought the Smith & Weston from under his body, and with the barrel no more than three inches from O'Donovan's face, fired. O'Donovan was thrown backwards. The round had caught him in the left eye, exiting the back of his head. He was dead before his body hit the beach sand.

Devereux tried to rise up and move, but fell back to the ground. His breathing was labored. He wondered if it was the effects of shock or the loss of blood. His shirt and pants were well soaked. If it were the blood loss, he probably would not make it. The sounds of police sirens could be heard some distance off. If he was to die now, it was okay. With that thought, Devereux passed into unconsciousness.

Chapter Eighteen

Devereux regained consciousness twelve hours later and then only for a few minutes. It was obviously a hospital room, intensive care unit most likely. Subtle background noise emanated from all the monitoring equipment. He was vaguely aware of a nurse looking down onto his face. Then a number of other faces appearing as he lapsed back into unconsciousness.

He remembered this later when his next episode of consciousness was longer and more lucid. It was two more days before Larry and Marge Neuson were allowed to see him.

Marge was the first to see him. She kissed him on the forehead and cried. It was disconcerting for her to see her Devereux this way. After all the usual things were said, Devereux speaking little, and then with difficulty, Marge turned to the subject she knew was foremost on his mind.

"What does this mean about, Brigid, Mason?"

Devereux did not respond for some time. Tears flowed down his cheeks. Marge wiped them away with a tissue. Devereux closed his eyes and said, "She's dead, Marge. They've killed her. Maybe before this, but surely now. Flynn knew there was no way to insure recovery of the photographs. He was only buying time. This I.R.A. gunman O'Donovan was here to kill me. Probably you and Larry too. Then he'd attempt to recover the photographs. If O'Donovan failed, then Flynn was no worse off than before. Plus he'd have his revenge. Now? Brigid would only be a liability. How's he to let her live with what she knows?"

Marge Neuson was at a total loss to say anything to comfort Devereux.

Devereux raised his eyes to Marge. They were no longer fogged by pain killing drugs. "I will kill Flynn if the police don't get him first. If they do, I'll see him dead anyway. People die in prisons all the time. I will find a way."

Devereux was tiring, so Marge kissed him and said that Larry was waiting to see him. Larry Neuson had braced himself with a couple of scotches. He was actually having more trouble coping with the near fatal attack at their house than his wife was. Devereux's exploits were one thing to read about but quite another to experience first hand.

"Jesus, Mason, you look — , you look — ah —"

"I look like shit, Larry, cause I've been fucking shot. Don't be an old woman,"

"Do you know what you did? You killed three I.R.A. gunmen. It was front page here in LA. New York Times, Washington Post, Chicago Tribune. London papers of course picked it up as a major event. And it's getting bigger. Once they connected me to you, I've got all the networks, CNN, wire services, tabloids, foreign press, you name it, after interviews. Hired a couple of temps and added additional telephone lines to handle the calls," Larry said.

"I hate to sound materialistic, Mason, but do you have any idea what this will do for the book? We're talking major seven figures, Mason. I've even obtained photographs of the bodies at the house from the coroner's office, unofficially of course, and for a considerable sum of cash I might add. I've also got pictures of the fourth guy who the police shot trying to get away in the Gas Company van. Crashed on Pacific Coast Highway then fired on the cops."

Devereux said nothing. Neuson continued, "The media is having a field day with this. There are already international complications. The State Department and White House are trying to figure a position. The British are wondering about the appropriate posture. The Republic of Ireland is uncomfortable. The Protestant militants in Northern Ireland are playing it to the hilt. And the I.R.A., the fucking I.R.A. mind you, is screaming foul.

Claims the attack was not sanctioned by the Provincial I.R.A. Claim it's some renegade faction. Gone to great lengths to disavow themselves even though all four men were known I.R.A."

Devereux responded weakly, "They may be right. Flynn looks more like he's broken with the I.R.A. Killed Dolan. Missed Adams. Missed the Prince of Wales. Power play may have failed." Devereux paused, then asked, "And what about Flynn?"

"Haven't got the old bastard yet. He's wanted now not only by the British, but also Dublin, and the United States. Hasn't returned to his home or the University. He's making great copy too. Guy had one helluva colorful past back in the early seventies from what the stories say."

"Brigid?" Devereux asked with dread.

"Nothing yet. I've talked to Lenox every day. They have nothing. No leads. I'm sorry, Mason." Neuson could see that Devereux was wearing down. "You sleep now. I'll look in tomorrow."

It was four days before Devereux left intensive care. Only then did the doctors agree to allow a meeting with police officials. The wound in his lower abdomen had been severe, hitting his liver and left lung. He had lost a considerable amount of blood and suffered a post-operative infection.

Since the group was quite large, Devereux was moved to a room used for media briefings. Present were Marge and Larry Neuson, the lawyer Banning, and an assortment of international law enforcement people. A large man with a tightly trimmed mustache introduced himself as Chief Inspector Lenox, Scotland Yard. A short middle-aged, affable man represented the Irish Federal Police, the Garda. There was a ranking F.B.I. official accompanied by two typically non-descript looking F.B.I. agents. A well dressed, attractive woman from the State Department contrasted against a no-makeup, no-frills female Orange County deputy district attorney. Three Orange County Sheriff's Department detectives and a doctor rounded out the crowd.

For almost two hours, Devereux answered questions about the attack. Technically, the local police were investigating a homicide. The doctor ordered a three-hour recess so that Devereux could rest before continuing. As the group departed for a long lunch, they had to run a gauntlet of reporters.

In the afternoon, Chief Inspector Lenox took over the questioning.

"The men you killed were known I.R.A. Garrett O'Donovan, from Belfast. He'd been suspected of being an Active Service Unit commander. That seems confirmed now with your information about the Opera House attack. Family history of association with the I.R.A. Father was I.R.A. His brother was killed participating in an I.R.A. attack." Lenox said. He showed Devereux a police booking photograph.

"He's the one that was about to do you in on the beach before you killed him."

Lenox held up another photograph to Devereux. "Magee, Brennan Magee. Nasty bastard. Unemployed mechanic. Suspected in two murders. Arrested five times for assault, convicted only once. Magee was from Belfast also."

"The other man you killed was Brian Kavanagh, recently from County Armagh. The fourth man, the one the police shot, was one Eoin Russell, also from Armagh. Both these gentlemen left Northern Ireland within the last year and entered the United States illegally. Irish friends in your Boston area we suspect. Both these chaps were wanted by the Crown for several bombings that resulted in loss of life."

Lenox looked straight at Devereux. "We know you were at the scene of the recent attack on the Grand Operas House in Belfast. You have identified Michael Flynn as the leader of the attack. What we want to know, Mr. Devereux, is the background of how you obtained such knowledge, and the identification of others that may have been involved in these murders. We are also seeking your testimony in British court after these people are apprehended and indicted."

"I understand you have the photographs of the other members of O'Donovan's unit, Chief Inspector," Devereux said. "Have you identified them?"

"Yes. At least three others. All with past I.R.A. associations. We suspect that they were part of a new unit we think may have been commanded by O'Donovan."

"But you haven't arrested any of them yet?"

"There is a massive effort ongoing to locate them, and of course Michael Flynn. The Garda is supporting the effort fully."

"But you have made no arrests yet, correct?" Devereux repeated.

Lenox reluctantly answered, "No. Not yet."

"And what is being done to locate Brigid Reilly?"

"Everything possible. Informers are being questioned. Known I.R.A. are being questioned. Mr. Devereux, I can appreciate ——," Lenox started to say but was cut off by Devereux.

"Appreciate? I don't think you can, Chief Inspector. So let me tell you clearly. You find Reilly. You find her alive. You do that and I'll testify. Against Flynn, especially Flynn, and these other assholes too. If she's dead, no testimony."

The woman, Helen somebody from the State Department said, "Mr. Devereux. We're talking about international terrorism here. The British government could bring legal action in the United States to force your cooperation. It also seems apparent that you broke a number of British criminal laws."

"I would suggest that it would be difficult to extradite, and the result unproductive at any rate," the lawyer Banning responded. "Mr. Devereux has made his conditions clear."

"I'm sure that you are aware that Ms. Reilly may already be dead," Lenox said, none too gently out of irritation.

Devereux glared back. "Get out. Everyone get the fuck out. I'm tired, Doctor."

Devereux was returned to his room.

Three days later, Devereux received a call from Chief Inspector Lenox. Lenox told him that the R.U.C. had arrested Erskine Colbert earlier that day. He was found at the home of a cousin in County Fermanagh. Unfortunately, Colbert was so far unwilling to give the police information about anything. The massive manhunt would continue. Although unsaid, Devereux knew it was not for the purpose of locating Brigid Reilly, but to catch or kill Michael Flynn.

Belfast and other parts of Northern Ireland looked now much like it had several years previous. Since the attack on the

Grand Opera House, British troops were again on the streets of Belfast and Derry, and patrols had increased along the border areas, particularly in County Armagh and County Fermanagh. The British had also re-instituted search and destroy patrols by the feared and hated British S.A.S. special forces. One such patrol happen upon a small farm in County Armagh.

Lenox called Devereux the following day.

"Mr. Devereux, I have excellent news. Miss Reilly has been rescued."

"My God," Devereux answered.

"A bit in a bad way I should say, but not life threatening or even serious."

"What do you mean?"

"She's suffered from being restrained. Major difficulty though is her hearing. Damage to her eardrums. Don't know the technical prognosis. Just received the news from my people in the field."

"What happened?" Devereux asked.

"Yesterday a British S.A.S. patrol was searching near the border in County Armagh. After taking fire and one casualty, the patrol attacked. The short version is they killed Jack Burns and Martin Kelly, the last two known members of Flynn's and O'Donovan's group. Miss Reilly was found alive."

"The soldiers used stun grenades to take Burns and Kelly. Unfortunately, its effects were just as traumatic on Ms. Reilly. The grenade creates a horrific noise when used in a confined space. There is disorientation for a number of seconds. Time for trained people like the S.A.S. to enter and selectively take out the bad chaps. Both Burns and Kelly were shot dead. Ms. Reilly was not wounded in the attack."

"I'll try to arrange contact with Miss Reilly as soon as possible. I am leaving immediately for the hospital."

Devereux was overcome with the news.

"Thank you, Chief Inspector. I appreciate your call. And I appreciate all your efforts."

"Mr. Devereux, are you all right?" Lenox asked.

"Yes. Just a little overwhelmed right now. Flynn? What's the news on Flynn?" Devereux responded, not without some difficulty.

"Little I'm afraid. Frustrating to say the least. Flynn is an extraordinary man. From an I.R.A. gunman of legendary proportions, to respectable academic, to apparently a leadership position in the Provincial I.R.A. The man is clever and undoubtedly not without extensive contacts and resources. Even if he's broke with the Provincial I.R.A. leadership, he'd have plenty of support both here in the North and in the Republic. Even in America."

"Are you suggesting Flynn could be in the United States?" Devereux asked.

"That's a possibility we cannot discount. However, I would see no danger to you in that, Mr. Devereux. You no longer represent a threat and Flynn has more immediate concerns."

Two hours later, Devereux answered the phone eagerly.

"Mason? Oh my God," Reilly said and wept uncontrollably. It was several minutes before she recovered.

"Can hardly hear, Mason. You'll need to speak up."

"I know. They told me about your hearing. Tell me how you are," Devereux said almost yelling for Reilly to hear.

"Hurt like hell from being tied up. Terrible headache. Nothing serious except for my hearing. Constant buzzing noise. Be seeing a specialist tomorrow. Doctors say only a day or so in the hospital here. But what about you?"

"I was shot. O'Donovan and his people tried to kill me. They're all dead now. It's over. When I see you I'll tell you the details. A few more days in the hospital for me too."

"Oh my God, Mason. How bad?"

"I'll live. Painful but not life-threatening."

"Mason, it's my fault. I told them where you were. They were hurting me. I was terrified. But that's no excuse. I almost traded your life for mine. I hate myself."

Reilly cried. Devereux could feel her sadness and sense of failure.

"There was no way you could have resisted. Look what happened to Kevin Flanagan. Do you blame Kevin?"

"They would have gotten the information in some other way," Devereux concluded.

"I love you, Mason. I must be with you. I'm leaving the day after tomorrow for Los Angeles. Where are you?"

"Are you up to traveling? Tell me about your injuries."

"When I see you, Luv. I'm up to it. It's you I need to get well," Reilly said. She was clearly still crying.

"Call me back when you know your flight. I'll arrange to have you picked up."

"I love you and need you with me too," Devereux said.

Marge Neuson picked Reilly up at Los Angeles International Airport late at night and brought her straight to the hospital.

After the initial kisses and tears Reilly said, "Where were you shot?"

"Here in the abdomen. Serious but no permanent damage. Lost a lot of blood. Some infection. They removed my spleen."

"What's that mean?" Reilly asked.

"Nothing. You can get along just fine without the spleen."

"And you? Your face? What happened to you, Brigid?" Devereux asked. Despite makeup, bruises were evident on Reilly's face.

"Just rough treatment. Only bruises. Nothing lasting. The hearing's the problem. Permanent damage the doctors say," Reilly said. "It will get better but it will never be right."

"What else did they do to you, Brigid?"

"Sore muscles from being tied for so long. And the burns of course. Cigarette burns. Not too bad now." Tears were forming. There were other things but they could wait.

"Tell me how you were rescued. How did you survive and the two I.R.A. guys get killed?"

"I was tied to a bed in a back room all the time. It was night and all of a sudden there was gunfire. It seemed like only moments later there was this unbelievable explosion. Think it knocked me unconscious for a time. Next thing I know two soldiers are cutting the tape binding my wrists and ankles. Fearsome types with painted faces. I guess they killed the two men holding me, but I didn't see that, thank God."

Within a few days, Devereux was released from the hospital. Marge Neuson insisted they stay at the Laguna Beach house. Devereux began working on assembling the book. He attacked the project, wanting to conclude as soon as possible. The sooner the book was completed, the sooner he and Brigid could leave. First to Antigua for a few weeks, then on to a new life. Wherever and whatever that might mean.

The text content of the book was more probing and opinionated than his previous works. For that matter, this book was as much text as it was photographs. It had also evolved into more a real life adventure rather than a documentary on the sectarian warfare in Northern Ireland. The extraordinary photographs were made all the more vivid as they became part of a real story with a beginning, middle, and bloody ending.

Devereux walked Reilly through the whole story documented by his extraordinary photographs.

"They never showed such photos as these in the papers," Reilly said referring to Devereux's shots of the carnage in the Opera House.

"What's it like to see such death first hand?"

"It's made me antagonistic to causes, to governments, to movements. You cannot experience first hand such death without being changed. It peels away all the bullshit of politics and causes. Touching and smelling the real thing changes you."

"This is Flynn and O'Donovan leaving my uncle's house on the night he was murdered?" Reilly asked, referring to a group of photos.

"Yes. Probably minutes after the shootings."

"This was probably the photo Flynn feared most. This would convict the bastard, but there's also lots of I.R.A. who would have him killed for such an act of betrayal. Even if he got to prison, he'd not survive for long."

The entire experience of looking at Devereux's photographs had disturbed the foundations of so much of her life.

Both Devereux and Reilly were recovering nicely. His daily schedule called for a walk on the beach in the morning, and another to take a break in the afternoon. Color had returned to his face. The Pacific Ocean in Southern California was not the same

as the Mediterranean, but it was an acceptable substitute. Devereux was the best therapy for Reilly's emotional injuries.

A slight, middle-aged man with thinning gray hair, with
black horned rimmed glasses and dressed in a baggy tweed
sport coat, approached the receptionist at the Neuson's office in
Santa Monica. The man walked to the desk with a decided limp.

"Can I help you?" The receptionist asked.

"I'm a police officer. Inspector Flynn with the Royal Ulster
Constabulary. That would be in Northern Ireland, my dear." The
man said. He held open a black leather wallet displaying a
document with his picture and an official stamp. The receptionist paid it only superficial attention.

"Do you have an appointment, Sir?"

"No. I'm afraid not, lass. But I'm sure Mr. Neuson will want
to see me. Please tell him it's about Mr. Devereux."

The receptionist called Larry Neuson's secretary and relayed
the message. Within moments, the receptionist asked the man to
follow her to Mr. Neuson's office.

"Please sit down Inspector —-. I don't believe I caught the
name from my secretary," Neuson asked.

"It's Flynn, Mr. Neuson. But I'm afraid I'm not really a police
inspector. But my name is Flynn. Michael Flynn," the man said
as he pulled a silenced nine-millimeter automatic from inside his
jacket.

"Jesus Christ!" Neuson exclaimed and made to rise from his
chair.

"Sit down, Mr. Neuson!" Flynn ordered sharply.

Neuson was scared as hell, but so angry at being face to face
with this murderer that he lashed back. "What do you want you
murdering bastard?"

"That's simple, Mr. Neuson. I want you to take me to Devereux."

"Why, so you can kill him?" Neuson responded.

"Perhaps. But that is not your concern."

"But it is, Flynn. If I don't do as you ask, then you'll shoot
me? So you assume that I'll trade my life for Devereux's, which
assumes that you would allow me to live, which would be ri-

diculous. Do you expect me to trade the dubious promise of my life for Devereux's?" Neuson said angrily.

"Please be calm, Mr. Neuson. If you raise your voice, it may attract your secretary," Flynn said calmly and continued.

"Let me put the situation to you in plain terms. You will take me to Devereux or I will shoot you and take your wife instead. I know she is here in her office. With this silenced weapon, no one will hear the shot that kills you. I will simply drag your body into the restroom. How long would you guess it would take before your secretary became worried enough to check your restroom? In the meantime, I have your wife in the same situation you now find yourself. What do you choose, Mr. Neuson?"

Neuson glared at Flynn. He knew that Flynn would kill him too once he had killed Devereux. There were no options without risking Marge's life. He was trading his wife's life for Devereux's. Maybe Devereux could once again beat the odds Neuson rationalized.

"Tell your secretary that you'll be out for three hours. No reason, or where you'll be," Flynn told Neuson.

Neuson rose to put on his suit coat. He was so scared he was shaking. The two men walked out of the office. Neuson told his secretary what Flynn had ordered him to say. She gave them a curious look, but returned to her work. They picked up Neuson's car in the parking garage, and were heading south on the 405 Freeway within fifteen minutes. Neuson drove. Traffic permitting, it was a fifty-minute drive to Laguna Beach.

Neuson was passed through the security gate at the Monarch Bay Community by the security sticker on his windshield and the recognition by the guard. Flynn took the keys from Neuson and exited the car first. Neuson unlocked the front door and entered the hallway. Flynn was behind him holding unto Neuson's suit coat collar. Flynn whispered for him to call for Devereux.

"Mason. It's Larry. Are you home?"

Devereux had been working in the family room on a laptop computer when he heard the front door being opened. It was eleven-thirty in the morning. Larry Neuson had said that he would be at his office in Santa Monica all day. Devereux had been attacked once in this house. He was hypersensitive. Something did not feel right.

He did not answer Neuson, even when Neuson called out again. He retrieved the .357 magnum revolver from behind the bar. Since the attack, the weapon was never far from his sight. Devereux then ducked behind the bar in the family room.

Receiving no response, Flynn whispered to Neuson, "Where is he?"

"I don't know. Maybe he went out. Maybe down to the beach," Neuson said, slightly louder than a whisper, hoping to warn Devereux.

Flynn pushed Neuson through the living room with its tall glass windows facing the ocean, then into the less formal family room, also with floor to ceiling windows. It was a magnificently sunny day. Flynn moved Neuson toward the windows to see if Devereux might be on the beach below. With his back turned toward the bar, Devereux came out with his gun leveled at the back of the man holding Larry Neuson.

"I'm over here."

Flynn swung Neuson around instinctively as a shield, with Neuson almost losing his balance. Devereux was shocked to the point of a moment's disorientation at seeing Flynn's face.

Without hesitation, Flynn fired three rounds toward the bar that Devereux was using for cover. Pushing Neuson in front of him, Flynn advanced toward Devereux's position. Neuson realized that he was the liability. Devereux would not shoot as long as Flynn used him as a shield. And if Devereux died, so would he. So he might as well try to resist.

Neuson pulled free of Flynn and moved from between him and Devereux's position. Flynn fired one shot that felled Neuson. However, Neuson's tactic worked. Devereux watched as if in slow motion, sure of his purpose, sure of his target. With a clear target Devereux marked a count to steady his aim and squeezed off two rounds at Flynn. The first round struck Flynn in the left shoulder, the second went wide as Flynn dropped to one knee. Flynn fired several shots into the bar. One found its mark, hitting Devereux in the right thigh.

Flynn rose to his feet and charged toward the bar, firing repeatedly, hoping to overpower Devereux. Devereux crawled out from the protection of the bar, close to the floor and fired three shots at the oncoming Flynn. One shot hit Flynn in the lower abdomen. Flynn tumbled over a coffee table and dropped to the floor.

Devereux too had been hit again by another round. The second shot had struck him in the left side, shattering a rib. That wound did not effect him as much as the thigh wound, but he could not really feel pain from either with the adrenaline and his rage.

He rose to his feet and limped toward Flynn. Devereux soon realized that Flynn had dropped his weapon. Flynn sprawled at an awkward angle with his back against a sofa and one leg over a cocktail table.

Devereux located Flynn's gun and kicked it across the room. Flynn was breathing hard and obviously in considerable pain. Blood was pooling beneath him.

"Are you in pain, Flynn? I hope the fuck you are," Devereux said, pointing the .357 at Flynn's forehead. "You deserve to die, Flynn, and I'm going to see that it happens."

Flynn mustered his strength. "If you kill me, I become another I.R.A. martyr, Devereux. Good for recruitment. Legendary gunmen dies. Dies on last mission with gun in hand. That's how the I.R.A. gets new recruits, Devereux. You've heard about the great funerals when an I.R.A. man dies. Best thing that can happen sometimes. Besides, imagine what it could do for your book if you don't kill me. Author captures Michael Flynn. The continuing media coverage of the trial would be free promotion for your book."

Devereux wanted to destroy this animal that had caused him so much pain. The man was cunning and dangerous. He could imagine a trial. Flynn would then truly become a legend, and a martyr.

"You think you're like Pearse or Collins. I've read much about them and I know you. You're not in their league, Flynn. If I let you live, you get to plead your place in history. If I kill you, well then, you'll just be remembered as another I.R.A. gunman, an old one, but just the same another footnoted name in a long line of killers. Only the I.R.A. will sing your praises around a campfire, or over a pint, or wherever you assholes do your bonding."

Devereux's rage got the best of him. He raised his foot and brought it down full force onto Flynn's right knee. His leg had still been draped over the cocktail table. The sound of the destruction of the knee was audible. Flynn screamed out with surprising strength.

"I understand Kevin Flanagan was knee-capped before he was killed. Is that something like what it feels like, Flynn?" Devereux screamed.

Flynn was in excruciating pain from the abdominal gunshot wound and now his damaged knee.

"You've got me, Devereux. You've hurt me. But I don't think you're up to killing me in cold blood. You say I'm a killer. Well, I kill for a cause. A cause I believe in. A cause I have been willing to die for. You'll kill me for what? Revenge?"

Devereux became incensed at Flynn's tactics to intellectualize the situation. His response was to move to the other side of the prone Flynn and drive a kick to Flynn's other knee.

Flynn writhed in a new wave of agony.

"I believe Kevin Flanagan was shot in both knees."

"Devereux, you're forgetting one thing."

"Which is what?"

"Reilly. You want Reilly—you can't kill me. If I die, she dies."

"Been out of touch, Flynn. Probably been here in the States hiding amongst your friends. So you haven't heard. Brigid Reilly is alive. She's here in fact.

Michael Flynn knew he was dead seconds before Devereux fired the last bullet from the .357 revolver into Flynn's forehead.

The effects of shock were starting to take hold. Devereux could hear sirens in the distance, but still called 911. He then crawled to Larry Neuson. God how he hoped he had not lost yet another friend. To his relief, Neuson was not only alive, but conscious.

"Mason! God, no!" Reilly screamed as she burst into the house.

Devereux lost consciousness before he could say anything to Reilly.

Epilogue

Neuson had been shot in the upper portion of his right shoulder from the back. The bullet badly damaged his scapula, which also reduced the projectile's velocity, thereby minimizing otherwise more serious damage. The bullet had exited his chest a few inches over his right nipple. There was damage to his lung, but the surgery was successful. Neuson left the hospital after one week.

Devereux had also been fortunate. The thigh wound missed the fibula and did not damage major tendons. The most serious problem with the abdominal wound was the shattered end of a rib. The surgery cleaned up the bone. There was no damage to any organs. Except for some highly visible scars, Devereux's recovery was full, with no lasting physical consequences.

The Orange County District Attorney's office debated only briefly as to charging Devereux with any criminal action. To the police and the deputy D.A., it was obvious that Devereux had gone way beyond self-defense in the killing of Michael Flynn. It was equally obvious that they would be unlikely to win an indictment, much less a conviction. Everyone involved felt that justice had been served.

Devereux spent the next six weeks in Laguna Beach recuperating and loving Brigid Reilly in a newfound freedom. Together they completed the book. Reilly arranged a long leave of absence from her firm. She was not sure she would ever go back to her job, or even to Belfast.

Neuson was overwhelmed by the impact of Devereux's completed work. He had seen all of the pictures, but Devereux's design of the work, the sequencing, the sizing of the photographs, and the narrative itself combined to make for an astounding effect.

"This is an extraordinary work, Mason. We'll have all the major houses bidding on it."

"I'll leave it to you, Larry. I'll call you in a month."

"In a month? Where are you going? I'll need to discuss details as we negotiate, Mason."

"I'm going to the Caribbean with Brigid, Larry. You don't need me for what you do best. I'll call you, Larry."

Devereux and Reilly left the next day for the Caribbean island of Antigua for an indefinite stay.

THE END

www.ingramcontent.com/pod-product-compliance
Lightning Source LLC
Chambersburg PA
CBHW030407030726
47497CB00002B/515